Lost Birds

Lost Birds

BIRUTE PUTRIUS

BIRCHWOOD PRESS

Published in the USA by:
Birchwood Press
Send inquiries to birchwoodpress@gmail.com
www.birchwoodpress.com

BIRCHWOOD
PRESS

ISBN 978-0-9965153-0-6

Book interior layout by Darlene Swanson • www.van-garde.com

Contents

For Max and Anna
and Algis

Becoming American

Irene Matas, 1950

It took eleven long days and nights to cross the Atlantic Ocean on the General Howze, a GI troop transport. For five days it stormed, raising mountains of water that made me feel so small. Everyone was sick, including my mother. My older brother, Petras, couldn't get out of bed for two days, which made my mother frantic since the men and women were separated on different levels. My father took care of Petras as best he could until the sea finally calmed. The next day, my mother stood with me and my brother on the deck, holding our hands as she pointed to the schools of flying fish leaping out of the blue water. "Fish can fly!" I said, delighted, not knowing it was possible. When I turned to look at my pale brother, I saw he was smiling, his eyes shining as he stared at the magical creatures that were part bird and part fish.

On the last day of our voyage, our family stood on deck watching the great city of New York in the distance, with its towers touching the sky. It was so amazingly different from our displaced-persons camp in Bavaria, where I was born after the war. When we reached New York Harbor, we disembarked like birds thrown out of our nest, staring at the immense forest of skyscrapers. I was a timid girl, and the huge city scared me. Everything seemed too big.

"So this is America?" my mother asked my father.

"Well, it isn't Kaunas," he answered, his face exhausted by the journey. The sharp October wind blew newspapers and dust across the grimy street, clearly distressing my mother, who craned her neck to see the tops of the buildings.

"Oh, Viktoras, it's so big, and there's no grass. Where will the children play?"

My weary father put a reassuring hand on her shoulder. "Don't worry, Dora, Mr. Jankus said there was a part of Chicago as green as Samogitia."

That same day we boarded the train to Chicago.

Our American sponsor, Mr. Jankus, met us at the train station and shook my father's hand heartily. "Welcome to Chicago," he boomed in American-accented Lithuanian, a cigar hanging loosely from his protruding lower lip, sending smelly puffs into the city's gloom. "I'm George Jankus, and this is my wife, Adele."

"Viktoras Matulaitis," my father said, introducing himself and his family.

"I'd change that name to Victor Matas if you want to get work here," said Mr. Jankus.

"Is that so?" asked my father, shooting my mother a worried look.

"My last name used to be Jankauskas, but no one in America could pronounce it."

I stood below the thicket of grownups, my skinny blond braids freshly redone with large plaid bows, noticing how our sponsor's belly strained the buttons of his brown pinstriped suit.

His wife, Adele, a tight-lipped woman wearing a hat like a plate of flowers, blinked nervously as she escorted us to their blue Studebaker. My parents, Petras, and I stood there in our wilted, refugee-camp clothes donated by St. George's Church. The Lithuanian-American parish had sent boxes of used clothes to the displaced-persons camps in Germany after the war. Its members had agreed to sponsor Lithuanian families wishing to immigrate to Chicago, promising to help them find shelter and work.

Mr. Jankus escorted us to his Studebaker, where our cardboard suitcases were swallowed up in the trunk. My parents and brother squeezed into the back seat of the car while I sat on my father's lap. Mr. Jankus drove us to the South Side, pointing out the various factories where my father might find a job. "There's more work in Chicago than pigs in the stockyards," he said, grinning, the foul cigar bobbing up and down as he spoke. We stared out the window at the industrial neighborhoods filled with factories and brick two-flats, searching for the green part of Chicago that looked like Samogitia. The South Side was one poor neighborhood after another, filled with Negroes, Gypsies, and runaways from Eastern Europe.

Clutching my father's hand, I stepped out of the Studebaker as Mr. Jankus walked to a decrepit storefront that was to be our new home. Once he unlocked the front door, we stepped inside a large room with shelves along three walls, which smelled of mold and stale tobacco. The only light came from the streaked and dusty storefront windows, while the rest was a dark cave with one light bulb hanging over a wooden table. Two beds and a dresser stood forlornly in the back of the store. A dust-covered treadle sewing machine sat abandoned in the corner, and an old stove hunched close to the sink, next to the minuscule bathroom.

Holding our suitcases, we stood there, disappointment shrouding us. No one said a word until Mr. Jankus tried to cheer us up by telling us that the church had finally found a used refrigerator.

"It's coming tomorrow," added his wife as she handed my mother a bucket with rags, soap, brushes, and a can. "Missus, these are some cleaning supplies," she instructed, pulling out a can of glass wax.

"Call me Dora," said my mother.

Mrs. Jankus looked up impatiently and cleared her throat. "Dora, this is for cleaning windows. You pour a bit of this on a rag and make circles until you cover the window. Then you let it dry and wipe it off with a clean rag. She demonstrated by smearing the cloudy pink liquid on a small section of the dirty window while my mother studied the perplexing ritual.

Afterward, Mrs. Jankus went to the car to get a bag of groceries and some old sheets. Her husband told my father how lucky we were to have Lithuanians help us. "When we came to Chicago in 1914, no one helped our folks. Hardly no food on the table and everyone worked the stockyards, even us kids. You read that book *The Jungle* by Mr. Upton Sinclair?"

My father shook his head. "As a high school teacher in Lithuania, I read a great deal, but never any books in English."

Mr. Jankus shrugged. "I didn't read it either, but they say it tells a sad story about the Lithuanians working at the stockyards, but it's different now that the unions cleaned up the stockyards. Maybe I could fix you up with a job there?" He took off his brown fedora and scratched his short gray hair, the folds of his chin jiggling. "Nobody fixed us up with a job when we came here. Heck, we almost starved. We at St. George's remember those days, so we weren't going to let that happen to you DPs. At church, you'll meet the Vitkus family, one of the other DP families our church sponsored. They live right down the street," he said, pointing out the dirty front window.

Mr. Jankus shook his head. "It's such a shame how the horrors of World War II just continue. Those damned Communists just swallowed all of Eastern Europe like it was theirs. Sons of bitches," he mumbled under his breath.

My father thanked him and shook his hand.

"Mr. Matulaitis, you call if you need anything," said Mr. Jankus, the cigar still clenched between his teeth. "This is a great country.

You work hard, you can make it here. Ain't that right, Adele?" His wife looked at us sideways, as if she wasn't so sure. She opened the door and turned back to us, her purse locked safely in the crook of her elbow. "Nice meeting you," she said mechanically as she nodded to my mother, ushering her husband out and closing the door behind them.

My father seemed both grateful and burdened by this help.

"What's a DP?" my brother wanted to know.

"Displaced person," my father said, frowning as he looked around the dank and dismal store. "I want you to remember this," he said, looking into our eyes with such seriousness. "We're not immigrants like the Jankus family. They came to America long ago looking for work and a better life. We are exiles. Never forget that. We came to this country for shelter until the Soviets leave our country and it's safe to return home. It won't be long now. The Free World will never stand for an occupied Europe. They'll make short work of Stalin, and then we'll go back home to Kaunas." He patted our heads and smiled. Ever the teacher, he added, "There are fewer than four million people in the world who speak our Baltic language, one of the oldest languages, the closest to ancient Sanskrit on the tree of languages. We must keep it alive until we return so that the Russians don't wipe us from the face of the earth."

Petras and I hadn't known we were exiles. We knew we were Lithuanians, but now we were also DPs and exiles. This sounded serious, but we weren't sure why. While examining the room, Petras mumbled his complaints under his breath, "This place doesn't look any better than the camp we left behind in Germany. I thought America was rich."

"I thought we were going to a home with flowers and apple trees." I was looking around the scary and lonely store with nothing on the shelves to sell. If this was America, I hated it. "Mama, I want to go back home, to our camp," I whined, on the verge of tears. "To the Danube to catch minnows in my bucket." I had an aching longing for our refugee camp, a converted cavalry stable where we had lived in one small room.

"Irena," my father interrupted, "don't you remember how every time it rained, the smell of horse manure returned?"

For me it had been cozy having my family tucked in tightly around me. I held onto my mother's skirt for comfort until I noticed a gaggle of children with their faces pressed to the front window, straining to see who had moved into the old store. There were two Negro boys and three young girls with dark eyes and long tangled hair and small gold earrings, smiling and waving their arms as if they wanted us to come out and play. Petras looked to my father for permission, but my mother hissed, "Gypsies," and I could see by the look on her face that she didn't like them. "They used to steal my father's horses in Lithuania."

"Dora, please! These are children, not horse thieves." My father gently chased them away from the windows while my mother wondered what she could do to cover the windows. Newspaper would have been fine, but since we didn't have any, she pulled out the tin can of glass wax and some old rags. "This will give us some privacy." Petras and I were told to smear the pink liquid onto the windows while she went to open cans of soup for our supper. We had hardly finished a row of cloudy circles when one of the Gypsy girls returned and pressed her face against the glass, flattening her nose and sticking her tongue out. I laughed and also stuck out my tongue, and we made faces at one another. Soon they were all back at the window. I drew a funny face on the window with the glass wax and the Gypsy girl clapped. Soon Petras and I were dancing and making faces, laughing so hard that my mother came over to chase the children away so we could finish smearing the windows.

That night, I slept curled into my mother in one narrow bed while my father slept with my brother in the other bed. Our khaki GI-issue wool blankets from the camps were as scratchy as ever. The night seemed long, and I felt far away from the only home I had known. When I woke in the middle of the night, I could feel the bed shaking as mother cried into her pillow.

"Why are you crying, Mama?" I finally asked.

My mother wiped her tears on the blanket. "I'm worried about your grandparents in Kaunas," she whispered. "I miss them so much."

"Tell me again about your house in Kaunas," I asked, knowing how she loved to describe it.

My mother didn't say anything for a moment and then sighed deeply. "It had many rooms filled with light," she whispered the familiar version in my ear. "With china teacups and silver candlesticks and flower boxes filled with red geraniums in every window." It soothed us both to imagine those rooms. "When I left my home in Kaunas, I thought it was only until the war ended. But now an Iron Curtain has come down in Europe, sealing it off from the rest of the world, and there's no going home." She wiped her tears.

In the morning, when I opened my eyes, I thought I was back at the DP camp, and it took me a moment to realize it was the store in Chicago. And yet something had changed. The gray and dingy room was transformed by the rosy glow of the glass wax. The sun shining through the bubble-gum pink of the smeared windows bathed the room in a cheerful glow like a fairy-tale spell. The sheets on my bed shone, as did my mother's sleeping face, no longer tired and worried. In this light, she looked younger. Everything in the grim storefront had been magically transformed.

When I woke my mother to show her, she squinted into the bright light, indifferent to everything. "Irena, go back to sleep," she murmured, turning away from the window, leaving a mountain of a shoulder.

But I couldn't go back to sleep. This was a magical hour. Waving my hands back and forth, I saw they were glowing. A man walked by outside, and I could follow his dark pink shadow across the large windows. I was enchanted.

Later that morning, while my parents were busy with cleaning the store, Petras and I ventured outside to see how America looked. My parents said we had to stay on our block. Old two-story brick apartment buildings lined the street, and at the corners, a few small stores like ours—one sold fruits and vegetables while another sold cigarettes and held racks of newspapers and magazines. We went to the end of the block and found one of the Negro boys who had peered into our window the day before. Soon the tangle-haired Gypsy girls appeared, and they were all speaking words I couldn't understand.

"Are you American?" they kept repeating. I smiled and shrugged, not understanding a word. Pointing to myself, I said, "Irena, DP, exile," but they all looked at me as if frogs were leaping from my mouth. The oldest girl pointed to herself and said, "Marlena," while the younger ones introduced themselves as Delphina and Seraphina. The Negro boy's name was Lovey. And just like that we were pulled down the block to play in a trash-littered lot they called a "prairie." We swarmed an old fallen tree like busy ants. "This is our ship," my brother said to me, pointing to the tree. "And here is your sword," he yelled, handing me a long stick. "We're sailing the seas through storms to fight off Russian pirates." Holding his stick, he yelled, "Attack," as we bravely fought the spindly branches.

Every day, we ran around the block with the Gypsies like feral children, faces smudged with dirt, climbing fences and playing tag in the cinder alleys until dusk. Being the youngest, I often tripped and fell, skinning my knees bloody on cinders, crying and screaming while my mother tried to pick them out with a pair of tweezers.

"Are we Americans, Mama?"

She glanced up at me. "No, we're Lithuanians. And we'll go back home as soon as our country is free again, God willing." She picked out a few more cinders as I screamed, but then her nerves gave out and she dabbed iodine on and bandaged my knees, hoping for the best.

8

"Do you have to play with those rough children?"

"They're my friends, Mama."

By the end of the second week, my father had changed our last name to Matas. He counted himself lucky because a Lithuanian acquaintance got him work at the Nabisco factory in Marquette Park instead of the stockyards, and my mother got a job cleaning offices downtown at the Prudential Building. In each place, there were other Lithuanians who would help them. Though my father could speak four languages fluently, he knew very little English, so teaching was out of the question. Few of his friends, who had been accountants, lawyers, or writers, could resume the kind of lives they had left behind. My father worked the day shift while my mother took the evening shift so that someone would always be home to care for us. Before long, Petras enrolled in the Precious Blood Catholic School, got his uniform, and left for school down the street. I started morning kindergarten, and in the afternoons I stayed with Mrs. Vitkus, who lived across the street from the church in a one-room attic. Her daughter Magda was older, but she still played with me. Her son Algirdas, whom the kids called Al, never wanted to play with me, but he followed my brother like a shadow. Now we had some Lithuanian friends and it was easier to speak to them.

It turned out that Lovey, who lived in the large brick apartment building next door, was in my kindergarten class. His brother, Charlie, walked to school with Petras, who now wanted to be called Pete. Instead of Irena, the nuns started calling me Irene, as did my friends.

Before I met Lovey, I had never seen a Negro before and so I kept examining him as if he had stepped out of a storybook. One day, when he came over to play and asked for the bathroom, I took him to the small one in the back of the store. I had never seen a penis before, and I was amazed, wondering what it was and why I didn't have one. I bent over, curious to get a better look and was about to ask him why he peed standing up when my mother came in and shrieked, "Irena, what are you doing?"

I jumped, knowing from her tone of voice that I had done something wrong. "Nothing," I answered. "Lovey had to use the bathroom." But I could see from her expression that I was in big trouble, though I didn't know why. After sending Lovey home, she spanked me and sent me to the corner. "Never do that again," she said sternly. I stood in that corner feeling angry and confused, still unsure of what I had done wrong.

A week later, my brother and I went to play jacks with Charlie and Lovey on the stoop in front of their apartment. Charlie wanted to know why my brother had no little finger on his right hand.

"Boom in Germany," Pete said in his halting English, making explosive sounds.

"Did the Nazis shoot it off?" asked Charlie, looking excited.

Rubbing the nub where his finger used to be, Pete tried to explain how he was playing war games in a bombed-out tank, throwing empty cans at his friends in a field full of war junk. One day he found a half-buried Nazi helmet with a bullet hole and put it on. One of his friends threw something at him, and it blew up, sending shrapnel flying, slicing through Pete's finger and gashing his leg. He told this story with plenty of miming and explosion sounds. Then he pulled up his pant leg to show the scar on his leg. "Hospital," he said proudly.

Charlie and Lovey had that soft look on their faces, as if they were seeing a miracle—Saint Pete of the missing finger, already a child war veteran. I hated Pete's missing finger because he poked it in my face whenever he teased me.

Sometimes my brother had nightmares about the bombing, but mostly he made drawings of planes bombing cities, or fighter planes dancing loops in the skies, with machine-gun bullets flying in all directions. As he drew them, he'd make gunfire noises or imitate the whine of falling planes as they crashed. My brother had fled to the West with my parents, through a rain of Allied bombs, escaping the Soviets. He drew those pictures for years after we came to Chicago. Even Charlie started to draw them, though he had never been in a war.

At the end of October, Lovey, dressed as a cowboy with chaps and a gun, came over and told me to find a costume because we were all going trick-or-treating. My brother put on his helmet with the bullet hole, and a khaki shirt that one of the GIs had given him— his cherished souvenirs. Charlie was a pirate with a scarf and eye patch. The wild Gypsies came as themselves with their liquid eyes and pierced ears, their full skirts and jewel-colored blouses patched or ripped in a dozen places. I wondered why their mothers didn't scrub their dirty necks the way my mother did. Though I loved how wild they were, I was careful because they would curse you out or bloody a nose if they got mad.

Lovey could see that I was upset about not having a costume, so he brought over an empty cereal box, cut out the tiger mask on the back, attached a rubber band, and showed me how to wear it. Lovey always took good care of me. He gave me a paper sack and taught me how to say "trick-or-treat."

Bundled in our coats and scarves, we set forth. The streets were dark and filled with monsters, witches, and princesses. The smell of leaves burning filled the air as I skipped alongside Lovey, my pigtails bouncing as we went from house to house, fear and excitement coursing through me. I had never seen so much candy. Every time I got a piece of chocolate, I ate it quickly before anyone could take it back. By the time we had circled two blocks, I had a stomachache and Marlena laughed at me. Delphina, shivering with cold in her thin jacket, asked to wear my blue gloves with the knitted tulip pattern that my mother had made in the camp. Reluctantly, I gave them to her and didn't real-ize until it was time to go home that she hadn't returned them. Because I knew my mother would scold me if I came home without them, I went with Lovey to Delphina's apartment building. While he waited on the street, I went to knock on the door. A large woman opened it, wearing a long green lace dress with a pink sweater. A dozen bracelets clanged together on her arms as she called Delphina. The smell of spicy cooking wafted out from the kitchen. When I asked Delphina about the gloves, she lied, saying she had given them back to me and that I must have lost them. When Marlena said, "But I saw you..." her sister elbowed her in the side, and Marlena shut up. Suddenly four women gathered around Delphina like a protective shell around a pearl. The large woman growled in a foreign language and slammed the door shut. "Dirty DP," I heard the girls shout through the door. "Go back to your own country." I wanted to yell that we couldn't go back; the Russians had our country, but I was so mad, I almost cried.

When I told Lovey about Delphina, he told me to wait out-side while he went to talk to her. It was cold, but I waited, hands deep in my pockets, as jack-o-lanterns winked on porches and ghosts and goblins ran through the streets. The wind whooshed through the fallen leaves, making them dance madly. Just as I was beginning to feel hopeless, I saw Lovey coming toward me, smiling with his straight white teeth and laughing eyes as he pulled my blue gloves out of his pocket. "There you go, princess," he said, his soft eyes shining with pride. I was so grateful, I hugged him. Prince Lovey had rescued me from the ogre. I wanted to sprinkle rose petals on his royal head. I hoped Delphina, the stupid witch, was sprouting hairs on her chin, and dark vapors were circling her gnarled body.

By Christmas vacation, English words were starting to come more easily. It wasn't as hard as I thought. Sister Mary Constance said I was a quick learner and gave me a blue enameled medal of the Virgin Mary, which I never took off but hid under my blouse whenever the Gypsies came around.

A week later, when my father brought home a small Christmas tree, we made ornaments out of white drinking straws, cutting and stringing them into elaborate stars and snowflakes. Mr. Jankus came by with a cooked ham and a box of second-hand clothes from the Lithuanian relief fund. From his back pocket, he brought out a pint of whiskey, which he shared with my father. I got a blue wool coat with a missing button and a funny smell that my mother said was mothballs. My mother said she had loved to dress elegantly before the war, in high heels and a fox-collared suit. "That's how I caught your father's eye, at the radio station where I worked in Kaunas."

In the DP camp, my mother had learned to knit and sew all of our clothes, including my underwear. They all had that DP look. I searched through the box of donated clothes to see if there was something that looked more American. There was a blouse with a lace collar, but when I picked it up I saw that it had brown stains under the arms, so I quickly put it back. From the bottom of the box, my mother pulled out a huge bosomy iridescent blue dress, which she later cut up and then sewed back together with the ancient sewing machine. Her new sheath shimmered when she moved. She also made me a plaid dress with a white collar so that we both had dresses for Christmas that were American-looking. No stains under the arms.

Under the tree, there was one present for each of us—my father got a new tie, my mother a bottle of Evening in Paris cologne, my brother a stamp album with a large envelope of stamps, and I got a Negro boy doll with a striped shirt and overall shorts that I had been admiring at the drug store. Wide-eyed, I kissed its nose and called my first doll Lovey. I didn't let go of it all day, even eating dinner with it on my lap. I would let Magda play with it but not the Gypsy girls because they might break it or not give it back. It was a great Christmas.

On New Year's Eve, I was about to have my first party. Not a big party—just the Vitkus family from down the street. All day my mother had been cooking, and the smell of ham was mouthwatering. She had made an apple cake earlier and was now humming Lithuanian songs as she peeled potatoes for a *kugelis*. My father came in the door, dragging the cold in behind him. He pulled a bottle of brandy and chocolates out of a bag—such luxuries for our family.

"It smells so good in here, Dora." He laughed and kissed my mother. "What a party we'll have, eh?"

My mother wiped her hands on her apron. "Like the old days." She pulled her apron off and smiled at my father, so stylish in her blue dress and high heels.

He nuzzled her neck. "You smell good and look beautiful, Dora."

"In this old dress I made?" She pushed back an errant strand of hair, pleased by the compliment. It was true. My parents looked transformed.

My brother and I had hung paper chains around the front of the store, which we called the dining room. I was excited because Magda would be coming over with her brother, Al.

Before long, the Vitkus family knocked on the glass-waxed front door. Jurgis Vitkus wore a woolen jacket, his shirt frayed at the collar, while his wife, Regina, wore a beige wool dress with an amber brooch she had brought from Lithuania. Both husband and wife were rather thin, and while the wife hummed with nervous energy, her husband simmered with subdued anger. Like their parents, Al and Magda both had dark hair and eyes, but Magda was beautiful. My father always said she had the face of a medieval icon—innocent and ageless.

After dinner, my parents, who had toasted the New Year with numerous shots of brandy, asked me to recite the little German ditty they had taught me in the refugee camp. I felt shy to say it in front of Al and Magda, but my mother insisted, giving me a little push. She told me to curtsy, so I did, holding out the skirt of the dress my mother made, feeling my big red bow bob along with me.

"*Deutschland, Deutschland, uber alles, zwei kartoffeln, das ist alles.*" I curtsied again and felt the blood rushing to my face.

Mr. Vitkus burst out laughing and clapped. "Germany, Germany, over all, two potatoes, that is all. Ha! You've changed the national anthem of the Third Reich!" He laughed again. "Hitler boasting of his thousand-year reign. All that was left of that reign—two potatoes! And rubble."

My father added, "Thank God we ended up in a camp in the American Zone in Germany, rather than the British, French, or—God forbid—the Russian Zone. We finally got some food."

The adults decided to play cards. Mr. Vitkus drank too many highballs and began to curse the Communists again. "The French, Danish, and even the Russians went home after the war, but we couldn't go home. Why?"

My father studied his cards and slapped one down on the table. "It's as if the war never ended in Eastern Europe."

My mother took the cigarette out of her red mouth and blew a string of smoke up in the air. "Remember how the KGB agitators showed up at the camps urging everyone to return to a free Lithuania, saying that Uncle Joe Stalin said we had nothing to fear. We later heard that those who were caught in the Russian sector of Germany were either sent to Siberia or shot at the train station in their home country." She shook her head. "As if we'd ever trust Stalin."

"The women caught in the Russian zone were raped," Mrs. Vitkus whispered behind her hand. "Which camp were you in?"

"Dillingen, and you?"

"Hanau, thank God. The KGB came to our camp as well."

Mr. Vitkus put out his cigarette. "Remember how after the Soviets invaded in 1940, there followed a reign of terror, and how anyone could be declared a Soviet enemy and put under arrest or deported without any legal process?"

My father added, "What I remember is how, in June of 1941, many thousands of men, women, and children were being deported to Siberia. It only stopped when the Germans invaded Lithuania. And then what a disaster for the Jews." He shook his head as if trying to erase the memories.

"What a horror," said Regina. "I can't bear to think of it."

"Tell me, why didn't the Americans come to rescue Lithuania or Latvia or Estonia?" Mr. Vitkus demanded as he scooped up the cards on the table. "The Allies signed the Atlantic Charter promising to protect the sovereign rights of those forcibly deprived of them. God, I memorized those words! Thousands of anti-Soviet partisans are still in bunkers in the woods, fighting as they wait for Allied help."

"Stalin knew that everyone was exhausted by the war," said my father.

I rolled my eyes. War, war, war. That's all they ever talked about.

Magda and I took our dolls and went to rummage through my mother's box of fabric scraps to see what we could use. I tied a piece of gauzy fabric on my Lovey doll, like a babushka.

Behind me, I could still hear them talking. "Remember V-E Day? How we all celebrated, thinking we could go home again?" Reshuffling the deck, Mr. Vitkus began to drum his war stories again. "Millions of refugees marching across Europe at the end of the war—stateless, without countries or passports."

Regina Vitkus added, "Running from the Soviets into a bankrupt and bombed Germany."

"Enough please, it's New Year's." My mother slapped another card down. "Can't we forget these conversations for just one day?"

"You're right, Dora," said Regina. "Let's talk about something more pleasant."

No one said anything for a few moments, and then my father looked up. "We're finally moving out of this place."

Hearing this, I turned around and asked my father, "Are we going back to the DP camp in Germany?" The adults laughed.

"No, we're moving to Marquette Park, right here in Chicago."

"Really?" Regina's head shot up. "We'll miss you all so much." She looked over at her husband.

Jurgis shrugged, looked at his daughter, Magda, and drank down the rest of his highball.

Across the room, the news hit me hard as tears welled in my eyes when I realized we'd be leaving Magda and Al, and Lovey, Charlie, and even the Gypsies, though they had made me mad. Pete had the same stricken look in his eyes. Neither of us could stand any more change.

"I don't want to move," I announced loudly.

My parents looked at me with puzzled expressions. "Why, Irena?" asked my father. "Do you love this dirty store so much?"

"My friends are here."

My mother waved her hand in dismissal. "Who? Those Gypsies? Bah! Forget those dirty girls. They're nothing but trouble. You've been running wild with them ever since we moved here, and I don't like it."

"What about Lovey?" I pleaded, tears threatening.

My mother shrugged. "Who—that Negro boy? Don't worry, you'll make new friends. I hear there are nice Lithuanian boys and girls in that neighborhood for you to play with."

"I don't care," I said. "What about Magda and Algis?"

"You'll be fine, Irena, you'll see," said Mrs. Vitkus. And with that the adults returned to playing cards and drinking.

Pete went to show Al his stamp collection while I went over to the window to sit with Magda. Hugging my Lovey doll, I scratched a peek hole in the dried pink film on the windows and another hole for Magda. Together we watched the snow falling in thick clumps, piling up on the sidewalks, on the cars, on the trembling bare branches of the elm trees. The night was still and bitterly cold as we watched the lights in the other apartments and houses across the street. We sat there until we heard the bells of Precious Blood Church ringing in the New Year on the South Side of Chicago. Somewhere outside people were cheering and blowing horns. The noise scared Magda, so she held my hand. It seemed all of Chicago was celebrating, but I felt a helpless sadness coming down on me like the snow piling up outside. The war and the refugee camps of Europe seemed far away. My parents' home in Lithuania was behind an Iron Curtain. We had started our new life in America, and it was safe here. But on this night I saw that war wasn't the only heartbreak.

As I was kneeling by the window, my knees began to hurt. Though they had healed long ago, I could still sometimes feel those forgotten sharp cinders my mother hadn't managed to take out. When I looked closely, I could still see them, submerged below my scarred knees, like black pebbles beneath ice, remnants of old pain.

Lost Birds

Agota Janulis, 1951

As Agota Janulis straightened the *Life* magazines on the table, she stopped to consider a cover photo of a hospital nursery filled with rows of babies. War veterans had returned to marry their sweethearts, and now they were having babies, so many that it was called a baby boom. She thought of it as atonement for all the deaths of World War II. The world had gone mad, and now everyone was trying to pretend life was back to normal: having babies, moving to the suburbs, trying to forget names like Hiroshima, Auschwitz, Normandy, and Dresden. She threw the magazine down with a disgusted huff. Why was everyone in such a hurry to forget? What happened to the need for mourning the dead, for grieving losses?

To the rest of the world, it was 1951, a time of technological hope and progress, but Agota's mind was stuck like a needle on a bad record, refusing to go forward. Like a somnambulist, she mopped and dusted and swept the fourteenth floor of the Prudential Building while her mind replayed the recent traumas of the war. It was as if she lived two lives simultaneously.

Regina Vitkus, a dark, compact woman who cleaned alongside Agota, shuffled in like a wraith, wearing a faded housedress. Dunking a mop into the soapy water of the bucket, she clamped the wringers shut with her foot and pulled the steaming mop back out. Agota thought Regina looked as thin as that mop. Still lost in thought, she stared at the rising steam. Six years already since she'd left her farm in Lithuania. A year ago she had come to Chicago from the DP camps in Europe like so many others. Now they were seen all over Chicago—walking ghosts, like Regina—blinking in the foreign sunlight, startled by their new lives. Lithuanians weren't the only ghosts—there were Jewish, Latvian, Ukrainian, and Polish ghosts as well. All of Eastern Europe had infiltrated Chicago. Sick with nostalgia for their lost homelands, they didn't have the hopeful looks of the immigrants who had come before them.

Turning to her reflection in the office window, Agota saw that her broad, fleshy face looked older than her thirty-eight years. After all the hunger and deprivation of the war and post-war years, it seemed she couldn't stop eating in America. Outside, the last wisps of color still hung on the horizon. She watched as the evening colors dispersed, dissolving into gray. Below, a flock of sparrows lifted from one building, swarmed, and finally settled on the window ledges of another high-rise. Once she had seen a hawk nesting on a ledge nearby, obviously lost. These birds didn't belong in the city. On the tracks below, an elevated train clamored loudly, scaring the birds away. The grating and rumbling sound reminded her of the cattle cars headed for Siberia, crammed with men, women, grandparents, and babies. The Soviets had deported the best and the brightest. Those who died on the way to the frozen north were left at train stops like cords of wood. A teacher and a judge had asked her husband, Pranas, to help them to escape to East Prussia, the frontier heavily guarded by the Soviets and their dogs. Afraid of the danger, Agota had begged her husband not to do it, but he wouldn't listen. "Mind your own business," she told him. "Wars come and go. We have to wait until the madness passes." But her husband brought the madness back to the family. One night when returning from the border, a neighbor stopped him before he reached home to tell Pranas that the NKVD was waiting for him. Someone had betrayed him, so he escaped to the woods to join the partisans. That was June 1941, during the first Russian occupation. The following week the deportations stopped when the Germans marched into Lithuania, with the Soviets in retreat.

The Lithuanians were so thankful the deportations stopped, but soon enough they realized this was not liberation but a new occupation. This time, the Jews were rounded up, and the horror began anew, as some were taken to ghettos in the cities while others disappeared into the woods to be shot. By the end of the German occupation, the Jews of Lithuania, who had lived side by side with their neighbors for six hundred years, were suddenly gone. Agota winced, remembering how one of her neighbors took part in the shooting squads and was shunned afterward by his neighbors as a "Jew shooter." When the war shifted again as the Germans retreated, the Soviets returned for Lithuania's third brutal occupation, this time to stay. Then thousands of Lithuanians—anyone with education, land, wealth, or anti-Soviet activism, the best and the brightest of Lithuania—fled like a flock of lost birds, knowing that death or deportation awaited them at the hands of the Soviets. Unable to go south to Poland or north to Latvia, most fled west into the maw of the war; only a few found fishing boats to take them across the Baltic Sea to Sweden. The rest fled in wagons, bicycles, or on foot.

Agota remembered the morning the Russians returned. Her young son Jonas had been having nightmares, so she held him as they both sat rocking, keeping watch out the window for her husband, who had left the night before to help a relative. She heard a rumbling in the distance, as if a storm were coming. She dressed her son and went into the kitchen where her father-in-law stood at the door already clothed, his suitcase packed. When she asked him why he was up so early, he turned to her. "Haven't you heard the artillery thundering? The Russian front is approaching. We have to leave." With a start, she realized that it was not an oncoming storm but artillery that she heard. As her father-in-law went to harness the horses, he told her to pack as much food and clothing as she could fit into the wagon.

Before the sun was fully up, people began swarming through their village, warning that the Russians were only an hour away. They advised us to hide the men because the Germans were seizing them for forced labor. Stuck between one madman and another—Stalin or Hitler—as the bombs came closer and louder. Jonas cried, calling for his papa, but Agota was too busy to comfort him. If she left her husband behind, would they find each other later? She was packing smoked sausages when Pranas ran into the house, and she dropped a large jar of preserves when she saw him. She started to clean it up, but he told her to leave it. The wagon was already out the gate when she jumped off and ran back to the house to get her mother's photograph. Then she took them all, not able to leave them behind, but like so many other things, they got lost in the war.

Leaving the land that was theirs for so long was like tearing something out of Agota's entrails. The soil that had been mixed with the blood and bones of her ancestors was sacred to her. And now it felt as if someone had ripped her away and thrown her into the world, raw and unprotected.

Could it be that that morning was only a few years ago? Agota looked at the last wisps of color on the horizon. It was so strange to be up so high above the city, to be able to see Lake Michigan as it curved toward Indiana, to see so far on the flat plains. Some evenings she felt she could see so far she could almost make out the broad expanse of the Baltic Sea, where she used to gather amber on the shores after storms. And beyond, to the birch forests where she used to fill her basket with mushrooms after the rains, and where, if she looked hard enough beyond the birch trees, she could almost see her home.

A flood of memories came to her, spilling out—her small village, circle dances at a wedding, the lowing of cows in the meadow, the orchard filled with fragrant apples, the smell of freshly cut hay, the white birches lining the way to church, the smell of hams and sausage hanging in the smokehouse. Those were young days, full of promise when she had so many endless days ahead.

Suddenly two women stormed into the room with a handful of tickets. Marcele Gudauskas, the general's daughter who worked on the floor below, marched in like she owned the place, followed close behind by Dora Matas, elegant even in a scarf and apron. "Hello, Agota, we came to ask if you're going to the picnic tomorrow."

"What picnic?" asked Agota, suddenly weary. Gone were the birch trees, the hay, and the smoked hams. It was toilets and dirty tile floors again.

"The Daughters of Lithuania are having a picnic at the Ragis Farm," said Marcele. "They're trying to raise money to build a youth center."

"I don't think I can go," said Agota. When she looked at the two slender women, she felt fleshy and old.

"Oh come on," said Dora, "come out and have some fun." Dora turned to Regina. "And bring Algis and Magda. My Petras and Irena have missed them since we moved to Marquette Park."

"It's for a good cause," said Marcele. She pressed the tickets into their hands. "And besides, we all need to get out and dance with our husbands again."

Feeling a bit bullied, Agota pocketed her tickets and sighed deeply as she watched the women leave.

"What is it, Agota?" asked Regina. "You look so sad tonight. I'm usually the one who's sighing."

"It's nothing." Agota tried to smile. She knew that Regina had her own problems with a husband who drank too much and a daughter who wasn't right.

"No, tell me, what's bothering you?" Regina asked once more.

"Just remembering the war again. I try not to think about it, but it's no use. It haunts me. Some days I feel like I'm a hundred years old."

Regina put her sandwich down. "I'm the same. I keep replaying the day Magda almost died, and I try to imagine what I could have done differently to save her." Regina rubbed her temples. Her eyes always looked wary, as if she'd already seen too much.

Agota looked at Regina as if she were speaking in riddles. "But Magda's alive."

"She's alive but not the same. The little girl I brought into the bomb shelter was bright and lively. The one I pulled out was like another girl altogether. Later, the doctors said it was brain damage. I don't know how to explain it, but something in Magda died that day."

Agota had seen Regina's ten-year-old daughter, but she had always assumed that she was retarded. "What happened?" she asked softly.

"When we were running from the Red Army, we were almost left behind because of Magda, who was not yet five. After I finished packing the wagon, I couldn't find her. I searched until I finally found her in the bathhouse digging to bury her toy tea set the way she had seen us bury our silver service earlier. She wanted to make sure her favorite toy wasn't damaged or lost." Regina shook her head, sipping coffee. "After we crossed the border, I heard the air raid signal before I heard the planes overhead. The British bombed during the day and the Americans during the night. Grabbing Magda, I ran for shelter, pushed by a river of people until I lost sight of my husband. I held Magda's hand tightly, afraid to lose her in the crowd. We scurried down to the cellar of a bombed-out building where only the outside walls were left standing. There was nowhere else to hide. We were cockroaches fleeing into the cracks and crevices of a ravaged town.

"The door to the cellar closed and everyone huddled together, the stench of nervous sweat filling the dim room. Outside, the percussion of bombs started. Far away at first, but getting closer. Soon you could hear the whine of bombs before they hit. The noise became unbearable. Magda screamed and cried while I prayed as the ground beneath us trembled, and the walls rattled. A bomb hit nearby, and the room shook as dirt and dust rained down on us. One woman became hysterical, yelling that we'd be buried alive. She panicked and fled as two men ran after her, trying to calm her. I stood to look for my husband, shouting his name. Magda, afraid to be left behind, began to cry, and I felt her small hand slip out of mine as another bomb hit, knocking us to the ground. A corner of the room collapsed, leaving it open to the dangerous sky. I choked on the dust and the dirt of the explosion. People were shrieking and climbing out of the shelter. Two women lay dead in the rubble. I screamed for my daughter, looking for her. Jurgis found me and we searched together, but Magda was nowhere.

"And then we saw her tiny hand. The rest of her was buried under dirt and rubble. I started digging, crying her name and clawing the earth until my nails were bloody. Jurgis finally pulled her out, and I wiped the dirt from her face. Jurgis listened and heard a faint heart-beat. We knew that if we could only find help, she might live. He climbed out to look for help. I held her as the bombers flew away. Then I looked up at the now-quiet sky and wondered whether to curse God for a world in which bombs fell on helpless children or whether I should thank God for the little bit of life that was still left in Magda."

"Regina, how terrible. I'm so sorry." Agota bit her lip to keep from crying. Another variation on the horror stories they all told one another.

------◈◈◈------

At midnight Agota put away her cleaning supplies, said good-bye to Regina, and left the office building, taking a bus filled with babushka-bound ladies, grimy factory workers, and janitors. Sitting in the back of the bus, she opened a window and stared at the anemic mannequins in the store windows lit by weak fluorescent lights. A lone man walked down the empty street. She watched him for a long time until the bus pulled away with a sigh.

Everyone sat silently with tired faces. A young woman in a blue jacket had fallen asleep with an open book still in her lap. An old Negro woman in a worn brown coat sat down heavily next to her. Agota looked at the woman's hands—working hands also. They all worked as if in a dream, as if they had died already, and Chicago was some gray purgatory. Before she came to America, she had never seen a Negro, an Irishman, or an Italian. This country was filled with the refugees of the world. That was America. How many lost flocks gathered from around the world?

Once home, Agota went to her children's room to check on them. Jonas had kicked off his blanket, so she carefully covered him and kissed his forehead, thinking of Regina's daughter, Magda. Suddenly she wanted to hold Jonas close, so thankful he had survived the war intact. Then she kissed Ona and went to the kitchen. On the table, she found a letter from her brother in Lithuania and opened it quickly. Reading letters from her family was like deciphering a code. Everyone had to be so careful about what they said because Stalin seemed to have spies everywhere. Every word had to be wrapped in shiny paper like a piece of candy to elude the Soviet censors. And the constant talk of the weather—the only way Agota knew if they were in trouble was when they wrote about the terrible storms. But this letter brought news of a death: her great-aunt *Teta* Ona had died of pneumonia. Agota made the sign of the cross and stared at the Formica table, aching to be at her funeral, to see her beloved face once more before it was returned to the earth.

And what about the rest of the family? Sleep often eluded her as she worried, constantly anxious over what Soviet fate had befallen them. Only prayer helped soothe her.

When Agota woke in the gray dawn, she had been dreaming about *Teta* Ona catching lightning bugs with her in the meadow behind their village. Across the room, the nylon curtains billowed in the morning breeze and for a moment she didn't know where she was, until it finally sifted back to her that it was their apartment in Bridgeport.

Pranas stirred from his side of the bed. It seemed to her that he was leading a separate life, waking before dawn to work long hours at the stockyards. He came home tired, his clothes smelling of death. She didn't see him much except on weekends. Pranas turned over. "Go back to sleep. It's Saturday."

"I can't," she snapped.

"Then come back under the covers and I'll help you sleep." He gave her a playful smile and pulled her over to him.

"Stop it," Agota said, getting out of bed and putting on her bathrobe and slippers.

"What's wrong?" he asked, getting up on one elbow.

"Nothing," she said as she scooted out to the kitchen.

As she stood over the white enameled sink, filling the tea kettle, her son came into the kitchen in his pajamas with his stamp album under his arm and sat down at the yellow Formica table. Jonas was such a serious boy for an eight year old, a collector of things—stamps, bottle caps, bugs, anything. Was he always so serious or was it the war that made him so?

"Jonas, do you remember Sapnai?"

The slender boy shook his head and looked up at her, concerned. "Do you think we'll ever go back there?" he asked, his sandy hair falling over his eyes.

Agota cut thin slices of farmer's cheese. "When we left Lithuania, we thought it was only for a few weeks or months until the war ended, or until President Roosevelt and Churchill talked to Stalin at Yalta. But now I don't know when we'll be able to go back."

"I don't want to go back there," Jonas said, frowning. "It's full of bombs, and there's no TV."

Agota was stunned. "But it's our home. My family is there. Your father's family too."

"This is my home. In Chicago."

"You go over to your Irish friend's house and watch the *Lone Ranger* as if there's nothing more important in the world. Don't you realize your uncle is still fighting in the woods with the partisans right this minute?" Agota shuddered to think of the Soviet Army searching for these men. The war still hadn't ended there. "Lithuanians are still being deported to Siberia as you watch your silly TV program."

"It's not a silly program." Jonas frowned. "I want to stay here."

Agota was too upset to say more. It had never occurred to her that her children would want to stay here, that they might become Americans. She finished cutting thick slices of rye bread and took the whipped butter out of the Frigidaire. God willing, we'll return home soon, she said silently like a prayer.

"Morning, Mama." Ona cheerfully padded into the kitchen. Her daughter was born in the displaced persons' camp in Europe and was the only one in the family who had never seen war.

"Sit down, Onute. While I make pancakes, I want to tell you and Jonas a story about my childhood."

Jonas made a face. "Again?"

"It's about *Teta* Ona, my great aunt, may she rest in peace." She blessed herself. "I got a letter that she died, and you'll never know her." Agota took a deep breath. "Onute, you're named after my *Teta* Ona. And, you know, you're starting to look a bit like her."

Ona rubbed her eyes. "Was she pretty?"

"Yes, with wheat-colored hair like yours and the same blue eyes." Agota gently stroked her daughter's hair. "She came to stay with us between the wars when Lithuania was still independent. I remember that day, nothing moved but the white smoke from the chimneys—the whole world still as I sat at the window waiting for my *Teta* Ona. At first, we were so busy with preparations that we didn't notice what she had brought with her."

"What did she bring?" asked Ona. "Gifts?"

Agota shook her head. "My grandmother liked to watch for omens. In Lithuania, everything was carefully watched for signs of good fortune or bad. Luck, illness, death, and a good harvest could all be foretold by the cards, or dropping hot wax into water, or even watching the storks in their nests." Agota looked at her children and thought that no one had ever foreseen a life in Chicago.

"And because our heads were filled with excitement over her visit, we never noticed that *Teta* Ona had brought a *domovoi* with her. We should have known because she came from Russia, which is filled with evil spirits."

"What's a *domovoi*?" asked Jonas.

Agota smiled, glad he was asking. "Like a house spirit, an imp.

It wasn't until after the first week that we finally noticed that the *domovoi* had decided to make his home in our pantry. He rattled around so much that no one dared go in there except my grandmother. I was so afraid that I never went by that door without blessing myself and spitting three times over my right shoulder, and even so the hair on the back of my neck would stand up."

"Mine too!" Ona shivered and grabbed her thin braids.

"Just before Saint John's eve we went to church, leaving Grandmother at home. As soon as our wagon was out of sight, she took out a cross, some holy water, and magic roots from the Rowan tree that had been struck by lightning. For protection, she draped herself with rue. Once she was armed and uniformed, she opened the pantry door and told the imp to get out. Then she blessed herself three times and went into the battle."

"Did it kill her?" asked Ona, biting her lip.

"Almost," answered Agota. "When we returned from church, we found her unconscious on the kitchen floor, and the pantry was a mess of overturned shelves and broken jars. In a fever, she mumbled nonsense for three days. When she finally came to her senses, she told us how she had fought the *domovoi* and cornered him with her last bit of strength, pouring holy water on him and banishing him to the marshes. The last thing she remembered was a howling and whistling."

"Was the *domovoi* gone then?" Ona listened, her pupils wide and dark.

"Yes, it was gone, and we had a celebration. My papa danced with me for the first time and pointed to the lightning bugs, saying, 'Look, Agotele, the lightning bugs are dancing with us.' I loved when Papa called me Agotele, such a sweet way of saying my name, like when I say 'Onute' or 'Jonukas.'" Agota realized that no one called her that anymore, not even Pranas.

Agota heard her husband noisily brushing his teeth. Why did he have to sputter and snort so?

"Mama, do you think we have a *domovoi* in our pantry?" asked Ona, looking around the kitchen.

Pranas came into the room. "What's this talk of *domovoi?*"

"There are no imps in America," answered Jonas very seriously. Agota realized that she felt the same way, as if America lacked the magic of demons. She thought of the skyscrapers and wondered how a *domovoi* could survive there.

Pranas laughed. "My son, the expert on imps." He stretched and yawned. "I feel so lazy today."

Agota turned to him. "I bought some tickets for a picnic at the Ragis farm, but I don't feel like going."

He perked up. "I heard about it at work. They're raising money for a youth center near Marquette Park. The Matas family moved there. Maybe we'll move there soon."

Agota looked up. "Move?"

Pranas shrugged. "Come on, let's go to the picnic. It'll be good to get out into the country."

When the bus arrived at the Ragis Farm, Agota stepped off and stood transfixed until Pranas asked her what was wrong. "It smells like home," she said, looking at the fields and nearby forest preserve.

"Of course it smells like home. We're at a farm, not the city," he chuckled.

Agota smiled, breathing in the air like an old friend. She took Ona's little hand, and together they touched, petted, and talked to all the cows and sheep. When her daughter ran off to play, Pranas asked if Agota wanted to go mushrooming.

She didn't say anything, but her eyes sparkled as she looked at her husband. She hadn't been mushrooming since she left her village. He took her hand, and together they walked through the cool woods like young lovers, dappled sunlight playing over their faces, as the leaves and twigs crunched underfoot. Agota felt drunk with the smells of the forest, caressing each tree until she spotted some mushrooms and ran to pick them, greedily gathering them in her skirt the way she used to with *Teta* Ona. Suddenly she stood up, and all the mushrooms fell to the earth. She fell to her knees, unable to breathe.

"What is it? What's the matter?" asked Pranas anxiously.

"I want to go home."

"We can't go back yet. We have to wait for the bus to take us."

"Not there. Back to Lithuania." Tears were streaming down Agota's face. "I want to go home."

"What are you saying? Dearest, you know we can't go home." Pranas stood there helplessly.

"We should have stayed in Lithuania."

"We'd be in Siberia if we did. Do you think that the Communists would have allowed us to stay on our farms? My God, have any of our relatives stayed on their farms? They've all been moved to Communist collectives or the cities." Pranas trembled in frustration. "Don't you think I also want to return?"

Agota sobbed as he sat down next to her, stroking her hair as he held her, not saying anything, only feeling the sun warm their cheeks. The stillness seemed to soothe her until she finally quieted. When she heard an unfamiliar bird singing in a clearing, she turned to look for it, seeing a wisp of color. When she leaned over to get a better look, the bird flew to another tree. Behind her, she heard twigs breaking and when she moved, she thought she saw something. What was it? She pushed herself up to get a better look. Pranas stood up as well, brushing the leaves off his pants. The lacy sunlight between the trees was moving. The branches were swaying in the breeze. Agota held her breath, waiting for God knows what.

And suddenly there was little Irene Matas, holding a Negro doll and pulling Regina's daughter, Magda. It was strange to see those two girls alone in the woods. Agota remembered Regina's tragic story and thought of telling it to her husband when suddenly Ona ran out from behind the trees and startled them both. "Where have you been hiding?" asked her daughter. "I've been looking for you everywhere."

"Oh, you surprised me!" said Agota, laughing quietly.

"You thought it was a *domovoi*?" Ona stood beaming, her blond braids shining in the sun.

Jonas came from behind another tree. "Mama, she's such a pest, chasing her friends, yelling that she's a *domovoi*, and she's gonna get them." Jonas raised his hands and turned to his sister. "I'm going to get you, you little brat." Ona screeched with delight and pulled her mother, who protested weakly but ran along. Jonas growled and threatened while Ona screamed and laughed until she caught up to Irene and Magda. "Watch out before the *domovoi* gets you." When the girls saw Jonas chasing them, making horrible faces and sounds, they screeched and ran.

"Enough," said Agota, between gasps of breath. "Let's go back to the picnic." She stopped, still laughing, marveling as if something in her had thawed ever so slightly for the first time in many years.

The sun was starting to slip behind the trees when they heard the women back at the farm singing the old songs. Marcele and Dora came out of Mr. Ragis' kitchen with steaming pans of potato *kugelis* and smoked sausages with sauerkraut. "There you are! I was beginning to worry," said Regina as she served cold borscht, giving Agota and Pranas extra helpings. Everyone ate until they heard the accordion begin to play the old songs.

The sun had set, and in the twilight a string of lights swayed gently in the breeze. When the accordion began to play the "Windmill Dance," Agota and Regina joined the circle of dancers. The two women danced and whirled as if they were still young. Afterward, when Agota took Pranas' hand, he looked up at his wife, a bit surprised, as she pulled him toward the other dancers. Suddenly the stout couple began dancing a fast polka round and round, as Pranas twirled his wife faster and faster while she laughed at the sheer physical pleasure of the dance, dizzy with the whirling. When the music stopped, they were both flushed with excitement. Magda and Ona clapped from the sidelines while Irene chased lightning bugs with a half dozen other children. When the band started playing a waltz, Pranas took his wife in his arms as they danced around slowly, both of their hearts still racing. He held her closely and murmured in her ear, "Agotele, you're so lovely tonight."

"What did you call me?" asked Agota.

"Agotele, why?" he asked.

"I just haven't heard anyone call me that for so long."

"Really? Well, then it's about time," he said, kissing her on the cheek.

The couple bobbed and swayed softly to the waltz music. Agota pressed her flushed cheek close to Pranas as her eyes misted over with tears, but through the blur she strained to see if the lightning bugs were dancing along with them.

Blue Tango

Vida Bartulis, 1952

Each morning, Vida and her mama would watch Papa through lidded eyes like thieves, impatiently waiting for him to slam the front door and head for the bus stop. They would both wave good-bye to him through the dime-store lace curtains, and as soon as he was out of sight, Mama would whoop, "The critic's gone."

Sometimes they'd spend the whole morning cooking, making dozens of marzipan cookies and eating them all before Papa came home. Sometimes they'd fry up some of Mama's favorite *ponchkas,* big dough balls filled with lingonberries. Once they spent a whole day making round wafer layers, placing them all over the house to cool—on tables, radiators, and dressers, even on the radio. Then Mama put all the wafers together with a delicious vanilla cream. She called it a Napoleon cake and it became Vida's favorite. They ate half of it and gave the other half to Regina Vitkus because Mama loved Magda, her sad daughter.

Mama played tangos all day long, stacked on the record player. That summer, she dressed both Vida and her friend Irene with scarves and jewelry, painting their faces with ruby lipstick and blue eye shadow. When Vida put on Mama's fringed shawl, Mama called her a little Gypsy. Vida liked "Tango of the Roses" best, but in the end Mama always put one special tango on the record player. Whenever she played it, quiet tears pooled in her eyes. It was called "Blue Tango" and Mama said it was the song of lost dreams.

Some days they would walk with Magda down to the pond in the cemetery and have a picnic under the birch trees. A sad wooden statue of Jesus watched over them, sitting with his head resting in one hand, a troubled look on his face like an old grandfather, worrying about the sins of the world. Mama said all the country roads in Lithuania bristled with shrines of the worried Jesus.

Mama would put down a blanket and take out berries and canned whipped cream, and she'd spray mustaches on their faces. They'd march around like soldiers saluting one another. Afterward, they'd spend the day lying on the grass, watching clouds and eating donuts while Mama wove stories and sang her favorite songs. As she sang, a white butterfly flew from flower to flower and then fluttered in circles around Mama's head. "In Lithuania they used to say the soul of one of your ancestors was visiting whenever you saw a white butterfly," she murmured. "Maybe it's my grandmother come to visit."

The fun stopped when Papa came home. He'd give them that narrow-eyed look like they'd just stolen something from him. Mama tightened up when he walked in the door with his sly fox face. She got quiet and careful. Some days she could joke him up a bit, but if he wasn't in the mood, he would chew her head off. Those were the times Vida saw Mama disappear, go somewhere far away in her mind. Mama would cook and talk, but Vida knew she wasn't there. It gave her the heebie-jeebies.

The year Vida turned six, Mama got sick. Vida played with her even though Mama had to stay in bed. Vida would paint her face like they used to, and she'd play Mama's favorite tangos on the record player. Vida and her friend, Irene, would run to the store to buy cookies and donuts, but Mama just didn't get any better.

The afternoon in June when Vida tied twelve ribbons in her hair, Mama quietly died.

At the funeral, Vida watched her father crying, but she just couldn't cry. She felt like she had turned to wood like that statue of Jesus down at the cemetery. As if something in her died too. Sister Kunigunda brought her class to the funeral home, but Vida didn't want to see any of them, not even her friend Irene.

Vida stared at Mama in the casket, but it just didn't look like her, more like a big wax doll someone had put in a box. Papa told her to kiss Mama goodbye, but she couldn't. She walked up to the casket and tried poking Mama's eyelids to see if they would open. They felt papery. At the cemetery, they put her in the ground under the birch trees like she wanted, but with no statue of the worried Jesus to look after her.

After Mama was gone, Papa hired a housekeeper named Marcele Gudauskas to cook and take care of Vida, but Vida wouldn't have anything to do with the woman. Papa introduced her as the general's daughter and told Vida to shake her hand and curtsy. "She's quit her job downtown to take care of you. She'll teach you good manners." Mrs. Gudauskas of the arching eyebrows penciled in carefully, of the ruby lipstick that smudged on her horse teeth, and the cold blue eyes that bore into Vida. "Delighted to meet you, my dear," Mrs. Gudauskas said. Vida stared at that grinning mouth and heard those soft words, but those icy eyes betrayed her.

And sure enough, the next morning Mrs. Gudauskas spent the day telling her what not to do. "Don't slouch: sit up straight, Vida. Don't talk with your mouth full, chew your food slowly, and no elbows on the table, dear." The litany continued until Vida could hardly move without the woman barking orders.

The following week, Papa also brought home his friend Jurgis Pocius, who liked to be called Mr. George because he thought of himself as a sophisticated man like George Sanders in the movies. Vida thought his bow tie looked like it was strangling his red face. He became their pig-faced boarder, and together the men would drink whiskey and play cards at night. One night, Mr. George put Vida on his lap, and she could feel his fingers clawing her under her dress, but she didn't say anything. She just pushed off his lap and went to her room, vowing never to let him near her again.

On Saturday, Papa and Mr. George brought two women home. Vida had never seen them before. She could hear them talking and playing cards. But when she heard the tango music, she peeked out her door and saw Mr. George dancing with a stout dark-haired lady in a ruffled dress. Pretty soon he was lifting her dress and clawing her too, but she didn't seem to mind. She pulled him over to the crimson sofa, and they both fell on it like they were wrestling. When Papa took the blond lady to his room, Mr. George turned out the lights, and Vida could hear him making his pig sounds.

She snuck into the kitchen to get some cookies, but while she was there she got the white bread, soda crackers, and all the other dull food Mrs. Gudauskas kept around the house and took them back to her room. She sat on her bed and ate until she felt numb. Only then could she fall into a heavy sleep.

Some mornings Vida went to school with Irene. Sometimes she waited until Sister Kunigunda rang the bell for them to come in from the schoolyard, and then she would quietly leave. On those days, she would walk to the cemetery and sit with Mama all day. Sometimes Magda came with her because she never went to school. Vida liked her because she never said much, only held her hand when she was sad. Sometimes Vida would hum tangos for Mama or bring her donuts or cookies and leave them on the grave for her. Often she would eat her lunch while sitting on the part of the grave she thought was Mama's lap. Sometimes she'd take a nap there and dream about Mama. One day she noticed how gray the headstone was, so the next time she brought crayons and drew pictures of flowers and trees on the cold stone. Once she even brought some ribbons and tied them around the headstone.

One day seemed to blend into another. The school year was coming to an end, but even Irene couldn't cheer Vida up. And then one day the doorbell rang, and she opened the door to find a bulky man in a wrinkled coat, holding a scuffed suitcase. He had the beginning of a beard on his long yellow face. He grunted hello and walked right into the living room. When he took off his coat, she saw how dirty his shirt was. He asked where her father was, and she told him he was at work. "Good," he mumbled as he collapsed on the sofa, curling up for a nap. She could hear his snores all the way in her room, and she wondered what other monsters were going to move into their house.

When Papa came home, Vida could see he was unhappy about their visitor, yelling that there was no room for him, but the man just yelled back for him to get rid of his intolerable boarder. Mr. George looked terribly offended and retreated to his room. They continued to argue and drink well into the night, but Vida could see Papa was losing. He seemed to be afraid of this strange man.

The next morning Papa told her that her Uncle Apolinaras was going to live with them. Vida was shocked to find out he was her uncle, but even if he was, she still didn't want him living with them. Her father was about to wake Apolinaras from his drunken sleep, but at the last minute he changed his mind, and with a wave of his hand he left for work.

As soon as the door closed, Vida turned to look at her uncle, still sleeping on the sofa, feeling frightened by his bulk and strangeness. For the first time, she was anxious for Mrs. Gudauskas to arrive. She jumped a little when she saw his eyes pop open.

"Has the critic gone?" he asked. Vida was surprised that he knew the name Mama had called Papa.

"Yes," she said tentatively.

"Great," he said, getting up from the sofa, a wide-toothed grin on his grizzled face. "Let me wash up and shave and then we'll find something to eat."

When her uncle emerged from the bathroom, he looked like a new man: clean-shaven, hair combed, wearing a fresh shirt and pants. He was almost handsome, and he smelled good. In the kitchen, he went through all the cupboards and the refrigerator.

"Vida, there's nothing to eat here, child." He pulled out some flour and lingonberry jam he found hidden at the back of the cupboard and, rolling up his sleeves, he made a dozen doughy *ponchkos* filled with jam. They deep fried them and devoured them just as Mrs. Gudauskas of the-thousand-rules-for-living walked in the door.

"There, that's better; now let's visit your mother," he said softly.

"Where are you going?" asked Mrs. Gudauskas, screwing up her face when she saw the mess in the kitchen.

Uncle Apolinaras and Mrs. Gudauskas glared at each other for a few uncomfortable moments. Then he smiled and said, "I'm Vida's uncle." He looked her over and rejected her. "I don't think we'll be needing your services in this house anymore. From now on, I'll take care of Vida."

"Look here, it's not your place to tell me what to do." Her face matched the color of her ruby lipstick.

"Yes, yes, well, get along now, out you go." Her uncle ushered the general's daughter out the door, with her protesting the whole way. After it was closed, he started laughing, and even Vida smiled.

As they walked to the cemetery, Uncle Apolinaras told her about his travels to France, Australia, and Canada after the war. He talked all the way to the cemetery, but he stopped when they got to Mama's grave. He stared at the cookies and the moldy donuts, at the crayon-colored headstone, at the tattered ribbons flapping in the breeze. For a long time, he was frozen in his silence until Vida sat down on the grave and said, "Mama, your brother's here to see you." Suddenly her uncle fell on his knees, tears streaming down his smooth cheeks, as though he were the one who had lost his mother, not Vida. After he wiped his tears, he gave Vida a huge bear hug, holding her close, telling her how much she reminded him of his sister, how much fun they'd used to have as children. He said the war had changed everything and how sad he was that he hadn't seen her before she died because he had promised her he would.

"You miss her, don't you, Vida?" he asked, his voice cracking.

"Yes," she said, her chin quivering, "very much." And for the first time since Mama died, Vida could feel a shudder of release as tears trickled down her cheeks. And then a flood of tears opened, followed by painful sobs, her face buried in her uncle's embrace. He murmured comforting words and held her until she had cried herself out and finally could only whimper. Once he had wiped her tears, she saw a white butterfly hovering nearby. It followed them part of the way past the other graves as they walked back through the park. Vida kept turning to watch as its delicate wings quivered and fluttered. She wanted to tell her uncle about how Mama said butterflies were the souls of ancestors visiting, but she didn't want to break the spell. The butterfly followed them and then flew away to the dahlias. Vida raised her hand for a little wave good-bye.

When they reached home, her uncle sat her down on the crimson sofa while he went through the record collection in the cabinet. He finally brought out a record with a jacket tattered from use. Carefully taking it out of its sleeve, he placed it on the record player, and Vida smiled as the first scratchy notes of the "Blue Tango" filled the living room.

Where Death Lived

Irene Matas, 1952

Each morning, my mother sat behind me weaving blue satin ribbons into my braids as she hummed the song about three brothers going to war. I could feel her breath on my neck and smell the yeasty warmth of her body and her Evening in Paris cologne as she twisted and plaited my hair. And yet it felt as though a part of her was far away. Perhaps she was thinking about the war again. Because I was a post-war baby, I could never get her attention as well as the war had, and sometimes I longed for her and missed her even when she was sitting right next to me.

That Tuesday in June, after she tied fat bows at the end of my blond braids, she handed me my sack lunch and dutifully kissed me. I walked to Vida's house, as always, knocking on her door, but no one answered. At first, it felt odd walking to school alone, but soon Magda, who didn't go to school, joined me at the corner. She walked with me, singing snatches of cartoon songs, but said good-bye once I entered the schoolyard.

I sat in the warm, stuffy classroom, but I couldn't concentrate, wondering if Vida was sick. My Catholic uniform felt too tight, making me itchy and restless. I was tired of fingering the same places on the well-worn wooden desks, of kicking the same black iron legs, of smelling the wax and chalk dust in our room. I was even tired of the view out of the second-story windows of our brick grammar school. The view changed with the seasons and weather—clouds drifted in and out, skies turned from blue to gray, trees lost their leaves and filled out again, but the telephone wires and spidery water towers were always the same. Bored and restless, I longed to run outside in the wind, to twirl in circles until I was dizzy, and roll down a hill until my clothes were grass-streaked.

The nun droned on in the front of the room. When she walked between the rows of desks, I could smell her soap and hear the crisp swish of her black habit and the clatter of her rosary beads as they hit our desks. I looked at her and wasn't exactly sure if she was human. Once, when Connie O'Connor asked the nun if she had hair under the stiff white thing on her forehead, we were shocked to see Sister Kunigunda's rigid face break into ferocious laughter. It took her a couple of minutes to contain herself, and then the nun bent over and whispered conspiratorially that she had purple feathers instead of hair. We all nodded solemnly, our suspicions confirmed.

Outside, the birds jumped excitedly from branch to branch in the elm tree. I was lazily printing my name, Irene, at the top of the blue-lined paper when Sister Kunigunda opened a note delivered from the office and announced that something terrible had happened. We all stopped and looked up.

"Let us pray for Vida Bartulis' mother, who died yesterday," she said, starting a prayer.

I looked over at the empty place where Vida usually sat and felt so shocked and sad. I knew that people died. My uncles had died during the war, and there was Jesus, who was always dying on the cross in every room, but I still couldn't understand how one of our mothers could die. While I knew that Vida's mother had been sick, but we all got sick. It frightened me to think that parents could die, because they seemed so powerful, so important. How could they die? These fearful thoughts gnawed at me, but lightly overlaying this fear was the excitement that something huge had happened, something never before experienced, something very mysterious.

Sister Kunigunda announced that the whole class would walk to the Gudaitis Funeral Home after lunch for Vida's mother's wake. I had no idea what a wake was. I only hoped it had nothing to do with waking the dead, as in the story the nun once read about Lazarus.

As the lunch monitor passed out the chocolate and white milk to each row, we took our sandwiches out of our paper sacks. My mother had made me a sausage sandwich on black bread, which daily embarrassed me because it was big and clumsy. When I took a bite, the tomato dripped down my arm. I peeked over to see what Connie O'Connor was eating. I was so envious to see her bologna sandwich on white bread—so neat, no odor, very American-looking. Though I had often begged my mother, she refused to buy what she called cotton bread, claiming Lithuanian black bread made you healthy and strong.

After lunch, Sister Kunigunda lined us up in two rows—one for the girls and one for the boys.

"Irene Matas, you can go to the front of the line," she said, giving me a little push. I didn't know why she put me there—maybe because I was Vida's friend. But all of this scared me and made me nervous. Sister cautioned us to be very good, for we were going to visit the dead. She said that Vida's family was in mourning and that if anyone laughed or giggled or fooled around, they would have to deal with her and the yardstick when we returned. Death was serious. All of these warnings and threats immediately made us all want to giggle nervously and fidget.

Sister Kunigunda and her two anxious rows of uniformed first graders obediently walked down Sixty-Ninth Street to Western Avenue, until we finally reached the Gudaitis Funeral Home. Magda followed us all the way there, waving to her brother, Al Vitkus, and me. I looked at Al and saw that he was too embarrassed to wave back, ignoring her until she finally turned around to go home. I was starting to realize that there was something not quite right about Magda. The fact that she didn't go to school like the rest of us was strange enough, but there was something childish about her that confused me.

Like soldiers in formation, we marched up to the front of a blond brick building with its fancy shirred nylon curtains and blue-canopied door. This was the Funeral Home where Death lived. Though I had often passed this place on my way to the drugstore and wondered what went on in there, today I wanted no part of it. None of us wanted to go inside. We could see it in each others' faces.

When Sister Kunigunda opened the heavy wooden door, the building swallowed us in its cool, perfumed darkness. There seemed to be no air, only the choking smell of roses. It was so dark that I bumped into Connie.

"Cut it out, Irene," she hissed.

"I'm sorry," I whispered nervously. It took a while for my eyes to adjust to the dimness, and then I saw a room that looked like a tiny church filled with flowers. At the front, people dressed in black were crying into their hankies. Somewhere creepy organ music was playing, and I thought that maybe I had stepped into a horror movie. I stared at the strange box in the middle of all the flowers, seeing an unfamiliar and powdery woman, painted like a big doll. For a moment, I thought that it couldn't be Vida's mom, that maybe they had put a statue there instead, like the statues of saints in the church.

The nun instructed each of us to go to the open casket one at a time and kneel down to say a prayer for the soul of Vida's mother—one Hail Mary would be sufficient. Then we were to pay our respects to Vida and her father, to tell them we were very sorry for their loss. Then we were to sit quietly until everyone in class was finished. Filled with tension and uncertainty, we sat down and waited as Sister Kunigunda went to talk to Vida's father, who was very upset. When Vida turned around to look at us, I nervously waved to her, but she seemed to look through me.

Soon Sister Kunigunda came back and pushed a reluctant Al Vitkus up to the front. She told me I was next. My stomach dropped as I watched Al kneel down in front of the casket lined with pleated satin. If that was Vida's mother, then they had done something very strange to her to make her look like that, and I didn't want to go anywhere near her. I wanted to run outside and cry. Instead, I followed Al, kneeling by the casket and blessing myself. My knees still bothered me whenever I knelt, those old cinders still stabbing me from when I had skinned them in the alleys. I gave up my pain for Vida's mother's soul, but I couldn't pray. Instead, I stared at her lying on a white satin pillow. So this was death. It was hard to believe this was the same woman who would dress Vida and me like Gypsies and dance the tango with us, laughing so hard she'd have to hold her sides. Once, we ate too many cream puffs and felt sick afterward. I had always envied Vida because her mom was more like a kid, always joking and laughing, so unlike my mother. Now it seemed strange to see her so still, the rosary wrapped around her papery hands as if she were praying. I started having strange thoughts: *what if she suddenly opened her eyes or said something or sat up?* Then I saw that her lips were open just a bit, and there was something weird in there, like cotton. I could hardly breathe.

Sister Kunigunda tapped me on the shoulder, and I shot up like a rocket, stumbling over to Vida, who looked as if nothing in the world was ever going to make her happy again. My heart ached to see her so alone and motherless. It made her different from the rest of us who still had two parents. We would always say she was the girl whose mother had died.

"I'm so sorry about your mother, Vida." My eyes smarted as they filled with tears. Her face twitched with pain. I wanted to cry and to hug her, but I was too stunned. "I'll see you, OK?" I whispered, wiping my eyes with the back of my hand.

She stiffened but didn't look at me. I could see she wanted to die too.

I said the same dumb things to Mr. Bartulis and waited in one of the pews as the rest of the thirty-two kids in my class went up one-by-one to experience the same frightening yet fascinating ritual. We were missing math and the spelling test. Sickened by the cloying smell of roses and the crushing grief, I felt faint until Al Vitkus knocked me in the ribs with his elbow.

"Wake up, Irene." I almost crumpled, and a nervous giggle trembled through the pew. The nun frowned at Al, raising one finger in warning and giving him "the look."

Finally, when everyone finished, we walked through the darkened funeral home out into the busy street, squinting in the bright glare of the sun. Great green maple trees swayed in the breeze and flowers flaunted their blooms. The whole world looked filled with color and life. Bright cars still moved, and people still walked as if nothing had happened. As we walked back to school in two straight rows, the smell of roses stuck with me, forever reminding me of death.

When we returned, Sister Kunigunda took Al into the cloakroom with her yardstick. We winced, hearing the nun whacking his behind. Then, as if nothing had happened, Sister emerged with her long, tense face, not saying another word about Al or Vida and her dead mother. Instead, she got out the Bible storybook and started reading about someone named Abraham. I couldn't listen. I just stared out the window and wondered if those birds would keep singing and those trees keep right on growing if I died.

———

That evening, when I padded into the kitchen in my slippers and sat at our Formica table, I asked my mother to describe something from her house in Kaunas. It was a game we often played when I was younger. "Have I ever told you about my grandmother's opal ring from St. Petersburg?" she asked, smiling. "She used to keep it in a tiny blue enamel box on the dresser."

"What did it look like?" I wanted to know. "It was oval and sparkled in many colors. She gave it to me when I married your father, but I had to give it to a farmer in exchange for food during the war." She looked at her hands, but soon I could see her eyes glaze over with that familiar sad look as she busied herself with making dinner. The clock ticked loudly above the Singer sewing machine as I sat at the kitchen table absent-mindedly rubbing the flowered oilcloth cover. My mother was humming the familiar windmill song as she peeled potatoes. Suddenly, she stopped to stare out the window, a potato in one hand and the peeler in the other, as if she still saw that opal ring. I wondered why it held my mother's attention better than I did.

I went into the living room to watch the Jackie Gleason Show on TV. My father sat in his favorite chair while Antanas Balys, our shy, reclusive boarder, sat on the couch. As we three watched the show, I heard my father's newspaper fall. A minute before, he had been reading it, but now his eyes were closed, and his chin rested on his chest. A cold jolt ran through my stomach. I knew he was dead, like Vida's mother. As I quietly rose to take a better look at him, he snorted and opened his eyes, scaring me, so I almost jumped. When he saw me peering at him, he smiled, mumbling something about being tired. Across the room, Antanas Balys laughed his shy, little-boy laugh into his thick fist as if I had played a good trick on my father. I bit my lip and shrugged, never quite knowing what to make of this boarder of ours.

"What is it, Irena?" asked my father.

Pulling myself together, I asked the first thing that popped into my head. "Papa, you know Magda Vitkus?"

"Yes, of course. Why?"

"Why doesn't she go to school like the rest of us?"

"She's a little slow, you know." He frowned and touched his head, picking up his newspaper again.

"Oh," I said, but I didn't know what he meant. It confused me.

In my bed that night, I couldn't sleep for a long time. There were too many things in life that baffled me completely. What was wrong with Magda? Was Sister Kunigunda human like the rest of us? Why did Vida's mother die? And was my mother or father going to die too?

One thing I knew for sure—Death lived right down the block and his breath smelled of roses. I would never walk by the funeral home again without feeling a shiver down my back.

Later that night, before I finally dropped off to sleep, I thought about my mother braiding my hair. I said a prayer that she wouldn't die, but as I said it, the strange thought came to me that some hidden part of her had already died during the war.

Lachryma Christi

Irene Matas, 1953

At the age of seven, I became a wretched sinner. When the year started, I was an innocent, still unaware of the sins of the world. It was the year I had yearned to be a nun like Sister Margaret, who looked like Grace Kelly in a veil. Every morning at Mass, I watched her gentle face framed by her wimple, doe eyes yearning for heaven as we sang the Latin hymns—*Tantum Ergo* and *Salve Regina*. Someday I was sure the Pope would declare her a saint like Saint Theresa, the Little Flower. I prayed to Saint Theresa, staring at her statue with burning intensity, waiting for a miracle to happen the way they did in the *Lives of the Saints* that Sister read to us daily. In that book, miracles were as common as the milkman leaving a bottle at our doorstep, as miraculous as the ragman in his wagon down the alley, paying us money for rags. Miracles were God's way of saying "I'm still here." They happened to saints all the time, so my friend Vida and I thought they might happen to good girls who prayed a lot, sang hymns in Latin, and recited the Catechism. The statue of Saint Theresa might move, or bleed, cry real tears, or even walk off its perch in the nave of the Nativity of the Blessed Virgin Mary Church to talk to us. Sister would be so proud of us then.

Lately, Sister Margaret was preparing us for our First Holy

Communion. She gave us holy cards whenever we were good, and at Mass we traded them until our Daily Missals bristled with them. Once, Sister gave me a card with St. Lucy with her eyes on a tray. No one wanted the martyr cards. Vida got Saint Agatha holding her lopped-off breasts on a tray. They didn't look real—more like scoops of strawberry ice cream with a cherry on top. Too embarrassed to keep it, Vida threw it away in the alley trash can. The holy cards we coveted were Saint Anthony, who found lost things, or Saint Jude, the patron saint of hopeless causes, whom you called on whenever there was trouble.

A month before our First Communion, as Easter approached, Sister Margaret gracefully walked into class, her habit swishing behind her, smelling of baby powder. She announced that those of us who already had our Communion outfits would be able to participate in the Easter Sunrise procession. That day, I begged my mother to get my dress right away. We went to three stores on Ashland Avenue where dresses seemed to have yards of tulle, pearls, and silk flowers—lily of the valley was the most popular, followed by stephanotis. I found the perfect dress—satin with a row of small seed pearls down the front. My veil had matching pearls along the headpiece. I wore it with white gloves, white nylons, my first garter belt, and a scratchy crinoline slip. I looked beatific.

During recess the next day, all the girls excitedly compared their Communion dresses, describing them in detail. They were made of silk, brocade, or fine lace; the skirts pleated, or puffy with petticoats underneath; the veils accented with lace, glass diamonds, or silk flowers. We were all the little brides of Jesus. As expected, pretty Milda Gudauskas said she had the most beautiful dress with embroidered roses on silk, with a crystal raindrop on each rose. Her veil and even her shoes had the same crystals. My friend Vida and I were mad with envy. But poor Vida seemed to have the ugliest

Communion dress—plain white, no pearls or lace, and no embroidered flowers—nothing but a plain, round collar and long sleeves. It sounded more like a nurse's uniform than a Communion dress. Vida didn't want to talk about it. I was sure that her mother, who died the previous year, would have hated that dress.

Recently, after Vida's Uncle Apolinaras left for work in New York, Mrs. Gudauskas returned to keep house for Vida's father. I was angry that Mrs. Gudauskas had bought her daughter, Milda, the prettiest dress, yet had managed to find the ugliest one for Vida. When I told my mother about it, she clucked her tongue, frowning, and the next day she bought a delicate lace collar you could tuck into the neckline. She sewed pearls on it by hand. I took it over for Vida to try. She bravely put it on and smiled, even though it only helped a little.

On Easter morning, my mother woke me to prepare for Sunrise Mass. I quickly dressed, and we walked to church in the dark. The girls lined up in their Communion dresses, our starched and scratchy crinoline slips chafing as we entered carrying calla lilies or baskets of white rose petals. As the sky began to lighten, Father Paulius, our regal pastor in his gold vestments, entered the vestibule. He waited until the first glints of the sun came up over the horizon, and then Al Vitkus, his altar boy, rang the bells, as the priest carried the monstrance into the church. Priests followed sprinkling holy water while altar boys waved censors, sending up clouds of incense. Finally, we girl brides entered, dropping rose petals on the marble floor, followed by the boys in their blue suits, marching solemnly. Even though the church was dark, I could see it was packed with people wearing their Easter best. As we entered, the pastor lit the large Paschal candle at the altar, a signal for the whole church to slowly light up until it blazed like the risen sun. The organ swelled as the choir sang out in full voice, "Alleluia, Alleluia, Christ is risen."

All the pomp and ceremony made my head swoon—the choir,

the pageantry, the smell of incense, and flowers. Tears threatened as I looked up at the cross and realized that Christ had finally risen to heaven after all of his sufferings. He was always in such agony on that cross. Our class had walked the Stations of the Cross on our knees on Good Friday, picturing every step of his torment and death. During Lent, we gave up candy and anything sweet so that we could add our little suffering to his great suffering. And now he was risen. Alleluia. I only hoped to be worthy of receiving him for the first time during my First Holy Communion in May.

But before our First Communion, we had to make our First Confession. The Monday after Easter, Sister Margaret rolled up her gigantic sleeves and quieted the clacking crucifix that hung on her stiff white bib. We could see that she meant business today. She called me up to the front of the class and gave me a stack of booklets to pass out to each row. Inside were long lists of sins with places to mark how many times we had committed each sin. After all, we were now seven, the age of reason, old enough to know what sin was. We memorized the seven deadly sins of gluttony, sloth, envy, lust, pride, wrath, and greed. Then Sister Margaret explained the difference between a mortal sin and a venial sin. A mortal sin sent you straight to hell while a venial sin sent you to purgatory—that muffled gray zone that was neither heaven nor hell. My homework for the rest of April was to scour my conscience for remembered sins. If we scrupulously confessed them all, we would be forgiven, making our souls as white as our Communion veils. Then we would be worthy of receiving the Blessed Sacrament.

After school, I went over to Vida's house as I often did and found that Mrs. Gudauskas, who usually gave us sugar cookies while we played Old Maid, was sick that week. We were on our own, so we practiced kneeling gracefully, lifting our faces, and sticking out our tongues for the host, hoping we looked holy rather than goofy during our First Communion. Piling books on the floor to use as the kneeler, we took turns being the priest, imagining the cookies were the host. As I was putting a cookie on Vida's tongue, Mr. George, their boarder, came out of his room wearing an undershirt tucked into his suit pants. He had moved back into Vida's house after her Uncle Apolinaras left. Mr. George's brown hair was sticking up on one side of his head. It was the first time I had ever seen him without his shirt and bow tie. We had had several boarders living at our house, too, who came and went. When we first bought a house, it seemed like the whole world moved in with us. My mother said they helped us pay for the house. I was always curious about what these boarders did in their rooms all day. My favorite boarder was Mr. Antanas, whose wife and four children got left behind in Lithuania. He was sad and sometimes drank too much, but he was sweet and quiet, so I always felt sorry for him. Mr. George, on the other hand, was an old bachelor, who was neither quiet nor sweet, and I could see by the look in Vida's large, gray eyes that she didn't like him one bit.

"What are you girls up to?" he asked, carrying a smelly plate with fish bones to the kitchen.

"Practicing for our First Communion," said Vida, very solemnly.

"No kidding." He padded over to watch us, scratching his hair back into place. "Hey, let me be the priest, OK? I always wanted to know what it felt like." He put his plate down on the cocktail table.

Vida frowned. "No, we can do it ourselves."

Mr. George paid no attention. "Oh Vida, don't be such a spoilsport." He smiled, showing his small teeth, his pug nose wrinkling. "This will be fun. Now, you girls kneel down here." He took the plate of cookies away from me and began to mumble as he made the sign of the cross.

I knelt down, closed my eyes and stuck out my tongue, waiting as he whispered something and put a vanilla wafer on my tongue. I could smell smoked fish on his fingers, and it made me slightly nauseated. Holding my breath, I blessed myself and stood up, returning to my pew, which was the couch.

"Well done, girls. You'll be the best in your class on Communion day." We practiced two more times until all the cookies were gone. Mr. George looked disappointed. "Do you both have Communion dresses?" His small yellow teeth peeked out of one side of his mouth like a row of corn kernels.

After I had described my dress, I ran to get Vida's dress and put the lace collar over it. Vida didn't say anything, curled up like a tight shell in the corner of the sofa, so I had to do all the talking.

Mr. George said that Vida's dress looked exactly like his mother's Communion dress. He told us how he treasured his mother's First Communion photo because she looked so innocent. He asked if we wanted to see it.

Vida shot up. "No, we need to do some homework," she said quickly, pulling at my arm.

I thought she was rude, so I protested. "Wait, Vida, let's see the photo first."

"No, I don't want to see it," she snapped back. "Let's go, Irene." Vida looked surprisingly upset. She was usually such a quiet mouse.

Mr. George smiled at me. "It's all right. Let Vida start her homework." He took my hand. "Come with me, dear, I'll show you the photo."

Vida tried to stop me. "Don't go, Irene," she pleaded.

Mr. George laughed as he pulled me into his room. He turned to Vida and bowed. "Don't worry, your little friend will be right back, as soon as I've shown her the funny old photos, including one of me in a sailor suit."

When I turned to look at Vida and saw her anguished face, distant alarm bells sounded.

Mr. George pushed the door closed with his back. "That little girl is too serious, don't you think?"

The small room had an old-fashioned bed and a matching bureau. Even though there was one window opened just a crack, with nylon curtains billowing in the breeze, the room smelled stuffy, as though it needed a good cleaning. There was a chair with some white shirts draped over it, and a pair of old brown lace-up shoes trying to hide under the bed. I noticed that Mr. George was wearing worn brown slippers with lumpy toes. He told me to sit down on his bed while he rummaged through a drawer of photos. The springs creaked as I climbed up and sat stiffly on the very edge, on the nubby green bedspread that was half off the bed.

He pulled out an old leather album and sat down next to me. "I finally found it. Let's see," he said, flipping the black pages. He showed me a yellowed photo of a serious boy with the same pug nose wearing a sailor suit. "That's me, can you believe it?" He laughed and showed another photo of his older sister, who lived in Australia. "Poor Vera never married." He patted me on the arm. "How could a woman with such a mean face find a husband, eh? She scared them all away." He laughed. "Not like you. You have such a sweet, pretty face. All the boys will want to marry you." He caressed my cheek, and I blushed, feeling uncomfortable.

"Come sit on my lap, will you? So we can both see these old photos better." Before I could protest, he pulled me up on his lap and put the album on my knees. "Let's find that communion photo. You turn the pages, and I'll tell you when to stop." I began to turn the pages filled with black-and-white photos, each held in place with little white corner holders. There were photos of people from long ago, some sitting stiffly in dark suits and long dresses, staring at me from the past. He talked into my ear, telling me stories of his grandmother, who was a servant for a rich family in Warsaw; his aunt, who owned a clothing store in Kaunas; and his grandfather, who once saw the Tsar in St. Petersburg. All the while his breath was a fish cloud surrounding us. And then he finally found his mother's photo in her Communion dress, which was even plainer than Vida's. Her hair was braided and curled like two snakes around her ears. She was holding a lily as she looked at the camera warily. "Isn't she lovely?" asked Mr. George. His breath, though still fishy, was now hot, and it tickled my ear. I wanted to get down and run out of the room, but one hand held me firmly, while the other hand slowly crept under my uniform skirt, sliding between my legs until I gasped in shock. When I turned to look at him, I saw he had his eyes closed. "It's OK," he cooed. "You're a good girl. There now, that's good, isn't it?"

I squirmed, trying to get off his lap, but his grip on me tightened. "Oh, you can't go yet." He kept touching me. Finally, I pushed his hand away, so embarrassed I couldn't even look at him. I shoved the photo album off my lap, and it landed on the floor with a thud, some of the photos slipping out. But just as I slid off and my feet thumped on the floor, he grabbed my hand and pulled me back toward him.

"Let me go," I pleaded, my panic rising.

"You don't need to go yet," he said as he put my hand on the swelling in his brown pinstriped pants, and I could feel something subterranean moving underneath the material. I pulled my hand away quickly, as if burned.

"I've got to go," I screeched, pushing him, desperate to get away.

"What's your hurry?" he said soothingly. "We're just starting to have some fun." He grabbed my hand again and smiled with those ugly little teeth.

"Please." I pleaded and tugged, but Mr. George held on tightly, hurting my hand.

"You won't tell, will you? I'll let you go if you promise not to tell." His smile now seemed cruel.

My chin quivered, and tears threatened like an approaching storm, but choked with fear, I couldn't say another word.

"If you promise not to say anything, then I won't tell anyone about the sin you just committed." He still smiled, but his eyes threatened.

I nodded, tugging with all my might until he finally released my hand. Wrenching open the door, I lurched out of the room, desperate to escape. Too ashamed to look at Vida, I fled and didn't stop until I got to my house and found Magda waiting for me on the front stoop. I told her I couldn't play and ran up the stairs, ignoring her hurt look. To avoid my parents, I rushed to my room and closed the door, crawling into my bed, still trembling with fear. Every time I thought of Mr. George, I shuddered, feeling spoiled and dirty. Pulling the covers over my head, I squeezed my eyes shut, hoping the memory would vanish.

Later, when my mother called me to dinner, I said my stomach hurt, so she brought me tea and a hot-water bottle and felt my forehead. I shifted my gaze, my face burning with shame. With all my heart, I wanted to tell her, but I was too ashamed. After she left, I hugged the hot-water bottle for comfort throughout the night. Each time I fell asleep, calamitous monsters and beasts chased me in nightmares. Flailing and tossing, I hardly slept all night. In the morning, my mother noticed that I was exhausted and haunted. Touching my forehead, she checked for fever, wanting to know if my throat hurt. I shook my head. In the end, she looked out the window at the gray, drizzly day and decided I should stay home from school. I covered my head with my quilt and finally slept. When I awoke that afternoon, the whole world seemed to have changed. Nothing seemed safe or happy anymore. There was something dark in the world that spoiled everything.

The next day I walked to school, feeling burdened with hot shame. Though I sat in my same seat, I couldn't look at Vida or Sister Margaret. Usually, I was so eager to raise my hand to answer questions or volunteer for some task, but today I kept my eyes lowered, and my hands folded, trying to hide behind Allen Braun's big head. Sister Margaret went through penmanship, arithmetic, and spelling, and then it was time to get out our catalog of sins to see if we had anything new to add to our list. With our pencils, we marked each time we had lied to our parents, stolen, cursed, or had impure thoughts. I felt sick to my stomach. The bowels of hell were going to open and grab me for one of their own. I turned crimson and kept my eyes down, with the booklet covering my face, hoping the nun didn't notice my blushing.

Sister Margaret repeated her little speech about Confession wiping our slates clean of any evil stains on our souls. All would be forgiven by the priest in the confessional so long as we confessed all of our sins.

That sounded so soothing. Could it be true? I could be forgiven, and my soul would be cleansed and pure again. The shame would continue, but my soul would be saved. I held on to that thought with all of my being until a new worry started. How would I find the words to describe this sin if Sister hadn't even mentioned it? Searching through the entire catalog of sins, I couldn't find it anywhere. There were no words for it. Now it seemed as if, everywhere I looked, sins were lurking like cockroaches ready to scurry the minute you turned on the light.

During recess, I sat on a bench at the far end of the playground, hoping to be left alone, but Vida came and sat down next to me, looking anxious and uncomfortable. "Irene, are you OK?"

I couldn't look at her, but I nodded my head and mumbled, "Yeah."

"You know something, I don't like Mr. George. Do you?" she asked very softly. "He's a bad man."

In that instant, I realized that she knew what had happened in that room, though I also hoped we would never speak of it. And just as suddenly, a new possibility arose. I wondered if it had happened to her as well, though I couldn't bear to ask her. "No," I spit out, my anger suddenly rising. "I hate him."

"Me too. From now on we'll go to your house after school." Vida scratched her knee and sniffed loudly. We watched Al Vitkus run by, chasing a ball, followed by Paul, who nimbly jumped over the rope that the girls were getting ready to twirl.

"Yeah," I agreed. "My house from now on." And the subject was closed. Neither of us could bear to talk about it, both buried under boulders of guilt.

The days plodded on mercilessly until the Saturday before May Day. Our First Holy Communion would be tomorrow, but today was our First Confession. The class lined up in rows in front of the confessional with our lists of sins in hand. I stood watching as each of my classmates stepped inside the wooden booth—a torture chamber. Struggling to find the words, I fidgeted and squirmed, wondering what would make this sin seem less huge. Over and over, I searched to find the words, but nothing came. Al, who stood in front of me, slipped into the other side of the confessional. I could hardly breathe. Milda came out of the near side, leaving the door wide open, waiting for me, but I was paralyzed and couldn't move. I could only stare at the empty cubicle with a cold heart. Sister Margaret came by and gave me a slight shove toward the door. I took three faltering steps on wobbly legs and knelt down, folding my hands. As I waited for the priest's little window to slide open, I felt sick. Struggling for the right words, I braced myself. On the other side of the confessional, I could hear the priest absolving Al, giving him penance—five Hail Marys and five Our Fathers. I was sweating so hard my scalp itched and my heart banged a rhythm in my ears. Let this be over with quickly. I prayed to Saint Jude to help me with this hopeless cause. But what if the priest was horrified by my sin? What if he started to yell at me, and the rest of the class heard? What if Sister Margaret found out and kicked me out of school? What would my parents think?

Suddenly, I flinched as the little door slid open, and I heard Father Paulius mumble something. Through the confessional screen, I could smell the priest's shaving lotion. I took a deep breath and plunged in. "Bless me, Father, for I have sinned. This is my first confession," I said in a quivering voice, swallowing the tears that threatened. "I lied to my mother ten times and to my father eight times." I started my confession with the easy sins—stealing change from the hall table and envying Milda's communion dress. I wrestled with my conscience right up to the very end of my confession. Then it was time to tell him the big one. I hesitated when the priest asked me if that was all. My face turned a moist red. I stammered and hemmed and stammered some more. "There is one more thing," I started.

"Well, get on with it," the priest whispered forcefully. "Others are waiting, my child."

I was holding my breath. "All right," I said as if I were diving off the high board. "I went over to my friend's house after school, and we were practicing for our communion…"

"I don't have time for the whole story, just tell me the sin." His whispers were getting louder with impatience. "Oh," I said, gulping down my panic. "Yes, well, it happened so quickly that I didn't realize…" I trailed off, not knowing what to say next. I was feeling light-headed. I wanted forgiveness, but no matter how much I wanted it, I just couldn't spit it out. I simply couldn't. My dry mouth was open, but nothing came out. The priest finally asked me if I was finished. I whispered a defeated, "Yes" and tears welled up. He absolved me and gave me the same five Hail Marys and five Our Fathers that Al Vitkus got. In shock, I stood up, opened the door of the confessional, and stepped out like a robot, to return to my pew. I knelt down and glanced up at the cross where Christ looked up to heaven with those sorrowful eyes. I was a doomed sinner—all alone with my huge sin. If God didn't strike me dead on the spot, then surely the Pope would excommunicate me. No *mea culpa* could help me. I was damned for all eternity. I said my penance, but I knew I was unforgiven.

The next day I put on my Communion dress and veil and went to church with my parents, simply going through the motions because my heart had turned cold. My mother kept asking me if I felt all right. All the other girls were excited, dressed in their Communion regalia and holding the pearlized prayer books Sister Margaret had given us. The procession marched to the front pews, where we waited for the sacrament of Communion. The statues of saints seemed to be glaring down angrily at me. We walked up one-by-one and knelt down and raised our heads, stuck our tongues out, and waited for the holy wafer just like Vida and I had practiced. Only now I wondered if it would burn my sinner's tongue. I remembered Sister Margaret had told us a story about a man who ate meat on Friday, saying he didn't believe in the holy day of fasting. He ate a piece of bologna while looking at the crucifix in his kitchen and was struck blind right on the spot. Would the same thing happen to me? Would my limbs shrivel like that poor boy I once saw at the carnival? Would my mind go bad like Magda's?

The altar boy rang the bells for Communion. One-by-one, my classmates knelt down at the altar until it was my turn. The priest said the blessing, and I was almost in tears when he put the wafer onto my tongue. I quickly closed my mouth, blessed myself and went back to my pew, waiting for catastrophe to strike. The wafer stuck to the roof of my dry mouth, and I couldn't peel it off with my tongue. I knelt, waiting for it to melt away, wondering how God was going to punish me. My guilt tore at my soul.

When Mass finished, I walked out of the church, blinking in the May sunshine. Everyone was to go to the auditorium to get their formal portraits taken before going home to celebrate with their families.

My mother had invited our family friends, who congratulated me, giving me presents of a gold cross and savings bonds that I didn't deserve. My mother had made roast beef and mashed potatoes. My father brought out a special bottle of wine that he had saved for this occasion called Lachryma Christi—the tears of Christ. I wondered if the tears tasted salty like my tears when they rolled down into the corners of my mouth. Later, when I found a tiny bit of the wine left in a glass in the kitchen, I drank it, though the taste was awful. If only those tears could make me a good girl again.

<hr />

A week later, Sister Margaret passed out large envelopes containing the formal portraits from our First Communion. I looked at Milda's photo in her lace dress, a rosary dangling from white gloves, eyes cast up towards heaven. She looked as if she'd just seen the Beatific Vision, a beautiful innocence beaming from her face like the morning sun. My photo looked different from the others. I saw at once that it was the face of a sinner—troubled and haunted. As I looked at the other portraits around the room, I realized they all looked saintly—all except one other face whose large gray eyes had the same haunted expression. Vida and I looked at each other's Communion photos and recognized our kindred souls.

Stalin on Talman Street

Jurgis Vitkus, 1953

I n the gray Chicago dawn, Jurgis Vitkus woke in tears, keeping his eyes shut, not wanting to face the day. He had been dreaming about Magda's tea set again. It had been his daughter's favorite toy, and she would make him drink from the tiny cup before she was injured. Life in Lithuania had been a sweet dream before the war. He had loved his farm—earth so black and rich you could spit on it and something would grow. Marriage to Regina had brought his beautiful children—first Magda and later his son, Algis.

A familiar wave of nausea washed over him. No good thinking about the past—that life was gone like the loud dead, whose shrill demands still haunted his dreams. He got up, but his head pounded so much he had to hold it. On the other side of the bed, Regina turned over. He tried not to wake her because she worked nights cleaning offices downtown while he worked days at the stockyards so that one of them would always be home with the children. Algis went to Nativity School, but it was no use sending Magda to school.

Sauerkraut—that was the answer to his hangover. He quietly shuffled to the kitchen, only to find Magda already pouring milk into Algis' cereal bowl. Jurgis greeted his children as he took out the leftover sauerkraut and picked up the Lithuanian paper—March 5, 1953. No news from Lithuania—only the local gossip: a folk dance group from Detroit was performing at the Auditorium on Halsted Street, the Lithuanian government-in-exile was having new elections at the Knights of Columbus hall, keeping alive the memory of an independent Lithuania, impatiently waiting and preparing for the day it would regain its freedom from Soviet occupation.

When Regina walked into the kitchen complaining that she couldn't sleep, Jurgis, who had been reading about the local soccer games, the marriage, birth, and death announcements, and the self-congratulatory articles by local businessmen, suddenly slapped the paper with the back of his hand. "They call this a newspaper! The parish bulletin has more news than this. Bah! What's happening in Vilnius or Kaunas?"

"Well, that's a fine good morning! Are you starting that old litany of yours?" Regina filled the teakettle with water and set it on the stove.

"Regina, this drives me crazy! What's going on there? Lithuania is as quiet as a tomb since the war. Once that Iron Curtain came down like a lid on a casket, everything became mute." Jurgis threw the paper down, fed up with not knowing if his family was still alive. At least his wife's family was still in Lithuania, while his family had been sent to Stalin's gulags.

"Regina, I had that dream again," said Jurgis, raking his thin dark hair with his fingers.

His wife, who had been staring out the window at nothing in particular, turned to him, whispering, "About Magda's tea set?"

Jurgis nodded; his heart felt squeezed. "I broke it."

"You know, you've wrapped yourself in sadness like a shroud. I can't even remember the last time I heard you laugh." Her pointed chin quivered as she spoke. "The past is gone like a swift-moving river, and it's time to start a new life. This is Chicago, not Lithuania. Aren't you at least happy for your children that we finally made it to Marquette Park?"

"Chicago, Chicago—what kind of life is this?"

⸻

That evening, after work, Jurgis and his young children ate the borscht that his wife had left them and washed the dishes, and then he put Magda and Algis to bed. He looked at his beloved daughter, almost thirteen—so beautiful, so loved, and so damaged. It broke his heart as he kissed her forehead and said good night. He paced restlessly until he knew his children were sleeping soundly. He was so agitated that he decided to go to the tavern for a quick drink. Leaving the radiator warmth of his brick two-flat, he could smell the sour-sweetness of the Kool-Aid factory. He walked down Talman Street, past the rows of brick houses, past the Sinclair station, to his favorite bar, the Amber Tavern. On Sixty-Ninth Street, between Western and California, there were a dozen bars or more, each known for a slightly different clientele. The Liths Club catered to the rowdy soccer teams, the Vytis Club was for patriots and politicos, the Playhouse for artists and intellectuals with clever "Second Village" take-offs of Second City, and the Continental for those world-weary cynics who suffered no fools. There were other bars for a neighborhood crowd, but the popular Amber Tavern took them all in, from the seasoned alcoholics to the pubescent local students.

Jurgis finally reached the Amber Tavern, where a group of disgruntled husbands banded together with some congealed bachelors and a small group of randy soccer players. They all had nicknames like Felius the Poet, Mr. George, and Captain Eddie—men as colorfully idiosyncratic as their names. Some eventually managed to get married, while others spent lifetimes hanging out on their bar stools, checking out the young girls who came in. Three or four shots of Asbach later, they were all best friends, singing in three-part harmony of their lost loves, while the bartender, Willy, played his accordion:

> The third brother rode off to war,
> leaving his beloved
> weaving the finest wedding linen
> and quietly weeping at the loom.

They sang the old patriotic songs about their lost homeland, which would make Captain Eddie, who was neither a captain nor an Eddie, tear up. Felius, the resident poet of the group, had a golden goatee and an affected manner that irritated some so that they might have written him off as an insufferable pedant, but they forgave him because he had memorized the great poet Maironis. Education was still education. Felius stood up from his barstool to declaim a poem by Brazdzionis:

> Gray hills hold up a sky
> That hangs so low, so low,
> And you walk on foreign soil
> Like an orphan, crying.

Captain Eddie started blubbering in his drink again. "Here's to you, Felius," he said, raising his glass. "That's beautiful. That damned war made us all orphans." He belted back a shot of brandy and coughed.

"Captain, you're like an old woman," laughed Willy, a veteran of the 1918 war for Lithuania's independence. "You'll stay a bachelor forever. Women want someone strong and brave, like Felius here." He winked and clapped Felius on the back, laughing. Jurgis, like half the men there, privately wondered if Felius was a bit fey. The poet forced a half-smile, looking around uneasily. Jurgis wondered if he realized he was being mocked, because Felius always bragged about being a great ladies' man—very debonair and Continental, like a young Cary Grant with a slight bohemian flair. No one believed a word.

Willy, a bear of a man, took off his accordion and pointed to the map he had tacked up on a wall. "Will you look at this," he said in his gravelly voice, his finger jabbing at the map. "Once our country stretched from the Baltic Sea to the Black Sea, but now I can't find it anywhere. It was swallowed by a giant pink glob that calls itself USSR. That's the wretched fate of small countries. Look how China swallowed up Tibet."

Jurgis raised his glass. "To Lithuania, may she spit on Stalin's grave." Half the bar spat at the mention of Stalin's name and then raised their glasses to toast a free Lithuania.

Just then, the front door opened, and a well-endowed bleached blonde entered, followed by a group of teenagers dressed in their national costumes, followed by an older group dressed in their Sunday best.

"Hey, Willy, what's going on?" asked Valentinas Gediminas, a plump dumpling-faced man who still lived with his mother but spent most evenings at the Amber Tavern.

"It's a folk dance group from Detroit," answered Willy. "They're having a party in the back room."

The whole place started buzzing like flies before rain. The soccer players immediately glued themselves to the young girls, while the older bachelors flirted with their mothers. Mr. George, the unctuous old bachelor, goosed one of the girls, who blanched and ran off to her mother.

Jurgis stayed at the bar with the laconic Antanas Balys, both sorrowfully sipping Canadian Club, trying to banish the gloom that sat on him like a long spell of bad weather. Jurgis was about to order another shot from Willy when he heard a laugh that was strangely familiar. That laugh made ten years drop from him like an old coat no longer needed. When he turned, he saw a woman with brassy bleached hair swept to one side, and a face so vividly painted, it would take two bars of soap to clean it. She didn't exactly look familiar, but still, he knew that laugh from somewhere.

"Excuse me, Miss, do I know you?" asked Jurgis.

"Silvia Degutis from Kretinga," she answered crisply, "but now I teach this dance group in Detroit."

"Silvia Degutis! Don't you remember me? Jurgis Vitkus. We were in school together."

"Jurgis!" squealed Silvia. "How wonderful to see you. How are you? Tell me everything." He looked her over, marveling that she had not only grown plump but also changed so much that he could no longer recognize her.

"Oh Silvia, what can I say?" He shrugged dolefully. "Stalin ruined all of our lives. My family is gone." He shook his head. "My daughter," he stammered hardly knowing how to begin. "My daughter was buried in an air raid shelter during the war."

"Oh, my Lord, may she rest in peace." Silvia blessed herself.

Jurgis shook his head. "No, no, she lived. It's just that her mind was affected. She's not right." He tapped his temple.

"I'm so sorry." Silvia took his hand and held it while Jurgis looked at Silvia and saw that her eyes were those of the girl he remembered. He nodded, swallowing the tangle of emotions that were rising in his chest like heartburn. "And how has life treated you, tell me?"

Silvia hesitated. "I shouldn't complain, really. It's just that my mother is still in Lithuania." Her chin quivered. "I worry." Jurgis could see that she wanted to say more but was afraid her emotions would spill over. Silvia smiled weakly. "Enough of these sad stories. This is a party for my dance troupe, so let's have a drink to the old days and old friends reunited." There was something curious in Silvia's eyes that Jurgis liked. It was a spark, an amusement that life had not been able to extinguish.

Felius the Poet insinuated himself between the reunited friends, asking for an introduction to Silvia. When Willy picked up his accordion and started playing the sorrowful but sexy "Tango of the Roses," Jurgis asked Silvia to dance.

Silvia continued, "The hell with Stalin, I say. He's killed so many already, and if you spend the rest of your days mourning, well, then he's taken your life as well. But not me! I'm going to dance and laugh enough for ten people. I owe the dead that much." Silvia gave Jurgis a kiss on the cheek and smiled. "By the way, did you hear what Stalin said recently during one of his speeches?" They tangoed listlessly around the room.

"No, what?" Jurgis didn't really want to hear it.

She lifted her fist in mock oration: "I am prepared to give my blood for the cause of the working class—drop by drop."

Jurgis frowned. "Yes, so?"

"A note got passed up to Stalin at the podium. It read: 'Dear Comrade Stalin, why drag things out? Give it all at once!'" Silvia winked and chuckled, going off to join the rest of the Detroit crowd. Felius the Poet, who had been standing nearby, followed Silvia into the back room like her shadow.

Left on the dance floor, Jurgis felt strangely abandoned. He wanted to talk to Silvia some more, but his head was spinning from too many drinks. The accordion music started wailing a new tango and dancers slithered around him. It felt crowded and hot. Tonight, like so often before, the past was threatening to bleed into the present.

Suddenly, Jurgis needed some air to clear his head. It was time to go home to his children. Leaving the stifling warmth of the bar, he stepped into the cold and foggy night filled with streetlights surrounded by yellow haloes. In the fog, he stumbled into a mailbox, and a dog started barking loudly in a backyard. As he staggered down the dark street, the accordion music slowly faded away.

Oddly, it felt as if he had never seen these streets before, as if he had suddenly woken from one dream into another. He wanted to find Talman Street, but there were no familiar landmarks; nothing was recognizable. The streets were utterly deserted as Jurgis trudged on, stumbling and lost like an orphan until he finally saw someone coming toward him. Perhaps this person might help him find his way. He stopped to watch, realizing that the person looked familiar. The man turned onto the walkway of a nearby house and banged loudly on the front door with his fists. Soon, the lights turned on, and Mr. Gudauskas came to the front door. The stranger kept saying something, but Jurgis couldn't hear it. Then, Mr. Gudauskas slammed the door, muttering curses under his breath. He watched the man walk to the next house and bang on that door. As he got closer, Jurgis noticed his Russian uniform. *Just like the NKVD*, he thought, *who only come in the middle of the night.* Jurgis felt an unexplained wave of terror and numbness as he remembered a night in June 1941 when the NKVD had come to his farm. It was a warm night, so he had gone to sleep in the hayloft where it was cooler. His wife and daughter were visiting at her mother's farm. To Jurgis' horror, the Bolsheviks took his brothers and parents into the back of a truck and drove away. He had cowered in the hayloft, hiding as he quivered in fear, afraid they would find him. Later, he learned that many thousands had been taken on those June nights and put in cattle cars to Siberia. The NKVD hadn't found him, but sometimes Jurgis wished they had. The burden of his cowardice weighed heavily on him. Not that he could have saved his family, but he hadn't even had the courage to try.

Jurgis felt his guilt sitting on his chest like a giant boulder, so heavy he could hardly breathe. He crouched down behind a hedge and watched the man walk toward him, stalking him from house to house until he finally recognized him—the bushy mustache, the thick eyebrows. How could it be? Yet, there was no mistaking him. It was Stalin himself, trudging down Talman Street, knocking on every door. The blood rushed to Jurgis' head as Stalin walked right by him, beating his breast as he softly muttered, "*gospodi pamili, gospodi pamili*," the Russian Orthodox prayer for God's mercy.

"I'll give you mercy," yelled Jurgis as he jumped Stalin from behind the hedge. "The same mercy you showed my family," he said as they fell in a heap. The two men rolled around the lawn in an agonized struggle. Jurgis felt thumbs digging into his throat as if Stalin wanted to squeeze the life out of him. He choked and gagged, battling for breath, until with a last bit of strength, he threw Stalin off with a hoarse roar into the night. Now he had the man and was going to show him no mercy. He wrestled him into a chokehold, and squeezed with all his might until he heard his neck snap. Suddenly Stalin began to fade and slowly disappear into the night air like a wisp of smoke from a pipe. Jurgis was stunned. He looked behind the hedges, checked behind the parked cars, and even lifted the lids of garbage cans. Nothing. He ran from one side of the street to the other. Everything was empty and still, shrouded in fog. Jurgis searched in all directions, trying once again to decipher the topography of his neighborhood. Had he been walking all night? Where was home? What about his sleeping children? How could he have left them? Jurgis walked until he reached a corner and saw a dusty road lined with birch trees. It was the familiar crossroads by the Akmena River that he remembered from long ago. He could hear the dry rustling of the grass as it was scythed. He could smell the sweetness of the hay. If only he could get to the end of the road, he would see his mother's weathered face. She would be picking cherries in the orchard. His brother would be sharpening his scythe. His wife, Regina, would be bringing cucumbers in her apron, and his little Magda would be waiting for him, wanting to drink tea with him in those tiny cups. They would stop what they were doing to wave to him with their white handkerchiefs.

Jurgis opened his eyes to a sparkling dawn of fluffy clouds in a Delft-blue sky—the kind of morning that should fall only on Easter Sunday as if God had just scrubbed the world clean. Inexplicably, he felt light-hearted. He found himself curled up like a stray cat on the hood of Mr. Matas' green Hudson as Magda pulled his arm to wake him. When Jurgis looked around and saw he was on his own street, he hugged his daughter fiercely and realized sadly that he hadn't done that in a while. Magda smiled shyly and together they walked to their front door, as Jurgis stooped to pick up the Lithuanian newspaper. He stopped on the stairs, shocked when he saw the giant headline:

March 6, 1953—Stalin Dead!

"I don't believe it," he hooted, and for a brief moment he wondered if he had killed him. He shook his head to erase last night's strangeness. "Now this is what I call a piece of news!" Jurgis sat down on his front stairs and started to laugh so hard that he woke his wife. Regina, surprised to hear the unaccustomed sound, came outside in her blue chenille robe, her hair still in pin curls, to see what was happening. It didn't take long before she caught the contagion and giggled, intoxicated to hear her husband's laughter again after so many years.

The Talman Rains

Ona Janulis, 1953

Neighborhoods can have a slippery luck depending on who moves in or out. Luck, like weather, can waft in like a soft breeze or mysteriously float away like a drippy fog. On a windy day in March 1953, Ona Janulis moved into her new home on Talman Street, changing the luck in that blue-collar neighborhood, which was never too good to begin with, but was about to take a peculiar turn for the worse.

Talman Street was lined with an elegant canopy of tall elm trees and working-class brick two-flats. In this corner of the South Side of Chicago, an earlier group of immigrants from Ireland still worked at the local Nabisco factory. The arriving Lithuanians were more-recent immigrants who mostly worked at the other end of the olfactory spectrum—the stockyards.

Ona sat on the front steps of her new red-brick house hugging Margis, her beefy basset hound. In her old school in Bridgeport, she had been taller and heavier than most of her classmates. They called her "Fat Ona" and it made her feel clumsy and shy. She couldn't help it if she was big-boned. She was hoping for a fresh start at her new school.

While Ona sat brooding about her past mistreatment, her

father and brother tried to wedge a bed through the front door, grunting as they tried to push it through. Having saved for years, her parents were proud to move into this neighborhood so full of tree-lined streets. Ona watched her brother, Jonas, struggle with the bed, when suddenly a neighbor sprinted across the street yelling, "He's dead, thank God Almighty, the monster finally died!" Jonas dropped his end of the bed while the neighbor dashed up the stairs and clapped Ona's father on his broad back, causing the bed leg to slip out of his callused hand. "I just read about it," said the neighbor excitedly, the newspaper still tucked under his arm. Pranas Janulis scratched his ear, looking confused.

The neighbor put his hand out. "Mr. Janulis, welcome to the neighborhood. I'm Jurgis Vitkus, remember me? Your wife, Agota, cleans offices downtown with my Regina. We met at the annual Daughters of Lithuania picnic. My wife told me you were moving here, but this is a day for celebration for more reasons than that. Wait here." The neighbor sprinted back into his blond brick house across the street. Pranas shrugged his shoulders and returned to the business of moving the bed. But no sooner had Pranas taken three steps into his new house than Jurgis returned with a bottle of cognac tucked under one arm and two shot glasses in his hand. "Come, let's drink to his death. I hope it was a terrible one."

Pranas finally lost patience. "Who the devil died?"

"What, haven't you heard? Look at this wonderful headline, will you?" He shoved the paper under Pranas' nose. "I've never seen better news. Imagine, Stalin finally died—we outlived the bastard." Mr. Vitkus poured cognac into two glasses and handed one to Pranas. "Now that he's dead, perhaps Lithuania will be free again, and we'll be able to go home."

Pranas shook his head, laughing. "Well, I'll be damned!" He lifted his glass. "I'll drink to that, all right!" He swallowed it in one gulp and coughed. Jurgis poured another shot. "Welcome to Marquette Park, Mr. Janulis."

"Call me Pranas."

Next door, a stocky man with ginger hair came out of the house to see who was moving in. His red-haired daughter followed him and waved hello to Ona.

"Jesus, not another dirty DP family moving in," he said to his daughter. "No wonder the Irish are moving out. This used to be a fine neighborhood."

"Shh, Daddy, they'll hear you." The girl looked mortified by her father's remarks.

"They can't understand us. They're all fresh off the boat," he said, turning back into the house, followed by the girl, who gave Ona an apologetic smile.

Ona's father scratched his head, frowning. "Ah, don't pay attention to those Irish. They've forgotten what it was like to be new in this country."

The March winds blew the elm branches wildly. The sky was darkening, and storm clouds were brewing. The two men stood silently for a moment. "Come inside," said Pranas. "Gladly," said Jurgis. "I heard this joke about Stalin on Dora Matas' Lithuanian radio program. Stalin goes to heaven at night, just like the NKVD is known to do, and Saint Peter is puzzled, so he stops him at the pearly gates. 'I'm afraid there's been a terrible mistake. You can't come here. You've robbed your people of all their worldly goods.' Stalin smiles, sure of himself. 'No mistake. Isn't it said in the Bible that it's easier for a camel to go through the eye of a needle than for a rich man to enter into the kingdom of God?' 'Yes,' says Saint Peter, frowning. Stalin continues, 'Well then, didn't I save my people's souls by turning them all into paupers?'" Jurgis' voice drifted away as the two men went inside.

Ona stayed on the front stoop, eyes open wide in her moon face, watching the treetops do their mad dance with the wind, waiting for the thunder and the rain to start. There was something about a fierce storm with the wind lashing the tree branches that she found exhilarating. Whenever she heard distant thunder, she ran out to meet it and watched as the storm broke over the city.

Before long, the diminutive Regina Vitkus came from across the street with a large pot of borscht to welcome her friend Agota to the neighborhood. She brought along her squirming son, Al, telling Ona that they would be in the same class at Nativity School.

Agota came out to greet her. "Come in before you get wet. Where's Magda?"

"My daughter wanted to stay home. She doesn't like to go visiting."

Ona saw that Al wasn't happy about visiting either. "I remember you from the picnics at Ragis Farm."

"Aren't you the girl who told us about the ghosts in your family?"

"The *domovoi*." She smiled, pleased that he still remembered.

"Why don't you two play some checkers?" suggested Agota.

"I can't," said Al, his eyes darting around. "I gotta do homework." He bolted desperately back across the street before anyone could protest.

"I'm afraid my son is not ready to play with girls yet. Please don't be offended," said Regina. Ona smiled, but she was disappointed.

That night, because the visiting delayed the moving in, Ona slept in her bed that was still in the living room. For a long time, she couldn't fall asleep, listening to the wind and rain lash the tall windows, but then she noticed the Irish family next door. From behind the nylon curtains, she could see their kitchen window. Ona watched them with rapt fascination through a scrim of rain, hoping this girl next door might become a new friend. Probably not, though, because this family seemed so different from her own, so

American. They ate strange food, arguing loudly. They were so emotional, not like her family, who seemed to go about their daily life never saying what they really felt, but these folks yelled and cried.

The next day her bed got moved into her new bedroom, but she still watched the Irish family whenever she could. One night she saw the red-haired girl out in the backyard catching lightning bugs and putting them into a jar. Ona was horrified to see the bugs blinking on and off in the jar, so she waited until the girl was gone and then crept into the neighbors' yard to let the bugs go.

"Hey, whatcha doing?" The Irish girl with a halo of red hair was standing in a lit doorway.

Ona was so startled that she flopped on a bed of snapdragons and clumsily got up to see what damage she had done.

The red-haired girl laughed, "You sure flattened those flowers good."

Ona nodded sheepishly.

"Why are you stealing my lightning bugs?" asked the redhead.

"I'm not stealing, I let them go. If you keep them in a jar, they'll die."

"So what, they're only bugs."

"It's cruel," said Ona brushing the dirt off her pleated skirt. "They're alive, just like us."

"So, bug lover, what's your name, anyhow? I'm Connie." She smiled and looked Ona over. "You like to jump rope or ride a bike?" Ona shrugged shyly, never having done either. Even so, the two girls quickly became friends in the easy way that nine year olds do. In the following weeks, Connie introduced Ona to the world of Barbie dolls, Monopoly, Old Maid, and TV. Ona watched the Roy Rogers Show at Connie's house, and afterward Connie put on her Dale Evans cowgirl outfit: the fringed skirt, the boots, and the six shooters. Ona swooned with desire for that outfit, but Connie wouldn't let her wear it, saying it was too small for her.

Connie inspected Ona's homemade flowered dress with the lace collar. "Don't you have any sweater sets or pedal pushers? Something more American?"

That day, Ona went home feeling disturbed. She begged her mother for a pair of pedal pushers, wanting desperately to fit in. Agota didn't like her young daughter to wear short pants, but she finally had to give in and make them just so that Ona would stop begging.

By the end of the week, Ona put on the new flowered pedal pushers and proudly went to show Connie her outfit. At the end of the alley, Ona could see four girls playing jump rope.

"Hi, Connie," Ona said eagerly.

"Come play double-Dutch," said Connie. "First Vida's turn, then Irene's, and then you can have a turn after me. Here, turn the ropes," she said, handing them over. Ona remembered those girls from the Lithuanian picnics. They were DPs, too. She had watched these kids play in the alleys and streets until the streetlights went on, a signal for all to go home. Everybody's parents worked, so their kids ran the streets and alleys, wild like feral cats, jumping over fences, climbing garages, or playing in the prairies.

Though Ona was disappointed that Connie hadn't said anything about her new pedal pushers, she dutifully turned the ropes and listened to the singsong rhymes the girls were chanting.

"Engine, engine, number nine, going down Chicago line..." Dainty Vida skipped, and then Irene energetically jumped in, and finally it was Connie's turn. Ona turned the ropes hypnotically, listening to the whoosh-whoosh sound each time the rope turned, until she realized with a jolt that her turn was next. As she watched Connie lightly skipping over the ropes, she carefully studied this rope-skipping method as if her life depended on it. She was starting to wish she had stayed home, knowing how clumsy she was. When her turn came she jumped once, twice, and then Al Vitkus rode his bike down the alley, chanting as if singing a jump-rope rhyme,

"Ona, Ona, Fat Ona, going down Chicago line." Ona turned to look at him and tripped over the double rope, falling heavily on her knees. Her new pedal pushers were torn, her knees bruised. Al doubled over in laughter. Ona turned a moist red. The other girls laughed along, while Irene started to sing a popular polka tune: "I don't want her, you can have her, she's too fat for me, she's too fat for me, yeah, she's too fat for me…" Connie joined in with glee.

Ona felt a disturbing quiet come over her, as she calmly untangled herself, stood up, and started to walk back down the alley. Her feet seemed miles away from her head. Behind her, she could still hear the girls singing when she got to her backyard fence. "Hey, Ona, come back, we were just teasing," yelled Connie.

A light drizzle started to fall. Ona felt like crying, but no tears would come. She closed her eyes and lifted her face to the comforting rain as if the clouds were crying for her. As she opened her back door, she heard the rumble of thunder in the distance and stopped a moment, turning to listen before she closed the door.

<hr />

Saturday morning, Ona woke late, refusing to get out of bed. Her mother, sensing some upset, brought her some hot chocolate, saying nothing about the torn pants. Even her brother, Jonas, who normally stayed in his room with his hobby, collecting anything he could find more than two of, shared his Classic Comics collection with her. Ona read them all while petting her dog, and when she finally got up to wander through the house, Margis faithfully waddled behind her. As the days went by, she no longer watched Connie's family through the window. Now she closed the curtain, lest Connie see how foreign Ona's family was compared to her American one.

Outside the rain kept pelting down. The rain had stopped all over Chicago except for Marquette Park. At first no one took much notice, but before long it was evident that the rain was an affliction on this neighborhood alone, and the folks on Talman Street didn't know what to make of it. All sorts of remedies were tried: some spat three times to ward off the evil eye, others brought out family relics and prayed, while others sought out spells to break the curse. But the rain continued, merciless and relentless.

By the end of the week, the rain had gotten on everyone's nerves, and curses were flying. People began accusing their neighbors of causing it—the Irish accused the Lithuanians, who, in turn, accused the Communists. The Polish accused them all. Long-forgotten grievances, some going back several generations to the Old Country, were resurrected, and a leaden depression was beginning to set in.

Ona watched the rain, thinking that the whole neighborhood could wash away for all she cared. Each day it became more and more of an eyesore. The houses had been wet for so long that the bricks were developing a patina of green mold, and the wood was beginning to rot. Front lawns, once so proudly tended, now were squares of drowned grass. The smell of decay and mildew was daily getting stronger, but it was the riot of worms and slugs that was really getting on everybody's nerves. No one could take two steps without squishing half a dozen. Real estate values plummeted.

Ona sat at her window quietly, watching through lidded eyes.

Before long, the deluge wore the neighbors down, as anger turned into resignation and people began to dream of the sun with a terrible longing. A general gloom was settling over the neighborhood, now ashamed of its unfortunate state, the way a crippled man is sometimes ashamed of his deformity.

Finally, in desperation, St. Patrick's, the local Irish church, sent their new priest, the handsome Father Dan O'Malley, to bless the street. It was sunny when he left his parish but when he reached

Talman Street, he felt the despair as the rain steadily pelted the neighborhood. With two altar boys holding umbrellas, he marched boldly through the slanted rain, flattening armies of worms in his wake, as he sprinkled each house with holy water. He said his most powerful incantations, but even so, the rain defeated him.

The priest from St. Stanislaus, the Polish church, fared no better.

The Lithuanian parish, not wanting to take any chances with failure, called out Bishop Petraitis to stop the rain. The bishop was a tight-lipped man with ferret eyes and a reputation for casting out evil that had followed him from Kaunas to Chicago. He was a man who knew the power of ritual and uniform, so he ordered a full procession: a bevy of nuns, altar boys carrying crosses—the works. Bishop Petraitis decided to wear his full costume as well, complete with mitered hat and staff, and for good measure, he called out the local folk dancers in native dress.

The bishop had heard about the ceaseless rain, but he was quite unprepared for the dismal sight. A lesser man might have thought twice, but he simply steeled himself, opening his umbrella as he began the procession. The Lithuanians had all gathered to witness the miracle, while the Irish neighbors stayed dry in their houses, peeking suspiciously from behind nylon curtains.

Marcele Gudauskas approached the bishop, kissing his ring. "Your Eminence, we are so honored by your presence. I am Marcele Gudauskas, the general's daughter." She smiled, pausing for her credentials to sink in. "I live in that blond brick two-flat over there, the one with the row of neat evergreens." She proudly pointed across the street and then she bent conspiratorially to the bishop's ear. His lips tightened. This woman's gossipy familiarity was getting on his nerves. When the bishop stepped back, the officious woman pushed forward again. "Frankly, this is a curse, and I know who did it." She smiled and nodded knowingly at the dripping crowd.

"Who would curse us?" Mrs. Vitkus scowled as she spat three times to ward off the evil eye. This provoked a whole flock of spitters behind her.

"Who, in heaven's name?" The bishop was losing all patience.

"It's Antanas Balys across the street," said Mrs. Gudauskas. Those close enough to hear turned to look at the accused, while Antanas, baffled by their sudden attention, stood holding his umbrella, smiling uneasily.

Marcele Gudauskas continued. "Imagine, the miser never gives a penny for the Free the Captive Nations Fund when I come around to collect."

Regina Vitkus snorted dismissively. "No, no, it isn't Mr. Balys. The poor man's whole family was left behind in Lithuania. The Germans took him to the forced labor camps. He has a right to be miserable. Personally, I think it's Aurelia Norkus on the corner there." She motioned with her chin. "That no-good hussy flirts with all the men with her huge bosom." She stopped, blushing visibly as she realized whom she was addressing. "Excuse me, Bishop."

Soon the women were arguing among themselves as to who had caused the unholy rain while the bishop felt a migraine starting. He finally shut them up with a Latin prayer. The whole group prayed, sang hymns, and danced, and everyone got soaking wet, including the bishop. Even the Irish had to admit it was a great show.

Ona and her mother watched the procession from their front stoop. Ona was hardly eating these days and her mother worried that she was wasting away. With each passing day, her clothes got looser as Ona replayed the misery of that jump rope day over and over again. At night, she dreamed that she was back at her old school where everyone still called her Fat Ona. She couldn't bear to repeat that misery.

As she padded down the front stairs, curious to see how Bishop

Petraitis was faring, Margis waddled behind her and, seeing the crowd, emitted a half-hearted bark. Ona could see Connie standing on her porch next door, but she ignored her.

Out of nowhere, Magda Vitkus walked across the street and pointed to Ona. "She's the one." Everyone stopped, momentarily surprised that Magda had voiced an opinion. Al crossed the street to drag his sister back home but seeing Ona, he stopped. "Hey, I'm sorry I called you Fat Ona. I didn't mean for you to trip and fall. I was only teasing." Because she hadn't expected the apology, Ona didn't know what to say, but her smile started slowly, then spread like the dawning sun. Al flashed a quick smile, then quickly pulled his sister back home where his father waited on the front porch, carefully scrutinizing the bishop's every move.

The soggy crowd stood there waiting for a miracle, more resignation than hope on every face. It seemed as if the rain had finally defeated even the indefatigable Bishop Petraitis. The procession dejectedly dispersed, each member going home to dry off.

Once the group disbanded, Ona saw that Connie's naturally curly red hair had exploded into a kinky mess in the rain. She was about to go back inside when she heard Connie call. "Hey, I'm sorry too," she said sheepishly. "I didn't mean it."

Ona stood as still as a monument.

"God, you sure lost weight, huh?" Connie smiled. "You're looking great, no kidding."

Ona almost smiled at the compliment.

Connie persisted. "You wanna come over and play?"

Ona didn't say a word. Her grudge was an iceberg, but it was slowly starting to melt.

Connie watched the receding procession. "This rain is driving me crazy. Please, come over. I can't stand it anymore. I'm bored to tears here."

Ona let out a tiny sigh.

"We can watch the Roy Rogers Show," offered Connie. "How 'bout it?"

Ona hesitated. "Can I wear your Dale Evans outfit?"

"Sure," she said, "just come over, please."

Like melting ice, the anger that had held Ona finally gave way.

The next morning, Jurgis Vitkus, dreaming of sunny, arid landscapes, felt the sun creep in through his window, warming his face so that he woke with a smile. As it turned out, he was the first person on Talman Street to wake and see the sun. He quickly put on his robe and grabbed a bottle of cognac to celebrate the event with his new best friend, Pranas Janulis, across the street. In fact, all of Talman Street celebrated on that day.

Bishop Petraitis even declared a holiday to celebrate the end of the rains. Everyone called him a miracle worker. Even the Irish.

The Carnival

Al Vitkus, 1954

In Chicago, you could always tell what neighborhood you were in by the smell. In the Lithuanian neighborhood of Marquette Park, when the wind blew from the east, the sweet-sour smell of the Kool-Aid factory filled the air. When the wind blew from the west, they were blessed by the just-baked-cookie smell from Nabisco, but other neighborhoods were not so lucky. Whenever Al Vitkus rode by the Bohemian neighborhood, it smelled so bad he'd gag and stick his nose in his coat. He didn't know what their factory made, but the smell made him dizzy. One of the worst neighborhoods was the "Back of the Yards," a Polish and Lithuanian neighborhood with the misfortune of being downwind from the Union Stockyards. Al felt sorry for the people who had to live there, but his father always said a person could get used to anything, and Al figured his father was right since he worked there.

Once a year, the Union Stockyards sponsored a night at the Back of the Yards Free Fair on an old baseball field on the corner of 47th and Damen Avenue. Though it was called a free fair, you had to pay to get on the rides except for the night designated for the stockyard staff and their families. This year the carnival fell on the Fourth of July, one of the hottest days of the summer.

Al and Magda waited with their father for the Archer Avenue bus until it finally glided up to the corner. Magda sat down in the middle of the bus, and Al plopped down next to her, their father sliding in behind them. Outside the sooty window, the sun glinted off the broken glass in the street, the air was wavy, thick enough to swim through, and the asphalt so soft that shoes would stick.

The morning had gone badly for Al. Before his mother went to work, she had yelled at him for getting in trouble again with the nun. Yesterday morning, Al and his best friend Pete Matas had served as altar boys at Mass and were caught laughing during Holy Communion. As Maureen O'Malley raised her chin to receive communion, Al, who held the communion plate to catch any crumbs, studied the boogers in her nose and couldn't keep from laughing. He tried to cover it up with a cough, but that made Pete look over and snicker. The priest turned to give them both the fisheye, but it only made them shake harder with silent laughter. From her pew, the nun saw them, and later she called their mothers. As a result, Al's mother almost hadn't let him go to the carnival. He had to apologize to the nun and the priest and to agree to wash dishes for a week before she let him out the door. And since his mother had to work at the factory, he was going to the carnival with his father and sister.

Al sat on the bus brooding about his punishments, yet relieved to be allowed to go to the carnival. The mugginess of the day had glued his starched white shirt to his back, and his long pants felt itchy, making him squirm. He loosened his collar and stood up to open a window, but it was jammed. Someone had leaned a greasy head there, leaving a fuzzy round spot that made him queasy.

Next to him, Magda sat quietly with her hands folded on her

full skirt, as if she were sitting on a block of ice. Al loved his sister, but sometimes he wished she were more like other girls, instead of always embarrassing him by acting strangely. When she wandered around the neighborhood, his mother sent him out looking for her, even though she was fourteen and he was only eight.

He pointed to the greasy window. "Hey, Magda, would you lick that window for a million dollars?"

Magda looked at the greasy stain and shook her head, frowning.

Al laughed. "How 'bout the gum that's stuck to the bottom of my chair? Chew it for a million?"

"That's icky."

Al loved the million-dollar game. There were endless variations that he usually played with Pete.

Leaning over, Al whispered into Magda's ear. "Would you walk to Mass on Sunday naked?" He laughed so hard he snorted. "For a million bucks?"

"Stop, Al," she pushed him away.

"But just think, one horrible moment and then imagine what you could do with a million dollars."

Magda looked at him blankly. He scanned the bus to see what other horrible things he could tempt her with when the bus stopped to let in a huge woman wearing a well-worn red evening gown. She waddled down the aisle, her many bracelets clinking, and stopped next to Al with a smile that revealed three silver teeth.

"Hello sweeties," she said in a rough, gravelly voice, standing over them, even though there were other seats available. "Can you let me know when we get to Damen? My eyes aren't so good no more."

"We're getting off there too," Al said politely, but inside he was horrified. Was this woman going to stand over him the whole trip?

"You going to the carnival?" she asked.

"Yes," he nodded.

"Me too. I'm the palm reader there. Let me sit down here and I'll read your palm for nothing."

"Sure," Al said, standing up to be polite though he didn't really want to. The lady in red sat down heavily next to Magda, while Al stood over her, holding onto the rail. With a shock, he looked down to see that her low neckline revealed three breasts instead of the customary two.

"Let me see your palm," she said, taking his sweaty hand. The bus was getting hotter, and Al felt like a fly stuck to flypaper. Her hot, sour smell rose up to him, and he didn't know where to put his eyes. Every time he tried to look away, his gaze kept returning to her two huge breasts and the small one in the middle.

"A long life," she said, tracing the line near his thumb with her thick yellow nail. It made him squirm because he didn't want her to touch him.

"You will marry late in life." She examined his hand closely. "But first comes heartache." Al glanced back at his father, who smiled indulgently and rolled his eyes. The lady continued, "I see war for you, a terrible war. I'm sorry." She finally let go of his hand and turned to Magda. "You're such a dark beauty," she said, taking Magda's hand. "Hmmm, what happened to you as a child?" she asked Magda. "I see war, but not your brother's war. This war was in the past, you poor dear."

Magda jerked her hand away. "No war," she said too loudly, clearly upset by the woman's words.

Their father stood up. "Here is carnival," he told the lady in broken English. "Excuse, please."

"Well, I'm going, too," she said as she pulled her bulk out of the seat. "I'm sorry, I didn't mean to upset her. Sometimes I see things, you know?"

Al's father nodded but looked annoyed. The woman slowly

stepped off the bus with grunts and groans. Behind her, Al got off, and the smell of the stockyards hit him right away, making him gag.

His father leaned toward him and whispered, "I didn't like the way that pushy Gypsy upset Magda."

"How did you know she was a Gypsy?"

"It was obvious."

Not to Al. Maybe all Gypsies had three breasts—was that how you knew? He wanted to ask his father but was too embarrassed to speak of breasts. He remembered the wild Gypsies who lived in their old neighborhood, but, of course, they were too young for breasts. When he glanced at Magda, he saw two small mounds under her summer dress. He frowned. Did she already have breasts too? It was all too much for him.

Standing on the corner, Magda was doing that embarrassing flapping of her hand that she did whenever she got upset or excited. His father quickly grabbed her hand as they crossed the street, entering the gigantic gate of the carnival full of tents, rides, sideshows, games, and raffles. Magda eagerly pointed to the double Ferris wheel turning alluringly beyond the tents. Though excited by it all, Al swallowed hard, trying to fight his nausea. The usual stockyard smell was bad enough, but mingled with the smells of popcorn, cotton candy, and hot dogs, it had become completely unbearable. Al thought about all the poor animals being killed at the stockyards and turned into steaks and hot dogs. His father told him they used the whole animal; nothing was wasted. They even used the leftovers for dog food, and they boiled the bones. Al remembered the deli case with the cow tongue that his mother sometimes bought. It made him feel sick to his stomach. He looked around, trying to get his mind off the smell and there it was—a sassy red Corvette on a round platform, slowly turning as it shimmered with carnival reflections. This was the car of his dreams, the car he would own someday. He stood, worshipfully staring at the

Corvette the way old women stared at statues of saints. If he had this car, everyone would respect and admire him, even Joey Cicero who called him a dirty DP. Displaced person didn't sound so bad, but when kids shortened it to DP, it sounded like a cuss word.

His father interrupted Al's adoration of the Corvette to quietly ask him to keep an eye on Magda while he went to play cards with his friends from work. That bugged Al. Why couldn't she take care of herself? After all, she was older. He pouted, but in the end he knew he had to do it. He always watched out for her.

His father headed straight for the picnic tables, where a heated card game was in progress. All of the Lithuanians who worked at the stockyards had come for the free company night.

"Well, well, Jurgis Vitkus," said Captain Eddie. "Sit down, my friend, we'll deal you in."

Al's father loved nothing better than a good card game and some beer with friends. Sometimes when the men started their war stories, he drank too much, and it worried Al. Now, his father fanned his cards out and looked up to assess the other men. Then, each man slapped down his card like they were killing cockroaches, the whole time keeping up a running discussion on whether Nikita Khrushchev was going to be any better than Stalin.

Magda and Al walked around the carnival trying to decide what to do first. Near the arcade, he saw a tent painted with fantastic people—a snake boy, an elephant woman, and a giant, like illustrations from his old storybooks—mythological creatures, half human, half animal. If only Pete were here, he'd love this freak show. He and Pete spent hours poring over "Ripley's Believe It or Not," as if it were a game. As if they gave you a choice—believe it or don't believe it. They had both believed that there could be a seal boy who had little flippers instead of arms and legs, but they'd been suspicious of the half man. Pete just didn't buy it. He wanted to know how a man with no lower body could possibly go to the bathroom. That stumped Al all right. If Pete were here, he'd know the real from the fake.

When a mouse-faced man with a pointy mustache came out of the tent and started to bellow about the wonders of the world, Magda and Al strolled in, following the rest of the crowd. The man strutted back and forth in front of the curtain, telling the audience that they were about to see the amazing elephant lady. Al tried to imagine a woman with an elephant trunk instead of a nose and giant flapping ears, but when the curtain finally opened, he was disappointed to see an ordinary fat woman sitting in a stall with a long dress on. "This is bunk," he whispered to Magda, until the lady pulled up her dress, and Al sucked in his breath. Her legs were huge and stumpy, and her feet disappeared somewhere under all that rough flesh. It was true—she had the legs of an elephant. Maybe it was possible, after all, to be half animal.

At first, he was so engrossed that he didn't notice Magda smiling and nodding as she listened to some older boy, who was grinning and flirting. Al was stunned, not knowing what to do. He had never seen his sister with a boy before.

Suddenly, the announcer introduced the giant, and a curtain opened with a man twice as tall as the announcer, who stood next to him. The giant's eyes darted around, looking uncomfortable. He stood there hunched over, his long arms dangling at his side. In a singsong voice, the announcer asked the giant to turn around. He was so slow and clumsy that he tripped over his own huge feet and almost fell. Someone in the audience gave him the raspberry. Then, suddenly, the giant bellowed out a song, *La Donna è Mobile,* in the biggest voice Al had ever heard. Everyone clapped enthusiastically, and the giant grinned proudly as the curtain closed.

Al kept glancing uneasily at his sister, as the boy put his arm around her shoulder. Magda was starting to flap her hand, but the boy didn't seem to notice. The curtain opened once again, and the strong man came out, but Al was anxiously watching the boy whisper into Magda's ear. The poor wart lady came out covered in warts, and then the mouse-faced man announced that the snake boy was the next attraction. Al thought about witches' curses and spells, but when the curtain opened the stage was empty.

"Hey," shouted the announcer. "What are you doing down there? Get up here." He was talking to the boy flirting with Magda. Al noticed that her hand was flapping big time now.

The boy jumped on stage and smiled, winking at Magda. The announcer was telling everyone to step up closer. When he told the boy to pull up his sleeves, Al saw that his skin was scaly and crusty, but it didn't look like snakeskin. Everybody looked at him like they did at strange animals at the zoo. Al wondered where the boy's mother was. Was she a snake lady, or did she work at some factory like the rest of their moms?

People had started to yell rude remarks to the announcer about his freak show when he shushed everyone and asked the boy to open his mouth. The snake boy strutted around the stage a few times, and then he smiled and slowly opened his mouth, sticking out a forked tongue. The crowd began blessing themselves and spitting three times to ward off the evil eye. Al wished his mother, who believed in evil eyes and curses, had come with them; she'd know how to protect Magda. If only she were here instead of at the Kool-Aid factory. She was always at that factory. Or sleeping.

Al looked over at Magda, who was smiling at the snake boy. He had never seen her flirt before, and it made him feel a little weird. "Come on, Magda, let's get out of here," he said, taking her by the arm.

"No," answered Magda, a bit too loudly.

"What's your hurry?" asked the snake boy with a wink at Magda. "Stick around."

"We gotta go. My father's waiting for us." Al pulled a grinning and flustered Magda out of the tent. Once they got outside, his sister became upset, so he tried to distract her. "Look," he said, pointing, "there's the Ferris wheel." Magda's eyes widened. "Let's go," he prodded, pulling her toward the giant double wheel though he had never been on one and felt scared when he looked up at the top. He swallowed his fear as they stood in line and got on. A man shut the bar down over their laps, and the seat lurched forward, slowly ascending to the top of the wheel. When it stopped at the top, waiting for more riders to get on, Al closed his eyes, his panic rising. When he finally dared to open them a little, he saw the sun was setting. The whole neighborhood twinkled below—houses full of people living their family lives. The lively carnival music played, and the lights gleamed as the wheel finally started circling. They went round and round until suddenly they stopped at the top again, as one of the cars had a problem. The colorful carnival below reminded Al of brightly wrapped candy, the kind his mother kept in a glass dish on the buffet. He could hear the merry-go-round and the rifle shots from the arcades. Sparklers twinkled near the tents. Farther away, Al could see his father still slapping down cards on the table.

A cool breeze blew up from the lake, rocking their seat gently. Chicago was so flat you could see great distances from up high. A small streak of lightning blazed far away, near Lake Michigan. A storm was heading their way. Next to him, Magda hummed some familiar Lithuanian song, and Al realized he no longer smelled the stockyards, nor did he feel frightened. In fact, he felt light and carefree, as if his whole life was going to roll out like a magic carpet, and it was going to be good.

Suddenly, fireworks burst in the sky above them—huge colored blossoms of light. With all the excitement, Al had completely forgotten it was the Fourth of July. "Magda, look, aren't they beautiful?" He was filled with wonder. When the seat suddenly lurched, he turned to see Magda slinking down, making strange animal noises, as she tried to hide in the bottom of the car. Thankfully, the bar prevented her from moving too far, but their car swung back and forth.

"Magda, stop that. What are you doing?" He grabbed her, afraid she'd fall out. "Cut it out, you're scaring me."

"Bombs," screamed Magda, covering her face with her hands.

"Those aren't bombs, Magda, they're fireworks. It's the Fourth of July. Look, people are holding sparklers. Don't be afraid." He could feel her trembling, and when the next burst lit up the sky, she screamed and started to cry, burrowing her head into his shoulder. Al held her close and wanted to cry too.

At last the Ferris wheel started its descent, and when it stopped, Al helped a cowering Magda get out. Whimpering and crying, she held on to him, making him frightened and embarrassed as he took her to his father, asking him what was wrong.

His father held Magda like a little girl, stroking her hair, murmuring assurances that everything was all right, and then another burst of color exploded in the sky.

"Bombs," she cried, burying her head on his shoulder.

He spoke gently, trying to soothe her. "Not bombs, Magda, never again bombs, my sweet girl. No more bombs. Shh, don't cry. You're safe now," he said, frowning at each burst of color above them.

"What's wrong with her?" Al had never seen her like this.

"Nothing, she just remembers the war." His father held her with one arm and shooed Al away with the other. Al went to sit nearby, not saying anything, just feeling sad as he watched the fireworks. At the arcade, boys were pitching pennies onto glass plates, while others were throwing balls at milk bottles, winning large teddy bears for their girls. He watched them for a while and then returned to his sister. "Hey, Magda," he said suddenly. "Answer me this."

She peeked up from her father's shoulder.

"Would you let the elephant lady step on your bare foot for a million dollars?"

His father looked annoyed until he noticed that Magda had stopped crying and was shaking her head.

"How about this one," Al continued, trying to hide his growing smile. "Would you marry the giant for a million?"

Again, Magda shook her head.

Now Al was grinning slyly. "I know a good one. Would you kiss the snake boy for a million bucks?"

A tiny laughed bubbled out of Magda as she nodded.

"You would? Really?" Al made a face when his sister nodded again, this time with more enthusiasm.

"Now that's really icky." A crack of thunder seemed to split the sky, and a cool wind began to blow. Al felt a deep sadness settle over him. Magda was never going to be like other girls. She would always be different.

"We'd better go home," said his father. "There's a storm coming."

On the way out, his father bought a fluffy cone of pink cotton candy for each of them. They saw the Gypsy lady sitting in a booth, reading a soldier's palm while he stared at her three breasts. Near the exit, Al heard an announcement on the loudspeaker for the Corvette raffle. The whole carnival seemed to be gathering there, holding their raffle tickets like holy cards, muttering prayers to Saint Jude, patron saint of impossible causes. A cool wind from the lake blew dust around, ballooning the lime green, puffy dress of a blond girl with a sash that read, "Miss Stockyards of 1954" as she climbed the platform to choose the winning ticket from a large glass bowl. Al saw the snake boy waving good-bye to Magda, a half dozen raffle tickets held tightly in his hands. Magda shyly waved back.

When they got on the bus to go home, Al sat down by a clean

window, picking off the last globs of cotton candy from the paper cone and stuffing them in his mouth, enjoying the way they melted into sugar. Outside the bus window, the wind blew the trees. Closing his eyes, Al leaned back on his seat and didn't open them again until the familiar Kool-Aid smell greeted him, letting him know he was almost home. By then, the rain was coming down in hard sheets, and thunder crashed through the dark and empty, wet city streets.

Trains

Antanas Balys, 1955

Chicago winters are as long as old age and as cold as death. The north wind howls down over the plains, skittering across Lake Michigan, into the hub of the nation's railroads.

Antanas Balys bent into the frigid wind hissing along the snow-caked railroad yards, struggling to open the frozen latch on the old shed. Pulling the handle, he shook the weathered plank door until he heard the crack of release as a board broke. He was about to go inside when he noticed a trickle of blood running down his hand into his sleeve. His hands were so numb with cold that he hadn't even felt the splinter in his palm. With fingers as clumsy as frozen sausages, he couldn't grasp it to pull it out. His hands were as weathered as that old shed door—a landscape of calloused skin and dirty cracks that no amount of soap could clean. And underneath was the remnant of an older splinter that had been in his hand for years—a tiny piece of wood covered by layers of callus like a submerged branch in an ice-shrouded lake—a fossil of time captured in his skin.

He caught sight of his blood drops on the snow like tiny blooms, the only specks of color on the winter landscape. And strangely he felt a slight release. It made him want to yell and scream at someone, at the wind or the sky, but instead, he took a deep breath as a slow moan escaped, and the moment passed. If someone had heard his bitter complaint, he would have been ashamed, because so many others had it much worse, like his younger brother who had died so senselessly.

He often thought that if they had not been in their fields that day, the Germans might not have taken them for forced labor, and his brother, Stasys, might still be alive. The Germans forced them to dig muddy trenches during those last frantic months of the war while Antanas and his brother waited for the American GIs to arrive. Rumors were flying that they were near. As they waited for liberation, wearing their one-piece work clothes, they strung wires along the endless railroad tracks with Stasys getting sicker each day. Antanas begged him to hold on, telling him how they would eat meat again once the Americans came, how they would celebrate, and then how they would go back home to their families.

But Stasys was killed, not by the Germans or the Russians, but, ironically, by the Americans—a simple mistake made by a skittish GI at the end of the war when everything was chaos. Antanas tried to hold the wound tightly so that his brother wouldn't bleed to death, but he couldn't stop the blood that seeped into the dark soil. After his brother died, it took four men to hold Antanas down. He didn't remember the rest. Only the long stay in the hospital until his friend, Viktoras Matas, a teacher from his village, found him in the DP camp hospital in Germany and filled out papers so he could immigrate to America. Antanas hadn't wanted to go so far away from his family, but Viktoras patiently explained that the refugee camps were closing, and the Iron Curtain made it impossible to return home.

So he followed the others to America and now he was a broken and lonely boarder in the Matas house. Antanas wrapped his bleeding hand in his handkerchief and picked up his tin lunchbox, suddenly remembering this morning in the kitchen. He was going to make his lunch when he'd found the Matas girl, Irene, dancing back and forth with Magda, her blond braids swinging as they wiggled to some nervous music. Antanas thought it was comical and wanted to laugh, but he stopped himself once he saw how embarrassed Irene was.

"We're learning the cha-cha," she said sullenly.

"Go on, you're a good dancer," he said, patting her cheek, thinking she reminded him of his own daughter. "Magda too." He nodded as if to convince them.

Irene flinched and drew away. "Ouch, your hand feels like sandpaper."

"Oh, sorry." Antanas quickly pulled his hand away and thrust it deep into his pocket. *They must be rough,* he thought, because he could barely feel her soft cheek. Suddenly, the familiar feeling of self-consciousness returned.

"Have to go. Good-bye, girls," he stammered on his way out the door. Back on his farm he hadn't felt this way. Everything seemed natural there, but in America it was as if everything was wrong, especially him. Like some wounded animal, he was too shy to talk to people—Americans were out of the question. With other Lithuanians, he might be able to mumble a word or two, but with their children he was at a loss. They had an American veneer, as if they knew more than their parents. And maybe they did. They knew how to live an American life, something he would never become accustomed to. In Lithuania he had blended into the landscape like a rock or a tree, living a simple life, driven by the needs of the seasons, the animals, and the church festivals that marked the passing of time.

Only with Magda did he feel himself, because she had remained innocent despite her age. And that was because the poor girl had been damaged during the war. Damaged like he was. He could sit on the stoop and talk to her without feeling so terribly odd.

A train pulled into the railroad yard, and Antanas jumped at the familiar screech of train brakes, the scream of steel against steel. When he arrived in America, he spoke no English, but so many Lithuanians worked at the railroad yard that he hardly needed to apply. A friend from the Amber Tavern simply arranged it with the foreman. At the time, Antanas thought it would be only until he made enough money to return to his wife and four children. He sent them packages of heavy wool cloth, clothes, and shoes. He sent them anything he could, and still he worried how they survived without him since the war. His eldest daughter, only eleven when he left, was now twenty-two and about to marry, but he wouldn't dance at her wedding. Time was rushing by like a runaway train while he remained frozen to the tracks.

The Baltic countries had simply vanished, as if some wizard had put a kingdom to sleep for a hundred years. How long would this Communist spell last?

His small flask of whiskey helped on days like this.

A train whistle moaned, and Antanas looked up as if it were speaking to him. He had grown to hate everything about trains—the tracks that slashed the land, the shriek of whistles, the stench of oil, and the rhythmic clang-clang as they rumbled by. He had hated them from the first time he heard them when he was six and the railroad line came through a corner of his father's land.

At first he had been excited as he watched men laying down tracks. His father had been happy to get a good price for such an unusable patch. The day the first train was to arrive, people from three villages gathered on the small platform waiting to witness the momentous event. Antanas would have been the first one there had his father not told him to run an errand first. Delayed by his chore, he ran down the dirt road, but Old Juska got in his way with his cart and sluggish horse. The old man hadn't heard about the train and so was in no hurry to get to the Tuesday market to sell his surplus vegetables. He rode, biting pieces of hard cheese and peacefully singing snatches of a song about a girl with flaxen hair weaving a wreath of rue. The road was narrow, with a pond on one side and dense bushes on the other, making it impossible for Antanas to squeeze by the cart. He was frantic about missing the train's arrival.

"Hey, grandfather, can't you move a little faster," he yelled, but Juska was either deaf or stubborn. Impatiently, Antanas walked behind the cart, muttering angry curses under his breath, until they got to the next bend in the road where the station was finally visible. The old man stopped his cart to see why so many villagers were gathered. Old Juska stood up when he heard the rumble and saw the giant black engine turning the bend, like the devil himself, heading toward all those poor people waiting like lambs at the slaughter. Just then the engineer sounded his whistle like a chorus of demons. When the locomotive came slithering down the track like an oiled dragon, brakes squealing like a stuck pig, the old man grabbed his chest and let out a cry. The black dragon was belching smoke from the mouth of hell itself.

Antanas stared wide-eyed at the train, afraid to move any closer. He heard the old man gasp and saw his eyes bulge as he fell from his cart. His spooked horse turned and ran to escape the noise, leaving the old man dying.

Antanas had never forgotten that old man, and now, all these years later, it seemed to him he heard Old Juska's song still ringing in his ears. He had cursed the old man's slowness, while Old Juska had left him with a loathing of the infernal trains.

Antanas looked at his hands and realized that they now looked just like Old Juska's hands. His job was to repair the boxcars—tearing down the rotten or broken slats of wood and replacing them. Most of the work was done outside in the sweltering humidity of a Chicago summer or in the arctic winters when the workers kept a garbage can burning with scrap wood to keep the frostbite away. Sometimes he did odd jobs like helping Tomas uncouple the trains. One winter he slipped on the icy metal and broke his leg. Tomas crushed his thumb while helping him. This year Mike, the Irishman, lost a leg under the tracks.

The boxcars reminded him of the ones the Russians used to send Lithuanians to Siberia at the end of the first occupation in 1941. In June, the deportations began. They rounded up Mr. Lankutis, the nervous and irritable mayor; his deputies; Mr. Valaitis, the fastidious judge; the reclusive Tutlys family with their newborn; the merchants, Klein and Rosen with their families; and many thousands more on those June nights. Many teachers disappeared after the NKVD came knocking on doors. Young men and old hid in the woods. Antanas watched with his father, who shook with rage as the boxcars filled with neighbors and friends. They could see their frightened eyes begging for help. The Bolsheviks with their rifles, black leather jackets, and caps, showed no emotion on their stone-like faces. When the doors slid shut, the remaining neighbors and friends stood by helplessly wringing their hands until the trains began their long journey east. Cries to God, shouts of farewell, angry curses, children screaming—it was all too painful to bear. And with each trainload, Antanas wondered when he would hear the nocturnal knock on the door.

Then one morning he heard the planes overhead and turned to his neighbor, who asked, "Oh, you think the war has started?" The deportations stopped once Germany crossed the border into Lithuania, and everyone rejoiced—everyone but the Jews, who trembled at the sight of German soldiers. At first many in the country thought the Germans would liberate them from Russia. The Nazis did—and then they occupied it. The war raged on. Antanas was again a silent witness as German soldiers, along with the police, rounded up Jewish families and marched them away. He saw Mr. Weber, the dry goods store owner, who looked bewildered as his wife asked the rabbi where they were going. The rabbi, standing in his long black coat with his small brown suitcase, said nothing, only shook his head. Big Isaac, who sold ropes of bagels outside the churchyard, walked out of his house as ordered, and Antanas asked him if they were going to Siberia like the last group. Isaac frowned and said he didn't know. A policeman told Antanas to move along.

That night the Germans warned everyone to stay home. It was late when Antanas heard a distant shooting that seemed to go on forever as he sat listening by the small window. He knew then what had happened and was stunned into silence. That long column of people he'd seen were dead. Why? Why kill those innocent, wide-eyed children, hanging onto their terrified mothers or the grand-mothers shushing them? Those poor, innocent people. He watched the cold stars winking without care, and he felt a sinking in his heart like a rock dropping to the bottom of a dark lake.

The next day the town was half deserted, and people walked around feeling haunted. Stores were closed, windows were broken, and the synagogue was empty. The war continued. The Germans requisitioned livestock and emptied granaries and larders. They began to round up men for forced labor and conscription. One day, Antanas and Stasys were taken. It was finally their turn to be put on trains. They didn't even have a chance to say good-bye to their families. Antanas often thought about his wife on that day, quietly tending to chores, cooking supper, waiting for him to return from the fields, sending his son to tell him that supper was getting cold. She'd probably looked for him, wondering what had happened. They weren't able to contact each other until years after the war, after the Soviets returned to stay when he was already on the other side of the world.

His wife's letters were carefully written not to alert the censors. She had moved to an apartment in the city. Their farms were bull-dozed, turned into collectives. In 1952, she started to work in a radio factory while the children went to school. She sent a somber family portrait. He hardly recognized his children. His wife looked tired and older but, to his eyes, more beautiful than ever. There was a gravity in her look that moved him. She had been so innocent, so lighthearted, always singing snatches of songs, laughing easily at the antics of her children. He put the photo back in his wallet and looked up to see his reflection in the dark window. His hair, though turning gray, was as thick and unruly as ever, the same stubborn cowlicks sticking up. His small eyes looked grief-stricken.

The sky was darkening as he boarded the bus with the other men who lived in his neighborhood. Today he stopped at the Little Touch of Kretinga Restaurant for some borscht and dumplings. Afterward, he had a few drinks at the Amber Tavern so his sleep would be untroubled. The neighborhood tavern was lively tonight with Willy the bartender telling jokes while Captain Eddie argued with Felius the Poet over politics. Antanas liked these regulars but felt too shy to join in their banter until he had a couple of drinks. He had his usual seat at the end of the bar, next to Jurgis Vitkus. Only after Willy brought out the accordion and started singing that sad song about the innocent girl with the flaxen hair weaving her wreath of rue did Antanas join in sorrowfully singing in honor of Old Juska.

Time sat heavily on Antanas' soul and his days and nights were often too long. In the dark night while Chicago slept, he sometimes also slept, until he heard the lonely moan of the train whistle or the clanging sound of boxcars being pulled into motion. Then he would toss in his tangled bed sheets, dreaming of trains filled with anguished faces. In the daytime he lived a lonely life, but his nights were crowded with tortured souls—children in trains headed for the frozen wastes of Siberia, frightened children standing at the edge of a pit in the woods, children in trains to the ghettos or camps, young men in trains journeying to the war trenches. Each night they seemed to whisper their terrible grief to him while God never said a word.

Silvia's House of Beauty

Silvia Degutis, 1957

Silvia Degutis strolled down the rain-slicked streets of Chicago's South Side, humming the "Blue Tango" as a light drizzle pinged a rhythm on her plastic rain bonnet. Last night, the band had played that song at the Patriots of Lithuania dance at the Auditorium on Halsted Street, where she had tangoed with Felius the Poet, the most elegant and cultured man in Chicago. For a plump woman, Silvia was amazingly dainty, jumping and skipping over the muddy puddles as if folk dancing. Magda, who was walking nearby wearing a hooded plastic poncho against the rain, watched Silvia for as long as she could stand it before she joined in, skipping and jumping alongside her.

"Hello Magda, what are you doing out in the rain?" Silvia smiled and waved gaily, but she felt her spirit sink whenever she saw the poor girl wandering the neighborhood, walking aimlessly all day long like a lost child. Magda shrugged, her face blank. Silvia's good mood vanished as she sighed, and the South Side neighborhood once again resumed the gray and grimy look of a rainy October morning.

Together Silvia and Magda tramped past the Sinclair station, the Amber Tavern, and the other bars, restaurants, and delis that lined Sixty-Ninth Street, greeting the occasional neighbor with a nod. When she reached her beauty shop, Silvia said goodbye to the ever-wandering Magda and unlocked the front door, turning on the lights and taking off her raincoat and rubber overshoes. Then she went over to the large storefront window and flicked on the pink neon sign that read: Silvia's House of Beauty. In Lithuania, her name used to be spelled Silvija, but once she came to America, she took the J out so that Americans could pronounce it properly. The sign sputtered a few seconds and lit the window with a pink glow. Suddenly, the whole shop seemed happier, more alive with the promise of a day filled with beauty. The rosy light shone on Silvia's hands, and when she looked up, she saw her face reflected in the large window—glowing, younger. Bathed in pink, she smiled at her reflection, her bleached hair floating around her head like a cotton-candy halo. Something about this pink neon always mesmerized her, making her unable to pull away from its spell. This was her shop, a refuge of beauty, a place filled with the potent smells of permanent lotions and powder dye—alchemy and transformation. No matter what went on in the outside world, here she had a power all her own.

Captain Eddie, wearing his factory overalls, stopped on the way to work and rapped on the window, breaking the spell. Silvia politely nodded hello. Captain Eddie always clowned and joked behind the glass, trying his hardest to make Silvia laugh, while she always pretended to shoo him away. As he did every morning, he puckered his lips and blew her a kiss, flirting with Silvia, often asking her out, but she never took the bait. He was a bit too vulgar compared to Felius, who was a poet, after all, and could declaim whole tomes of Lithuanian poetry. Felius smelled of Italian hair pomade on his golden goatee, and his shoes were as shiny as his hair.

As Silvia readied the shop for business, she found herself brooding about last night. She had worn her best purple taffeta dance dress and a new pair of see-through mules with purple bows. Her blond hair had been dramatically swept to one side like Lana Turner's. She had done her best to look dazzling, but Felius had still flirted and danced the tango with Aurelia Norkus. If only that cow Aurelia would come to her beauty shop, she would fix her up good. She'd cut off her long chestnut hair and pull her nails out instead of painting them.

Some days it made Silvia gloomy to think about that perennial bachelor she loved. For four years, she had been trying to get this slippery man to the altar. A few more and she'd be too old to have children. But every time she mentioned marriage to Felius, he got as nervous as a bug under a broom.

A tiny bell tinkled as the front door opened to let in Elena Kazlas.

"Elena, sit down, my dear, get warm." Silvia danced over to her. "It's time for glamour."

Elena waved her hand dismissively. "Who needs glamour at the factory? Just give me my usual permanent. I'm only going to Nabisco later."

"Well, you never know. With my permanent you might catch yourself a nice Lithuanian husband."

"Oh, Silvia, there's no one at the factory. Besides, my father doesn't like it when I date."

Silvia knew Elena's father was a hard man who fought some private demons, using the bottle as his primary defense. *Another life shattered by the war, and yet we all carry on,* thought Silvia as she dragged the giant hot-curl machine, a cross between Sputnik and an octopus, over to Elena and began to clamp the tentacles to her head.

When she was done, Silvia went over to one of the mirrors to study her image, licking her finger to smooth the arches of her penciled eyebrows above her iridescent blue lids. She checked her thick pancake makeup to make sure not a bit of skin was left uncovered. Rubbing the little globs of accumulated lipstick from the corners of her full mouth, she thanked God she no longer looked like the refugee she had been after the war. Turning on the radio, she heard Harry Belafonte singing "Jamaica Farewell." Silvia put one hand on her stomach and the other in the air as if she was taking an oath, and she started doing the cha-cha. The front bell rang again, and Dora Matas walked in. Elena sang along with the radio, "Down the way where the nights are gay…"

"Well hello, ladies, it may be damp and cold outside, but it's tropical in here."

"Hello, Dora, get comfortable while I heat up the beeswax."

Dora Matas took off her fox-collared coat and sat down in a turquoise vinyl chair. Silvia came back with a pot of wax and applied it to Dora's upper lip. She put a strip of gauze over the wax and waited until it cooled. Then she quickly tore the strip from her upper lip.

"Jesus and Mary," yelped Dora.

Silvia examined the fuzzy hairs stuck in the wax. She touched Dora's skin, which was red and puffy but successfully hairless.

Seeing Elena's horrified face in the mirror, Silvia said, "If you want to be beautiful, you have to suffer." She put some cream on Dora. "A man gets older when he feels it, but a woman is older when she looks it, true?"

"Yes," said Dora. "And I resent it bitterly."

"What's new at the Lithuanian radio program?" asked Elena.

"Nothing! What a dreary little hour. There's never any real news, just picnics and dances and deaths."

"Dora," said Silvia. "I love your program; Felius and I listen to it all the time."

"I tell you I don't know how much longer I can bear to read all that dreary Cold War news."

"But you're so good at it," said Elena.

"Elena, you may be too young to know this, but there hasn't been any good news since the war ended. And I'm not even sure that was good news."

"The Korean War?" asked Elena.

"No, the real war. World War II."

"But that was so long ago," said Elena.

"Eleven years is not so long ago unless you're twelve years old," said Dora.

"It's been eleven years since the war," said Silvia as she mixed the powders for Dora's brown hair dye. "Eleven years," she repeated as she mechanically painted the dye on Dora's head with a brush, her thoughts returning to the war that had separated her from her parents. She had thought it was only going to be a brief separation: perhaps a month or a year at most, not eleven years. She had been twenty-one when she had said good-bye to them. Soon she would be thirty-three.

"Silvia! You're painting my forehead with that dye. Be careful. That stuff stains." Dora mopped her forehead with some tissues.

"I'm terribly sorry, Dora. I was just thinking about my mother. I always worry about her as the winter approaches."

"How is she?" asked Dora.

"How can she be? She's alive, thank God. Not like my poor father, may he rest in peace."

Dora smiled wistfully. "You know what I remember best about my mother before the war? She had twelve pairs of Bally shoes in all colors. Imagine an even dozen! All Bally. And I can't even afford one pair."

"Shoes are my weakness too," said Silvia. "Not Bally, of course, they're too costly, but I can never get enough shoes—the fancier the better."

"What do they look like?" asked Elena from across the room.

Silvia's eyes were bright with excitement. "Black velvet high heels with rhinestone bows all over. Bought those shoes for my first date with Felius. I have silk slippers with ostrich feathers, and red satin sling backs with stars on the heels." Though Silvia wore a size sixteen dress, she was vain about her dainty feet.

"When did you first go out with Felius?" asked Elena.

"Four years ago, when I moved here from Detroit. I used to work at the General Motors plant. Made good money there, but once I came to Chicago and saw how many Lithuanians were here, I decided this was the place for me. And, of course, I met Felius."

"So when are you two getting married?" asked Dora.

"When Lithuania is free."

"What?" Dora was taken aback.

"Felius always says he'll marry me when Lithuania regains its independence."

Dora was outraged. "Is he crazy or just stupid? Look what happened last year in Hungary. Look how their revolution got crushed, for Chrissake. No, if Felius waits for that, you'll both be gray before the wedding bells ring."

Silvia frowned. "Come, let me shampoo you."

"Listen, Silvia, I hate to be the one who tells you this, but that man goes from woman to woman like a bee in a field of flowers," said Dora.

Silvia didn't want to hear it. "Women always clamor to dance with Felius because of his fancy footwork, that's all. He can work his way around the dance floor faster than anyone else." Silvia's face softened, remembering Felius' flourishes. What a couple they made. "My dresses just fly behind me, my white crinolines showing." Silvia sighed. "Dancing is my passion, you know."

Dora shook her head in disbelief. "Well, Silvia, I have some news for you, and it's not from the Lithuanian radio station. I think Felius is a confirmed bachelor, about as confirmed as they get. I think you better wake up before it's too late."

"That's not true," said Silvia, pouting.

"I'm saying even if Lithuania became free tomorrow, I don't think that man would marry you or anyone else." Dora slapped her thigh for emphasis.

Silvia was taken aback by Dora's pronouncement. "He would, I know he would." Her voice quivered slightly, betraying her words. Silvia used to think Felius was so loyal to his principles whenever he stated his patriotic preconditions for marriage, but lately she didn't know what to think. Her eyes filled with tears and the mascara burned.

"Silvia, I've got the most wicked idea," squealed Dora, excited like a schoolgirl. "In fact, it's brilliant. If he says he'll marry you when Lithuania is free, then we will give him Lithuania's freedom." Dora had a mischievous grin.

"What? I don't understand." Silvia sniffed back the tears that were threatening.

"Silvia, don't I read the news on the Lithuanian hour?" asked Dora.

"Yes, I listen to you every night."

"Well, Silvia, make sure you listen on Saturday before you go to the Daughters of Lithuania dance. And make sure Felius is over that night. We'll see what he says after he hears this news. The man's a liar, and it's about time you realized it. I'll bet my job on it."

"Won't you get fired?" asked Elena.

"Only if I'm lucky." Dora laughed shrilly. "Don't worry, I'll retract it all the next day. I'll call it misinformation. But for one night we'll all pretend it's true. We could all use one good night of celebration, couldn't we? And in the morning, we'll all sober up again." She laughed and pointed to Silvia. "Especially you."

"If only it were true. I'd immediately go home to my poor mother in Palanga." Silvia sighed deeply.

———————

For Saturday's dance, Silvia bought an iridescent, silver organdy dress and had some satin high heels dyed to match. She painted her eyelids blue, colored her lips red, and dotted pink rouge on her cheeks—finally achieving a face as colorful as an elaborate Easter egg. And to finish the effect, she dusted her blond hair with silver powder. Felius' favorite dinner—roast duck filled with prunes and apples—waited in the kitchen.

Outside, it was cold and slushy. The wind was picking up and by night the slush would solidify into ice footprints and tire marks.

Silvia sat with Felius in the radiator heat of her apartment listening to the Lithuanian Hour on the radio. Polka music and folk tunes followed announcements of deaths and weddings while Silvia was practically holding her breath until she heard Dora's voice announcing the news. First she read the local news and then she announced that the Russians had captured the last Lithuanian partisan in the forests near the Baltic Sea. He had been in hiding since the end of World War II. The Communists blamed him for many acts of aggression against the government.

Felius stopped gnawing on a crispy duck wing. "Every year they capture the last partisan in Lithuania. How many of them can be left in the woods? How can they survive with the NKVD dogs on their trails?"

"Shh," said Silvia, "Dora is saying something about Khrushchev."

"In Moscow this morning, Khrushchev announced that he was removing the Soviet Army from the Baltics and finally restoring Lithuanian independence. Yes," said Dora on the radio, "you heard it right, Lithuania is once again a free country."

Silvia jumped out of her chair and flung herself on Felius' neck. "Did you hear the news? Lithuania is free! That means we can finally get married, just like you said. When shall we set the date?"

Felius was completely stunned by the news. "My God, I can hardly believe it, after all this time, it's free. And so suddenly, so unexpectedly. This calls for a huge celebration. Let's buy some champagne and meet everyone at the dance." He kissed Silvia and put on his jacket.

"Champagne, yes, we can toast our wedding," said Silvia as she put on her coat. "Now there's nothing in the way of our getting married."

Felius was too astonished by the radio news to take in her words. "Can you believe it, Silvia? Free again! I can't wait to see our friends. This will be some celebration tonight." He turned around and went to the telephone. "But wait, first I'm going to call my boss at the printing press and tell him what I think of him."

Silvia was alarmed. "Wait, don't do that. You'll get fired."

"Ahh, I've hated that crappy job for years. If he doesn't fire me, I'm going to quit anyway and go back to Kaunas."

Silvia fretted and finally blessed herself while Felius called his boss and told him, in his thick accent, exactly what he thought of him.

The Knights of Columbus hall was filled with cheering people. Everyone was wild-eyed with disbelief at the good news. Champagne corks were popping every few minutes as every table stood to toast Lithuania's newfound independence. Mr. George got misty eyed and sheepishly came clean to his dance partner that he had a wife left behind in Lithuania. Mr. Janulis had already made arrangements to sell his house. He said he'd called his brother in Boston, who had been waiting for years in anticipation of such a day. When his brother came to America he had refused to leave Boston to come to Chicago where there were better jobs, wanting to be closer to Lithuania so he could be on the first boat back to his homeland. After tonight's news, his brother was taking all his money out of the bank first thing on Monday to buy his boat ticket. No planes for him, thank you. He came by boat from Bremerhaven and by boat he'd return, taking the first train to the Lithuanian border. He didn't care if he had to walk the rest of the way to his village by the Baltic Sea. "Now there's a true patriot," said Felius as he climbed on a table to declaim some patriotic poems. Everyone sang the national anthem and got rip-roaring drunk, especially Felius. Finally, Silvia was able to capture him for one tango as he draped himself on her, swaying around the dance floor, his sweaty cheek plastered to hers. A mirrored ball was spreading tiny lights all around the room. Silvia kept cooing about weddings and children, while Felius cooed about getting a plane ticket to Kaunas.

When the music stopped, Silvia noticed that the silver powder from her hair had left a metallic sheen on Felius' face and shoulder. He tried to brush the silver powder from his shoulder but only succeeded in spreading it onto his sleeve. Silvia sighed. So far things weren't going as planned.

"Look what you've done to my good suit. Do you know how much this suit cost? What is this stuff in your hair? You look like one of those aluminum Christmas trees tonight. Get that crap out of your hair." He excused himself to the bathroom as Silvia sat down, watching him cross the dance floor and detour over to Aurelia Norkus' table. She watched as he complained about his soiled suit. She watched as Felius started to dance with Aurelia, and her heart sank as she watched him kiss her neck and take her into the coatroom.

Silvia sat alone at her table with the silver powder around her shoulders like magic dandruff. Her mascara trickled down her cheeks, her tears blending the silver with the blue of her eye shadow and the pink of her cheeks. She wiped her tears with the back of her hand, and her face looked like a smeared painting. For a long time, she sat there watching everyone in the hall rejoice at the news of freedom. She watched them dance and drink and kiss and laugh, feeling as if she could no longer be seen, as if she had simply disappeared.

When a cork popped behind her, Silvia jumped. The war came back in a flash as she remembered the morning she had left her home by the Baltic Sea. They packed food, buried their silver behind the back steps, and left their dog still tied in the yard, thinking they would return as soon as the Russians and the Germans left. At the bridge, a soldier was stopping everyone. Silvia's father was held and interrogated. Her mother was frozen with fear and told Silvia to get in their neighbor's cart and that they would meet her on the other side of the bridge. Silvia did as she was told and never saw them again. She came to America like an orphan. By the end of the war both her father and her fiancé, Donatas, were dead. But she didn't find this out until much later when letters were finally allowed.

"Can you believe this?" Dora sighed as she plopped down next to Silvia. "Everyone bought my story, and they're all delirious. Oh, my Lord, I feel terrible. What was I thinking of to pull this hoax? I won't be able to face anyone for months. And my husband's going to kill me." Dora buried her face in her hands.

"You did it for me, Dora. Thank you. You're a good friend." The two women sat dejectedly in a sea of celebration.

Dora looked up at Silvia and moaned. "And I saw that cad Felius in the coatroom with Aurelia. You know, they deserve each other."

"Maybe they do," said Silvia mechanically.

"You look a mess. Your face looks like it melted. Here, take this." Dora gave Silvia an embroidered handkerchief that smelled of Evening in Paris, and Silvia wiped the smeared paint off her face.

Dora put her arm around Silvia. "Listen, don't feel bad. I always say it's better to know he's a rat before you're married than after you're stuck with him. Look around, there are better men to be had."

"I think I'll go home," said Silvia.

"Me too. I feel too guilty to face anyone."

"Do me a favor," said Silvia. "Get my coat out of the coatroom. I don't want to go in there."

"Of course, my dear. You wait right here."

Silvia sat watching Valentinas Gediminas dancing a dramatic tango with Lucy Gudauskas in her green satin sheath. Curly-haired Elena Kazlas in a blue chiffon dress waved as she danced by with her father. It seemed as if hours had passed. It seemed as if Silvia had grown old in this dance hall. Dora brought her coat and left.

"May I have this dance, Silvia?" said a voice behind her.

Silvia turned to find Captain Eddie. "I heard the news today about Lithuania, and I wanted to celebrate. I came to dance with you."

"Me? You came to dance with me?" squeaked Silvia in a small voice.

"Is there someone else here? Maybe you're hiding them under your skirt?" He tried to pick up her skirt playfully. Silvia pushed his hand away. "Are you sitting on someone?" Captain Eddie smiled. "Of course it's you I want to dance with."

Silvia laughed a choking laugh, startled by the happy sound coming from her.

"Ha, I finally made you laugh."

"It feels good, especially tonight."

Captain Eddie took her in his arms and started dancing slowly, rocking back and forth like a father cradling his child. Spotlights of red and blue were swirling around the dance floor. A soft blue light landed on them, making Silvia's hair shine like the moon.

"Silvia, you've never looked more beautiful than you do tonight. There's a tenderness in your face." Captain Eddie smoothed her hair and laughed at the silver sheen that remained on his hand. "Your hair is like snow in the moonlight. You women know such magic. Look, you've turned my hand to silver."

Silvia looked at Captain Eddie, almost handsome in his brown double-breasted suit, smelling of spice. He was so solid and substantial, not like her slippery Felius. The blue spotlight stayed on them a bit longer, working its magic. Silvia sighed, her blurred face perched on Captain Eddie's shoulder, smiling a crooked smile while little spotlights danced by like harbor lights on a June night near the Baltic Sea.

Sunday Dinner

Milda Gudauskas, 1958

That Sunday, like all others, the Gudauskas family walked to Nativity Church on Sixty-Ninth Street. Milda and her brother Paul looked like miniature versions of their parents—Paul wearing the same gray hat and coat as his father, Milda wearing the same white gloves as her mother, and the same patent leather purse hanging from the stiff crook in her arm.

As they passed their neighbors, Mr. Gudauskas greeted them with a dignified nod. Though he had been a lawyer in Lithuania, in Chicago he could only find work at the Nabisco factory, a fact he tried to hide from the neighbors by wearing a suit over his factory overalls and carrying his lunch in a briefcase, saying it was important to maintain one's dignity, no matter what circumstances life provided. Milda couldn't figure out why he was so embarrassed, considering everybody else's parents worked at the stockyards, which to her mind was a lot worse than Nabisco. Maybe it was to make up for his wild sister, Lucija, whom everyone called Lucy, who had a bit of a reputation in the neighborhood. Or maybe it was because his wife was the general's daughter, a proud fact he dropped into as many conversations as he could.

When they had first come to America, Marcele Gudauskas cleaned office buildings downtown, and later worked as a housekeeper for the Bartulis family after Vida's mom died. But recently she had quit because of her migraines. These days she chaired the Daughters of Lithuania meetings, taught at the Lithuanian Saturday School, and made sure her children practiced their piano and took dictation in Lithuanian daily so that they could read and write in their native tongue. In her spare time, she collected china teacups and embroidered the family crest on everything.

In church the family followed Mr. Gudauskas down the center aisle to the front pew, his head held high, not even a nod to friends. Just as Milda was about to slide into the pew behind him, she thought she saw something furry slithering on the floor and, trying to avoid it, she tripped over their neighbor, Magda, who always seemed to be in the wrong place. Milda caught herself before falling, but not before making enough noise for everyone to turn in her direction. When she saw Magda's brother, Al, trying to smother his laughter, she was so embarrassed, she erupted in a nervous giggle. Her brother Paul tried desperately to suppress his bubbling laughter, but Magda didn't even try to restrain her amusement, laughing loudly as she pointed to Milda.

Her father's face tightened. "Milda, what the devil!" he whispered in her ear through clenched teeth. "People are staring at us," he hissed, squeezing her arm so tightly she let out a yelp. "Shush, control yourself." Her father gave her one of his narrow-eyed looks that riveted her in place. Milda got quiet, but she could see Paul's shoulders still bobbing up and down with laughter. Paul never learned; he still sometimes got the strap from their father, but Milda never forgot those red welts on her legs. She had learned to be a good girl. Sometimes other kids thought she was too good, but the grownups always pointed to her as an example of excellent behavior.

After Mass, the family milled around outside the church, greeting friends and neighbors. Mr. Gudauskas argued with Mr. Matas and Mr. Vitkus about what should be done to help free the Captive

Nations, as the Baltic countries of Lithuania, Latvia, and Estonia were now being called. Milda just stood around smiling politely, watching Irene Matas chatting with Vida and Ona. With a familiar sinking feeling, she realized that they never even noticed her. How she wanted to simply walk over and join Irene's circle of friends, but she didn't have the courage, nor would she know what to say to them.

Soon everyone started to go home for Sunday dinner, which was early, in the European tradition, around two in the afternoon. Milda's grandmother, Marijona, who no longer went to Mass because of her arthritis, had made a pot roast with potatoes and carrots. While Milda set the table with the good china and the damask tablecloth, her mother brought in the cold borscht and dilled cucumber salad, all the while clucking her new Russian phrases to her children. Since coming home with her new Russian phrase book, their mother kept encouraging Paul and Milda to repeat them because the Cold War was getting worse. They might expect the Russians on their doorstep at any moment and must be prepared.

"Great," Paul whispered to Milda. "When they arrive, I'll be able to look them in the eye and say, *Eto karandash*—this is a pencil."

Milda smiled and was about to put another plate down on the table when she turned to ask her brother, "Is Aunt Lucy joining us today?"

He scratched his flat crew cut and gave her a look. "Are you kidding?" Most Sundays Aunt Lucy went to church with them, but stood in the back with the soccer players and left early to meet up with her friends at the Diamond Head Restaurant and Bar. She often brought Milda the colorful paper umbrellas from her tropical drinks. By now Milda had a whole collection of them.

At last they sat down to Sunday dinner, another formal occasion when no one said much. Milda was about to put a potato in her mouth when suddenly something furry brushed against her leg. She dropped her fork and let out a tiny squeak. It felt like a dog or cat had brushed against her, but they didn't have a pet. Her father pivoted his irritated gaze her way. Ignoring him, Milda lifted the damask tablecloth to peek under the table and was shocked to see a hairy face peering back at her with an embarrassed smile. He put his finger to his lips to signal her to be quiet. The poor thing was covered with hair and had a long tail and hooves instead of feet. It looked like a cornered goat—eyes darting in all directions. Milda couldn't take her eyes off him, even though her mother told her to get back up and eat like a lady.

"Milda, stop that this instant," her father threatened.

She poked her head back up and told her parents there was some kind of animal under the table.

Her mother sliced her a look. "Really, Milda, stop being annoying," she said, her lips compressed with disapproval.

Only her grandmother looked at Milda, totally perplexed. "What is it, dear?"

Paul bobbed his head under the table. "She's lying," he said flat as a pancake. "There's nothing there."

"No, I'm not," she argued, poking her head back under the table to make sure she hadn't imagined it. The goat-man was still there, curled up, looking uncomfortable, motioning for her to go away.

"Sit up and stop that nonsense, Milda," her father raised his voice and eyed her suspiciously, as if she were playing nasty tricks. "This is all very annoying." He ran a hand through his slick, dark hair. "You know it's not good for my heart to get angry."

"I'm sorry." Milda decided to say no more.

Across the table, her mother carefully placed another bite of roast beef into her red-lipsticked mouth, trying to ignore the breakdown of their Sunday ritual, while Milda bit into a dilled cucumber and watched as their eyes glazed over. Only her grandmother studied her carefully as she sipped her Sunday glass of sweet wine, a mysterious half-smile on her face.

After dinner, her father went to his weekly meeting of the Lithuanian government-in-exile, a group of educated men who were the hope of Lithuania to carry on its government until the Soviets left. As soon as he left, Paul and Milda turned on the Ed Sullivan Show. During a commercial, Milda crept back to the dining room to peek under the table and see if the goat-man was still there. To her relief, he was gone.

That night she tossed and turned, dreaming that she was in a school play and when she tried to take her mask off, it stuck to her face, smothering her. In the dream, she tried to scream and woke making muffled animal sounds.

At school the next morning, Sister Bonaventura prattled on about the many miracles of Mary. When she asked for an example, Milda raised her hand but then behind her she heard Al Vitkus say under his breath, "It would be a miracle if we could get outta here." The rows on each side started tittering.

"Algis Vitkus, was that you again?" asked Sister Bonaventura.

"No, Sister, I didn't say anything."

"Liar, come up here this instant."

Every day it was the same thing. All through fifth grade Al Vitkus got clobbered by the nuns. Why hadn't he learned to stop being so devilish? Milda nervously chewed the eraser on her pencil as she watched Al walk down the aisle to his doom. For a moment, he looked up at her, and when she saw the fear in his eyes, it made her stomach churn. Milda winced, closing her eyes as Sister Bonaventura awkwardly waddled her bulk over to Al. When Milda opened them again, she saw the goat-man sitting up on the file cabinet behind the nun. It so jolted her that she almost fell out of her seat. He waved to her, smiling impishly, and jumped down. She looked around the room, but no one else seemed to notice him.

Next to the goat-man, Sister Bonaventura slapped Al, first with her forehand and then with her backhand. "This is your daily bread,

Algis Vitkus," chanted the nun as Al's face twisted, but he didn't cry.

Suddenly the goat-man picked up sister's habit and peeked under her skirt. Milda could see the nun's black stockings like giant sausage casings around her thick legs.

Milda stood up. "Stop it, don't do that," she hissed to the goat-man.

"Who said that?" Sister Bonaventura bellowed like a wounded elephant. The whole class turned to look at Milda, who looked around, feeling trapped. Al Vitkus was staring at her with his mouth open.

"Milda? That wasn't you, was it?" Sister Bonaventura couldn't believe it.

"No, Sister, I mean, I wasn't talking to you," she said in a nervous, squeaky voice.

"Well, to whom were you speaking, Missy?" Sister's fat lip curled like a caterpillar.

Behind her, the goat-man laughed so hard he was holding his sides.

"Him," Milda said pointing to the goat-man. Sister Bonaventura turned around in one direction and then in the other. The class started tittering again. Milda was beginning to realize that no one else saw him.

"Milda, is this some joke?"

"No, Sister." Her heart pounded in her throat, as she wondered if the nun was going to slap her next.

"I don't like jokers, Milda, you know that." The nun listed down the aisle to Milda's desk.

"Sorry, Sister…" She bit her lip to keep from crying.

"I'll let you go this time." She leaned over, and Milda could smell the sourness of her anger. "But no more outbursts or you'll be next, do I make myself clear?" She wagged her arthritic finger in Milda's face.

"Yes, Sister." Milda kept her eyes lowered so as not to see the goat-man or Sister's accusing eyes. While the nun waddled back to her desk, Milda sat, her hands folded, hardly breathing or daring to move until she felt a tap on her shoulder that so startled her, she almost jumped out of her seat. It was Irene Matas, slipping her a note. It read: "That was so cool Milda! I always wanted to tell the old bag to stop it." Milda had never gotten a note in class before, but that day she got four more before lunch.

As she walked down the hall after school, she almost bumped into the goat-man around a corner.

"What are you doing to me?" she demanded through clenched teeth, so angry she wanted to scream, but was afraid someone might hear her. The goat-man just shrugged his shoulders and skipped away down the hall.

"Hey, wait a minute, I want to talk to you," she yelled, running after him, just as Al Vitkus came around the other corner.

"Yeah, I wanted to talk to you too." He squirmed a bit. "Hey…ah… thanks for standing up for me today. Nobody's ever done that before." Al smiled his crooked smile. "And I sure as hell didn't expect it to be you."

Milda stammered, not knowing what to say. "I…uh, didn't mean…"

"Well, I guess I owe you one. Come on, I'll buy you a vanilla Coke down at Country Maids."

Milda looked at him sideways, too stunned to answer. It was the first time Al Vitkus had ever said a word to her. They both stood there for what seemed a century. The very idea of going to Country Maids made her knees tremble, but before she could run home, Al whisked her away, blabbing a mile a minute about Corvettes and Thunderbirds.

Country Maids was filled with the kids the nuns yelled at. Some of the older kids were smoking, and a bunch of girls were trowelling on pancake makeup and ratting their hair. An eighth-grade girl was kissing a boy in one of the booths. Milda felt as if someone had taken her to another planet. Just as she was about to tell Al she was going home, Irene Matas and Connie O'Connor grabbed her off to one of the booths. Al brought her a vanilla Coke while Irene shared her fries.

"You know, Milda, I used to think you were stuck up, but you're not half bad," Irene said, biting into a fry.

"Yeah," added Connie, "if you only relaxed a little and weren't such a goody-goody." Connie smiled. "And you know something, I never realized that you look a little like Annette Funicello. I bet if you cut your braids you'd look just like her—really pretty."

Milda smiled and nervously ate a fry. "You think so?" She couldn't believe her ears.

That night Milda stood in front of the mirror in the bathroom, studying her face: tight pursed lips like her father's, hair severely parted in the middle and pulled into two tight dark braids, but it was her eyes—angry little coals—that bothered her the most. She had been looking at this face every single day, yet it was as if she were seeing it for the very first time.

Then the nightmares returned, as she dreamt that she walked to school with a blouse but no skirt, just her underpants. Though she desperately searched for her skirt, she couldn't find it anywhere. Sister Bonaventura was horrified and told her to come get her daily bread. The whole class laughed as the nun threw sharp pencils at her head.

She woke feeling something sharp sticking into her scalp, and when she put her hand to her head, it felt like a halo of burrs or a crown of thorns. When she went to the bathroom to look in the mirror, she saw that her whole head was covered with dozens of little ringworm curls, all stationed in place by crisscrossed bobby pins. In her drowsiness, she felt confused. Had she done this last night? When she pulled the bobby pins out and brushed her hair, it was shorter and full of curls. She must have cut it, too, but she couldn't remember doing it. Brushing her dark wavy hair, she decided it looked pretty.

On her way downstairs, when she spotted the goat-man's tail wagging under the table, she smiled and went into the kitchen for breakfast. But when her father looked up from his newspaper and saw her hair, he screwed up his face like he had eaten some bad cheese.

"Who do you think you are, some kind of Brigitte Bardot? Next thing, you'll be wearing lipstick and high heels? What will the neighbors say if they see you looking like that?"

"I think she looks pretty," her grandmother said unexpectedly. "Very soft and flattering, Milda. Reminds me a little of our Lucy."

"Lucy!" her father snorted. "Lucy is a disgrace. No daughter of mine is going to walk around looking like a streetwalker. Mother, give me the shears."

Grabbing a hunk of Milda's hair, he was ready to cut it off when her grandmother took his arm. "Son, give me those scissors," she said sharply, staring right into his eyes. Her father's lips pursed; his face strained with anger. His wife said nothing but went upstairs to nurse a migraine.

"And Lucy never looks like a streetwalker," Grandmother hissed. "Why would you say something like that about your own sister? Why, she's beautiful." She took his scissors away, and Milda let out a sigh of relief.

Still steamed, her father straightened his tie, picked up his briefcase, and left for work.

Her grandmother came up to Milda, putting her arm around her. "You look great," she said as they both stood at the door watching him walk down Talman Street.

As usual, he ran into Mr. Vitkus and Mr. Janulis, who were on their way to catch a bus to the stockyards. Her father stood there solemnly like an undertaker in his dark suit, pretending he had some important work to do, when suddenly Milda saw the goat-man trot by, waving and smiling. She watched him take her father's tie off and unbutton his shirt until his factory overalls peeked out. Her father looked around confused, but the goat-man continued. Her father jerked around, flailing his arms, swinging his briefcase, trying to catch the joker, but there was no one anywhere near. The men stared at the Nabisco overalls peeking out underneath his shirt.

"What the devil's going on here?" Mr. Janulis asked, looking at the overalls. "Are you all right?" He thought that Mr. Gudauskas might be having a seizure or a heart attack.

"Why, look, it's a Nabisco uniform," said Mr. Vitkus, looking puzzled.

"Well, you certainly don't have to undress in the street," said Mr. Janulis with a snicker.

Milda's father turned red as a raspberry, sputtering and stammering, not knowing what to say. He tried to straighten himself. "I'm perfectly fine."

Mr. Vitkus snorted a laugh and leaned over to Mr. Janulis, whispering loudly, "What an old hypocrite, pretending he's got some fancy office job all this time when he's just working down at the factory." Mr. Janulis laughed into his fist. "In Lithuania, we used to say that you can dress a bear like a prince and make him dance in the square, but when the circus is over, he still walks on all fours." Mr. Vitkus bellowed out a laugh.

Milda's father didn't say a word. He just buttoned his shirt, put his tie in his pocket, and went to work, leaving the other two men snickering in the street.

Standing at the door, her grandmother also laughed softly into her hand, trying to hide how much this scene tickled her. Milda was about to close the door when she saw the goat-man leaning against a tree, waving to her. She smiled and waved back, as though he was an old and trusted friend.

Lucy in the Sky

Milda Gudauskas, 1959

Milda's grieving grandmother, Marijona, always said that if no one prayed for a soul, it became lost. To her, the very air was thick with souls. "Milda," she'd say, as she fingered her rosary, "pray for each dead member of our family." Together they'd name each one, counting them out on their fingers. Sometimes Milda would even dream of her ancestor spirits following her everywhere she went, commenting on every aspect of her life like a Greek chorus.

When her father died of a heart attack the previous summer, she prayed hard for him because he was such a stern and powerful presence in her life. But when her Aunt Lucy was killed while crossing Western Avenue, Milda didn't pray for her, though she couldn't say why. Maybe it was because Lucy was the modern aunt, the one everyone said was a bit crazy, the one who spoke English when everyone else spoke only Lithuanian, the one who liked to drink and swear and flirt with married men. They said she had a failed romance with Valentinas Gediminas, one of the curdled bachelors who sat at the Amber Tavern most evenings. They said she had a broken heart because he wouldn't marry her. They said she was drunk the night the car hit her.

Maybe because Aunt Lucy wasn't much of a believer, Milda

thought she didn't need prayers like the others, but she was wrong. Lucy needed it more than any of them. Her soul was lost, not in the way the church taught, but because she, more than any of them, had broken with the past—that long string of souls reaching back to the beginning. She always thought of them holding hands like children on the playground playing Red Rover. Lucy had broken the chain of hands—no telling what that meant.

It wasn't, however, apparent right away. In fact, her family continued to lead their everyday lives, mourning their lost ones. They still went to church on Sundays and all the holy days of obligation. Milda still prayed for her dead family, naming all but Lucy on her fingers the way her mournful grandmother had taught her. And she continued to be the best student in her sixth-grade class, even though she now hung out with the cool kids.

Then came May Day.

On May first, Milda was chosen to crown the statue of the Virgin with flowers. Dressed like Mary in a long blue gown with a veil, she felt like a pastel nun as she led a procession of girls dropping rose petals and singing, "Oh Mary, we crown thee Queen of the May." She was about to climb the ladder to put the flowers on the head of the statue when she had a strange thought. *If Mary was the mother of God, why didn't they call Joseph the father of God? Was it something about the Immaculate Conception or was it the Virgin Birth?* She could never get that straight. But she knew that Mary never had sex. *So, if Joseph wasn't Jesus' father, and God was his true father, then was Mary God's wife? Then she should have her rightful place in the Trinity—Father, Mother, Son, and Holy Ghost. Only then it would be the divine square rather than the mysterious triangle. Or maybe Mary was God's daughter-in-law.* All this confusing genealogy of the divine was, for some reason, bouncing around in Milda's head as she crowned Mary in the courtyard. If only she could ask Sister Petronella about it, or even the handsome Father Mike, but she didn't dare.

Milda remembered how the priest had called Irene Matas a blasphemer for questioning the raising of Lazarus. Irene had merely asked if Lazarus had been green or moldy, or if he had smelled bad after being raised from his grave. Milda thought it was an interesting question, but the priest didn't think so.

The question was never answered, but that didn't matter. What mattered was that Irene had dared to pose such a question. That was monumental. For Milda, it was a moment of pure clarity. The idea of questioning dogma became a new way of looking at the world.

After the May Day procession, she went home, as usual, to do her homework. She was on the second page of her history report on the Crusades when Irene came running in the door.

"Milda, come quick, you won't believe this, but there's a miracle happening right in front of the Gediminas house on Talman Street. The Virgin Mary's appearing and she looks just like you did today in the May Day procession."

"Are you kidding me?"

"No lie, honest to God." Irene crossed her heart. "Hurry up, before she disappears."

As Milda ran down the street with Irene, her mind whirled with its new habit of questioning. Why was it always Mary who appeared at these miracles? How come they never saw Jesus or Joseph or any of the apostles at Lourdes or Fatima?

When she reached the Gediminas house on Talman Street, she glimpsed a patch of fog, and, oddly, something was glowing inside the fog. As she got closer, she could see that there was a woman in blue robes floating in the clouds. Her head was turned the other way, but she had her hands out in the traditional Holy Virgin pose. It looked like an authentic miracle all right. Milda moved in closer to get a better look. So many people had gathered there already. Her friends and their mothers and grandmothers were reverently blessing themselves. Only Magda seemed unaffected. She was walking among the worshipers, softly singing a Lithuanian lullaby. Milda squeezed through the crowd toward the apparition and was about to kneel when she saw the Virgin's face and froze. It couldn't be. With a shock she realized it was not the Virgin Mary appearing in front of the whole neighborhood, but her dead Aunt Lucy, the loony one who had died. It struck her like a thunderbolt.

"Well, well, Milda," whispered the apparition. "About time you got here."

"Aunt Lucy," Milda stuttered, hardly able to talk. "What are you doing here?" She was both startled and confused.

"I'm waiting for Valentinas Gediminas to come out of that house to declare his undying love for me," answered the spectral Lucy. "Right here in front of all of these God-fearing people, the way he used to declare it in the back seat of his old Plymouth."

Milda looked around. No one seemed to have heard her. "Why are you impersonating Mary? Everyone thinks you're the Virgin with those robes."

Aunt Lucy choked back a laugh. "That's a good one."

"But you're an impostor, Aunt Lucy," Milda whined.

"So? I got the idea from watching you do your impersonation this afternoon."

"But that was May Day," she protested.

"Well, this is V-V Day—Victory for the Virgin." Aunt Lucy chortled. "Valentinas Day. Where is that bum anyway?" Aunt Lucy looked around. "I loved that lout for most of my short years on earth." She was getting worked up. "Valentinas Gediminas, the one I worshiped and adored, the one I lost my virginity to, the one who left me. I'm back to torment him for as long as he tormented me. Look at him peeking out from behind his mother's lace curtains. Ha! He knows it's me. He's afraid to come out. He's making it in his pants, he's so frightened." The aura of light around Lucy was getting brighter. She blazed like some Old Testament prophet. Her anger fueled her like propane in a lantern. The people gathered around "oohed" and "aahed" at the bright light. Rosaries were pulled out of pocketbooks.

"Milda, go tell that miserable excuse of a man to come out here."

Reluctantly, Milda went inside the brick two-flat and found Valentinas Gediminas cowering in the corner of the fussy living room.

"Wh-what's she doing here? Why doesn't she stay dead like she's supposed to?" Valentinas was chewing his mustache nervously. "What does she want?"

"She wants you to tell everyone you love her. You know, a declaration of love from you."

"Really?" He was astounded. "That's all she wants? To tell everyone I still love her?" His face softened. "To think that she took this love for me to her grave and beyond." He shook his head, looking like a boy about to cry. "Such is the power of love."

Milda wanted to say that it was anger and revenge that was powering this return from the grave, but she kept quiet. Valentinas pulled some paper out of a drawer and began to compose a love note. His handwriting was as thin and spidery as the hairs on his head. When he was finished, he thrust it into her hands and told her to deliver it to Lucy quickly.

As Milda watched Aunt Lucy read the letter several times, she wondered how much her aunt knew about God. Maybe she could answer all of those burning questions that plagued her so.

Lucy slapped the letter with the back of her hand. "Ha, he says it was his mother's fault. She didn't want him to marry me. What a coward! He couldn't stand up to that battle-ax. Did he think this would be enough? Did he think that I bothered to come all the way from the other side for this puny little letter? I want a declaration of love that the whole neighborhood can see."

"Like a sign?"

"Bigger," she bellowed. "And tell him I'm not moving until I see it."

"OK, Aunt Lucy, I'll tell him, but before I go in, can you answer one question?"

"Maybe," she pouted.

"What about the Virgin Birth? Did Mary really become pregnant without doing it? Why did God arrange it that way?"

"Do you really think God cares about the Virgin Birth?" Aunt Lucy laughed. "He doesn't care about stuff like that."

"Are you sure?"

"Don't worry about God. Worry about your ancestors. You'll never find a more resentful bunch than the dead."

Milda was amazed to hear that her grandmother had been right about the power of ancestors.

———◆◆◆———

The following week, news of the apparition was spreading. Milda's whole family came to see Aunt Lucy. Her grandmother cried when she saw her daughter. She asked about Milda's father. "Ah, Mama, he's as cranky as he always was," said Aunt Lucy. Milda's mother was shocked at first and embarrassed, telling Lucy to vanish before anyone else in the neighborhood recognized her. "I always knew you were different, Lucy, but I never expected this," she said, looking sideways at Lucy, then looking to see who else was around. Grandmother Marijona had many questions about all of her family and friends who had passed over. Milda realized that her grandmother knew more people who were dead than alive. She was the last of her generation still living in this neighborhood. Two school friends still lived in Lithuania, also isolated leftovers from a time now gone. They wrote occasional letters in shaky handwriting, which her grandmother read with a magnifying glass. From across the room, Milda saw her tears magnified as she read with the glass close to her face. The news from Lithuania was always sad. She saw the longing in her grandmother's eyes to join the dead—a whole tribe waiting for her.

Though they lived in Chicago, the second largest city in America, Milda's grandmother often said that their neighborhood of Lithuanians felt like a village. One-by-one, the people in the neighborhood began to recognize Lucy. Old friends and acquaintances dropped by to say hello. Some were shocked; others took it in stride, while a few called Father Mike to investigate, hoping that their Lucy would be declared a saint.

Father Mike explained that two miracles were needed in order for Lucy to be considered for sainthood. Things like miraculous healings or rosaries that changed from silver to gold, or strange lights or whirling discs in the sky—and a waiting period during which the Pope must declare her Blessed.

"Piece of cake," said Lucy when she heard the news. That afternoon, as the neighborhood gathered to watch the appearance of one of their own potential saints, the silver fillings in their mouths turned to gold.

"Rosaries, the priest said rosaries," Milda muttered under her breath, "not dental fillings."

"Don't be boring, Milda. You worry too much about the rules. Relax, you're too intense."

Milda thought she was relaxed. But one day in religion class, as Father Mike droned on about the Annunciation, one of his favorite subjects, explaining how Mary got pregnant the night the angel whispered in her ear while she was sleeping, Milda thought of blowguns with sperm in them. *Was there a way for sperm to get from the ear to down there*, she wondered?

"God doesn't care about the Virgin Birth." She hadn't meant to stand up and say this, but there she was blaspheming in front of the whole class.

"Where did you hear such a thing?" asked Father Mike.

"Lucy told me," she said in a nervous squeak.

Father Mike looked around. "Lucy who?"

"Not here," she gestured out the window. "Lucy in the sky, you know, my Aunt Lucy."

The priest frowned.

Several days later, Father Mike was in front of the Gediminas house performing an exorcism, sprinkling holy water and commanding Aunt Lucy to be gone with all of her minions from Hell.

"Fat chance," said Aunt Lucy. "I ain't leaving until I get my declaration of love, and if it doesn't come soon, I'll make life hell for one Valentinas Gediminas."

Valentinas came out the next day with placards declaring his love, but it wasn't enough for Lucy. The next day, he had larger signs printed and posted on every telephone pole, but it still was inadequate. Aunt Lucy wanted more; she wanted bigger. A love letter went up on the corner billboard, above the Sinclair station, but Lucy wasn't satisfied. Valentinas, frantic to show his love, was running out of ideas.

That night, Milda's dreams were tortured by groups of ancestors watching her every move. She felt cowed by the intensity of their interest. Long strands of DNA, like the tree of life, filled her dreams with her dead family attached in a twisting chain. There was nowhere to hide, no one to confess to. This was beginning to feel more oppressive than the church with its dogma. Milda went to Lucy for help.

"Silly girl," said Lucy. "Your ancestors are also there to help you, not just to judge you. Ask them for help when you need it. Honor them when your life goes well."

"How do I honor them?"

"Get some photos, light a candle, and say a prayer. It's elementary. Life is hard and short, but it's also sweet and simple. Relax, Milda, and have some fun."

At the corner store, Milda bought some candles, and she took out photos and started praying, mostly that her father wouldn't come back the way her aunt had. Her mother thought she was becoming odd. She even sometimes saw Sister Petronella and Father Mike watching her with suspicion. But in her grandmother's eyes, Milda was the family hero.

One night, after lighting her candles, she prayed for Aunt Lucy to finally get her declaration of love. That night she dreamt of her dead father, flying a plane and writing in the sky. It looked just like Valentinas' spidery handwriting.

When Milda awoke, she decided her dream was promising and ran to tell Valentinas about it. He was overjoyed, kissing her on both cheeks and then running out the door. She later heard that he had rented a skywriting plane, making a huge heart in the sky with "I Love Lucy" in big white puffy letters.

No one in the neighborhood paid any attention. Everyone thought it was an advertisement for the TV show of the same name. But Aunt Lucy was ecstatic. "There, he finally did it so the whole neighborhood could see he really loved me." She glowed warmly and faded away slowly like the letters in the sky. The last Milda saw of her, she was smiling beatifically and blowing kisses to Valentinas. He cried copious tears at her fading, finding he loved her far more in death than he ever had in life.

Valentinas still spent time in the Amber Tavern with the other confirmed bachelors, only now, whenever he had too much to drink, he cried over his lost love, Lucy. He spent the rest of his days in lovesick mourning while Milda spent her nights trying hard to relax under the gaze of a new cosmology. Lucy was never declared Blessed, even though Milda's grandmother's arthritis mysteriously vanished the day Aunt Lucy left. They both lit candles and prayed especially long and hard for the soul of their own dear Lucy.

Miner's Lake

Irene Matas, 1960

Day by day my mother grew weaker until she could no longer work. When the doctors said she needed an operation, I panicked, remembering how Vida's mother had died when we were in first grade. Last year, when Milda's father and her Aunt Lucy had died, I got frightened again. I didn't want my mother to die. But what was death anyway? It seemed to me that people just disappeared from life. Where did they all go? The nuns said souls went to heaven and hell, but all I sensed was their endless absence.

My father tried to reassure me that my mother would be fine, but I could see the fear in his eyes. I repeatedly went to her door, not wanting to disturb her, but listening for any noise that might signal distress. Even though I was only fourteen, I was beginning to realize that there was something dark in the world that could claim mothers, fathers, and aunts, something underneath ordinary daily life that tugged at it, that wouldn't let people simply live their lives without worry and grief.

Our neighbor Mrs. Vitkus came over with Magda, bringing soup for my mother and potato *kugelis* for the rest of us. She moved the medicine bottles to the side and put down a bowl. "Borscht," she declared, "is good for the blood." As my mother ate, Mrs. Vitkus told her about a Lithuanian camp in Michigan, a farm that the Lithuanians had recently purchased from the Amish near Miner's Lake. Her son Al was going, as were Milda, Ona, and Vida, and many of the other kids from Lithuanian Saturday School.

Just as I was perking up and wanting to hear more, Mrs. Vitkus scooted us out of the room. "Irena, take Magda to your room to play while I talk to your mother." As I was leaving, I heard her say, "Why don't you let your kids go camping, too? It'll give you a chance to rest, and it'll be good for them to get out of the city. They say the camp has rolling meadows and an oak forest just like Samogitia."

Magda sat down on my bed and said nothing for a while. When she picked up the stuffed dog on my bed and hugged it, I plopped down on the bed next to her as she looked around the room. "Where's your Lovey doll?" she asked me. I had forgotten about that doll. When we first came to America, my parents had given me my first doll, a Negro boy, whom I named after my first American friend. Magda used to love that doll. But that was so long ago. Magda and I no longer played together, and I felt bad because I had outgrown her.

"I don't have the doll anymore, Magda." I couldn't remember what happened to it. Had I lost it? Had I left it in that old storefront where we first lived? And I wondered what had happened to my old friend Lovey. Was he still living in that apartment building on the South Side of Chicago that was now a Negro neighborhood? Were the Spanish Gypsies still living there? On the South Side, the dividing line between the Negro and white neighborhoods was Halsted Street, but the line crept west every year. Maybe one day I'd see him again in Marquette Park.

Magda, Al, and I used to play in the streets of our old neighborhood, but now I felt shy whenever I saw Al. He was starting to look cute in his jeans and white t-shirts.

That evening, after Mrs. Vitkus left, my father told my brother and me that we would be going to a camp in Michigan in two weeks.

Tomorrow we would buy cots and camp clothes. It felt odd because I had never gone shopping with my father before, nor had I ever been away to camp. The thought scared and thrilled me, but under all the fear and excitement was the nagging worry about my mother.

The day we were to leave for camp, I went to kiss her good-bye. She was sleeping on her side, her hands tucked under her chin. I didn't want to wake her, but I just couldn't leave without saying good-bye. I tiptoed to her bed and tapped her on the shoulder. She groggily opened her eyes and stretched, sleepily wiping her mouth. I bent over to hug her and suddenly started to cry. "Don't die," I whispered.

My mother hugged me to her. "Ah, don't worry, I'll be just fine. You have fun with your friends, and I'll be fine. You'll see." She kissed me on the nose.

"Just get better, OK?" My voice cracked.

That afternoon, all the kids I had grown up with were gathered at church with our suitcases and our cots, waiting to board the bus that was to take us to Michigan. I sat next to Vida and saved the seat across the way for Milda and Ona. Al Vitkus got on the bus and sat with Pete, Paul, and Jonas. "Just think," Al yelled as the bus pulled away, "two weeks with no parents, no nuns or priests." He let out a hoot. "One more year and we'll be done with that stupid grammar school. Yahoo!" The other boys whooped and hollered.

I wanted to yell along like we used to in the old days, but something was happening to me. Tall and skinny with fat blond braids, I felt self-conscious about everything. My breasts were beginning to show, and I was embarrassed, slouching to hide them. In fact, everything mortified me—my braids, my clothes, my face, my voice, and most of all my period. I hated it.

By the time we drove through Illinois, Indiana, and half of Michigan, I was wilted and sweaty. After Ludington, I began to see the Amish farmers who lived in this part of central Michigan. A bonneted girl in a long skirt tended neat rows of green onions and tomatoes, while a boy wearing suspenders over a white shirt was loading milk cans onto the back of a wagon. The sun glinted off the silver can and blinded me for a moment. When I looked up again, I saw the bearded father in his field. I thought this was how my grandparents must have lived in Lithuania. It felt as if the past and future were divided by a bus window. The past was outside with its buggies and old-fashioned clothes, and we were the future whizzing by in a silver bus.

When we reached camp, I could see Miner's Lake shimmering in the distance, down a sloping hill, beyond farm fences and the crowded maple trees. I wanted to jump into that cool, sparkling lake, but we had to get our luggage first and find our tents.

Dragging what I swear was the same DP suitcase we'd had in the refugee camps in Germany, the one we had lugged to America, I looked around, embarrassed as usual, hoping Al didn't see me with this relic from the war. Finally, I found the canvas-and-wood cot with my name on it, awkwardly balancing it on my hip and lugging the suitcase along while trying to follow my group. Ahead, I saw Al, his suitcase on his shoulder and his cot under one arm. He made it all look effortless.

"Hey, Irene," he said. "You need some help with that?"

I turned red and stuttered, "No thanks, I can do it." I made a monumental effort to lift my heavy suitcase and ended up dropping it and tripping over my cot. What was it about Al that made me so clumsy? Every time he came near I turned into a total oaf. It was so humiliating that I vowed to stay away from him, but it was no use, I couldn't keep it up for long. Pretty soon I'd be slyly looking for him again. It was torture. Thank God the boys' and girls' camps were separate, getting together only for bonfires and swimming.

"Irene Matas," called a big girl with too many freckles. Her name was Daina, a high-school senior who would be our tent leader. She had legs like thick sausages and no waist. Daina helped me drag my suitcase into our tent, set up my cot, and shove my brown suitcase under it.

Our first night, the boys joined us for the bonfire as the counselors explained the history of the Amish people who had come to America in the 1700s and had never changed with the times. The counselors also told us the many legends about Miner's Lake. It was a place where miners used to pan for gold, and it was said that the unlucky miners still haunted the weathered barn near the lake. Indian legends about the lake warned that the Indians refused to swim there. They said that Miner's Lake wouldn't freeze over in the winter unless someone drowned in it that year. The lake spirit required a sacrifice and for many years, it seemed a sacrificial victim always arrived before the ice did.

That night I couldn't fall asleep, listening to the mysterious whoosh of the wind through the oak trees, the chirping of the crickets, and the whine of a mosquito somewhere near my ear. What were my parents doing at home? Homesick and tired, I worried about my mother. Would she die while I was at camp? My eyes filled with tears. How did Vida bear it when her mom died?

Getting my flashlight, I wrote my mother a letter, telling her about the Amish and how pretty it was in the woods. I told her to rest and get better soon, and felt better thinking I could mail it in the morning.

The next day, the girls' camp marched along the dusty road in twos, towels draped over arms, suntan lotion ready for an afternoon at the lake. The day was hot and muggy, and the bees buzzed lazily in the Queen Anne's lace on the side of the road. As we passed an old crab-apple tree, I picked a small sour apple, took a bite, and spat it out. It was so sour that my mouth puckered, sending a shudder through me.

Soon the boys came marching in cadence from their camp, chanting some silly ditty until they reached the crab-apple tree, which they stripped like locusts. An apple came zinging by my ear and hit Ona on the back.

"Hey, you stupids!" Ona bellowed, turning to look at the culprits. Another apple whizzed by and skidded down the road. I turned around to see Al Vitkus lobbing an apple in my direction. I took two steps back to get out of the way and bumped into Vida, who grabbed me to keep me from falling.

At the front of the group, Daina turned around. "Who threw that? Was it Al?"

Three guys named Al shook their heads. Al Vitkus looked around and saw Algimantas, Alfonsas, and Alfredas. They had all shortened their names to Al. In Marquette Park, if you stood on a corner and yelled "Al," a dozen guys would turn around.

Daina threatened them all with a raised fist: "One more apple and the whole group will march back to the kitchen to scrub pots instead of swimming."

The apples dropped, and the boys got back into formation. Al Vitkus threw his store of apples into the cow meadow. The boys' counselor looked sheepish, unable to discipline his group.

When we got to Miner's Lake, we climbed over the rail fence because the gate was padlocked. Then we half-slid down a sloping path to the lake, where a roped-off section had been created for swimming. The sun was strong, and I was feeling sweaty and dusty.

Daina drilled us on the safety rules and how to team up with a buddy whenever she blew the whistle, how we couldn't swim past the ropes, and how there was no roughhousing allowed. When she blew the whistle, the boys ran into the water first, splashing and yelling, diving and hooting. I didn't want to go in with all those boys, but Vida was too hot to care. She dragged me into the water before I had a chance to protest. When I tried to hold back, she splashed me until I was dripping wet. I noticed that my hands were covered with flecks of gold. "Look," I said, showing Vida. The water was filled with tiny flecks of gold that sparkled in the sun. In the places where the water wasn't disturbed, the gold sat on the bottom, shining like in a fairy tale.

"It's fool's gold," said Vida. "Mica. That's why they call it Miner's Lake." She cupped her hands, trying to capture the gold flakes.

Nearby, the boys had organized swim races at one end of the swimming area. Al was the best swimmer, effortlessly gliding through the water like a dolphin.

Soon, the girls organized their own race. Al came to watch, smiling at Vida with her Gypsy good looks, so dark, pretty, and petite, always so quiet and mysterious. She wasn't swimming because of her period. The boys all seemed to love her long wavy hair. Even when I let my braids out, my hair was frizzy instead of wavy.

It was hopeless, but I felt a bit better when I looked over at Ona, who used to be fat and was still a bit pudgy. Al came over to give the signal to start the race, and we jumped in. Milda was the fastest, but Ona and I kept trying to reach the ropes, swimming just a little faster each time, determined to beat Milda. When we heard Daina blow her whistle, we buddied up and held hands. When Daina blew the whistle again, we all rushed back into the water, stirring the mica flakes again, making the water sparkle with gold. Ona was getting faster in our underwater race to the ropes.

Al came over to watch us, and I could see by the look on Ona's face that she was determined to win. "This time I'm gonna beat you," she said. She was showing off for Al, but I wasn't going to let her embarrass me. Not with Al watching. He yelled, "Ready, set, go" and we all dove in. I swam until I thought my lungs were going to burst, but I wasn't going to give in easily. I swam and swam until I felt lake grass brush against my face, and realized I had gone past the ropes, beyond the sandy area. I surfaced the same time Ona did, both of us gasping for air. When Ona couldn't reach the bottom, she panicked and grabbed me, and we both went under into the sudden silence of the water. Underwater I could see her frightened face, her braids floating around like twining snakes. In a panic, she grabbed my shoulders, pulling me down into the lake weeds and muck. We struggled, and I could feel Ona pushing me down farther as she climbed on my shoulders. The lake grass was twirling around my arms and legs. We had churned up the mud on the bottom, and now clouds of it were rising. I struggled to free myself from Ona's legs, but they were wrapped around me like a vise. Scratching and pulling at her legs, I strained to shove her off but I couldn't. In her panic, Ona kept pushing me under so that she could stay above the water. I thrashed and struggled in my own panic, desperate for air. My lungs were bursting. I was swallowing muddy water. Above me the sunny surface of the water shimmered as I reached for it, my hair floating past my arm, the lake grasses drifting with it. My arm seemed pale and iridescent. The bright flakes of fool's gold sparkled around me like a heavenly vision, the sun glinting in streaks through the green water.

I felt Ona loosen her grip as the lake grass slowly swirled around me. Suddenly I realized that I could just disappear from my own life. There would be no more Irene Matas. It was amazingly quiet. I had always heard how when you're about to die, your life flashes before you like a speeded-up movie, but at that moment, the *Chicago Sun-Times* newspaper appeared before me. I saw the date and the headlines, and I watched it open page by page in slow motion like an old movie. Each page turned, as if I had all the time in the world, until it stopped at a page toward the back of the newspaper—the obituary page. In no hurry, I scanned it, reading snatches of lives, until I found a small box on the lower right-hand side, and I read the small headline: "Young Girl Drowns in Lake in Michigan." I slowly read my obituary—my whole short life—before I blacked out.

The next thing I knew, I was being dragged out of the lake by Al. Bits of green waterweed still clung to my arms and hair. Suddenly I could hear the noise and the din around me again. Al flipped me over on my stomach like a dead fish and began to push on my back. I coughed and coughed, sick with overwhelming nausea. I sat shivering with deep cold, covered in mud, lake weeds and grasses still curled around my arms. Ona sat next to me crying, her thighs scratched bloody. She was covered in grasses and mud too. We both looked like Creatures from the Black Lagoon.

"I'm sorry, Irene. I didn't mean it. I just panicked. I've never been out that far before." Ona was crying, and the tears were making clear pathways on her muddy face. Next to me, Vida and Milda were both crying too. Dizzy and nauseated, I finally threw up the muddy water I had swallowed, and I was too sick to even feel embarrassed. All I wanted to do was sleep, even though my eyes hurt from the water and the gritty mud. Daina covered me up with some towels and told me to rest.

I must have fallen asleep until the nurse came to examine me. "You're a very lucky girl," she told me. "You're going to be all right. You just need to rest for a day or two."

Vida told me that they had rescued Ona but that no one had seen me because of the muddy water. "Al was the only one who knew you were there, so he jumped in to look for you."

I looked over at Al and tried to smile.

He said, "You were on the very bottom of the lake. I couldn't even see you, Irene, but I could feel your hair and pulled you up. You were still alive, thank God."

I was still alive. It seemed strange to have come so close to dying. All I could think of was how sad my mom would have been. Somehow my mind couldn't take it in, but my body was grateful to be breathing. Though I had read my obituary, I was still alive.

The whole camp seemed to be gathered around me, looking at this girl who had been snatched from the muddy lake bottom, snatched from clammy death, brought back to life right here in front of them. Better than a campfire skit.

Daina held onto me and told me I was going to be just fine. When she draped a towel around my shoulders, I pleaded, "Please don't tell my mother about this."

"I can't do that, Irene. I have to tell your parents."

"Oh, please, my mother's sick. I don't want her to worry."

"It's not up to me, Irene, but I'll see what I can do." Daina looked concerned as she patted my arm.

Vida and Milda were both wiping away tears.

Soon Daina blew the whistle three times, and we all got up to return to camp. We paired up by twos and walked up the dusty slope. The mud on Ona had dried and caked with flecks of fool's gold that still glittered in the sunlight. As the campers helped me climb over the rail fence, an Amish family drove by in a horse and buggy and a young girl in a bonnet pointed to Ona and me, as if we were subhuman. She stared until the buggy disappeared over the hill. Strange how I no longer felt self-conscious. I was caked with mud but didn't care.

Turning to take a last look at Miner's Lake, I saw the sun still gleaming on its surface, but no matter how brightly it shimmered, I knew there was a darkness underneath. It was the same darkness that was underneath everything. I now knew what it was. It had almost taken my life. As I walked back to camp that afternoon, I felt that no matter what else I did in life, I would never forget the taste of cold mud from the bottom of Miner's Lake.

For the next two days, Ona never left my side and couldn't seem to do enough for me. Apologizing over and over, she made a pest of herself, but I still had a hard stone of anger in me. Everyone came to visit me and brought me candy and cookies from their packages from home. At first, I couldn't eat any of it, but by the second day I was starting to nibble at a Mars bar that Vida gave me.

The next morning, Vida brought me a letter from my mother. I stared at it, afraid to open it. In the letter my mother said the operation had been a success and that she was feeling much better and was even getting out of bed a bit. The doctor told her she would be back to normal soon. She told me to have fun at camp and not get into any trouble. I was so relieved at this news that I started to cry. When Vida asked me what was wrong, I answered, "Nothing, my mother's better."

"Well, that's great, so why are you crying?"

"I thought she was going to die."

"Why?"

I wiped my tears on my sleeve. "I kept thinking about your mother, Vida. How she seemed fine and then all of a sudden, she was sick and died. How did you stand it?"

Vida didn't say anything for a few moments. "It was the worst time of my life. I never felt so alone."

"I'm so sorry, Vida. Your mother was so much fun. I wish it hadn't happened."

Vida smiled wanly. "Me too."

That night I finally felt good enough to go to the campfire. I sat with Ona, Vida, and Milda as usual. The bonfire was just beginning to burn in the dark night. The cicadas pulsed in rhythm, and a quiet wind rustled the tall oak trees. Al came over and squeezed in next to me. I was so glad to have him near.

"Hey, you look a hell of a lot better than the last time I saw you, Irene." He laughed a little. "For a moment, I thought you were going to be the sacrifice the Indians said happened every year in the lake."

I winced. "I forgot about that legend. That's really creepy, you know."

"How are you feeling?"

"Much better." I smiled, realizing I no longer felt as clumsy and oafish with Al. "Listen, I never got to thank you for saving my life. Thank you so much, Al." My chin trembled as I said this, feeling bound to Al forever for his gift of life.

Now it was Al's turn to look uncomfortable. "It wasn't such a big thing, Irene. Anybody would have done it." He cleared his throat and glanced down at his hands.

"But nobody else did. It was you, and I'll never forget it, Al." I took his hand and squeezed it, and he smiled and squeezed back.

We sat there for a long time, watching the leaping flames of the bonfire light up the velvet night. Suddenly, a huge burst of sparks rocketed from the fire, sending bright arcs into the star-filled night, as the whole camp seemed to let out a collective sigh of awe.

Southside Miracles

Irene Matas, 1961

This school year was not turning out as I had hoped. Here I was, sitting in the principal's office for the sixty-millionth time, listening to Sister Devota give me the business as I slouched down into the green vinyl chair, trying to disappear. Twirling a strand of hair around my finger, I wondered what was happening to me. I was changing and it wasn't for the better.

"Sit up straight, Irene. I just called your mother and told her I'm sending you home."

Aw hell, I thought as I left the school, dread knotting my stomach all the way home. My goose was cooked. I'd be grounded till Judgment Day. When I got home, I opened the back door ever so slowly and carefully, hoping to sneak into my room without running into my mother. But there she was, waiting for me. "I'll teach you to shoot the priest," she screeched, quivering with anger, wearing a black sheath and slippers. When she got the call from the nun, she had been getting ready for her weekly appointment at Silvia's House of Beauty. I swallowed hard and hung my head, staring at my black shoes, hoping to look contrite, when suddenly my mother took off her house slipper and whacked me on the back. I was so startled, I almost burst out laughing.

"But Mama, he didn't even feel it," I squealed, trying to shield myself from the slipper blows.

"Sister told me he was dripping wet," yelled my mother.

"Yeah, but he had on way too many clothes during Mass. He didn't even feel the squirt gun."

"I'll show you to shoot the priest," she said, smacking me on the butt with her slipper.

Quickly running to my bedroom, I locked the door, leaving her slapping it with the slipper. It seemed to me that my mother had been more easygoing before her hysterectomy. Afterward, she became short-tempered.

"Open this door. What are people going to say? You're becoming an American hooligan," my mother yelled from behind the door. "Chicago is no place to raise a girl. It's a city for gangsters."

I rolled my eyes, able to repeat the text by heart.

"And you—a priest shooter," my mother continued. "For Christ's sake, your uncle was a priest, and the other one was a partisan who lived in an underground bunker in the woods for three years. One day, God willing, we'll return to Lithuania, but how will you ever fit in?"

"Leave her be," said my father, who always quoted Maironis poems about the storms of youth when I got into trouble. Whenever my father intervened, it was a huge relief. For some reason, he seemed to understand my turbulent nature, often saying it reminded him of my mother when she was young, though I couldn't imagine her ever getting into trouble. My mother seemed to be often sad and disappointed in life in America, in perpetual mourning for her lost life in Lithuania.

Flopping on my bed, I stared at my James Dean poster, thinking I was never going back to Lithuania no matter how many relatives were still there, no matter how many Russians left the country. Lithuania sounded positively medieval to me, so Soviet Bloc. They probably didn't have TV or washing machines. Nope, Chicago suited me just fine.

That night I dreamt that I was hiding in a deep forest where uniformed nuns and priests hunted me. When I woke in the dark, I got dressed and tiptoed out of the house, going down the street to see my friend Connie O' Conner. I threw some pebbles at her window, but no one answered. I whispered Connie's name a few times and threw some more pebbles until I finally saw her face.

"Irene, what are you doing here?" Connie's pale face was like the moon, her frizzy hair flattened by sleep on one side.

"Come on, get dressed," I said in a loud whisper. "We're going to the carnival."

"The carnival! Are you crazy? It's the middle of the night."

"Come on, Connie, it'll be fun. We'll be the only ones there. It'll be so cool."

"All right, all right, hold your horses."

Three o'clock in the morning and not a soul in sight except Magda, who sat on her front porch in her nightgown staring at the stars.

"Hi, Magda," I said. "Don't tell anyone you saw us, OK?" She nodded. I had watched and worried over Magda for years, always admiring the way Al looked out for his damaged sister.

Connie and I walked through the night streets, past the rundown Sinclair station, the Amber Tavern, Silvia's House of Beauty, and the dark schoolyard, until we reached the deserted carnival in a large empty lot. The carnival looked so sad at night without its garish lights and loud music. The booths were boarded up, and the Ferris wheel seats swayed and creaked in the wind. A trailer at the back of the lot had a light on, and some insomniac was listening to Roy Orbison on the radio. We walked the sawdust-strewn dirt humming "Only the Lonely." It was quiet and eerie enough to put us in the mood for moony thoughts of the future. We climbed on the Tilt-A-Whirl and watched the few lights that were still on in our neighborhood.

I sighed heavily. "I'd like to go somewhere where nobody knows me. Maybe run away with James Dean and spend years riding on his motorcycle."

"Yeah, that might be a little difficult since he's dead," Connie snorted. "But I'd like to do the same thing with Al Vitkus."

I swallowed hard. Al had always been my secret love.

"Al told me I look like Sandra Dee." Connie smiled. "Isn't that cool?"

"Not even," I snorted. "With your frizzy red hair? That's a good one." Why hadn't Al told me I looked like Sandra Dee? At least I was blond. My mother always told me I was born with a thirty-year-old face that I would eventually grow into.

I started walking around the carnival, and soon Connie caught up with me. "Hey, Irene, I've been meaning to thank you for not telling Sister Devota about my water gun."

"Yeah, sure, nobody ever thinks Saint Connie could ever do anything wrong."

"Aw, come on, Irene, don't start that again. It was no use both of us getting into trouble."

"But how come it's always me, Connie? You do the same things, but you never get blamed for anything. It's always me. Well no more, you hear me, Connie?"

The next day, I decided it was time for a change. It seemed like everywhere I went, people saw trouble coming. The whole next week I was as quiet as Milda Gudauskas. Sister Devota didn't call me into the office, and I was even doing my schoolwork. Nobody could believe the change in me. By the end of the week, everyone seemed to be watching me and wondering what was up.

"I bet you're faking," said Ona.

"Am not!" I answered.

"I bet your mother gave you hell," said Al.

I coughed and looked away.

"Maybe you've changed," said Milda.

"Yes, I have," I vowed, putting my hand on my heart.

"We'll see," said Vida.

By the end of the week, I was feeling itchy, afraid that my friends were right. I really wanted to be good, but it was so boring. That afternoon Al stopped me in the schoolyard.

"Everybody says you've become scared, Irene." He raised his eyebrows in challenge.

"Shut up, I have not." Why did I have a crush on this guy?

"Oh, yeah, well, prove it then," said Al, smiling.

I looked at his full lips—pillow lips, not like those skinny lizard lips some boys had. I looked at his blue eyes, and my heart took a leap, but I wasn't going to let him see my attraction. "I don't have to prove anything to you," I said defiantly. "I can do anything I like."

"Well, I dare you to light a cigarette in the confessional," said Al, a slow teasing grin spreading.

"What? You must be nuts!" Why did I think he was cool?

"Last week, I saw you smoking at Country Maids," he continued his teasing. "Don't tell me you've become a chicken?"

"Oh, yeah, well, I'll be there after school if you will." As soon as I said it, I knew that trouble was getting ready to head my way, but I just couldn't bear it if Al thought I wasn't cool.

"Hey, wait a minute, I was just joking," he said, suddenly concerned.

"Oh, now look who's chickening out." I turned and walked away, leaving Al looking uneasy.

After school, Connie and I waited around the schoolyard until everybody went home, and then we snuck into the church. I had blackmailed the unwilling Connie into coming along. We found Al waiting for us in one of the pews. He tried to talk me out of the prank, but I was determined to show him I could take his dare. The empty church seemed dark and spooky. We all squeezed into the confessional box, and I lit a cigarette. Before long, we started coughing as smoke filled the tiny space.

"I'm getting out of here. I can't breathe," said Connie.

"I think I hear someone; hide the cigarette," said Al.

"Oh, no, I'll get expelled," I said in a panic, throwing the cigarette out the little window.

"Be quiet, maybe they won't find us," said Connie.

We sat huddled until the noise stopped.

"My foot fell asleep. Do you think they're gone?" asked Al.

"I smell smoke," said Connie.

I pulled the curtain aside and saw an open hymnal smoldering.

"Oh my God, the church is burning," I said. "Get some water." As I scrambled for the baptismal font, Al ran to get the holy water, and Connie ran home. I ran back, flinging water hysterically in the direction of the smoke, managing to miss the smoldering hymnal altogether and splashing the wall instead. A less hysterical Al threw water at the hymnal, and I heard the hiss of fire being doused.

"Dump this in the trash, while I clean up this water," I said.

As I was frantically looking around for something to wipe up the mess, I noticed a huge weepy stain spreading over the wall where I had thrown the water. Taking off my half-slip, I tried to mop it up when I heard steps. My head whipped around just in time to see Sister Devota coming in the door.

"Who's that?" asked the nun. "What's going on here?"

I quickly put on my wet slip and was desperately looking for a hiding place, but when I realized I was cornered, I dropped to my knees, raising my hands. "Miracle...a miracle...it's the Virgin Mary."

Sister Devota came running over, giving me the fisheye. "Irene, is this one of your pranks?"

"No, Sister, look, you can see her smiling face over there. Can't you see her?" The stain was slowly spreading over the wall.

"Where? That stain?" The nun stepped up closer to get a better look.

"Yes, Sister, see that splotch over there? That's her robe."

The nun squinted her eyes. "Well, it does look a little like…" She sniffed around. "What's that smell? Is that smoke?"

"Yes, Sister, I came in here to say a prayer when suddenly there was a great puff of smoke. I ran over to see what was happening, and when the smoke cleared, this miraculous vision of Mary appeared, and I fell on my knees before her." My telling had been coached by years of watching Jennifer Jones in *Song of Bernadette*. It was Sister Devota's favorite movie about the miracle at Lourdes, and she showed it every year.

"I wonder why she chose you," the nun murmured. "When I've been waiting my whole life."

"Sister, look, she's holding something," I said, pointing to a splotch on the right. I could tell I had her by the look on her face.

"Where, Irene?" The nun's usual harsh features were softening, as if the weight of many years was dropping off.

"There, Sister, I think it's a baby. Don't you see him?" I asked, pointing.

"Why yes, I think I do," said the nun, standing for a long time lost in her private thoughts, her face a blaze of ecstasy. Then, abruptly, she blessed herself. "Wait here while I get Father Mike." With that, Sister Devota ran out of the church, her veil flying behind her.

Left alone, I cautiously got up to look around for the others. "Good old Connie, the escape artist, did it again. She must have a nose for trouble. And that stupid Al, this was his fault. Wait till I get a hold of him," I was mumbling to myself when suddenly I heard someone coming. It was Father Mike and Sister Devota, and they brought the Good Samaritan Club, that bunch of do-gooders, with them. I was sure I was in for it now, but then I heard the hysterical nun yell, "Look, look, it's the Blessed Virgin." She fell on her knees, and some of the more impressionable girls knelt down next to her.

"I see her too, Sister."

"Me too, me too!"

It didn't take long for everyone to see her. Everyone but me. I couldn't believe they had fallen for that one.

Word of the miraculous apparition spread quickly through the neighborhood. Soon lines formed around the block, as people battled their way into the church to see the miraculous apparition on the church wall. The amazing wart lady from the carnival was miraculously healed of the millions of warts that had covered her entire body for years, but afterward she cried about losing her job with the carnival. A few days later, Milda's mother's migraines disappeared soon after touching the stain. Mr. Vitkus recovered from his asthma. Soon other parishes came to see the miracle, as spontaneous healings were becoming a daily event.

Before long, miracles were becoming as contagious as measles all through the South Side. Soon girls in neighboring parishes began seeing all sorts of things. At St. George's, the local Czech church, a girl named Sophie said she saw the statue of Mary crying or maybe sweating. True, upon investigation, it was found that condensation had formed on the statue, but it never dried out. Everyone rushed to see the new miracle and to touch the sweat. The local health department sealed the statue in a glass coffin in case there was a health hazard. A number of cases of gout were cured there.

St. Stanislaus, the Polish parish, had a miraculous spring burst forth at the foot of Mary's statue. Everyone ran to get some of the holy water. Numerous cases of rheumatism and eczema were cured. Every home had a vial of the holy water until the Department of Water fixed a broken water main.

Random reports of miracles continued throughout the South Side for the rest of the year.

Meanwhile, I was getting a reputation of a different sort. Parents who had once warned their girls not to be like Irene now nagged their kids to be more like me. People began to look at me as if I were already canonized, wanting to touch me, ask my advice, and mostly just tell me their problems.

The Channel 9 news team came out to interview me, and the whole neighborhood watched TV that night. The next day, the local papers carried my story. Even the *National Enquirer* was talking about a cover story. Bishop Petraitis declared a holiday from school and everyone had a celebration. I was becoming a local celebrity. Little souvenir pictures of me standing by the miraculous apparition were being sold at the church kiosk.

The strange part was that I really did change, no longer doing crazy things to get attention. I even started praying, saying the rosary, and going to Mass. My mother thought that in itself was a miracle. Everyone encouraged me. Everyone but Connie.

"That was no miracle and you know it," said Connie, sarcasm curling her lip. We were at our old hangout, Country Maids, drinking vanilla Cokes out of paper cones set into little metal holders. A morose song about a grisly car death called "Teen Angel" was playing on the jukebox.

"Well, maybe at first I thought it wasn't, but now I'm not so sure," I tried to explain.

"What! That's just a stain on the wall." Connie was outraged.

"How can you be so sure?"

"I don't believe this," said Connie, slapping her forehead. "I was there, remember?"

"I know that the water on the wall caused that stain, but people have been cured, Connie. Me, of all people, I caused a miracle, and it's changed people's lives."

"Cut the crap, Irene. I know you, remember?"

"Oh sure, Connie, you liked me just fine when I was getting into trouble every second, but now that I'm not screwing up, now that people admire me for a change, you can't stand it, can you? You know, I think you're jealous." I couldn't admit to Connie that there was a small part of me that was secretly afraid she was right. No matter how hard I tried, sometimes my skin would start to prickle with the effort of being good, but I wouldn't let anyone know how hard it was, especially not Connie.

Connie got up to leave. "Tell it to the Pope. I ain't buyin' it." As she opened the door, I spun around on my stool. "Maybe I will," I yelled.

<hr/>

It was true that Connie was jealous, and it was eating her up. And now that I wasn't catching all the flak at school, somehow Connie kept finding herself in trouble. She had been to the principal's office three times, and Sister Devota was threatening to call her mother.

"Why can't you be more like your old friend Irene?" asked the nun, pointing to me one day.

Connie's face was getting as red as her hair. That was it. Something inside her snapped. She decided to end this charade, not able to stomach one more remark about what a good girl I was. She told Sister Devota the whole truth about the miracle. The nun listened quietly until Connie was finished, while I gulped, thinking the jig was up.

"Liar," screamed the nun, not about to lose her long-awaited miracle. "I saw that miracle with my own eyes," she said, turning to me, "didn't I, Irene?"

I nodded, my mouth twisting, trying to smile. It was all beginning to get to me.

Connie was suspended from school for the rest of the week.

When I went over to her house after school, I found her at home watching *Queen for a Day*, wondering how those women could scream so over winning a stupid washing machine. She said she had come up with a brilliant plan. She was going to cook up her own miracle since nothing had happened as yet at St. Patrick's Church.

Somehow, she talked me into coming with her to the Irish church. It must have been the heavy armor of guilt we Catholics wear. We sat down in a pew, waiting for the church to empty, and then Connie went to unscrew the statue of Mary from its base. She figured if she moved the statue to the middle of the church and knelt before it, waiting until somebody found her, she would swear the statue came down to her. But the screws were tight and no matter how hard she twisted and turned, those screws were not budging. She tried to use the screwdriver like a crowbar to force the statue off its base, but it slipped and jabbed her palm. Screaming with pain, she watched the blood trickle down her wrist. I ran to help her, but when I heard Father O'Reilly muttering in the yard, I panicked, not knowing whether to run or hide. Before I could decide, Connie had a blinding flash of inspiration and jabbed the screwdriver into her other hand and threw it under the altar. When Father O'Reilly found Connie, she was standing with outstretched arms, both hands bleeding. When he asked her what was going on, she answered with one word—"Stigmata."

The Irish parish was overjoyed. Finally, they had their own miracle, and a fine one it was with the lovely O'Connor girl and their own statue of the Blessed Mother, and once Mrs. Shaughnessy's rash was cured, that cinched it. Now the old parish had a reason to celebrate. A parade was planned with Connie O'Connor at the head and all the fine colleens following her. It was to wind up in the parish yard with Irish jigs, shamrocks, and all the usual shenanigans.

The morning of the parade, all went according to plan. Connie waved to the crowd with bandaged hands. When she spotted Al Vitkus and Joey Cicero, Connie waved like a beauty queen on a float. Al and Joey did not wave back. I came with them to witness her moment of triumph and smiled to see her so honored.

Al hooted. "Ah, go on, just 'cuz everyone else had a miracle, you guys had to cook one up too. Who are you trying to kid?"

When Connie saw that Al Vitkus and the handsome Joey Cicero were making fun of her miracle, she was devastated. She turned to me, frowning, as if I had talked them into it.

The Irish began to grumble. Thomas Kelly yelled back: "And what about your miracle? You don't suppose any of us believed for a second that the stain on the wall was the Virgin Mother, do you?" The insult to my reputation stung. Soon insults were flying in all directions, and it didn't take long for fists to fly.

Connie was mortified. No news teams or newspapers, just a huge brawl started by Al. She sat down on the curb getting ready to have a good cry, while I watched her from across the street. We eyed each other warily, not quite sure how we felt, but then a spurt of laughter bubbled up from deep inside me, which I attempted to hide with my hand. Seeing this, Connie tried to suppress her giggle. That was my cue to cross the street, biting my lip to keep from laughing, though a snort of repressed glee escaped. By the time we reached each other, hysterical fits of laughter overtook us. We cackled and squawked so that tears ran helplessly as we fell on each other, slapping our thighs, sides cramping, shrieking like banshees. Even Al stopped fighting and came over to see what was so hilarious, the laughter so infectious that soon he began to hoot with laughter. We all fell on the ground with cackles, doubled up and braying, slapping the sidewalk, trying to catch our breath. We laughed so damned hard that it was a downright miracle we didn't just bust a gut.

Frozen Waves

Elena Kazlas, 1962

Some women have very short love lives. For them, love blows into their lives like a tropical virus, leaving them weak and trembling like a newborn lamb. And even after it's over they shake their heads in wonder at the ferocity of what hit them. That's how love was for Elena Kazlas.

Elena stood on the chocolate wafer line at Nabisco watching the one window in the factory, waiting for it to turn from black to gray, signaling that her shift was almost over. Down at the end of the line she heard Odell Givens singing "Good Morning, Heartache" again. Odell sang those sad Billie Holiday songs so often that even Elena knew them by heart—"My Man," "Everything I Have is Yours," and Odell's favorite, "Gloomy Sunday." Odell said all kinds of people committed suicide the year Billie Holiday sang it. Elena just shrugged. *Imagine killing yourself over a love song*, she thought. Sounded like nonsense to her. She had never understood those songs about men leaving women broken and alone like orphaned birds. Love was something foreign to her.

Elena shoveled cookies onto a corrugated paper tray, then bagged it and sent it on the upper conveyor belt. The chocolate on the cookies didn't smell right, and it didn't taste like it was supposed to. The line boss said this chocolate was too green, not ready for eating until it sat for some time. Elena didn't eat the chocolate wafers anymore because she remembered Aldona, the new girl who had recently come from Lithuania, who tried to save lunch money by eating Mallomars all day long while on the line. Before her shift ended, she threw up right on the conveyor belt. Management had to stop production until it was cleaned up, and then they fired her. The next day they told the ladies on the lines not to eat green chocolate.

On the next line, Isabel stood watching a mountain of Lorna Doone cookies come down the wide belt from the floor above. All the while she cried about her husband, while using a long stick to straighten the rows so they wouldn't pile up. These women on the lines were always wailing over men. It didn't matter whether they were Lithuanian, Irish, Mexican, or even the Negro women who were moving into the neighborhood, their stories were all the same. Isabel's husband was seeing someone on the Oreo line, Silvia's husband was coming home late every night, Mary's boyfriend had fallen in love with the bottle, and Odell's husband had vanished years ago. Agota Janulis was the only woman on the line who was content with her husband, Pranas. Agota always told Elena that a good man meant a quiet life, and a bad man meant tears. You just needed to pick carefully, like fruit down at the market.

The other women always kidded Elena about her manless life.

"Who you saving it for?" Charlotta would ask her.

"Leave her alone, she's waiting for the right man, that's all," said Agota.

"She's waiting for a man with a gold-tipped one," Odell would say with a wink. They cackled like hens at that one. Elena just watched the chocolate wafers marching by in straight rows, all those hands a blur of snatching them up in little trays, then sending them down to the next station, where Agota sealed them shut and sent them down to Odell, who put them in boxes.

Elena figured her father had been enough man for one lifetime. Always so particular about how his daughter looked, what she did, and whom she dated. He liked her to look plain, bland like his food. But now he and his diseased liver were buried and silenced, and Elena liked the quiet of her life. She felt like a modest jewel, muffled in gauzy cotton like her mother's amber brooch, which she kept in a little box.

Having spent years being a dutiful daughter, she was now blessedly free, and it was intoxicating. For the first time in her life, she dared to join a group—the Baltic Chorale, a group of singers who met in a room behind the Amber Tavern every Saturday afternoon. And she started saving money for a vacation—not to Union Pier, Michigan, like the other Lithuanians, but a luxury vacation to Bermuda during some cold February. She had always hated Chicago in February, a month in which the whole city turned as gray as the slush on its dirty streets. Instead, she was going to take two weeks in February as though they were chocolate bonbons and fly to a resort hotel to sit on a palm-covered beach, drinking rum punches with little pink umbrellas, and toast those back home still wading through grimy slush in their galoshes. She cut out tropical pictures of white sand, coconut palms, and big hotels to put on her Frigidaire and began putting money into an empty Hills Bros. coffee can. There was no way she would be the same person once she came back from that trip. And there was no telling what could happen on such a vacation, whom she might meet, or how it could change her life. She would return with tropical memories and souvenirs that were unlike anything those Union Pier vacationers found on their drab beaches.

One Tuesday in June, not unlike any other in Elena's life, a man named Johnny Charbonneau replaced Captain Eddie as the new box man. He came up like a feral cat that first day, grinning and introducing himself to the line. Odell was just finishing her rendition of "Stormy Weather."

"What do you pretty ladies got to sing the blues about?"

"All you slick men, that's what," said Odell, laughing loudly.

"Slick, I ain't slick, I'm smooth, ain't I, sugar?" Johnny put his arm around Elena, pulling her to him, a touch that was electric, coursing through her body like a flame, melting some long-frozen part of her. Elena blushed and giggled, startled by how good it felt. She had never seen anyone like Johnny. He looked like some tropical hothouse flower to her, something exotic that didn't grow in Chicago. He had a Southern drawl and long blond hair combed back into a duck's tail, with eyes so alive they took her breath away. This man was hungry for everything life could throw his way, nothing careful or measured about him. When she stared at Johnny's smile, her soul, which had long ago shriveled to a raisin, now grew plumper. Johnny's smile—his even Chiclets teeth were mesmerizing, casting spells on her.

The next day Elena found herself spending part of the week's Bermuda money on a shampoo and set at Silvia's House of Beauty. As Silvia piled curls high on Elena's head, ratting each curl to make it stiffer, she kidded Elena about finding a man as good as her faithful Captain Eddie.

At work, when the line broke down as it sometimes did, Elena surprised Agota by asking if her lipstick was on straight. Agota bobbed her head up and down like those dog statues in the back windows of cars, as she watched Elena walk right over to Johnny, who was stacking boxes. He looked up and said, "Hey, sugar, what's doin'?"

"Line broke down," Elena answered, blushing.

"Oh, yeah, good, maybe I can cop a cigarette." Johnny put down the box and walked out to the loading dock with Elena dogging his heels.

She asked shyly, "Where are you from, Johnny?"

"Where was I from last or where was I from first?"

"I didn't know it was such a complicated question," said Elena, smiling nervously.

"Cleveland last, Florida first."

"Wow, from Florida." Elena was impressed.

"I ain't from the wow part of Florida, honey. Where you from? You got some kinda accent."

"I was born in Lithuania."

"Lithu-what? I never heard of it."

"It's in Europe. Well, now it's part of Russia."

"I bet they got some good cookin' there. You a good cook, honey?"

"I don't know," Elena stammered.

"Maybe you'll invite me sometime. I get tired of eating alone in restaurants." Johnny cocked his head and looked her over.

"Well, maybe you could come Saturday for some dinner?" The blood in Elena's head was pounding. If he didn't answer instantly, she was going to pass out.

"Downright pleasure, ma'am," said Johnny, blowing out a smoke ring. "You know, I like you." Johnny flicked his cigarette out from the dock and flashed his cat grin at Elena.

By Saturday afternoon, Elena had bought a new blue dress at Goldberg's Fashion Forum, gotten her hair piled on her head at Silvia's, and picked up a choice roast beef at Balta's Meats, a Napoleon cake at the Tulips Bakery, and the best brandy. She picked all the dahlias in her stingy backyard to put on the table, and she put on her mother's amber brooch for good luck. By the time Johnny rang her doorbell, Elena was a swoon of colors, perfumes, and emotions as she answered the door.

At first, dinner was uncomfortably quiet as Johnny kept pouring brandy into the cordial glasses. Elena felt like a wooden puppet, always politely smiling, serving food, but part of her was shyly hidden. When she looked at Johnny's big-toothed smile, she suddenly felt like that green chocolate on the assembly line—somehow not ready yet. It wasn't until Johnny went to look for some dance music on the radio and took her in his arms to dance that Elena finally looked into Johnny's eyes and found herself at home like a sore foot finds its worn slipper. Taking a deep breath, she melted into Johnny's arms, swaying back and forth to Frank Sinatra.

Johnny slept in her bed that night and in the morning Elena woke up on his shoulder. It felt so strange, so reckless, so unlike any other morning of her life, that it was sheer intoxication. They didn't get out of bed until the late afternoon. They rolled around and made love again and slept like they were children, and there was nothing in the world calling them. Elena heard the Janulis family, who lived in the downstairs flat, going down the back stairs on their way to church. Hours later, she heard them return. She could smell Agota cooking Sunday dinner. And still, she stayed in bed, legs wrapped around Johnny's. When she finally got up to make some apple pancakes, Johnny wolfed them down as if he'd never eaten one before.

"I knew it. I can spot them every time. I knew you was a good cook the moment I laid eyes on you. Come here, sugar, you're as sweet as these pancakes." Johnny kissed her hard, like he was devouring her the same way he ate those pancakes, with an insatiable hunger.

That week, Johnny slept at Elena's every night, and soon he moved in with his small scuffed suitcase. Elena spent every penny she could spare on Johnny—the best dinners, cigars, and records. Always she'd bring home a surprise and bring it out with their brandy. The coffee can with the Bermuda fund hadn't seen a penny since Johnny came. She'd wash his hair and trim his nails, polish him like an icon until he shone. She liked taking care of him. At night, she curled into his body, feeling ripe with him, liking the smell of him on her skin. Before long, she wanted to keep him, lock him up safely like her mother's amber brooch.

The women at Nabisco warned her to go slowly. Agota tried

to tell her to go out with nice Lithuanian boys, saying she wasn't so sure about Johnny. Elena thought it was because her friend was old-fashioned and didn't understand Americans. Even Silvia at the beauty shop had heard Johnny was a smooth one. She tried to tell Elena to be careful, but Elena wasn't listening. He was hers, as much a part of her as her arms or legs.

Elena began to talk to Johnny of love and marriage, not realizing how love-phobic he was. She noticed a change immediately, as though he became too itchy, his eyes darting in all directions as if looking for the door or checking for the nearest road.

One hot July morning Johnny said good-bye in his casual way. Elena didn't yet realize that he meant forever. Later, when he didn't return, she crumbled, hardly able to breathe without Johnny. And in her wild abandoned surprise, her lovesick stupor, she didn't even notice that her coffee can had been emptied. Every day for two weeks, she called in sick. From downstairs, Agota brought her pots of soup and dumplings. When Elena finally returned to work, no one mentioned Johnny. Everyone helped her bag her quota of cookies. When Elena finally asked Captain Eddie where Johnny had gone, he told her that Johnny had come by to get his last check. Someone said he had bought a used car and was heading south. When Captain Eddie saw her stricken look, he told her, by way of condolence, that there were running people and staying people and damn if they didn't sometimes get together, and someone got hurt.

Odell sang the blues through the rest of July.

In August, when the weather got sticky and hot, Agota took Elena with her to the Lithuanian resort in Union Pier, Michigan, for a three-day weekend. Elena sat like an invalid on the beach, hardly noticing where she was, and not even realizing she had missed her period. She found herself humming snatches of Odell's blues like they were lullabies. Agota tried everything she could think of to cure

Elena's lovesickness, but Elena looked incurable. If only she would cry or scream in anger, but she was too numb.

On the last day, Agota took her friend to a Lithuanian picnic at the Lankutis resort. Tables were set with potato *kugelis* and smoked sausages and sauerkraut. A band was playing tangos, and stout couples turned dramatically to the Latin rhythm. Elena sat in an aluminum chair with a physical ache so strong she felt as if she had lost an arm. Agota brought over a plate of food, but Elena pushed it away.

Agota asked, "What did you like about Johnny? I could never understand what you saw in that hillbilly."

"That's what I liked about him. He was so different, so foreign."

Agota laughed. "Foreign? He was an American through and through. You're the foreigner here."

Elena shrugged. "He had this mouth I liked." As Elena said this, she realized that she always thought of Johnny's mouth or his hungry eyes. She could hardly remember the rest of Johnny. The rest was vague and fuzzy like his past. She was stunned to realize that she knew next to nothing about this man of hers. And for the first time since Johnny had left, something inside seemed to release a bit.

The band stopped playing, and Mr. Janulis took the accordion and started to play the old songs. From all sides, people joined in the singing, forming a huge circle, swaying arm-in-arm. Even Magda joined the circle and sang snatches of songs. Elena didn't pay much attention, but something insistent in the accordion made her foot twitch to the tempo of those harvest songs she remembered singing. A long-forgotten rhythm was taking over her body. And when she heard the owner of the resort, Bronius Lankutis, a recent widower, sing a lament in his soothing tenor, "Oh, well, let me fill you with hot tears," Elena woke from her mournful lethargy, feeling as if she could listen to that voice forever—a tenor so clear and healing, it was like balm. His voice cast an old spell, like something long forgotten. Suddenly, she felt as though she were ten again and had never left Lithuania, where all her days were filled with birch forests. This was not about love. Love was madness. This was about a cure for love. As she stood there listening to the songs, Elena decided she was going to marry Bronius Lankutis and spend all her Februarys at his resort growing hothouse flowers, and staring at the frozen waves of Lake Michigan.

Agota was surprised when Elena asked if her lipstick was on straight. She nodded and watched as Elena walked over to join the circle and link her arm to Bronius' arm as if they were two links of an unbroken chain. Agota smiled and walked over and took her husband's arm, and together they joined the others to make another link in an old and familiar chain.

Secrets of Life

Irene Matas, 1963

A dolescence is like doing the cha-cha. Two steps forward into the dark mystery called adulthood, cha-cha, followed by two steps back into the stifling coziness of childhood. Cha-cha back and forth. I was doing that dance big time in 1963—the last innocent year, when the Kennedy brothers were still in the White House and political assassinations only happened in history books. The country's innocence would soon be shattered in November with the Kennedy assassination, and afterward a whole generation would veer into cynicism and mistrust.

But in April of that year innocence still prevailed as I contemplated my transformation—not the superficial makeovers in women's magazines, but a grand transformation of life. At seventeen, I looked around my South Side Chicago neighborhood for a role model, but couldn't find anyone to emulate. I didn't like the look of the unhappy mothers I knew, some with education and status before the war but now working the night shift at factories or cleaning offices. During the week, my mother's face congealed into a resigned sadness, but sometimes, on weekends, she would have company over. Then she would tell lively stories about the golden days of Lithuanian independence between the wars, when she used to stroll down Freedom Avenue in Kaunas wearing fox collars and cloche hats. "I used to look like Greta Garbo in *Camille*," she would sigh. "Your father looked like Ronald Coleman in *Lost Horizons*. What a time we had," she would say sadly, as if all life had stopped after the war.

The nuns at Maria High School didn't look any happier, always smelling of baby powder and chalk but often looking sour, as if life had played a dirty trick on them. The single women from the neighborhood were a mixed bag. Some looked slightly overdone, like Silvia in her beauty shop, painting on a vivid face. Others like Elena were quiet and muffled, hiding from life and all of its appetites. And yet, I was amazed to hear that both Silvia and Elena had recently married despite their old-maid status. There were other women with reputations, like the loose Mrs. Paskus, who had run away with Mr. Teodoras, the alcoholic ballet teacher. These were not the models I was seeking, but the more I looked around, the more dismal it looked.

And then one weekend, after a performance of the Lithuanian Opera, my mother threw a party, and Aurelia Norkus came into the room as if she owned it, wearing a long tight skirt with a dramatic cape, her hair piled high on her head, and large hoop earrings framing her face. Her eyes were direct, not demure, as she stood with one hand on her hip—defiantly blowing cigarette smoke into the sky like an offering to some unknown god. I instantly worshipped her, even though Aurelia was thirty-four years old, a fact that would have made her an old maid in the eyes of the other women, except that she was so exuberantly different that none of the South Side categories suited her. She was dark in a world filled with dishwater blondes—beige people with blurred features. Aurelia looked like New York, while the rest of the women looked more like Gary, Indiana.

I studied her, trying to decipher the code that made Aurelia such a different species, noticing how the men also watched her, stealing glances while their wives chattered on. This was a woman who knew the secret weaknesses of men and held them in her palm like an amulet. By comparison, the other women around her looked harmless, sanitized. Aurelia was telling Felius about a Fellini film festival where she had seen *La Dolce Vita*.

"I saw that a couple of years ago," said Felius the Poet, the local bohemian who usually held court at the Amber Tavern. He was thrilled to discover another foreign-movie enthusiast. "Have you seen *Jules and Jim* with Jeanne Moreau?"

Aurelia continued as if she hadn't heard him, gesturing with her cigarette as she spoke. "There's a redemptive scene at the end of *La Dolce Vita* that's so moving, don't you think?" She looked at Felius expectantly, but he only stared blankly. As if picturing the scene, she added, "These Italians emerge from a castle after a night of debauchery into the brightness of a Mediterranean morning on the beach. They're repulsed by a monstrous fish washed up on the shore—a symbol of their own corruption—while Marcello is seared by the face of an innocent girl standing nearby—a symbol of what he's lost." She narrowed her eyes and took a deep drag on her cigarette, satisfied that she had painted the scene successfully.

My mother smiled and waved her hand dismissively. "Oh, those crazy Italians!" Everyone else looked at each other, puzzled.

"What does she mean—a monstrous fish?" My father shrugged his shoulders.

Aurelia realized she hadn't quite captured her audience. "Well, you simply must see it. It's a fable for our times," she said as she sashayed off to the kitchen, with Felius watching her every move.

I followed her, wanting to ask her about the secrets of life, to sit at her feet like an acolyte until I had learned the complicated arts of this brand of womanhood. Aurelia lit her Marlboro with a Dunhill gold lighter and poured herself a crystal glass of Chivas, while I finally worked up the courage to talk to my idol. "That movie sounded interesting. Tell me more about it," I asked, smiling shyly.

Aurelia looked at me blankly for a few seconds, then took a long drag on her cigarette and let out a plume of smoke. "It's about life with a capital L," she said through lidded eyes as she turned to walk away.

The next day, after school, I sat at the Little Touch of Kretinga Restaurant, where I worked, checking the Catholic newspaper, the *New World*, to see if *La Dolce Vita* was on the Legion of Decency's condemned list. It was, and it was playing at a little art house downtown. Time for a field trip.

All teenage girls need to do things in pairs—the minimum required number. Since I needed a companion in my transformation process, I asked Vida, who lived across the street, but she shuddered at the idea of seeing a condemned movie. "It's a sin, Irene."

On Friday, before walking into religion class, I stopped in the bathroom and looked at my dowdy uniform—navy skirt and a matching bolero jacket with a white blouse underneath. *Too ugly for words*, I thought, as I rolled up my skirt until it was the fashionable length and tried to tame my dirty blond hair with a brush. In class, Father Miknaitis was warning the girls about the dangers of sex. "You've got to be careful with boys this age," said the priest. "They've only got one thing on their minds, if you know what I mean." That was my cue to whisper loudly, "No, what?" The girls sitting around me tittered.

"Oh, I heard that, Irene, and frankly I'm tired of your dirty whispers." His upper lip curled.

That shut me up. I thought I was funny, not dirty. Hearing Father Miknaitis say that made me wince. I knew I wasn't one of those goody-goody types like Milda, and that kids used to call me Bad Irene in grammar school, but, geez, I felt like a little kid when it came to sex. Sure, I'd kissed and necked with Al Vitkus until my lips were swollen, but I was still a virgin and sex was a complete bafflement. Father Miknaitis' angry stare drilled into me, making me feel dirty.

Suddenly Connie O'Conner raised her hand and asked, "But Father, doesn't everything on earth procreate? If that's how God created us, then how come it's such a sin?"

The priest's anger swiveled from me to Connie like a giant searchlight in the fog. "Well, Constance, now what would happen if we all just followed our basest animal instincts to procreate? Just think about that for a minute," he said, his anger rising.

Connie wisely said no more.

He scanned the room filled with pubescent girls, took a deep breath, and plunged back into his lesson. "That's why we have marriage. It's the job of the church to control these base instincts. God gave us a body, but he also gave us a spirit, which he didn't give to the animals," he soldiered on, jabbing his finger in the air. "God gave us a soul so that we could control our animal instincts. Now, isn't that right?" He made a point of looking at Connie and me.

How does this celibate priest know so much about sex? I wondered, but no longer had the courage to ask anything. I was just grateful that Connie had saved me from his wrathful glare.

After class, when I walked into the cafeteria and spotted Connie ahead of me in the line, I picked up my lunch tray and followed her to her table. "Oh my God, thanks for saving me from Father Miknaitis," I said, putting my tray down. "You know, sometimes I think he gets a kick out of talking about sex to a room full of young girls." I was beginning to move from shame to anger.

Connie opened her carton of chocolate milk. "Come on, he's a priest. They don't think that way."

"Heck, he's just like any other man, only he's got a skirt on, that's all." I spooned the chipped beef onto white bread and rolled it up before taking a bite. "That poor priest doesn't stand a chance in a class of girls swimming in hormones."

"Get out!" Connie snickered as she ate the canned peaches and drank the syrup. "Where do you come up with this stuff?"

I told Connie about meeting the sophisticated Aurelia and wanting to go downtown to see *La Dolce Vita*. Connie was intrigued. "Did you ever see *Breakfast at Tiffany's*?"

"Yeah, sure, I loved it, why?"

"I just cried when Holly Golightly sat on her windowsill singing 'Moon River.' I want to be like her."

"Yeah, like who wouldn't want to be Audrey Hepburn," I said, handing Connie my canned peaches.

———————————

The following Sunday, I told my father I was going to Marquette Park to watch the soccer matches—the Lithuanians were playing the Estonians. Then I met Connie in the public restroom in the park, and we both changed into tight sheaths, high heels, and scarves. Dime-store makeup and sunglasses helped us achieve a cheap Holly Golightly likeness. On the way to the bus, we ran into my brother, Pete.

"Hey, what's going on? It's not Halloween, what're you two dressed up for?" Pete cleared his throat, trying to hide his laugh.

"Pete, just don't say a word to Mom, OK?" I felt more wary than insulted.

"Don't worry, but, geez, Irene, you look kind of sick with that white lipstick. You sure you're OK?"

"Yeah, it's not white, it's nougat, Pete. I think it's cool."

Connie and I quietly brooded about Pete's comments, worrying about how we looked as we headed for the elevated train to downtown. Something had happened to us lately—we had suddenly become makeup crazy, hair crazy, clothes crazy, and, most of all, boy crazy. All that craziness was exhausting and confusing. It seemed not long ago that we were all playing with dolls.

On the train, I sat studying the women, trying to determine who'd done it and who hadn't. I was sure that once you had sex, it was stamped on your face forever. You were a changed woman. No one talked about sex, exactly, but everyone knew it was going on somewhere. Heck, kids were being born every day.

I took out a pack of my mother's cigarettes. "Let's smoke when we buy the tickets so we look older."

"You know I don't like to smoke," said Connie, twisting her gum around her finger.

"Don't be silly, everyone who lives downtown smokes. If you don't smoke, they'll know you're from the South Side."

When we got to the theater, Connie and I lit our cigarettes. "Blow the smoke up in the air like this," I said, in imitation of Aurelia. "And for God's sake look bored, like you do this every day."

We walked up to the ticket booth, both putting our hands on our hips, blowing strings of smoke in the air. We handed the man a five-dollar bill and said, "Two please," in our most bored voices.

No one noticed; no one asked our ages as we ducked into the movie house. I fell in love with Marcello and decided that Anouk Aimee, with her icy beauty and brains, was even cooler than Audrey Hepburn. Now this was what life was really supposed to be about: jumping into Roman fountains, staying up all night for parties, glamorous clothes, and handsome men.

"I hate doing so much reading," said Connie, complaining about the subtitles. "They're too fast. I keep looking at what's going on and I forget to read. I don't get this movie."

"It's about…ah, you know, real life, not our dull life. This is how you're supposed to live." I felt uplifted by the movie, as if I was finally being taught the secrets of life.

"There's a guy over at the end of the row, and I think he's playing with it," whispered Connie. "Just don't look."

"Don't be silly. I'm sure he's only brushing popcorn from his lap," I said.

"Come on, the movie's finished, let's get out of here." Connie grabbed me, pulling me out into the lobby. The projectionist whistled at us as we were leaving.

Afterward, we walked down Michigan Avenue past the Art Institute and sat on a bench in Grant Park, looking at the windows in the highrises. Who lived there? Were they happy? What did they do? I turned to

Connie. "We may have grown up in one of the grittiest, most factory-choked neighborhoods in America, but we aren't going to stay there and rot like the others." I scanned the rows of buildings facing us. "And one of these days we're going to have a drink over there at the Tip Top Tap at the top of the Allerton Hotel," I said, pointing to the sign on the tall building.

In the next few months, Connie and I saw *Last Year at Marienbad*, *L'Avventura*, *Breathless*, and *Hiroshima, Mon Amour*. Coming out of the theater, Connie squinted in the bright light. "Don't take me to no more movies where people's skin is falling off. I'm not gonna sleep right for a week. That was horrible. I don't know what that Hiroshima movie is gonna teach us about being sophisticated."

I didn't know either. The scenes of Hiroshima had so shaken me that I could barely speak. Why were humans so cruel to one another? "We're going for a drink." We were ready for the Tip Top Tap.

The maitre d' paused too long before showing us to our table, making Connie nervous. When he handed us a menu, I told him that we were only having drinks. His eyes narrowed suspiciously as I lit a cigarette and blew the smoke up toward the ceiling.

"A couple of Pink Ladies, please," I said, full of bluff, in my best I-do-this-every-day voice. Connie looked out the window, trying hard not to giggle from nervousness. I had already coached her to say our wallets were stolen if we were asked for identification. Connie was sure that we would be thrown out and humiliated at any moment. She bit her lower lip and concentrated on taking off the opera-length gloves I had taken from my mother's drawer.

The maitre d' nodded wearily. "I'll tell your waiter."

I looked out the window at the expensive stores along Michigan Avenue. I could see the Wrigley Building and the Chicago River winding around toward State Street. Lake Michigan was the huge blue blur in the other direction. Someday I would live in one of those high-rise apartments along Lake Shore Drive and shop at Saks Fifth Avenue, have a boyfriend like Marcello, and swim with him in Roman fountains. Someday I would live a glamorous downtown life, not that sad little South Side life that seemed to make all the women I knew so unhappy.

That is, if the atom bomb didn't get us first, like in Hiroshima. I remembered crouching under desks during atomic alerts in grammar school. Like that was going to save us.

The waiter brought two pink, frothy drinks in champagne glasses. I drank it down like it was a strawberry shake and ordered another.

"I like this stuff," said Connie, licking the pink froth from her upper lip.

We had another round and were wondering what to do next when I spotted Aurelia Norkus in a corner of the room, sitting by herself.

"Oh my God, it's her. Should we say hello?" I couldn't believe my good fortune as I stood to walk across the room, my head slightly dizzy, filled with an unexpected confidence even though it seemed as if my high heels had grown an inch or two while I was sitting. Connie followed with exaggerated care.

"Why, hello, Miss Norkus, so nice to see you again."

Aurelia said nothing.

"I'm Irene Matas. We met at my mother's party after the opera," I continued uneasily.

"Of course," said Aurelia unconvincingly.

"You were raving about *La Dolce Vita*, so my friend and I decided to see it after your recommendation."

"Really? How did you like it?" asked Aurelia, blinking at us with an amused smile.

"It was just like you said, life with a capital L. This is Connie O'Connor," I said, presenting Connie. "May we join you?"

"Actually I'm expecting someone. Perhaps another time." Aurelia looked around.

"Oh! Well, naturally. Next time." Embarrassed, I turned to leave and to my horror I saw Vida's father entering the restaurant. I moved back and stepped on Connie's foot with my high heel. "Ouch, what are you doing?" Connie let out a squeal of pain.

"I'm sorry. Let's get out of here before Vida's father sees us and tells my parents." I skittered to the side of the restaurant, waiting by the busboy station until he sat down at Aurelia's table. Then I paid the bill and left quickly, with Connie limping behind me. "I think I'm going to be sick," I said.

"Yeah, me too," added Connie. "That pink stuff was too sweet." We found the bathroom, and I threw up while Connie splashed cold water on her face. Black eyeliner ran into beige pancake makeup and smeared her pink lipstick.

"Why would Aurelia be having drinks with Vida's father?" I stopped to look in the mirror. My face looked blurred. "It just doesn't make sense. She could have anyone she wanted."

"Oh, shut up and let's go home." Connie looked pale and tired.

The next week, as I was on my way out the door to my usual Sunday jaunt, my mother stopped me at the door. "Irene, I found these matches from the Tip Top Tap on your desk. Are you smoking?"

My eyebrows shot up, and I stopped breathing momentarily. "No, Mama, maybe they're Dad's."

"Your father went to the Tip Top Tap?" My mother stared at the matches, suspicion rising like heartburn. I couldn't wait to get away from her questioning eyes.

"Do you know what happened to my opera gloves?"

I hesitated. Should I plead ignorance or should I confess? I already felt guilty about the matches, so I decided to confess.

"I forgot to tell you, Mama. I borrowed them."

"Taking my things without asking isn't borrowing, Irena. Please give them back to me."

"OK, but..." I bit my lip and looked around. "They're not here. They're at Connie's house."

I was grounded for a week. A fine rain splattered my windows as I sat in my gingham bedroom, staring at a woman walking in the rain, thinking about foreign movies and wondering why Aurelia would be with Vida's father.

<hr />

Though our hearts were no longer in it, the next week we decided to see one last movie, *Jules and Jim*. We went to the park and, as usual, changed into straight skirts, sweaters, and heels, teasing our hair into a fine pouf and slathering on makeup. On the way to the bus, Connie and I ran into Felius the Poet and Valentinas Gediminas, who showered us with admiration.

"Hey," said Felius, poking Valentinas. "We've got some good-looking rookies here. We're going to a party. You gorgeous ladies wanna join us?"

"No, thanks," said Connie politely. "We're going to the movies to see *Jules and Jim*."

"Great movie," said Felius. "But see it next week and come with us to Aurelia's house instead."

My head snapped to attention. "Aurelia Norkus?"

"Yeah, right there on 71st, across from the park," said Felius, jutting his goateed chin toward the end of the street.

"OK, sure," I said, giving Connie a little shove.

Connie protested, but I started following the men. "I need to go," I whispered.

The apartment was dimly lit with brick-and-board bookcases and strange black-and-white woodcuts. The Danish couch and chairs were filled with older men and women, so we didn't know where to sit. Harry Belafonte was playing on the record player, and three couples were dancing the cha-cha. Across the room, Aurelia stood near the small mirrored bar wearing a Chinese red silk sheath, her dark hair in one long braid down her back. She was discussing Sartre with a handsome man who looked familiar. I looked around carefully to make sure Vida's father was nowhere around.

"What'll you rookies have to drink?" Valentinas Gediminas asked us.

"We'll have two pink ladies," said Connie.

"This isn't a bar. How about a highball?"

I nodded as Connie poked me in the ribs with her elbow. "What're we doing here?"

"I gotta figure this Aurelia out, Connie. She's got half the Amber Tavern in here. I see these guys at the soccer games. I thought she'd have better taste." After we got our drinks, Felius the Poet got up to declaim sad poems about the Iron Curtain.

"Why are they all speaking Lithuanian?" asked Connie. "I feel like I'm back at the foreign movies but without any subtitles."

Someone started playing the accordion, and everyone sang the old folk songs until Aurelia went over to put a record on the turntable. I watched as couples joined to dance. When the music changed to a cha-cha, I saw Connie dance by with Felius the Poet, smiling and waving with the tips of her fingers. Where had Connie learned to dance with such style and confidence?

I sat down on the empty couch, and a familiar-looking man sat down next to me. "Smoke?" He offered a pack of Kents, and I took a cigarette and held his hand as he lit it. "I've never seen you before at Aurelia's parties," he said.

I blew smoke up in the air. "This is my first," I said, trying to sound blasé. I couldn't place his face.

Aurelia slowly walked toward us. "Well, well," she said, taking in the situation. "Hello, Apolinaras, I've been looking for you."

"I've been talking to this young lady."

"I see." Aurelia frowned, standing in front of us, her arms crossed. I couldn't tell if Aurelia was annoyed or amused, but when I heard the man's name, I suddenly knew him.

"I remember you," I said. "You're Vida's uncle from South America. I'm her friend, Irene Matas, remember me?" I smiled, happy to see him again. "She told me you had moved to New York."

"Yes, I just got transferred back here. So you're my niece's friend, eh? You girls have sure grown up quickly." Apolinaras smiled stiffly as he shot a look at Aurelia, who was relishing this turn of events. He squirmed a little longer before politely excusing himself. "I think I'll get a drink."

"Moon River" started playing on the record player and I went to look for Connie, knowing it was her favorite song, but she was nowhere to be seen. Some couples were necking in discreet corners. Opening the door to the bedroom, I whispered Connie's name. When my eyes adjusted to the dim light, I saw Aurelia kissing Apolinaras. Embarrassed, I closed the door quickly. Standing in the hallway, I heard Connie's voice in the bathroom. "Let me out, you creep," Connie demanded. I knocked on the bathroom door. "Connie, are you all right?"

I heard muffled talk. Suddenly, Connie bolted out of there with her lipstick smeared, rolling her eyes, while Felius the Poet sauntered out, smiling as he combed his hair over his bald spot.

"Let's get out of this zoo," Connie whined. "That guy followed me into the bathroom, and he was on me like syrup on pancakes."

"You're kidding." I winced.

Connie and I came out of the dark apartment, squinting, shading our eyes from the sunlight. We walked across the street to the park and sat on the empty swings, watching as a blond boy of about five climbed the red slide, while his mother stood at the bottom ready to catch him.

Connie wiped her lipstick off with a tissue. "You and your big ideas. I wish we hadn't gone to that party."

I squinted in the bright sunlight. Life, I saw, was full of messy situations and mystery. There were questions I wouldn't be able to answer no matter how many transformations I went through. And it seemed the business of sex was the messiest and the most mysterious one of all. I looked up at the blond boy, laughing as he went down the slide. He was so innocent and wonderful. "This reminds me of the part in *La Dolce Vita* where Marcello goes out on the beach after the party and sees that young girl, and he feels so decadent compared to her innocence."

"Yeah, I didn't get that part," said Connie. "Did you? What was with that monster fish on the beach?"

I almost laughed. "I didn't get it either."

<hr />

When we got up to walk home, we spotted our school friends, Al Vitkus and Joey Cicero, driving by in an old green Dodge. We waved, and they stopped and beeped. "Hey, you girls look great," Al yelled out the window.

I smiled shyly, my heart always thumping a little harder whenever I saw Al. "Hi, guys, where are you going?" Al and Joey looked like a breath of fresh air after our experience at Aurelia's party.

"I don't know. Nowhere really." Al shrugged. "We're just driving around. Wanna come?" His smile lit up his whole face.

I tried to hide my smile as I looked over at Connie. "Sure," she said, nodding eagerly.

We happily climbed into the back seat of the car as Al shifted into drive, and we all glided down the grimy streets of South Side Chicago, looking out the windows, wondering what to do next.

Those Chicago Blues

Irene Matas, 1968

We were sitting in a bar on Wells Street in Old Town, listening to Muddy Waters and laughing for no reason, when suddenly I touched my face and felt tears. Was I crying because Muddy Waters was on stage wailing the blues, or was it because I had taken LSD? "There's only the thinnest thread," I said in my purple haze, "between laughter and tears. The thinnest thread," I repeated, as my voice bounced back from the four corners of the room. My whole being flowed into the bar stools, the pipes overhead, the music, and the people.

"Yeah, Irene, keep taking that stuff and there's going be the thinnest thread between you and a lunatic," said Connie, her thin mouth stretched into a sneer.

I could see she was in no mood for pharmacological enlightenment, but I couldn't help myself. "Lunatic. Luna. Someone deeply affected by the moon." I smiled beatifically, and the blue-and-rose stage lights pulsated wildly, extending like haloes around each person in the room. The speakers throbbed. Everything was divinely aglow. A gathering of saints. A redemptive rally of former sinners. A vision from the Old Testament. All God's children were saved, and Muddy Waters would lead them beside the river, the beautiful, beautiful river. My eyelashes fluttered in religious ecstasy.

Connie leaned in closer. "Irene, your miniskirt is sliding up halfway to China. You're putting on more of a show than Muddy Waters." I scooted off my torn plastic barstool and tugged my skirt back down to mid-thigh. Connie rummaged through her crocheted purse. "I've got some Valium in my purse if you need it." Her red Irish Afro was backlit by a blue halo, and her jeans were so tight that a roll of fat was pushing out of her waistband.

The smoke-filled air pulsed with the rhythms of "I've Got Those Walking Blues," as four couples danced lethargically in the corner.

"The blues remind me of death," I said, feeling profound.

"Everything reminds you of death." Connie looked irritated. It was probably her lousy-paying job at Piper's Alley in Old Town selling scented candles and lava lamps. A job like that would irritate a saint.

I leaned over to Connie's ear. "Death never walks alone. She always walks with her sister, lust." I was really tripping.

"And why is that, Irene?" asked Connie, as if it were an ordinary conversation.

"Because lust carries the seed."

"The seed?" Connie rolled her eyes. "Uh huh."

"Of life. The next generation. Always another generation. Like waves, they keep coming despite lassitude, drunkenness, boredom, satiation, and listlessness. Despite death." The door opened, and I could see the black night outside. "What's the point of life, Connie, if we're all headed in the same direction—death? Tell me, what's the point? Struggle or don't struggle, all the waves crash in the end."

"Baba Irene, guru to Lithuanians, wherever they may wander." Connie lit her Marlboro.

"Baba means wise man. Sounds like *boba* in Lithuanian. Means foolish old woman." I felt my mouth curl in disgust. "Sexism."

Connie grabbed her purse and stood up to leave. "I'm sick of this. Let's go home. I'm going to wake you early tomorrow for the

Democratic National Convention. Remember? We're going, in case you forgot."

The next day started out kind of pleasant for Chicago. Crowds of hippies were watching Alan Ginsberg chanting "Ooommm" in Lincoln Park. All of Lincoln Park looked stoned in an ecstasy of togetherness. There was a feel of festival in the air—music playing, people dancing. This was the dawning of the Age of Aquarius.

Connie wore bell-bottoms and a tie-dyed t-shirt while I wore my Lithuanian blouse with the red embroidery over frayed jeans and my favorite water-buffalo sandals with the strap around my big toe. I was covering the demonstrations outside the Democratic Convention for the alternative press, as I liked to call it, but in reality it was a throwaway paper that landed on the doorsteps of incense stores and head shops. Connie and I headed over to Michigan Avenue, where Lyndon Johnson was staying at the Hilton. Across the street in Grant Park, the serious demonstrators were gathered wearing khaki jackets and jeans, bandanas pushing down their shaggy hair as they shouted angry slogans through bullhorns and waved antiwar placards. Though I was against the war, some of these demonstrators struck me as a tad too self-righteous, their anger more put on than heartfelt—a bit like my Bolshie professors at the university, whose beliefs seemed to stem more from current fashion than conviction.

The chop-chop of helicopter blades snapped me to attention, as one landed behind a long line of National Guard troops on the park side of Michigan Avenue. They were standing at attention with their rifles in hand. Behind them, the Guard jeeps bristled with a grid of barbed wire in front of each car's grill.

"Geez, friendly looking group." I started to creep away.

"It's a police state," said Connie. "They're not kidding around here."

"Ho-Ho-Ho Chi Minh," some shirtless hippie taunted a young Guardsman, whose grinding jaws worked silently. Another hippie was putting a flower into a rifle stock.

"I say let's boogie on home." My stomach was beginning to churn with nervous tension.

"Nothing's going to happen," whined Connie. "This is just Mayor Daley flexing his muscles, showing off in front of his fellow Democrats, letting them know he's one tough son of a bitch."

"But he is one tough son of a bitch!"

"Yeah, well, never mind. We're here and we're staying. They can't frighten us away." Connie marched on, like the Taurus bull she was. The trouble with Connie was, she was a true believer. I, on the other hand, though anti-war, was a bit too cynical to truly be in the trenches, but also too curious not to at least put a foot in. One foot in, one foot out—my perennial stance.

I ran to catch Connie by her arm. "Hey, nothing's started yet, and I need to go over to Walgreen's for some tampons and a cup of coffee. My head is still throbbing from last night."

At Walgreen's, Connie sat at the counter sipping coffee, staring out the window toward Michigan Avenue, while I went to the bathroom and took some aspirin and some "window pane." At the very least, maybe the acid would give me some needed courage. When I sat back down, the waitress poured us another cup of coffee. I studied it like it was the Rosetta stone, pouring cream in, stirring it, and watching the coffee swirl around in the cup, and then I stirred it again. And again. "I wonder if coffee swirls in the other direction south of the equator," I said slowly, not daring to look at Connie.

"Coffee swirls in the direction you stir it, above or below the equator." Connie finally took a good look at me. "Oh bloody hell, don't tell me you took something while you were in the bathroom?"

"Just a touch," I said sheepishly.

"Now what am I going to do with you?" Connie was pissed.

"Nothing, why?"

"Irene, we're going to go yell 'hell, no, we won't go' to the assembled Democrats. We will do this in honor of your brother and Al Vitkus, who are both in Vietnam. Remember?" Her voice was rising like some Biblical prophet.

"Yeah, sure," I said, suddenly contrite. "For Pete and Al. You think I'm not going?"

"Irene, you're turning into a total head."

"It's only because I don't know how to live my life. It's all so confusing." I was beginning to feel remorse.

Connie sighed. "Come on. Just don't freak out on me." She didn't know anything about life either. She was just scared of acid, like I was scared of rifles and jeeps with barbed wire.

On State Street, the usual shoppers and hawkers thronged the street. When Connie and I walked toward Michigan Avenue, we heard the sound of a crowd yelling and figured that LBJ had finally arrived at the Hilton. Then we stopped, feeling confused and concerned as we noticed a group of kids, wild-eyed with fear, running toward us, followed by others. A group of long-haired hippies blitzed by, followed by a cloud of tear gas floating over from Michigan Avenue. We could feel the sting in our eyes and throats as we started to run back toward State Street.

Suddenly, the Chicago police materialized, their pale-blue shirts everywhere, their clubs cracking the heads of protesters and onlookers alike in a delirium of violence. A policeman grabbed Connie by her big hair, dragging her away to a waiting patrol car, while she screamed obscenities, writhing and kicking.

I wanted to help her, but I stood still, totally immobilized by fear. All around me, students cursed the oncoming threat. A policeman rained blows on a girl nearby as she screamed in pain, clutching her head, a trickle of blood between her fingers. I longed to help her, but I had turned to stone. My mouth was open in a silent scream. My whole life I had listened to my parents tell apocalyptic stories about the chaos of World War II. Now it was finally here—chaos, maw open wide, most ravenous of beasts, riding a tear-gas cloud, feeding on innocent blood. I had been waiting for this beast for so long, it was almost a relief to finally see it.

Suddenly, I felt a hand grab mine and I shuddered, prepared to die. As death's sour breath reached my cheek, I was ready to be the sacrificial lamb. Oh, lamb of God, who takest away the sins of the world, have mercy on me. The hand pulled me again, and I submitted, surrendering to the beast as it swept into the melee of screams, shouts, and curses. Still the hand pulled, and then a bus door closed behind me, and the bus driver hollered, "That's it. We're not letting any more in. No more room."

Bus 1968 to hell. The express—no stops, no transfers. I stood pressed against a hairy young man who looked like Van Dyke, or was it Henry Hudson? "Whew, that was close," he said.

"Where am I?" I tried to focus. Was this some post-death bardo state, or was I Alice in the rabbit hole? "Are you a Dutch captain on the Hudson River?" I asked.

"Are you crazy?" he asked back.

"Maybe," I answered, but I knew nothing. Looking out the window at the rough sea of violence swirling around the bus, I was in the eye of the tornado, an eddy in the storm. Who was stirring this? What hand had pulled me to safety, and why me and not those people out there? I started whimpering, thinking they were all from my grammar school. I knew them, didn't I? Why was one hurt and not another? Why did my brother Pete go to Nam? Why Al? I began to sob while Van Dyke held me.

I didn't know how long I stayed on that bus. Clinging to Van Dyke in my grief, I grew old there. I didn't know yet that his name was Joel. I only knew that my jeans were soaked with blood. Had I gotten injured? Nothing hurt. It took me a long time to remember the bathroom at Walgreen's. I had forgotten to use the tampons. The ambulances arrived, and they wanted to put me inside with those who had been injured. I wanted to protest, but I couldn't. The solicitude of attendants, nurses, and doctors was too much to resist. Why was all of this feeling so Catholic? Always the redemption of blood. Or was it a blood sacrifice? Martyrs, torture, flagellation, and the always-dying Jesus on the cross.

When the ambulance attendants lifted me onto a gurney, Van Dyke went along for the ride to the emergency room. The TV cameras were rolling. It was my finest hour. I was ready for my close-up, Mr. DeMille. It was faux, but I was a symbolic martyr of the Democratic National Convention.

It was only much later, after the LSD had worn off, that I began to feel embarrassed. Then I was totally mortified. Penitent. The doctors were not amused. My savior, Van Dyke, stayed with me, though I don't know why. We bailed Connie out and got her home. She was neither bruised nor broken as I had imagined. Just angry.

Chastised, I bowed my head, bad to the bone. I couldn't hold my head up or speak for days. I would have worn ashes and sackcloth, or joined the flagellants if there had been any around, but instead I scourged myself with a running inner monologue of self-loathing. I went to all my classes at Roosevelt University, worked my dull credit-office job at Marshall Field's, apologized over and over to Connie for doing too much acid, and vowed never to take it again. And I promised myself I would go see my parents the following weekend. I needed the stability of home.

The trouble with home was that it made me sad to go back to

my old South Side neighborhood, which always looked like one of life's forgotten backwaters. There was Life with a capital L, full of risk and excitement, and then there was this old life, cautiously lived, saved, and parceled out carefully. I knew every nook and cranny of that South Side life.

"We saw you on the news, Irene." My mother was studying me.

"You did?" I felt sick.

"Last week, during the convention. What were you doing there with all those hooligans?" My mother was looking at me the way Margaret Mead might have looked at those South Seas islanders.

"What did you see?" I asked warily.

"You were being dragged onto a bus. They kept showing it on every newscast. All the neighbors called to ask if you were all right. They saw you too." My mother bit her lip. "I was so embarrassed, Irene."

I didn't know what to say. Why did seeing parents mean being crushed with guilt? It made me remember an old Arab saying that said a man resembles his time more than he resembles his father. I guess the same held true for mothers and daughters. I marveled at how little I knew my mother.

"I was demonstrating against the war, Mama. For Pete and Al, so that they could come home." My face was turning red, as I wondered if my mother had seen my bloody pants. I didn't ask. I ate my mother's apple cake and drank her hot tea. The clock ticked loudly on the wall, the same yellow electric clock my parents bought in 1950. It reminded me of grammar school, sitting at the table, doing my homework for Sister Kunigunda.

My parents looked at me like I was an escapee from a perpetual Mardi Gras—colorful but not to be taken seriously. And I knew they were right. My mother poured more tea, and we were quiet, stirring our cups until she looked up. "Mr. Vitkus told me yesterday that his son was injured in Vietnam."

"What?" I was shocked. "Al was hurt?" I held my breath. It must be my fault. The acid, the demonstration, the tampons—something I did wrong.

"He said it was his leg."

"Will he be OK?" I felt sick. I hadn't had a letter from Al in many months.

"His father said it was nothing serious."

I wasn't relieved. I knew Al wouldn't tell his father if it was serious. "How about Pete?" My brother was due to come home soon.

"He's fine. He writes that he's in Saigon working in an office. I pray for him every day."

Pete was lying too. He was in Hue, but he didn't want Mama to worry.

When had my mother gotten so much older, so much grayer and tired looking? When had my father gotten so bald? It squeezed my heart to see them like this. I wanted to keep them young and vital, the way I remembered them from my childhood.

"Are you going to visit your old friends, Vida and Ona?"

"I don't have time, Mama. I have to write some papers for school."

"Vida's engaged, you know. To Jonas Janulis." My mother said those words like they were a charm—one of life's alchemical phrases.

"Yes, I heard." I knew my mother wanted me to dress like Jackie Kennedy, marry some nice Lithuanian engineer, move into a brick bungalow down the street, bring her grandchildren to dinner every Sunday after Mass, and send them to Lithuanian Saturday School. I wanted her to have that too. Who doesn't yearn to heal their mother's heartbreak? I just couldn't do it, even though life would be easier if I could. It was not in my nature to be so compliant. I was a wild card. Now I would have to play it to the end.

I kissed my parents and told them I loved them. My heart ached, realizing that I had taken a turn in life; I couldn't say exactly when it had happened, but it was irrevocably away from them. When I walked down the stairs of the brick two-flat and headed for the bus station, Al's sister, Magda, crossed the street, walking alongside me without saying a word. As we walked down Talman Street together, I remembered a day when Magda was about twelve, and I was about seven. She was walking ahead of me in the alley wearing a blue house-dress. I watched in amazement as she picked up her dress, pulled down her underpants, and squatted down to pee. When I walked by the place where Magda had been, I saw blood. My first thought was that she was dying, that something was terribly wrong with her. And after that, for months, I carefully watched her with apprehension, looking for signs of a fatal illness. I knew nothing about menstrual blood then. My mother had once mentioned that someday I was going to bleed, but that, God forbid, I should never tell my father or my brother about it. In my baffling ignorance, I thought I was going to have the stigmata. What else could it be? I knew more about the martyrdom of saints than I did about my own body.

It suddenly occurred to me that Magda was short for Magdalena, after Mary Magdalene in the Bible. Jesus had cast out seven devils from her. Poor Magda was as innocent as a baby, while I seemed to have the seven devils in me. I took Magda's hand and walked to the end of Talman Street, where I knew she would walk no farther. Magda had her perimeter in this neighborhood, like I supposed her brother Al had in Nam.

She smiled like the six year old she still was inside. Why had God done this to Magda? Was she the sacrificial Lamb of God? I felt a sudden sympathy for all of life's misfits—for the slow and the clumsy, for all the rejects and queers, for the deformed and the misshapen, for the odd and the slow-witted. I knew I was one of them. I hugged Magda fiercely like the sister I'd never had. Sisters in menstrual blood.

I took the bus to Loomis and got on the El. The wheels of the train screeched and clacked as I sat quietly, staring at the blur of broken back porches on the South Side. When the train slowed, I could see a window where a tired, middle-aged black woman stood at an ironing board, staring back at the train as it passed. Below, three boys were jumping from the rail of a porch onto a pile of old mattresses. Soon, the train sped up, the wheels clacking in rhythm against the rails, as the backyards and the sagging, rickety wooden porches of the South Side became a blur. My eyes brimmed with tears as the elevated train finally descended into the dark subway tunnel, into the underground below the city, sparks flying, wheels squealing, tracks clanging, and my confused heart beating out the seconds of my life.

War Wounds

Al Vitkus, 1973

The crisscross of bullets sliced the thick air as Al Vitkus struggled to reach the trees across the clearing. His feet were like dead weights and the radio on his back was so goddamn heavy he couldn't run, its straps like razors cutting into his shoulder muscles. Straining to get to cover to radio for help, he pushed himself with everything he had in him until he felt a hot, searing pain in his leg. At that same moment, he turned to see Bob Lund get shot through the neck, a look of such surprise on his friend's face. It was followed by a concussive blast. It seemed as if hours went by. The damp smell of rot rose in the clearing. Pain and black numbness, and then pain again when he opened his eyes to see the medics zipping the plastic body bag shut over his chest, right over his face. "Hey," he whispered in a harsh rasp. "Hey, I'm not dead yet, hey," he yelled, "I'm not dead."

Al awoke panicked, gasping for air, heart thumping, bathed in sweat. For a moment, he looked around, not knowing where he was, and then, of course, it slowly sifted back to him. He was in his old room, safe in his childhood bed where there was no danger, nor bullets, nor body bags. Yet, even though it had been a week since he had returned from Nam, he still didn't feel at home. It was so unreal to be in his room or sitting at the same kitchen table with his parents and Magda as if nothing in the world had changed, as if he hadn't entered the maw of hell itself. In Nam he had conjured up every detail of his house with such longing. It had calmed him, but now that he was actually home it felt wrong. He was what was wrong.

When he'd come back stateside, Irene Matas had been waiting for him at the airport, along with his parents and Magda. He had carried Irene's picture in his wallet the whole time he was away, written her letters, thought about holding her. He had thought about it so much it hurt. At night in the jungle, he had whispered her name like an incantation, a litany of love. She would heal him. Yet, when she finally stood there in front of him at the airport, looking even better than he remembered, he was so emotionally flayed, so unprepared for civilian life, that he could hardly look Irene in the eyes. The veneer of civilization had been stripped away, and only the raw animal in him remained, and he was afraid that everyone who looked into his eyes could see it. What he needed most now was time to grow a civilized skin again, and to once again learn the language of ordinary humans.

The following week he didn't return Irene's calls, pleading exhaustion to his family so they could tell her, but tonight she was throwing him a party at the old Amber Tavern. The thought of facing her and the old crowd filled him with leaden gloom.

It was past noon when he finally showered, dressed, and came out of his room to find his father watching the news as reporters grilled Nixon about the Watergate scandal.

His father stabbed his finger at the TV. "Why are they hounding him like this?" He stood and turned it off angrily. "Nixon's a good man," he said, shepherding Al into the kitchen.

Al sat at the table across from his sister, Magda. "He broke into the Watergate Hotel, right?"

"Speak Lithuanian, you're home now," his mother chided him good-naturedly as she brought a steaming bowl to the table like an offering. "I made your favorite mushroom dumplings."

"Nixon didn't do it," said his father, dismissing the idea with a wave of his hand. "Some hooligans broke in."

Al piled some dumplings onto his plate and passed the bowl to his father. "Weren't they spying on the Democrats?"

His father almost dropped the bowl in a fit of anger. "Look, in the Soviet Union the Communists have spies on every phone, in every house, workplace—everywhere. You don't hear them giving Brezhnev any trouble."

Al was confused. "Wait a minute. You hate the Communists."

"Yeah, I hate the sons-a-bitches. They took over our country." His father pounded the table with his fist. "That's why you were fighting in that son-of-a-bitch country! To stop Communism."

"Uhmm." That old rant again. Everything seemed so clear to his father.

"Nixon hates those Commies too," his father added. "That's why he's a good man." Jurgis Vitkus finally smiled at his son, satisfied that he had made his point.

Al couldn't give less of a shit about Nixon.

His mother tenderly put her hand on his, making him nervous and jumpy. "You know we watched the news every night while you were in Vietnam," she said softly. "We saw such terrible battles with wounded soldiers being taken away in helicopters. Was it as bad where you were?" His mother seemed to be holding her breath. Nausea rose in him like steam in the jungle.

"No, Mama, it wasn't that bad," he lied and watched as his mother visibly relaxed.

His father heaped sour cream on his dumplings. "War is hell, all right, and no one knows that better than your sister." Magda stopped eating when she realized everyone had turned to her. Al looked at his sister's placid face. At thirty-three, his sister was plumper than he remembered but with that same beautiful face as innocent as the moon.

"Yeah, I guess," Al whispered. He had been about seven when he realized that his sister was different from other girls. Her strangeness used to embarrass him, but he'd always felt a fierce protective love for her.

His father poured him a beer and Al drank it all at once. Then he had to force himself to finish the dumplings. When he stood to put his plate in the sink, his mother said, "Leave it, I'll do that." She was watching her son warily.

"Thanks, Mama, the dumplings were great." Why was it so hard to look her in the eyes? He cleared his throat. "I'm going over to Pete's for a while."

"Wait, I wanted to tell you Irene called again." His mother smiled coyly. "She said for you not to forget your party."

"Yeah, don't worry." Al looked at the clock. "I've got plenty of time." He raked his hair with his fingers. He had to get out of there.

"Bundle up, it's still snowing."

Al jammed on his jacket and was racing out the door when Magda stopped him, holding out his gloves. He thanked her and was about to go out when she stopped him again to wind a muffler around his neck the way she used to when he was in grammar school, and she would help him dress in the morning. She wound it round and round and suddenly Al felt as if he couldn't breathe, as if the body bag was closing.

"Magda, stop!" he yelled, pushing her aside to open the front door and gulp air.

"Sure, Al." She stood back, surprised by his reaction.

"I'm sorry, Magda. I mean...I don't want the muffler." Al unwound it, giving it back to her.

Suddenly he had to get away, down the front stairs of the stoop, the cold air a relief. Down the street, he saw Pete Matas getting into his blue Pinto. Pete had been in Nam. He knew. Only Pete had been stoned for most of the war. It was as if the world had split into two: those who knew what hell the war was and those who didn't. Al didn't know how to be with those who didn't.

"Hey, wait for me." Al was slipping and sliding on the packed snow as he ran to catch up with Pete. "Where are you going?"

"I dunno," said Pete, shrugging. "I just need to drive. I've been watching too much bad TV and that radiator heat, man, I just hate it."

"Tell me about it. I got to get away, Pete."

"Jump in."

Pete drove out to the Chicago Skyway and into Indiana, past the hellish smokestacks of Gary, right into Michigan, chain-smoking Winstons the whole way. Pete had been home for almost a year now and said it soothed him to take long drives along the lake. Sometimes he drove for hours; sometimes he drove all night. This time, he drove out to Union Pier, where he and Al used to spend their summer weekends with friends. Pete told Al how lately he had been visiting his childhood haunts—his old grammar school, high school, all his old hangouts, seeing old friends from childhood, even visiting the nuns and priests who had taught him. It was as if he wanted to find himself in one of those old familiar places, as if he had dropped his life somewhere like a lost ball that he hoped to retrieve.

Pete stopped the car at the public beach, and they walked down the wooden stairs to the snow-covered beach with the frozen waves at the shore. Walking the cold, deserted beach, they didn't say much of anything until they reached the old Lankutis resort where they had often stayed in years past. Farther out, the metal-colored waves crashed against the frozen shoreline. From afar, Pete spotted Elena Lankutis through the large windows of her solarium watering her many flowers—amaryllises in various hues, and blood-red poinsettias left over from Christmas. It was such a surprise to see such lavish blooms in the snow-covered landscape that they stopped momentarily to stare at the garish colors. Then Al and Pete kept walking until they reached the Point, the Arctic wind blowing off the lake, stinging their faces with cold. Sitting down on the craggy rocks, they looked back at the trail of solitary footprints they had left in the snow. Al noticed that his bad leg had left a deeper impression.

"Pete, what do you think of Nixon and Watergate?" Al stood up, took a few steps and sat down again, hardly able to sit still.

His friend looked at him as if he were speaking another language. "I don't give a shit about Nixon or his Watergate."

Al snorted a laugh. That was how he felt too, but he still felt as if he should care.

Pete watched Al's knee bouncing like a jackhammer. "Man, you look like you're ready to jump out of your skin."

"Tell me about it. How the hell did you handle coming home? I can't take it."

Pete blew out a long plume of smoke and flicked his cigarette into the water. "You remember how hard it was to get used to the war? Those first days when you practically shit in your pants at every noise."

"Yeah, so?" Al wanted the secret formula.

"Remember how after a while you stopped noticing the blood and bullets that used to scare you? How all of that slaughter started feeling routine? You remember that?"

"Yeah." Al rubbed his forehead, suddenly remembering the errand boy in Vietnam. He was just a local kid who ran errands in exchange for a little money. He couldn't have been more than ten when he died.

"What I'm saying is that you get used to anything. Take it easy. You'll get used to this too." Pete smiled and put his arm on Al's shoulder. "Look at me," he said, barking out a hollow laugh. "Relax, it gets easier with time. Grass helps." He snorted. "A helluva lot of grass."

"You know, Pete, I'm not sure I'm ready for your sister's party." Pete had told him about Irene's hippie, anti-war demonstrations, and about her taking LSD. Al had seen some anti-war demonstrators outside his base calling the soldiers murderers and child-killers. He had wanted to wring their necks like chickens. Who the hell did they think the soldiers were fighting for? He couldn't bear it if Irene was like that.

"Listen, she's been working her buns off for your party," said Pete.

"I just want everything to be like the old days." Al wanted to be the same man he had been before the war, but it was becoming increasingly clear to him how difficult it was going to be to get back to that man.

"Hey, forget it," said Pete, rolling his eyes. "Nothing's ever going to be like the old days, no matter how much you want it."

"Tell me the truth, Pete. Has Irene been seeing anyone else?"

"I ain't gonna lie, man. Not to you. Yeah, she went out with some guy named Joel from the North Side. I think she met him at some political rally or something."

Al felt like someone had punched him in the stomach. "The guy's probably got a deferment, right? Some draft dodger. Is she still seeing him?"

"Naw, Irene's always had a thing for you, man." He smiled and lit up a joint. Al noticed Pete's missing finger, another war wound. He remembered hearing how Pete had lost that finger playing with old German army ordinance in the DP camps in Germany after the war.

"Well, we better get back, or Irene will kick my ass," said Pete, handing Al the joint. Al shivered, wondering if it was from nerves or cold. Whatever it was, he wished he had taken the muffler Magda had wrapped him in.

That evening the Amber Tavern was decked out with balloons, streamers, and welcome-home banners. When Al and Pete walked in, everyone surrounded Al, cheering and laughing as they carried him to the back hall where there was a table with food. When they finally put him down, Irene came over and hugged him warmly. "Welcome home, soldier." She looked great, dressed in jeans and a blue sweater, her blond hair hanging down past her shoulders. She didn't look like a hippie to him.

"Thanks, this is a nice welcome home." Al could see that Irene had had a few drinks already. He didn't know why, but this bothered him. And, as if on cue, Pete handed him a vodka tonic as he toasted his return.

"Thanks, grunt," said Al, smiling.

"Takes one to know one," said Pete as he went back to the bar to talk to the old timers like Felius the Poet, Antanas Balys, and Valentinas Gediminas. He got a kick out of these old guys and their byzantine stories of past wars.

Connie came running over, pulling Al's old friend, Joey Cicero, behind her. "Al, look, he finally popped the question." Connie showed him her diamond-and-emerald engagement ring.

"Congratulations." He smiled but didn't know what else to say.

"She wore me down, pal." Joey laughed and clapped him on the back. "It's good to have you back, buddy."

Felius the Poet came into the back room with the rest of the usual crowd, holding a bottle of champagne to toast their war hero. Valentinas Gediminas followed with a tray of glasses. They drank and Joey poured the last of the champagne on Al's head.

"Hey, what's that for?" Al was ready for a fight.

"A baptism. Welcome back to civilian life, soldier, where the worst wounds are often hidden." Joey winked and handed Al a towel. "You're one of us now—a vet."

"You were in Nam, Joey?" This pleased Al enormously, and he wanted to ask him about it, but Ona Janulis and her brother Jonas pulled Al over to the table with Vida and Milda. They were laughing about old times. The whole time Al kept checking on Irene. He'd smile when he'd catch her attention, and she'd smile back. Connie put a quarter in the jukebox and "Bye, Bye, Miss American Pie" blared out. Everyone started dancing and singing along while Al sat back, remembering how he used to listen to that song in Nam and ask himself—will this be the day that I die?

Drinks flowed, snatches of stories got started but not finished, and new tunes played until Irene pressed the magic button on the jukebox. "Zorba!" she shouted, and the whole group assembled itself into a dance line just like the old days, locking arms, gamboling around in an arc based on what they remembered of the movie with Anthony Quinn. Irene tried to get Al to join them, but he said his leg bothered him. They played it over and over until everyone was overheated. Irene opened the door, leading the whole line as it snaked its way out into the street, slipping and sliding on the snow until Irene fell, taking Connie and Milda down with her like bowling pins. Al watched his old friends. They were innocents, like children, untouched by anything tragic, while he had seen too much. He watched his friends dance away and then he went into the bar to join Pete, who was talking to Joey Cicero.

"So, Joey, where were you in Nam?"

"I was in Saigon most of the time. Hey, Pete tells me you went back for a second term. Are you nuts or what?" Joey's Italian hands were flying as he spoke.

Al heard the *Zorba* music start up again. The nausea returned, always there, just below the surface. "Yeah, I'm nuts all right." His stomach was so tight it hurt. As he ordered a highball, he realized he was drinking a lot but he wasn't getting drunk, not even relaxed.

"Why'd you do it, Al?" Joey asked, wanting a real answer.

"I was in recon the first time, and most everyone got wiped out." Al ordered drinks for his friends. "I had the radio. You know what they say about us?" Al took a slug of his drink.

"What?" Joey shrugged.

"We have a life expectancy of less than five minutes during any firefight."

"Well, you proved them wrong then." Joey jabbed the air while holding his glass.

Al looked into his highball as if it knew his secrets.

"Was that how you hurt your leg?" Joey asked carefully.

Al nodded and looked up to see Irene dancing back into the tavern. She was showing him how to have fun again.

"So you went back to recon?"

"No, they put me with the medical corps."

"Oh shit, are you kidding me?"

"I had to go through the body bags and find their wallets, photos, letters, you know, personal effects for the relatives back home."

The three men stood there for a long moment, each lost in his own thoughts until Irene walked over holding her coat on one arm and Al's jacket on the other. "Let's go for a little walk, OK, Al?"

"Sure, Irene." He put on his jacket and followed her out the door. They walked arm-in-arm down the street, with Al trying hard not to limp. He could sense that Irene had a lot to say, so he waited for her to start.

"What's going on, Al?" she spit out at last. "You've been avoiding me all night."

"No, I haven't. I've been watching you all night long." They

walked down Sixty-Ninth Street past Silvia's House of Beauty with
Al apologizing along the way.

"That's the problem, Al," she explained, her words furred from
too many drinks. "It's like you're not even here, like you're watching
a movie about a welcome-home party." Irene looked like a rag doll
on the verge of tears.

Al wanted to hold her, comfort her, but he no longer knew how.
Instead, he took a cigarette out of his shirt pocket and lit it. "Irene,
it's a great party." He took a long drag on his cigarette and looked at
her watery eyes. "And you...well, you look really beautiful."

"Well, OK then." Irene smiled and took his cigarette out of his
mouth and took a drag the way she used to before he went away.

"I'm sorry, would you like a cigarette?" Al offered her the pack.

"No, I quit." Irene leaned over and kissed Al on the cheek and
then on the nose. Al kissed her on the mouth, but he was a million
miles away.

Irene touched his cheek. "What's wrong, Al? Tell me."

"Nothing—nothing's wrong." Al could hear the laughter from
the tavern, and he wondered if his rawness was visible to everyone.
He wondered if Irene could see it. Probably everyone saw it.

Irene's eyes bored into him. "Come on, Al, talk to me. Tell me
what's going on here. Is it something I did?"

"No, it's just this damn war." He took a long drag on his cigarette and watched a car drive slowly down the street. "I'll be OK, I
just need some time, Irene."

"I'm so sorry, Al. I wish I could make it all go away for you. Can
you talk about it?"

"Not tonight. Maybe some other time, Irene."

Irene rubbed her nose, trying her best to smile. "Is there someone else?" She couldn't look at him.

"No one else, Irene." He felt deeply ashamed, as if he were not man enough to face her and the welcome home party she arranged for him.

She stood in front of the beauty shop looking a bit sick until she doubled over, throwing up in the street. Al held her by the arm until she stopped.

"Sorry, I've had too much to drink." Taking a deep breath, she looked around and shivered. "Can we go back inside?"

Al flicked his cigarette into the gutter. "Listen, Irene, I think you did a great job with this party, and I'm so grateful. And, this is nothing against you, but I just can't go back in there." He shook his head. "It was a great party, Irene, but…" He hesitated, upset that he was stuttering his way out of this, not knowing what to say. "It's just…" He took a deep breath and plunged in. "I just have to go." Al knew there were a million things he wanted to say, but he just couldn't.

"But Al, this is your party. All your friends are here. Don't go." Irene's eyes pleaded with him. "We've just begun. There's so much I want to tell you, and so much I want to hear from you. Stay with me."

"I can't, Irene. Not yet. I'm so sorry." He took her hands. They felt like small fish in his large hands. "I wish to God I could, but I just can't."

"Yeah, OK," she said, unable to hide her disappointment. She slipped her hands out of his and back into her pockets—slender herrings returning home. "I was kind of hoping…" Irene smiled a crooked smile. "I don't know what I was hoping for. Oh hell, I was hoping to be swept off my feet." She laughed a little, but Al could see the tears in her eyes.

His heart was racing. He wanted to ask Irene about the draft dodger she had been with. He wanted Irene to hold him, to tell him that she still loved him no matter what, to heal him, but he was frozen like the waves on the Michigan beach. What he wanted was to get away from all of the raw emotions he was pushing down.

"Hey, I'm freezing and a little dizzy," said Irene, glancing back at the bar. "If you're not going back, then I am. To warm up if nothing else." Irene tried to take his hand, but he gently pulled it away. They stared at each other for a long moment.

"Thanks for the party," he said, trying to smile. "It was great."

"Yeah, you're welcome," Irene said quietly as she turned, quickly walking away.

He watched her go into the noisy tavern, wiping her eyes before she went back in. The snow started again as he slowly walked home, smelling the familiar scent of Kool-Aid from the factory where his mother worked. His leg hurt, so he walked carefully, his limp more pronounced than usual. He passed the old Sinclair station and the houses he had known on Talman Street. It all looked like a stage set for a bad movie.

A disintegrating Chevy drove by loudly chugging exhaust, leaving a noxious cloud hanging in the air. It backfired and Al jumped for cover. The smell reminded him of the plumes of napalm, of percussive grenades, the constant whoop-whoop of the choppers. Had it all been a dream? The familiar nausea returned.

When he reached his house, he sat down on the front stoop, smoking a cigarette to calm himself. His heart was still racing, and a crushing desolation was growing until it felt like it would swallow him. He looked up at the snow falling in the night sky and felt like the smallest speck in the universe. All of those deaths he had seen in Nam—too many to count. One death stood out from all the rest, though. It was the face of their ten-year-old errand boy who shined their shoes, bought them cigarettes and whores and anything else they wanted in Saigon. His name was unpronounceable, so everyone called him Beaver like the TV series. One day, while Al was playing blackjack with the guys, Beaver ran into the courtyard screaming hysterically. The soldiers grabbed their rifles, thinking it was Viet

Cong. And then Al saw that Beaver was running toward them, his arms held high and his body strapped with explosives. In an instant, Al knew they had to shoot him, or they'd all be blown up. He picked up his rifle and looked Beaver in the eye as he shot him.

The snow was falling unhurriedly in the dark night. He sat there for a long time watching the gossamer snowflakes float from the sky, watching as they piled up on his jacket sleeve and his leg, feeling as if he could sit there forever.

When someone tapped him on the shoulder, he shot up like a rocket, pushing whoever it was away. When he turned and saw it was Magda, wrapped in her quilted robe, he felt bad. "Sorry, you scared me."

She frowned. "It's cold out, Al."

"Listen Magda." Al shook his head. "I'm sorry."

She cocked her head to the side.

"I'm sorry about earlier too, with the muffler. When I got so upset." He shook his head. "Maybe I'm a little shell-shocked from the bombs." As soon as Al said that he regretted it, realizing that his sister had been shattered by a bomb. "Sorry, Magda, I didn't mean…" He stopped himself. Everything he did was wrong.

She came over and took his hand. "No more bombs, Al."

"No more bombs, Magda." His voice was muffled.

She stood there holding his hand until he could feel her start to shiver.

"You're freezing, let's go inside," said Al, as he led his sister up the snowy stairs. Only when he got to the door and touched his cheeks did Al feel the tears that had frozen on his face.

Chinese Red

Irene Matas, 1976

Last June, Vida and I moved to the North Side of Chicago, near Belmont Harbor. My old Lithuanian neighborhood had gotten too insular for me, too focused on holding on to its lost past. For me, Lithuania had become too much a myth of golden fields and thatched cottages with carved wayside crosses at the crossroads. The myth was beautiful, but it was crushing me. I wanted something else, something new.

I got a job as a substitute teacher and jumped from school to school until I finally got a long-term assignment in March at the freshman branch of Marshall High School on the West Side. The separate branch was called Dante, but the teachers called it the Inferno. But not me—I was an innocent idealist who longed to help the neighborhood that had rioted after the assassination of Martin Luther King Jr. I took the El and, full of zeal and good will, walked four blocks to the school, smiling and greeting women and children sitting on stoops. When I reached the school and saw the Black P Stone Nation, the most feared gang in Chicago, milling around at the entrance, I was rattled, but not enough to leave. Two armed guards were stationed at every door, because, as they said later, trouble seemed to visit often.

The first day, when I walked into the remedial reading class and found some students scanning the sports section, I was overjoyed, thinking that if they could read the paper, my job wasn't going to be as hard as people said. But when the students looked up and saw that a substitute teacher had come in, a low grumbling started, followed by a folding of newspapers and then some of the young men opened the windows and bailed out, without a direct word to me.

I stood at my desk, stunned by the sudden exodus.

As a freshman in high school, I had won a prize for a poem about the plight of blacks during the civil rights demonstrations I had watched on the nightly news. It hurt me to see dogs snarling at school children or when demonstrators got blasted by water cannons. Afterward, I vowed to help right the wrongs done to blacks, angry at the injustice of such discrimination.

Each week at school, I was happy to see that fewer students jumped out the classroom windows, hoping I was beginning to make some progress. During our preparation period, the teachers were expected to patrol the halls. About two months into my new job, as I was patrolling the second floor, Charles Washington, one of my students, came from behind and grabbed me in a chokehold, putting a knife to my throat until I felt the pain of skin broken. I stiffened in shock, recognizing his voice at once. Though I was trembling with fear, something elemental clicked in, some survival instinct, and a strange calm came over me. I started talking to him in a soothing, almost kidding voice. "Oh Charles," I said. "Come on, put that thing away before someone sees you," I said, gently trying to push the knife away from my throat.

"Where's Patricia?" he whispered thickly in my ear. "I need to see her right now." I could tell he was hopped up. Last week he had been expelled after being caught shooting heroin in the bathroom.

"Don't worry. I know her schedule," I cooed. "She's downstairs.

Let me take you to her." I felt him loosen his grip, and I just took his arm like we were about to take a leisurely stroll down to the park. Where did this cool-headedness come from? As we walked down the stairs, I spotted the two security guards at the front door but kept chattering to Charles to make sure he didn't panic. Behind Charles' back, I waved my arm, hoping the guards would spot him, but they didn't catch my semaphore. I continued down the hall to Patricia's class and told Charles the bell was about to ring in ten minutes and then he could talk to his girlfriend. While he looked through the small window in the door to make sure she was there, I gestured wildly to the security guards, who finally woke up and came over to investigate. Once they saw it was Charles, they quickly grabbed him and pulled him away to the office, as he cursed us, struggling to get away. As I watched them go down the hall, I was trembling, too stunned to move, belatedly paralyzed with fear. This could have been my last day. The vice principal found me in the hall and helped get me to the nurse's office, where my neck was bandaged and a report was filed. I sat there for a long time, trying to come to terms with what had happened, but I simply couldn't. There was no way I could ever return to this school. Before the day was out, I went to the principal's office and quit. Then I walked the four blocks to the El, shaking like a leaf, looking around at everyone I passed, as if each person was a threat. By the time I reached home, I was a wreck, locking the door and diving under my comforter.

For the next week, I sat home brooding, feeling shaky and unmoored, my confidence as a teacher lost. Each day, while Vida went off to work at the community theater, dressed like a chic Gypsy, I sat near the window immobilized, looking out at the gray street and the pale green emerging maple leaves trembling in the wind, feeling frozen by inertia, not wanting to do anything but read. Flattened by ennui and melancholy, I was hardly able to muster the enthusiasm to leave my apartment. I simply wanted to leave myself behind, like an old limp sock.

The truth was, I didn't have a clue what to do with my life. After the attack, I felt uneasy and jumpy but didn't want to move back home because the old neighborhood was slowly disappearing, and I didn't want to move in with my parents, who had recently bought a house in the Chicago suburb of Lemont.

I brooded while tearing through the novels of Dostoyevsky and Gogol, wallowing in the bleakness. But as the days warmed and brightened, I turned to something lighter—Anaïs Nin's journals. Reading her, the clouds of my gray Chicago life parted momentarily and I had a glimpse of a life unlike my own. This tiny bird-like woman seemed to have such a rich and full life. I envied her travels, her long conversations with interesting people like Henry Miller and Otto Rank, her romantic love affairs.

But after two weeks of Anaïs and ennui, I got a phone call from my old friend Milda Gudauskas, who was getting her master's in psychology in Los Angles. She said her roommate was moving out, so she wanted to know if I wanted to move in with her. I told her I'd think about it, but with each day that went by, it seemed like a better idea. My roommate, Vida, was getting married to Jonas Janulis at the end of June. It seemed all my friends were getting married and moving away to the suburbs, while I was one of the leftovers for whom wedding bells were not even a distant tinkle. And, besides, I couldn't bear to keep running into my old love, Al Vitkus, who seemed to go out of his way to avoid me since his return from Vietnam. Once, I even saw him cross the street to steer clear of me. It tore at me, but no matter how many times I tried to talk to him, he managed to slip away without saying much of anything.

I finally decided to shake myself out of my inertia. One of the images from Anaïs Nin's book had caught my fancy. Like the colorful rooms in a Matisse painting, Anaïs chose her peach robe because the color went so well with her Chinese-red walls. And just like that, I went to the hardware store to buy red paint, and my tiny kitchen was transformed, borrowing a tiny sliver of Anaïs' life. If that didn't cheer me up, perhaps it would brighten our kitchen in time to throw a going-away party for myself and invite all my friends. I couldn't stop myself from asking my brother, Pete, to invite Al to my party, hoping that if he heard that I was leaving Chicago, there might be a flicker of hope for a reconciliation. My heart was simple-minded and stubborn.

I called Milda to tell her that I would fly to Los Angeles after Vida's wedding. I had visited her last fall and had so loved being with her. Our week together had been filled with talk of books and music and movies. Life with Milda seemed to be just what I was hungering for—culture and the wider world.

A few days later, Milda's brother Paul called, asking if he could come to the party. He had just returned from a trip to the homeland and wanted to give us a taste of Lithuania and Russia, bringing some *krupnikas*, the Lithuanian honey liqueur said to cure ninety-nine ailments. Since he was the first of us to go to Lithuania, we were very curious to hear about it. All my life I had heard my parents curse Russia for occupying Lithuania after the war. Now, it seemed kind of exotic to have Paul arriving like a delegate from the other side of the globe—the enemy's side. He said he was also bringing some Russian herring and vodka, instructing me to boil some potatoes with dill because that was how they did it in Russia.

Paul was the Lithuanian most likely to succeed from our group, having graduated from Dartmouth. The rest of us hadn't gone farther than the University of Illinois in Chicago or Urbana. He was smart and funny, but with a self-conscious stiffness that was sometimes off-putting. I had never seen him wear a pair of jeans or a baseball cap. He always dressed elegantly, sometimes affecting a British Raj look from the last century, even sporting a thick mustache. In the summer, it was seersucker and safari gear, wearing a pith helmet to the beach or a white linen suit to a wedding. But we had all grown up together, so we forgave him no matter what he was playing at. He was Milda's brother, after all.

When Vida returned, she frowned when she saw the red walls. "What the hell kind of color is this? Opium-den red? Bordello red?"

"It's Red-Square red," I said flatly. "In honor of Paul's visit to Moscow and Lithuania."

She frowned. "A little dark and creepy, if you ask me."

"You think so?" I looked around the tiny kitchen. "I thought it looked so bohemian," I said hopefully.

"Bohemian? It's like a room in a crazy fun house—the kind you try to get out of as soon as possible." Her mouth twisted into a half smile. "And the paint stinks like hell. Did you forget about the party tomorrow?" she asked with an annoyed twang.

I opened the back door leading to the rickety back porch to air out the paint fumes. "It'll be dry by then," I promised, lighting vanilla-scented candles to mask the smell. I put one of the votive candles on the five-foot-high styrofoam dinosaur skeleton in the living room so that the ribs sent shadows over the walls. I'd show her crazy fun house. On the wall, over the brick-and-board bookcase, three black-and-white *Alice in Wonderland* prints by Tenniel undulated in the flickering candlelight. We fretted that the two circular wicker chairs that Vida had brought from her parents' house wouldn't be enough seating for a party, so she borrowed some folding chairs.

The party started early, as my newly married friends, Connie and Joey Cicero, came over to help me prepare. Connie, her frizzy red hair almost tamed, brought chips and dip and champagne. I lit the candles and soon Pete came in the door, bringing two younger girls I didn't know. Looking at their fresh faces, I realized that soon I'd be the last unmarried woman in our crowd, not counting Milda. I scanned the hall to see if, by some chance, Al had come with him.

"Don't look too hard," said my brother. "He's not coming." There was a note of fatigue in his voice, like we had played this scene once too often.

I frowned, realizing how transparent I was. "Did you invite him?" I asked. "I told you to invite him," I said, my anger rising.

"Sure," said Pete, shrugging. "But you know Al. He's not going out much these days."

I knew that all too well, but I was still hoping. I'd known Al since I first came to America. He and his sister Magda were my first friends. We all grew up together, and then one day I noticed I was falling for him. My love grew like a deep root in my heart, one I couldn't pull out without tremendous pain. But Al was an old wound by now. The pain of losing him was deeper than tears. I'd spent years waiting for him to heal, hoping he'd return to me, but when he didn't, I started feeling cast off. I rarely saw him anymore, and when I did, it was awkward for both of us. He'd returned from Vietnam looking so handsome, but something had changed. The war had broken him in some way, but he wouldn't talk about it. Words didn't work anymore, and when I looked into his eyes, all I saw was searing pain.

Soon Paul came in the door looking like Chekhov in a long black coat with a beaver collar, wearing a fur-lined Russian hat with ear flaps. "*Krasavitsa maya*," he said to me with his usual slight stutter and affected accent. He took off his dark overcoat and stood there wearing a tweed jacket with suede elbow patches, a pipe sticking out of the pocket. The rest of us still had remnants of that scruffy hippy look, which made him stand out all the more, but, then, I guess that was the point. He was as pale as ever, and his black-framed glasses slid down his nose, eyes at half-mast, always checking to see if he was impressing the rest of us.

"My sister called me from LA today," he said. "Milda said you're moving there. Is that true?" He put his arm around me, but I slowly eased away.

"That's right. Joining Milda as soon as our lease is up." I twirled around. "*Ochi chornaya*, California," I sang, mimicking the Russian songs I'd heard.

"California with the two of you—sounds like trouble," Paul added, chuckling, as he pulled out the promised salted herring and vodka from a paper bag and put them on the small table in the kitchen. "Did you boil some potatoes?" I put the pot of potatoes on the stove and told him they'd be done in twenty minutes.

"You and I should go out somewhere before you leave." He smiled and took my hand and held it.

"Yeah, sure," I answered, but I knew I wouldn't go. While we had been friends since childhood, and I liked him, I wasn't interested in anything remotely romantic with him. When he complained that the paint smell made him dizzy, I opened the kitchen door, and we moved into the living room. He took the curved pipe out of his pocket, packed it with tobacco from his pouch, and lit it, filling the room with a sweetish smell. Then the stories started, as he told us how Lithuania was so run down after thirty years of Communist repression. "The grayness of Soviet life is so depressing, and the lines for food are endless. Oh my God, I don't know how our relatives do it."

We drank a shot of vodka to the bleakness of it all. Then he proposed we toast to the sadness of our poor imprisoned Lithuania. "You wouldn't believe it," Paul said. "The Soviets wouldn't let me visit Lithuania unless I took a mandatory swing through Moscow first and then only five days in Vilnius at an Intourist hotel. My relatives had to come to see me because I wasn't allowed to leave the capital, as if I would infect the populace with my Western ideas. And the worst part was the constant sense of being watched. My hotel room was bugged, I had an Intourist guide everywhere I went, and, as if that wasn't enough, I was constantly followed by the KGB. It was like some bad Bond movie."

"Cool," said Pete.

Vida and Jonas came in with black bread and Lithuanian sausages from the deli in our old neighborhood and announced that they had brought someone from the Amber Tavern. "Hey, look who we found on Sixty-Ninth Street." It was Felius the Poet, the old skirt-chaser who brought every subject back to the most basic one—sex. His hair had thinned, and his ears had grown, but his smile was still infectious. He was always ready to party and have a good time.

"Ladies, your salvation is at hand," he said, eyeing Vida and me. "Felius is here to save you from your repressive Catholic upbringing." He laughed his sniggering laugh, his speech already slurred, and then he saw Paul. "Hey, is it true you went to Lithuania?"

"Yup." Paul poured a shot of vodka.

Felius belted down the shot and said with narrowed eyes. "So, you're probably working for the CIA, right?"

"Nonsense," Paul barked a staccato laugh. "Why do you say that? Is it because I finally got permission to go to Lithuania?"

Felius shrugged, smiling with one side of his mouth as he looked Paul over. He wasn't buying it.

We finally brought out the potatoes with dill and salted herring and put them on our thrift-store table. We tossed back the vodka and chased it with the food. Before long, Connie was drunk, laughing about the good old days when she was still single. "God, Irene, we used to have so much fun, remember? We were the wild girls." Her words were slightly slurred.

"Yeah, Connie. We had a lot of fun." Saying that made me feel ancient.

Joey tried to talk Connie into not drinking any more, but she wasn't having it. She leaned over and whispered in my ear. "He wants to start a family, but I'm not ready yet, Irene. I'm too young to be a mother." Her breath tickled my ear. "You know what I mean, don't you?" she asked, hugging me tightly.

"Sure, Connie." I said, but wasn't really sure of anything. Somehow it seemed that my friends' lives were setting like Jell-O in a mold, but my life was as unformed as an endless fog. Now here we were—our old gang of Lithuanian refugees, partying on the North Side of Chicago, far away from our South Side lives, still hanging on to one another for solace.

Paul poured me another shot of vodka and toasted Vida's upcoming wedding. I drank it down. The paint fumes and the vodka had gone to my head, making me a bit tipsy. I noticed that my vanilla candle had melted the styrofoam of the dinosaur's pelvic bones. I blew out the candle and walked over to the front windows and opened them, gulping down fresh air. It was late and the street was quiet. A cool wind blew off the lake, stirring the branches of the maple trees. The streetlights cast an amber glow, and through the tree branches, I could see the moon glowing behind a thick batting of clouds like a bandaged eye. The row of high-rises along Sheridan Road stood like phalanx along the lakeshore, blocking the never-ending wind. Someone was cooking cabbage, and the smell wafted up to the window, reminding me of home.

At what point did my life begin to diverge from the path of friends and family? I felt adrift, filled with doubts about my future.

As I looked out the window, a gentle rain started to fall outside, and a sadness fell over me. I was leaving my tribe. Opening the window a bit wider, I sat looking out over the city, and for a brief moment that feeling returned, as it had so often in the last weeks— the shock of fear as the cool blade of the knife pressed against my neck. As I touched my throat, feeling for the small scar, and closing my eyes, I could feel that familiar trembling start deep inside.

Vida came over to the windowsill and sat down, putting her arm around me. We had all had too much vodka. "Oh, Irene, I will miss you so much." She kissed me on the cheek. "What will I do without you?"

"You'll have a husband, remember?" I smiled sadly, realizing how much I'd miss her too.

"True, but he'll never replace you," she said, taking my hand.

"Thanks," I said, tears gathering, "I'll miss you too, Vida." I was grateful when our attention turned to the kitchen, where Paul was teaching our friends a bawdy Lithuanian song. It kept me from crying in earnest as Vida and I turned to look at them in the tiny Chinese-red kitchen, glowing in the candlelight, warm and cozy. Vida held my hand tightly, telling me we'd be friends forever. And with a deep sigh, I smiled sadly, already painfully nostalgic for what I was about to lose.

The Pull of Home

Ona Janulis, 1987

As her plane approached O'Hare, Ona Janulis-Tucker watched the city come into view. There it was again, Chicago—former hog butcher to the world, the hub of the nation's railroads, and home to the largest group of Lithuanians outside of Lithuania, and Ona's recently mugged mother was one of them. Guilt sat in the seat between Ona and her daughter, Amy. But even the heavy burden of guilt couldn't get Ona to move back to Chicago, and her mother refused to move to Portland.

At O'Hare, Ona rented a car and drove the Eisenhower Expressway to the Dan Ryan into the heart of the South Side, where she had grown up, showing Amy places of interest along the way.

"There's the Prudential Building, where your grandmother used to clean offices when she first came to America. Here's the University of Illinois, where I went to school," she said, pointing to her old Chicago Circle campus. "And this used to be the stockyards where your grandfather worked. And that neighborhood was called 'Back of the Yards' because it was downwind from the stockyards. The smell would make you gag." The deeper they got into the South Side, the more depressing it looked—old blue-collar neighborhoods dominated by gritty brick factories and the rusting equipment alongside them, the railroad boxcars that stopped traffic at the crossings, the broken-glass-strewn empty lots they used to call prairies, and the ubiquitous neighborhood taverns.

Even though the city was home to her family and friends, Ona had never liked Chicago. The South Side had once been filled with ethnic European pockets: the Irish, the Polish, the Bohemians, the Italians, and the Lithuanians. And the black neighborhood that moved a little closer every year, like a slow tide. From what Ona could tell, the tide had recently swelled to engulf her old neighborhood and, from what she could see, there were other newcomers from Asia and Central America as well.

Her parents had moved into their house on Talman Street the day Stalin died in 1953, the year it had rained for weeks. The stately elms that had once arched over the street had since been thinned by Dutch elm disease, so that now the block look shabbier, like a derelict with lost teeth.

When Ona pulled up in front of the brick two-flat, she knew her mother was behind the lace curtains waiting for her. In fact, she knew her mother had been waiting for her to come home ever since she had gone to Oregon for graduate school, hoping Ona would move into the flat upstairs to take care of her in her old age. She hated to think of her widowed mother so vulnerable and alone. Stepping out of the car, she looked up at the clouds floating by like tattered gauze.

After dragging their suitcases up the concrete stairs of the front stoop, Ona finally collapsed into her mother's soft embrace, suddenly realizing how much she had missed her.

"Why do you have to live so far away?" her mother asked, turning to embrace Amy.

"*Labas, bobute.*" Amy knew a handful of Lithuanian words and "hello, grandma" was part of her repertoire. Amy spent part of each summer with her Lithuanian grandmother, and she loved her softness and gentleness. She often asked her mother why her *bobute* seemed so lost in America, why she spoke such broken English, and why she had to live alone. Ona had no answers for her daughter, only the familiar choking guilt.

Agota took them to the bedroom and folded back the flowered bedspreads. "Your old room's waiting for you." Ona's bedroom still had the old fifties blond furniture, covered with crocheted doilies. It even smelled the same. The sunlight came in through the window at the same slant like a fat wedge of yellow cheese.

That evening her brother, Jonas, his wife, Vida, and their eight-year-old son, Alex came to dinner. Ona noticed that Vida had gained about forty pounds. They talked of old days, the picnics at Ragis farm and dancing under the stars, of Easter processions, scout camps, weddings, and funerals. All of this was so that they could knit together for a time, remember their shared history and give it to Amy and Alex so that they could be part of the tapestry of their past. That was what families did.

Before Vida left, she invited Ona over for a get-together with her old friends.

"Am I invited?" joked Jonas. "I'll bring the guys."

Vida choked out a laugh. "Are you kidding? Heck, no, this is a girls' night out. I'll invite Connie and Milda. Too bad Irene's in LA," she said, hugging Ona as she said her good-byes.

After Amy had gone to sleep, Agota poured her daughter a last cup of tea and asked her about her husband, Richard. "Why didn't he come?"

"He had to work." The lie slid off her tongue so easily. The truth was, Richard was having an affair. She hadn't told anyone about this, wanting some distance from him to think about what to do next. A physical distance was more tolerable than the emotional distance that had grown between them. It was almost a relief to find out about the other woman. Strangely enough, it didn't upset her as much as she'd thought it might. It felt more like lancing a painful boil.

"Too bad," said her mother, offering Ona another slice of her homemade lingonberry coffee cake.

"Maybe next time," Ona lied again, staring into her cup as if it would tell her why each year her husband felt more like a stranger. She taught her English classes while he taught his psychology classes. Each night she slept close to her edge of the bed, not even wanting to touch him. For a long time, she had wondered why they had so little to talk about. Now, it seems, there was an answer.

On Sunday, her mother insisted they go to Mass at Nativity. Ona wondered if the nuns who taught her had retired or left the convent. When they entered the church, it was almost empty, only a few gray heads here and there. The priest droned on in the front while Ona's mind drifted to her past. This was where she'd had her First Communion, where she'd gotten married. After Mass, she was happy to see Irene's mother, Mrs. Matas.

"Ona, how good to see you, my dear. It reminds me of the old days when all of you girls were still living in Chicago. But children grow up and go on to have their own lives. You're all young and educated and have your eyes set on better homes and schools in the suburbs. Where are you living now? I forget."

"I live in Portland, Oregon."

"So far?"

Ona shrugged helplessly and smiled, thinking that Mrs. Matas' daughter Irene now lived in LA.

Mrs. Matas turned to Ona's mother. "Someone told me you were mugged. Is that true?" She took Agota's hand in hers.

Agota raised her eyebrows, remembering her alarm. "Right on the corner, near my house. They grabbed my purse, and when I started screaming, they pushed me down. I'm lucky I didn't break a bone."

"How awful. I tell you, these colored gangs are just terrible. I've heard that Mr. Vitkus' car was stolen, and someone said that a girl was raped in an alley behind Western Avenue. It's getting more and more dangerous around here. The businesses are moving to the suburbs." Mrs. Matas shook her head, looking around.

"They weren't colored," Agota said flatly. "They were Lithuanian. The new ones who came after Gorbachev declared glasnost. I think they're with the Russian mafia. Didn't you hear about the Lithuanian prostitutes who were arrested on Sixty-Ninth Street last month?"

"No, it can't be true." Mrs. Matas sucked in her breath.

"You know, it was two colored boys who helped me out. Good boys from Kennedy-King College. They chased those hooligans down until they caught them. I was screaming the whole time."

"What's the world coming to?" Mrs. Matas shrugged. "Who would think that your own countrymen would do such a thing? And that those colored boys helped you."

Agota reassured her friend. "Oh, not all the new Lithuanians are like that, but you know what the Americans say about a rotten apple in every barrel."

Bushel, thought Ona, but didn't correct her mother.

Agota continued, "Most of the Lithuanians coming in this third wave of immigrants are good people, not exactly like us because they grew up under the Soviets, but good people nonetheless."

"Thank God for that," said Mrs. Matas, somewhat relieved.

Ona interrupted, taking her mother by the arm. "Well, we better go, Mama. I'm sure Amy is hungry." She wanted to cry, thinking of her mother being attacked. What would she do if her mother died?

"Ona, is this your daughter?" Mrs. Matas asked, opening her purse to pull out a dollar. "Buy yourself some chocolate, dear." She snapped her purse shut and looked around to see if there were any Mafia types hanging around before leaving.

As they walked to the Little Touch of Kretinga restaurant, Ona noticed that many of the stores were boarded up. Silvia's House of Beauty was now Darlene's and it advertised hair weaving. The Sinclair station was gone, but Ona was happy to see that their old hangout, the Amber Tavern, was still standing.

At the restaurant, Ona ordered potato dumplings and cold borscht. Her mother ordered potato *kugelis* and sauerkraut soup, and Amy ordered the combo plate so she could taste all of the Lithuanian specialties. They greeted Felius the Poet, who sat in a maroon vinyl booth at the other end of the restaurant. Mr. Jankus smoked his cigar at the counter while Antanas Balys paid his bill at the cash register. This was a favorite hangout for all of the regulars of the Amber Tavern.

Amy ate her cold borscht and was left with a red mustache. "Why don't you come live with us, *bobute*? It's much safer there. No one robs you."

"I don't know Portland, Amy. All I know is Lithuania and this little corner of Chicago. You'll see when you get older how hard it is to change or start all over again."

"Then why don't you go back to Lithuania?" Amy asked, as if all of life's answers were simple.

"Some of my friends have visited Lithuania. But I'll tell you, Lithuania is not the same and neither am I. And besides, how could I leave my children and my granddaughter here in America?" They all stared out the window at the four black girls playing double Dutch across the street. They saw Mrs. Gudauskas slowly wheeling her grocery cart behind her.

"When I grow up, I'm going to visit your old home in Lithuania," said Amy.

Agota smiled. "You know what? Maybe I'll take you there myself." She brightened. "That's a wonderful idea. Why didn't I think of it before?"

Sunday evening, Ona drove to Vida's house. All of her old friends who hadn't moved out of state now lived in the suburbs. Connie O'Connor, who used to be such a hippie, now looked hopelessly middle class. And Milda, who was always such a mouse, now resembled a smart ad for Barneys. Milda looked Ona over and smiled. "I see life has agreed with you. You look great!" Ona smiled, hoping her regular workouts had kept her looking fit, at least. She never wanted to be called "Fat Ona" again in her life. The wine was opened, and soon they began to talk about the old days and all of their friends.

"Whatever happened to Irene?" asked Ona.

"She's still in LA, married a producer," said Milda.

"What does he produce?"

"Nothing much, from what I hear. Irene's not happy."

Vida shook her head and laughed. "But that Irene was something else in high school, huh?" she marveled.

"God, I only wish I could have had half the nerve and guts she had," Ona said, as if reproaching herself. "I would have had a different life."

"I wonder…" said Connie dreamily.

Ona looked puzzled at Connie's vague reply. "Well, you should know, Connie. You were right there in the trenches with her."

Connie looked stricken. "Yeah, it's true, and I miss it to this day. Irene was such a blast."

As the evening wore on, Connie and Milda got their coats and said their reluctant good-byes, explaining that children were waiting at home.

Vida and Ona continued drinking. "You know," Ona confessed, "I guess I always wanted to be like Connie or Irene."

"Me, too," said Vida. "They got into trouble, but they had so much fun."

"We were always the good girls, huh?" said Ona.

"Yeah, we were always too scared of the nuns not to do the right thing," added Vida.

"Yeah, why were we so scared?"

"Because those nuns were intimidating!"

Ona stood up, smiling wickedly. "I've got an idea. Let's go over to the Amber Tavern to see who's left from the old days." The tavern was where their friends went after dances or parties, but it used to terrify Ona, Vida, and Milda because they were so painfully shy. Even when they finally found the courage to go, they would stand in dark corners watching Irene and Connie laugh, flirt, and dance as if they owned the place.

In half an hour, they were standing at the tavern door waiting to get buzzed in. That was something new, the owners more careful as the neighborhood changed. As Ona entered, she still felt that bit of fizz in her stomach, a learned emotional hiccup, like Pavlov's dogs.

The bar looked shabbier, the soccer trophies were covered with dust, the Hamm's beer sign still twinkled over the bar, and the sentimental paintings of Lithuanian village life still hung on the walls. Valentinas Gediminas and Antanas Balys were still sitting like fixtures on their barstools in exactly the same way that Ona remembered seeing them. But the bar also had some new faces—young men and women who'd recently arrived from Lithuania. They were talking to the old crowd —Captain Eddie and Felius the Poet— who the new Lithuanians referred to as the DPs.

Ona said hello to Felius the Poet, who smiled knowingly, as if running into people he hadn't seen in a decade or two was habitual for him. Everyone from out of town made it to the Amber Tavern sooner or later. It was a way of revisiting the past. This was a place where everyone knew your history, and there was no need to explain yourself. Before long, they fell into the same old conversations, as Valentinas bought the women a drink. Vida put a quarter in the jukebox and chose her favorite old standard, "Blue Tango." Suddenly the whole bar came alive as men and women coupled up, dancing around the room with fancy footwork, dips, and twirls. Valentinas spun Vida around the room with the familiar flourishes. Felius the Poet asked Ona to dance, raising his eyebrows and giving her a look as if to say—tonight is my lucky night.

Silvia, of beauty shop fame, walked in and squealed with delight. "Look, everyone's dancing!" Her husband, Captain Eddie, came to greet her, swooping the fleshy woman up in his arms as they cheek-to-cheeked around the room, his eyes closed, both of them smiling, pink-faced and cherubic.

When the door opened, and several young women walked in, Valentinas leaned over to Ona, asking for an introduction to the young ladies, disregarding the gap of thirty years between their ages. These guys were still on the prowl. She laughed at the human comedy unfolding right there in the tavern, and later, when Felius leaned over and boozily whispered in her ear that she was still a gorgeous woman, she appreciated the compliment from one of the old bachelors, a true cavalier.

Later, Ona danced with one of the beefy soccer players who hadn't yet learned the intricacies of dips and twirls. She'd had a lot to drink and had eaten too much at Vida's house so that the inept dipping and twirling made her dizzy and sick to her stomach. When the music stopped, she excused herself to go to the restroom. She entered the hallway in the back of the tavern just as Valentinas staggered out of the men's room. He grabbed her by the arm and said, smooth as velvet, "Not so fast. Where are you going, my darling?"

"I'm going to be sick. Please, let me go," Ona pleaded.

"Don't be silly," he said in mock seriousness as he pulled her closer to him. "We have to get to know one another better."

Too late. Ona threw up on his tweed sports jacket, while he stood there blinking in disbelief, almost stunned into sobriety. She didn't know whether to laugh or cry, apologizing over and over, but Valentinas just stood there with his arms outstretched like a helpless boy. Ona got some wet paper towels from the bathroom and started to mop up his jacket, but no matter how much she wiped, the jacket was a mess. She offered to pay the dry cleaning bill, but he just took it off and went back to the bar.

Vida, good friend that she was, took Ona to the bathroom to wash up, and when they returned to the bar, the magic was gone. Suddenly the club seemed as if it were full of life's leftovers, trying to recapture the past while the neighborhood underwent a painful transformation.

Still, somehow all of this had been good for Ona's soul, though she couldn't have said why. For this short time, she had stepped out of her ordinary life of grading papers, of dull rainy commutes to the college, of absent husbands and vanished dreams. Ona sat down on one of the barstools next to Felius the Poet, who said it was always good to see some of the lost flock return to the old neighborhood. It confirmed his belief in the futility of leaving home.

Ona laughed softly. Back in Portland, she used to feel the pull of home like a powerful undertow. Though she'd always resisted coming home to Chicago, she realized that, in spite of herself, it made her laugh and cry, and most importantly, remember whom she once had been. By comparison, her years in Oregon were like a fog. With a shock, she realized that even after all the years she had lived and worked there, Oregon was never really home. The truth of the matter was, she had left Chicago because everyone here knew her, and it seemed as if what they knew was etched in stone, unchangeable like the Ten Commandments. At the time, she had desperately needed to break free and redefine herself. Now, all these years later, it felt good to be back among those who knew your history, whom you didn't have to explain yourself to.

She turned to Felius. "You know, you're right, it's so nice to be back home." And quite suddenly, Ona found herself wondering how hard it would be to find a job teaching college English in Chicago. Some clockwork mechanism in her seemed to have shifted ever so slightly, allowing her to see new possibilities. She looked up at the lit Hamm's beer sign over the bar that had been hanging there forever. "From the land of sky-blue waters," it said. Her eyes followed the water as it trickled and flowed in waves and then fell over the edge of the waterfall, but then there it was, back again at the beginning. The blue, sunlit water kept on flowing down the same river, no matter what.

The Boarder

Irene Matas, 1987

October in Los Angeles is the month of sulfur and ash. All summer long the sun bakes the hillsides until the grasses and brush turn brown—tinder waiting for a match or a lit cigarette. It wasn't unusual to turn on the evening news and see the hills burning.

After picking up my son, Nick, from his Salvadoran babysitter, I headed home on the San Diego freeway, trying to avoid the section that had recently been scorched by fire. We stopped at the supermarket and came home to find the light blinking on the answering machine. It was my brother, Pete, in Chicago. My mother had had another stroke. It was really bad this time. She wasn't recognizing anyone and was paralyzed on one side.

That evening I sat in the rocking chair facing the window with my sleepy boy in my lap, as Los Angeles glittered below us. I hummed an old Lithuanian lullaby, only now it sounded like a dirge. Guilt weighed on me like an anvil. I wanted my own mother, to crawl onto her ample lap and cry.

Why had I stayed in California? Los Angeles was a city of amnesiacs where no one seemed to know how to live anymore. It was one of the most spiritually bankrupt places on the globe. My generation was doing the Great American Dance: step to the left, cut all ties, step to the right, tranquilize with TV, do-si-do, buy more stuff, turn around, pick a new partner, swing 'em round, and start all over again. We were like bad children, blaming our parents for our problems, complaining that we were never going to grow up, and endlessly playing until we trashed the planet. The old gods were dead, the old kings were dead, and we were all so lonely without them as we wandered from sea to shining sea without a clue.

I had started my dance in the heady 60s and danced myself into exhaustion. The baby boomers loved endless therapy, workshops and workouts, hoping to forestall death, remodeling and refashioning themselves so that they had no idea whom they were any longer. I wasn't surprised when my marriage failed. Only the act of giving birth had finally woken me, like some mythical sleeping princess. Only when my son was placed in my arms did I finally grow up.

⸺◈◆◈⸺

I flew to Chicago with my son to see my frail mother. By the time I got there, she had been transferred to a nursing home near the Lithuanian Center, which was not far from where my family used to go to the Ragis farm for picnics. By now the city had spread, the suburbs swallowing the farms. I took my son to meet his grandmother, wanting her blessing, but, in truth, I only prayed she would still recognize me.

Pete helped me push Nick's stroller into the red-brick building that looked clean enough, but which underneath the harsh cleansers still smelled of urine. It was difficult to find my mother—all those white heads and withered faces, those clouded fisheyes. We finally found her in the communal room, asleep in a wheelchair, her chin resting on her chest, in front of a TV with other old and withered people. I hardly recognized her. Her hair had turned completely white. It was strange how old people start to look alike, both the men and women, almost genderless, like babies. It was as if old age and infirmity were a country that they all came from. They came into this world helpless and helpless they would leave it.

This was the mother I had tried so hard to please when I was little, the mother I had rebelled against so harshly in my adolescence, the mother I had left in my adulthood. She looked so vulnerable here, washed clean of our shared histories. Funny to realize, after all this time, that I still wanted to please her, be her little girl, be loved and petted. "Everything will be all right," she would lie, the way adults often lie to their children. Her hands were folded neatly in her lap. I remembered those hands raw from cleaning office buildings. She had been pampered in Lithuania and wasn't used to such hard work. She would slather Nivea cream on to soothe her chapped knuckles. They looked healed now.

Why were our parents here? I couldn't imagine the crime for which they were being punished, a penance of old age and infirmity. Where was the life my mother grew up with, filled with all the generations tending one another? She would die and be buried so far away from where she was born and raised. Who will tend her grave in this Chicago suburb? Grief took the air out of the room.

When Pete woke her, she recognized neither of us. As he wheeled her, vacant-eyed, to her room, I bit my lip to fight tears. We sat down and began to speak in Lithuanian, but she made no answer, no gesture of recognition, only smiling politely. I hugged her, kissed her, held her hand, and stroked her white hair, but it was only when Nick started fussing and crying that she finally turned to me. "Where did you pull this one from?" she asked, reaching out for Nick's hand and smiling as if I had produced a rabbit out of a hat. My brother turned to me, smiling at the bluntness of the question. Yes, from where had I pulled this child? She had been too sick, too confused from her previous stroke to know what had happened to me in the last years, so far away in Los Angeles, while she was far from her home in Lithuania. My mother hadn't known that I was pregnant, so where had this child come from? I told her he was my son, and she took his tiny hand and smiled and then I saw her fading again into that wrecked body. I had wanted her blessing. I guess that was it.

I finally ran out of things to say, so I sat quietly, holding her hand, hardly able to breathe, hot tears running down my cheeks. We said goodbye an hour later and like survivors, we stumbled over to the elevator. I held Nick and kissed his forehead, wanting to plead with him not to put me in such a place when I got old and feeble.

While waiting for the elevator, I noticed a bulletin board with a photo of Al Vitkus and Magda as the volunteers of the month. I felt an ache to see them both. I had loved Al for years, but he had come back from Vietnam changed. I guess I had also changed while he was away. He was quiet and sullen. The war had done something to him. It seemed he no longer cared for me. Maybe if Al hadn't gone to war, if we had married, life might have turned out more comprehensible.

It seemed as if I was always waiting for life to begin. Life was not what was happening now, but what would happen in some mythical future. Maybe if I had married an ordinary guy who might not have been exciting, but he would have been decent. Someone who might watch too many ball games on TV instead of doing yard work, or who would never want to see foreign movies or the ballet, but would be there for me year after year—solid, dependable like the wonderful husbands of my friends. A man like my brother or Jonas Janulis, nerdy engineer-types who used to have slide rules in their pockets, but who now made such good solid fathers and husbands. Al might have been such a man.

My brother stood by the elevator, pointing to another sign on the bulletin board that read, "This month's birthdays," just like in elementary school. He recognized one of the names on the list. It was Antanas Balys, who had lived with us for many years as one of our boarders.

"It can't be him, can it?" asked Pete. When we asked the attendant where Mr. Balys was, we were shown a room. The attendant knocked on the door and walked in. "So, Mr. Balys, you finally have some visitors." We watched as he thrashed around in his bed, muttering to himself. We recognized him at once, though he had grown older and gray. The attendant checked his arms and legs, which were moving back and forth as if walking. Then I saw that he was tied to his bed: restrained by strips of cloth tied to his wrists and ankles. The attendant explained that he would walk out into the street otherwise. "He walks in his bed all day and night." She made finger circles on her temple. We walked over to his bed and introduced ourselves.

"How are you, Mr. Balys?" my brother asked in Lithuanian.

"Fine, fine," he answered in a gritty voice. "How are you?" He spoke in the old dialect of Samogitia, his corner of Lithuania. How was it he was here and none of us knew?

"I walked too far, you see," said Antanas, suddenly frightened. "I shouldn't have gone past the bridge. I should have stayed closer to home."

Pete and I looked at each other, puzzled.

"They came for me," he continued. "Those Germans. My wife didn't know." We watched his labored movements and listened to his strained mutterings, realizing he was in another place, another time. Reality had telescoped for him as he relived some portion of the war.

My brother tried to explain how he had been my father's neighbor in their village in Lithuania, how he had lived with us for many years as our boarder after we came to America. Pete asked him if he needed anything.

Antanas raised his voice. "They say the Americans are coming soon. Don't eat the bread, they put sawdust in it. Hurts your stomach." He thrashed about in his bed and then turned to Pete. "Where is he? Did they send him away?" Pete looked at me and shrugged, neither of us knowing what to do. "I shouldn't have walked there. Tell him not to go too far. It's dangerous," he said without looking at us, his eyes wide as he looked beyond us into his own version of hell.

"OK, sure, we'll tell him, don't worry," I said, patting his arm, which was still jerking back and forth. We told him that my mother was down the hall. Maybe they could visit each other. None of it seemed to register with him.

"When will I go home?" he asked, turning toward the window. We knew he didn't mean Chicago.

<hr />

That evening, after Nick fell asleep, my father and I sat quietly, talking over cups of tea. He said I reminded him of some tropical bird that flies into Chicago once a year and then flies back to the tropics. I nodded sadly. Of course, he was right; I was no longer part of their everyday life. I had mutated into some lost bird.

We talked about my mother. I told my father about our visit and asked him about Antanas.

Shaking his head sadly, he said, "Poor man left a wife and four children behind in Lithuania. He was a small farmer in my village, and we were friends before I went to school in Kaunas. During the war, the Germans were seizing able-bodied men for the forced labor. They took Antanas and his brother Jurgis right out of their oat fields while they were working. Antanas survived the war but broke down completely when his brother was killed. Near the end of the war, when the Soviets were returning to Lithuania, we all ran to the

West. We already knew what to expect because of the first Soviet occupation in 1940—confiscated property, jail, executions, and mass deportation to Siberia. And that was repeated in 1944.

"The rest of Europe rejoiced when the war ended, while those behind the Iron Curtain suffered a long occupation, forgotten by the West, which seemed indifferent to what went on there." My father stopped to drink his tea. I could see this conversation was difficult for him, bringing up old memories he'd rather forget.

"After the war we ended up in a displaced-persons camp that was run by American GIs and found Antanas in the camp hospital. When we realized we couldn't go home because the Soviets weren't leaving their conquered countries, it was a blow to us all. Later, when the refugees in the camps could finally apply to go to America, Canada, and Australia, they wouldn't let Antanas leave because of his nervous breakdown. What could I do? I signed papers saying I would take care of him. We couldn't just leave him there alone."

All of these war-torn lives. I was the lucky child who was born post-war. But I was born with the taste of ash, my mother singing dirges for lullabies in the displaced persons camp. When we finally came to America, we lived in a storefront. Later, we moved to a house filled with the boarders we took in to help pay expenses. We all ate our meals together. Sometimes Sunday dinner meant ten people eating my mother's pot roast and discussing politics, telling anecdotes, drinking cognac, and laughing or crying depending on the mood and the amount of liquor. There seemed to be rooms everywhere in that old house that various members of the household retreated to. Half of the basement had been turned into rooms for the boarders. The other half held the laundry and the coal chute with the large black furnace. I'd come down the stairs and run past the stove, sure that something horrible was chasing me in the dark.

We had a variety of boarders over the years. There was Captain

Eddie, a middle-aged bachelor, who always laughed to hysterics. There was also Teodoras, who lived there only a month but was my favorite because he taught me how to tango and flirt, and Antanas, who lived with us so long he became part of the family, like an eccentric uncle. He was a short, sturdy man who always seemed put upon and too lonely for any human to bear. Sometimes he drank too much. I had wondered why these people had no homes of their own. Where were their families? My child's sense of order had been disturbed by these solitary men. They disappeared behind their doors and led their secret lives. Captain Eddie even managed to get married and moved away.

Antanas was the only boarder who stayed with us after the others left. Eventually, my father remodeled our basement into a recreation room with a bar, sofas, and a piano. My mother had parties there after the opera or for the radio show where she worked. Antanas had a room in the back with a small kitchenette, though he still ate with us on weekends. I remember coming down to the basement to practice my piano lessons, turning on the light, and finding Antanas sitting in the dark, in the middle of the room, wearing a robe. It would always startle me, no matter how many times it happened. He would apologize with an embarrassed laugh like a little boy. He rarely laughed unless he was drinking. Otherwise, it looked as if his mouth wasn't used to it. Once, after too many highballs during some party, I heard him talking about how beautiful my mother had been at her wedding. There was a softness in his face that was uncharacteristic of him. Maybe she reminded him of his wife left behind in Lithuania. When I asked my father, he said that Antanas had been handsome in his youth, with so many girls after him, but had his eye on my mother. He and my father had both been rivals for my mother, but my mother chose my father instead of Antanas. "I don't know what she saw in me," he said, smiling as he remembered those long-ago days, but when he turned to me there was a twinkle in his eye. "She said I made her laugh."

It was painful to imagine my white-haired mother in the nursing home as young and beautiful. She was no longer reachable, having retreated into some deep part of herself that none of us could touch. Perhaps in some inner place she was still young and beautiful.

Antanas had worked at the railroad yards and saved every penny he made to send packages to his wife and children in Lithuania. I was a high-school sophomore when I saw him go on a bender that lasted three days. He cried and talked nonsense, so I asked my mother what was wrong.

"Leave him alone," she said. "The man is grieving for his dead wife."

A few weeks after his wife died, Antanas took his money out of the bank and decided to buy each of his four children a car. He bought four new, blue Chrysler sedans in cash and had them shipped to Lithuania at great expense. After that, he seemed agitated and angry and soon started drinking again, often staying out all night. My father would search the neighboring bars for him, sometimes finding him and other times not. Once or twice we got a call from the police saying that Antanas had been wandering the neighborhood in a drunken stupor, talking nonsense. This went on until he had another nervous breakdown. He sat in the basement crying about his wife and children. No one could talk him into doing anything—not eating or bathing, or seeing the doctor. "Why can't I go home?" he sobbed. "I want to see my wife's grave. Who's taking care of it?" he wanted to know. "I have three grandchildren I've never seen." He beat the table with his fist.

"Calm down, be reasonable," said my father. "You can't go there, and they can't come here, but maybe someday…"

"How long can a man wait?" he asked. My father had no answer. He too was waiting. All of them counting the years, waiting to return to old lives, but Antanas couldn't wait any longer.

I saw him a few times after that at the Amber Tavern. He seemed the same, only quieter, sadder, older. My father said he had moved in with another friend, an old bachelor. The two of them lived a quiet life in an apartment in Town of Lake.

With time I moved away from home and forgot about Antanas, forgot about my life as a refugee. Cutting my ties, I exiled myself from the cloistered community of Lithuanians and went to Los Angeles, where all the disillusioned go. Where once I had been a displaced person, I now became a misplaced person. What happens when you leave your people? Who are you then? My family had been forced into exile, while I went into voluntary exile from all that had rooted me, given me identity. I tried to reinvent myself like all good Americans do, but I failed. I was a boarder in my own life, as if I had no family, no roots, no graves to tend. And then I gave birth and then my mother became ill, and in that scramble of emotions, I ran into Antanas again, quite by accident, in the nursing home. Once again, he was my mother's neighbor, once more under the same roof, together again near the end of their lives, and yet neither one knew the other was there. God must love irony.

Antanas died a few months after my mother died. Once a year, like a tropical bird, I fly to Chicago to visit my father. It turns out that the ties of family and friends are still binding. Every year, my father takes the time to teach my son a few more Lithuanian words. Next year, Nick and I will spend the summer with him in Chicago. He hopes to take us to Lithuania someday to show us his ancestral home. With these small sacramental acts, something in me can heal a little each time.

This year I even worked up the courage to write Al Vitkus a

letter. When I go to Chicago, I hope to see him and my old friends Vida, Connie, Milda, and even Ona, who recently divorced and moved back to Chicago from Oregon.

When I visit my mother's grave, I put flowers there and then on Antanas' grave as well. They are in the same cemetery, the Lithuanian one. Antanas never returned home to his farm in Lithuania, nor did he ever again see his wife or his four children with their new blue Chryslers. He died thinking he was back in the Nazi labor camps, regretting having walked too far.

<hr />

It's October again, and the hills are burning as usual. Tonight I can see the ridge of the canyon burning like a snake of fire. There's an eerie beauty to it.

I, too, regret having walked too far and having walked so long. I find that I don't always feel at home when I get there. Antanas and my parents were homesick all their lives for that patch of earth where they were born. I too suffer a homesickness, but for something more elusive that I can no longer name.

A Foreign Country

Agota Janulis, 1988

For the second time in her life, Agota Janulis found herself in a foreign country. The first was when she fled Lithuania during the war and eventually came to Chicago. The second was the day she realized her neighborhood had changed so completely she hardly recognized it any longer.

When Agota first arrived in Marquette Park, she found an earlier wave of Lithuanian immigrants who had come at the turn of the century and built schools, churches, and a convent. Agota was part of a post-war second wave, adding a youth center, newspapers, restaurants, and even an opera company. Now, all these years later, most of the bars and businesses were closing as people moved away. Young Lithuanian families were moving to the suburbs, abandoning the old neighborhood to their aging parents, while African-American families moved in, changing the sounds, tastes, and even the religion of the area.

An insistent, percussive rhythm passed beneath Agota's living-room window. Peeking through the nylon curtains to see who was carrying the loud boom box, she clucked her tongue in disapproval as she unfastened one of the three safety pins on the bib of her apron to use as a toothpick. She surveyed her elm-shaded street filled with girls playing double-Dutch the way her daughter, Ona, used to. Across the street, grandmothers kept watch from front stoops as sullen teenage boys watched the girls through lidded eyes. The woman who lived in Regina Vitkus' former home walked down her front steps with a head full of pink rollers, her terry-cloth slippers slapping her heels, as she yelled at her two daughters to get inside. A young retarded boy sat on Marcele Gudauskas' old stoop with his grandmother, his tongue resting on his lower lip, reminding Agota of Magda, who used to roam the neighborhood like a stray cat. Next door, her neighbor, Mr. Lewis, who helped her whenever her fuses blew or the unreachable light in her bathroom needed changing, was watering his pink hollyhocks. Ever since the neighborhood had changed, she'd been a bit uneasy. If her Pranas were still alive, she wouldn't feel so vulnerable.

The third wave of Lithuanian immigrants had started to trickle into the old neighborhood after Gorbachev and his glasnost. They reminded her of her own family when they came to America. *Sajudis* was stirring talk of freedom in Lithuania, while Solidarity was doing the same in Poland. After all this time there was a glimmer of hope for freedom for Lithuania. But if by some miracle her country regained its independence from Russia, it would still be too late for Agota to return to her birthplace. Her life was almost over. More than half of it had been spent in this house on Talman Street.

She had never thought that this was where she would end her life, where she would be buried, so far away from her birthplace in Lithuania.

Ever since Pranas died, it was the loneliness of old age that she hated most. Daydreams filled her head of what her life might have been had she remained in her village with the company of those she had grown up with. How strange that the whole direction of your life could change in an instant. Ah, what's the use of old regrets? she chided herself.

⸻

Out her window, Agota could see Odell Givens, who used to sing the blues on her cookie line at Nabisco, crossing the street. She had recently moved into Ema Bartulis' old house—that sad house where her daughter, Vida, grew up motherless. The doorbell rang and Agota opened the front door to greet the gray-haired woman, who hadn't bothered to take off her flowered cotton apron to visit her neighbor. Odell had grown old and heavy since their days at Nabisco, with several folds on her neck holding up her chin.

"Well, good morning, honey, did I wake you?" asked Odell.

"No, no, of course not, welcome to my home." Agota nodded primly. She disliked the easy familiarity of Americans and had never gotten used to acquaintances calling her "honey" or "sweetie."

Odell shifted her bulk from foot to foot like a listing boat. Both women smiled politely for a few uncomfortable seconds, and then Odell came into the house.

"You know, don't you, that I moved into the house across the street about two weeks ago?"

"Of course, into Mrs. Bartulis' house. Remember, I brought you a box of candy and a tomato plant?"

"Oh, Lord, that's right." Odell laughed. "I swear I sometimes forget if I ate breakfast or not." She shook her head.

Agota smiled. "In my country they say that old age is no sweet roll."

"You're right about that. It ain't for sissies, is it?" Odell nodded. "How are your children?"

Agota smiled sadly. "My Ona got a divorce and moved back to Chicago with her daughter Amy. She teaches college on the North Side and wants me to move in with them, but I tell her that I'm used to my own home. And my Jonas has a house on the market for six months and no sale. He and Vida have no luck."

"Tell him to bury a small statue of Saint Joseph in the front yard. Make sure it's face down and toward the door."

Agota thought this sounded like some kind of voodoo.

"I'm telling you, works like a charm. Tried it myself. Learned it from a Polish lady at the factory."

Agota frowned. "Saint Joseph is a powerful saint."

"I guarantee he'll get an offer soon." Odell cleared her throat and shifted her weight for a few uncomfortable moments. Then she scratched her ear but wouldn't look Agota in the face. "And speaking of problems, I came to ask if you could help me with the one in my new house."

Agota's brow knit together. "Me? I know nothing about fixing houses. Get a carpenter."

"No, no, not that kind of a problem." Odell looked around the living room at the family photos, the crystal vase, the lace doilies, and the linen runner on the coffee table. "It's worse than that."

"Please sit down," Agota offered.

Odell sat down heavily on the slipcovered sofa. "My feet don't stop talking to me for a minute. And I can't take too much excitement because of my high blood pressure. My heart isn't strong anymore. You know I'm living with my daughter, Betty and my grandson, Darrell, a good boy. I want to make sure he stays out of trouble, keeps away from the gangs, but the world has become a dangerous place, not like when we were growing up, ain't that right?" Odell said nothing for a moment, and then she frowned and looked sideways at Agota.

Agota had forgotten how much Odell liked to talk, how she could go on and on, spilling out words from her generous mouth. She was known as the "clattering pan" on the cookie line. And whenever she finally stopped talking, she would sing those Billie Holiday songs so often that even Agota learned the words to "Gloomy Sunday" by heart.

"What year did you come from that old country?" asked Odell.

"1950."

"Same as me, I came from Alabama in the 50s looking for factory work. I was part of the Great Migration. Seven million of us left the South and now we're pushing into Marquette Park." She smiled broadly. "Only took a year out to have Betty. She's a good girl, works as a teaching assistant, going to school to become a teacher. Still goes to church with me on Sunday."

"Nativity?"

"No, Trinity Baptist on Damen. Used to be some Lutheran church. But I didn't come here to talk about churches. I need some help. I even had Reverend Williams come over, but he couldn't do anything with that spirit. She just kept right on talking her talk, you know?"

"No, what do you mean?"

"Well, there's a woman ghost in that house, and I can't understand a word she's saying. I thought that maybe she was, you know, Lutherainian."

"Lithuanian or Lutheran? I'm Catholic."

"Well, never mind. Anyway, I figure you might understand what that ghost is saying. I don't know what else to do. We're all scared to death. Thought you could help us."

"A ghost?" Agota's face puckered. "Please, what can I do?" She was uncomfortable.

"Honey, if you could just talk to her, find out why she's there. Maybe then we'd know what to do because, I tell you honestly, my nerves have just about had it."

"Oh, I can't help you." Agota wished Odell would just stand up and go home.

"Now, listen, you don't have to do a thing," pleaded Odell, grabbing Agota's hand. "Just listen to her. Just come over for dinner tonight? She always comes to the kitchen at dinnertime. Please come, just this once."

Agota didn't want to go to dinner to meet a spirit who spoke Lithuanian. She just wanted to shut the door behind this large black woman and pretend she had never had this conversation. But she was too polite to refuse her. "What time?"

"Six. She always comes around that time. You like barbecue chicken?"

Agota nodded politely, feeling angry with herself for not saying she was busy.

Odell looked relieved. "Thank you, you're our last chance," she said, pushing herself up from the sofa. "If this doesn't work, I'm putting the house up for sale. I'm not living with ghosts, no sir."

———————

That evening Agota put on her favorite navy dress, pinned an amber brooch on the collar, hung a gold cross on her neck, and tucked her rosary and her favorite holy card of Saint Jude in her purse. Her navy low-heeled pumps squeezed her bunions as she walked across the street for dinner, dressed as if she were going to the Lithuanian opera. Odell led Agota to her backyard, where her daughter was grilling chicken and her grandson was shooting baskets in the driveway. Agota was introduced and seated at the redwood picnic table.

"We don't eat inside no more," said Odell as she nervously turned a plastic fork over and over. When Agota raised her eyebrows in question, Odell shook her head. "Honey, we don't set foot in that kitchen during dinnertime. I make everything ahead of time and then we hightail it out of there. Here, try some of my corn bread. Chicken's almost ready."

Agota chewed the crumbly yellow bread, thinking how dry it was. The chicken tasted good but a bit burned and the greens were bitter, but she liked the black-eyed peas. Both Betty and Darrell ate quickly, looking as if they wanted to get away as fast as they could. Soon Betty got up, excusing herself.

"Girl, where you going?" Odell shot her question out.

"Night school, Mama." Betty looked sideways at Agota.

"Oh, yeah, sorry, sugar. I guess it's my nerves," said Odell, pushing her bulk up from the table and watching her daughter disappear down the gangway to the street. Darrell slipped out behind her with a wave, his basketball tucked under his arm. "Agota, we better go have our dessert in the kitchen."

"With the ghost?" Agota felt her skin prickle at the idea.

"I don't wanna go either, but how else you gonna hear what she wants?"

Agota wanted to spit three times to ward off the evil eye or any other bit of bad luck that lurked nearby. Touching the cross on her neck, she asked Odell, "You're coming too, aren't you?"

Odell took the hanky out of her apron pocket and blew her nose. "I am, though, God knows, I'd like to stay out here with the lightning bugs." The two women reluctantly climbed the five stairs that led to the small kitchen. "Cookies or ice cream?" asked Odell.

"Ice cream." Agota looked around the cramped kitchen, sitting uneasily at the round table by the back door, while Odell brought out some vanilla ice cream. "You know, ever since we worked at Nabisco, I can't stand cookies no more. Maybe I ate too many while I was there."

"I don't like them either." Agota sat wondering when it would be polite to go home, but then she felt a shivering and a tingling up her spine. She looked around and saw nothing, but thought she heard the faint humming of "Blue Tango." Agota had always liked this tango. It reminded her of her youth.

Suddenly, Odell dropped the ice-cream container. "Lord, that song scares me half to death. It always starts with that same old tune." She stood wide-eyed by the open refrigerator. Agota stooped to pick up the fallen ice-cream container, and when she got up, she saw a gossamer version of Ema Bartulis tango into the room, long hair falling in waves down one side and a Gypsy scarf around her hips.

"Oh-oh, I'm outta here." Odell opened the screen door and let it slam behind her. "Yell if you need help, but I'll be damned if I'd know what to do." Odell stumbled down the steps and fell into the redwood chair. "Oh, my heart is racing. Tell her to go haunt some-one else," she yelled from the backyard.

Agota felt a tingle of fear run down her spine. She blessed herself and asked the angels and saints to protect her in case this was an evil spirit. Then, taking a deep breath, she asked in Lithuanian, "Ema, why are you still here in your old house? You should leave these poor people alone. You're frightening them." Agota's heart was in her throat.

"What are these strangers doing in my house?" said the shimmering vision. "Tell them to leave. Who are those Negroes anyway?"

"They live here, Ema."

"But this is my house. I live here. Tell them to go."

"Ema, that was long ago; it's been many years since you lived here."

"It has?" Ema looked confused. "Who are you?"

"Agota Janulis from across the street."

"Agota!" The ghost's face lit up like Easter Sunday. She sat down at the kitchen table with her old friend as if it were 1950 and she had never died. "Agota, how you've aged. I didn't recognize you."

"I got old Ema, not like you."

Ema's face dropped and her chin quivered as if she were about to cry. "I died too young, Agota. It wasn't fair. I was so full of life, music, tangos."

"No, it wasn't fair," Agota agreed.

"And that stupid husband of mine—the critic—is he still alive?"

"Yes, he is."

"Why did I die so young? Was I a bad woman? No, it was my husband who should have died young. Then, what a time Vida and I would have had without his angry looks and lectures! We would have made Napoleon cake every night." Once again Ema looked stricken. "How's my little girl? I haven't seen her in such a long time. I miss her so. When I died she was so little. How could I leave her alone?" Ema looked out the window, as if she would see her daughter still playing in the backyard. "My poor little Vida used to come sit on my grave and pretend it was my lap, bringing doughnuts, ribbons, and pictures she'd drawn for me." Ema looked back over her shoulder. "She doesn't come to my grave anymore, so I came looking for her. You don't know how lonely it is for a soul to be stuck here on earth after death. But I'm a stubborn Samogitian. I refused to leave out of sheer terror that my Vida would have to grow up with my husband."

"Your brother, Apolinaras, came to look after her for as long as he could stand your husband."

"I saw him at my grave."

"You know, don't you, that your Vida married my Jonas and they have two children, one named after you."

Ema looked surprised. "Really? After me?" Ema stared off into the distance, her face glowing happily. "Imagine, my little girl is already a mother. I have grandchildren." The ephemeral Ema held her hands together as if in prayer. "She hasn't forgotten me?"

"No, of course not." Agota wanted to pat Ema's hand to reassure her, but she stopped herself in mid-air and pulled her hand back to her lap.

Ema's face hadn't aged in forty years, and Agota realized that Vida now looked older than her mother. "Why have you returned like those revenants in our villages?"

Ema laughed like the tinkle of a small bell. "Ha, my dear, you've forgotten that the world is filled with spirits. So many forgotten and lonely spirits waiting at their graves for loved ones to visit them, to pray for them. They're all around, and let me tell you that they're not all kind either!"

Agota suddenly remembered a year when she was a girl and her *Teta* Kotryna brought home a *domovoi* from Russia. That trickster took up residence in their pantry and wouldn't leave until her grandmother finally banished it to the marshes where all evil spirits lived. Her grandmother knew more about these old ways than she did. Agota no longer thought America had no spirit life.

"Why aren't you resting in peace? What do you want, Ema?" asked Agota.

"I want to see my Vida again, to make sure she's all right." Ema looked as if she'd cry soon. "Please, can you help me, Agota?"

"See Vida again?" Agota sighed deeply, wondering how she had gotten herself into this mess. "I'll try."

"Bless you, Agota, I'll wait here." With those words, Agota saw Ema dissolve into the ether. She sat there, too stunned to move or say anything until she heard Odell yelling to her from the backyard. "Is she still there?"

Agota put the melting ice cream back into the freezer and went outside. Odell was sitting in the redwood chair surrounded by lightning bugs winking happily in the starlit night. For a moment it looked as if Odell were a ghostly apparition in the garden. "No, I'm afraid she's gone."

"I'm afraid, too. Who was she and what did she want? I heard you two gabbing that foreign talk like you were old friends."

"It was Ema Bartulis." Agota suddenly felt so tired that she wondered if she had the strength to cross the street and climb the stairs of her house.

"Well? What did she want?"

"To see her daughter again."

"Daughter?"

"And she's still angry at her husband after all these years."

"Man trouble. Women always got man trouble. Well, I can understand that, honey. I had some too. Wouldn't mind coming back to scare the daylights out of one or two myself." Odell chuckled and stood up to take Agota's arm. "Come on, I'll walk you home." The two women waddled arm-in-arm across the street, and Agota was touched by this gesture of solicitude.

"Listen, don't put your house up for sale yet, Odell. I think Ema will rest in peace after she sees my daughter-in-law, Vida."

"What? This is your family's ghost? Then tell me why the hell isn't she at your house? Why is she bothering my family? We don't even speak her damn language." Odell had both her hands on her hips, infused with a righteous indignation.

"She used to live here. It was her house."

"Oh, Lord help us! I don't know how we got into this mess,

but Lord get us out." Odell prayed to the dark heavens and the pale sliver of a moon. "One week, Lord, I'll give you one week to rid our house of this ghost. If she's still here next week, we're moving in with my sister, Hortense."

Agota thought it was unseemly to threaten God that way. It was asking for trouble, in her opinion. She unlocked the front door and turned on the light. "Thank you for dinner, Odell." Agota burped and realized that the barbecue chicken had given her heartburn. She patted her chest daintily. "I must make some potato *kugelis* for you to try."

That next evening, Agota invited Vida and Jonas over to break the news to her daughter-in-law that she had just seen her long-dead mother, but no matter how many times she tried to broach the subject, she just didn't know where to begin. From the way Vida was looking at her, she knew she must be acting very strangely. Agota gave them a statue of Saint Joseph and told them to bury it in their yard in order to sell their house. And then, after much stuttering hesitation, Agota finally blurted out the news about Vida's mother.

"You're joking." Vida sat there wide-eyed, looking at her mother-in-law as if she were suffering from dementia. Agota assured them that she was not joking, nor was she losing her mind. "It was your mother all right, still in her old house across the street, and she asked to see you." Vida sat there totally dumbfounded and in shock. In truth, Vida had never gotten over losing her mother. For a long time she didn't say anything, lost in her own thoughts, but finally she looked up, eyes brimming with unspilled tears. "I can't believe it."

In the end, it took two days of calls by Agota and three phone calls from Odell to finally persuade Vida to return to her childhood home.

On Friday night, Vida stood in front of her old home in such a state of sadness, mixed with anxiety, that she faltered on the very first step. Agota held her up, giving both physical and moral support. The thought of seeing a ghost terrified her, but this ghost was her beloved mother, who had asked for her. How could she refuse her?

Odell opened the door and showed Vida and Agota into the kitchen. Vida looked around, studying the details of the house that she remembered. The furniture had changed, but it was still the same house with the same rooms. Odell put a plate of cookies on the table and went to join her daughter outside. Vida looked around nervously, and neither woman touched the cookies.

As soon as Vida heard the distant humming of "Blue Tango," her mouth dropped, too stunned to speak. She looked around and then crumpled onto the table in tears. Agota gave her an embroidered handkerchief she kept in her pocket. "There, there, dear, don't cry."

The ethereal Ema Bartulis danced into the room and went to look at Vida slumped on the table. "Is that you, my little Gypsy?"

When Vida raised her head, her mother peered into her face, studying her features. "Oh, my little girl, you've changed so much. So grown up. You look a little like my mother."

"Mama." Vida's voice sounded like a child's. "Is it really you?" Vida laughed through her tears. "I've missed you so much, Mama."

"Not half as much as I've missed you, child." She patted Vida's hair, but her hand seemed to disappear. "How are you? Tell me everything. Did you bring photographs of my grandchildren?"

Agota sat in amazement as the two women visited, heads together, crying and talking as if no time had passed since they had last seen each other. Vida told her mother about her life, her husband, and her children. Her mother wanted to know why she had gained so much weight.

"I keep trying to make your Napoleon cake, but it never turns out like yours. What's your secret, Mama?"

"Cognac. VSOP."

"Do you drink it or put it in the cake?" Vida laughed.

Her mother gave her the secret recipe and asked her to make it and bring it to her grave. "Have a picnic on my grave like the old days, light a candle, bring your family. And put one of those Jesus the Worrier statues on my grave to let him worry over my family so that I can rest in peace. You know the wooden statues of a sad Jesus sitting, leaning his head on his hand, as if saying, 'Ayayay, what a world.'"

"Mama, I used to visit your grave every day. I used to tell Papa I was going to school, but I would go to the cemetery instead and sit with you."

"I remember, my Gypsy girl. I was so happy when you came, but then you stopped. Why?"

Vida hesitated and then her voice dropped, "It was because of Mr. George."

"Mr. George?"

"Yes, I want Mr. George's thing to shrivel up. Can you arrange that?"

"Thing?"

Vida pointed a finger between her legs. She felt embarrassed. "You know, that thing men have down there."

"Vida, don't be crude." She started to laugh. "But why, dear?"

"He touched us, Mama. Me and Irene." Vida told her mother how the boarder had molested her and her friend. "It was awful, Mama."

"My poor baby. Why, I'll not only shrivel his thing, I'll...I'll cover him with boils that will burn. That louse, I'll show him what it means to touch innocent children. May his eyes rot in his head. May his tongue no longer fit in his mouth." Ema Bartulis was quiet for a long time. "What about your father? Did he know about this?"

Vida shrugged. "I don't think so."

"You tell your father I want a word with him, will you?" The light surrounding Ema blazed brightly, fueled by a righteous anger. "I want to give him a piece of my mind. Tell him to come here, or he won't like it if I have to go look for him." The glow flared up like flames around her. "And don't you worry, my dear daughter, I'll take care of that Mr. George. There's no hell to pay like a mother's anger."

It took several days for Vida to gather the courage to talk to her father, who was living in the Holy Family Villa retirement home. At first, when she told him about her mother, he refused outright, saying he had a weak heart, but afterwards his dreams were troubled—each night his avenging wife came to him like some Valkyrie. Finally, after several sleepless nights, he called his daughter to say he was coming.

For this occasion, Agota put on a simple gray dress and wore her flats. The afternoon was blustery by the time Mr. Bartulis finally arrived in a taxi, so he held on to his hat as he climbed the stairs. Agota was surprised to see how he had changed over the years—old, bent, and frightened beyond words to face his dead wife. His hands shook and his blood pressure rose as he reached the door of his old house on Talman Street.

Odell greeted them and showed them into the kitchen. She felt like her new home was turning into a social hall for Lithuanians—living, half-living, and dead.

It didn't take long for them to hear the soft humming of "Blue Tango." Mr. Bartulis stood by the door and wouldn't sit down. The man seemed to shrink into himself as he licked his dry lips and his fingers drummed nervously against the door, his eyes darting around the room. Agota had warned him that it would all start with the tango. He wanted to call his wife's name, but his throat was so dry his voice cracked. A vision of tiny lights appeared and gathered itself into his young wife, dancing a sultry tango.

"Lord, have mercy on me," whispered Mr. Bartulis.

Odell got up from the table as if she was getting used to these strange visions. "I'll let you family members visit while I go collect my thoughts in the backyard." When she opened the door, a violent wind rose, sending leaves flying into the kitchen. The door abruptly slammed shut, imprisoning her skirt. Odell shrieked as though it was her last hour. "Oh my God, she's got me," she screamed, tugging at her skirt for dear life.

The ghostly Ema came to her aid, attempting to open the door, but it was stuck shut. Then she tried to help Odell, tugging on the skirt until it ripped. Odell's eyes widened. "Is she trying to kill me? Tell her to stop."

Across the room, Agota hid her smile with her hand, watching this comical scene. "She's only trying to help you, Odell."

With outraged dignity, Odell finally managed to tear her skirt out of the door, but she lost her balance and tripped over a chair leg, falling heavily. "Ow," she bellowed as Agota tried to help her up.

"Oh dear," said Agota. "Are you all right?"

"No, damn it, I'm not all right." Odell rubbed her knees. "I'm going to have two big bruises on my knees and, look, I've skinned my hand. You tell that woman to leave me alone. She may be a ghost but she ain't seen nothing until she's seen me get mad."

Agota tried to control herself but couldn't. She collapsed into giggles, which she tried to stifle.

Odell's head whipped around. "What's so funny?" she asked, casting an irritated look at her neighbor. "You better not be laughing at me."

"No, no," Agota shook her head, but couldn't stop laughing. "Ema said you scared her."

"I scared her!" Odell was steaming mad.

"Yes, she said you fell so hard that the whole room shook and she thought it was an earthquake." Agota shrieked with laughter. "An earthquake," she repeated weakly, "right here on Talman Street."

Odell's mouth twisted into a half smile. "This damn ghost thinks she's a comedian." Odell shoved her kitchen chair back. "Tell her I'm going to get Rubina from Haiti in here to work her hoodoo and send her to zombie land." The fact that Odell didn't know anybody from Haiti didn't stop her bluff.

"Wait!" cautioned Agota. "Ema says she's very sorry that you hurt yourself. She asks that you please not tell your friend Rubina."

Odell walked to the door and yanked it open. "All right then, but tell her I'm getting mighty burned up about all this. Tell her to holler at her husband and get this over with before this storm comes in. I don't like sitting out in the rain."

Agota had almost forgotten about Mr. Bartulis in all the commotion. She looked at the old man, who was cowering in the corner, ashen with fear.

"My husband?" Ema turned her gaze to him. "This little feeble old man is my husband?"

Mr. Bartulis blessed himself. "Yes, Ema, it's me, dearest." His voice was shaky.

"Oh, so now I'm your dearest. Before I couldn't do one thing right; your harsh words followed me as Vida and I quaked in fear of you." Her eyes bore into him like the Angel of Death.

He fell to his knees. "Forgive me, dearest, my most precious, my holy wife. I was wrong to be so harsh. You were so full of life that I thought I'd lose you to someone else unless I reined you in. But I lost you anyway. Forgive me, please."

"Forgive you?" Ema stood looking at him, not saying anything. She had carried her anger to her grave, but now, here was this broken old man on his knees, begging her forgiveness.

"What about Mr. George?" she demanded. "Where is that horrible friend of yours?"

"He moved to Cleveland. Why?"

Ema told her husband about the molestation. Her husband listened as long as he could until he broke down sobbing. "I'm so sorry. I didn't know."

"Don't worry. I'm going to find this Mr. George and make his life a living hell. Shrink his thing like a shriveled string bean."

Mr. Bartulis gulped and felt his privates pucker. He could only stare at his wife in awe. "You are quite a woman, Ema. I've always thought so."

"Well then, dance the tango with me and maybe I'll consider forgiving you, old man."

He took a deep breath and held out his hand. Ema began to hum "Blue Tango," and she twirled and dipped before she took his hand. Her voice rose and she sang the words with feeling as they danced around the kitchen to the old remembered steps and flourishes.

Odell sat out in the backyard listening to Ema's song, hoping they'd hurry and get this over with. She knew white folks were strange, but these Lithuanians were stranger than most. She had a headache, her knees hurt, and a storm was headed their way. Agota came out to join her, and the two women kept a quiet vigil in the backyard with the distant lightning flashing over the rooftops and the wind blowing the trees in a wild dance of their own.

That night Ema Bartulis left Odell's house, and once Vida made the Napoleon cake and brought it to her grave for a picnic, her mother went to Cleveland to look for Mr. George. Odell was so thrilled to have the first quiet night in her home that she went across the street to kiss a startled Agota on both cheeks. "You're a miracle worker, you are!"

The next evening Agota brought over her famous *kugelis* to Odell's to celebrate, telling her it must be eaten with plenty of sour cream. "Honey," Odell made a face and grunted. "I don't know what in God's name, that dish is, but I'll tell you something right here and now. I can't stand no sour cream. I don't know how folks can eat that nasty stuff."

Odell put it on the redwood table and asked Agota to serve the potato casserole. Darrell came over to taste it and smiled sheepishly as he reached for the ketchup. Agota watched him, horrified, but said nothing. Odell followed his example.

As was proper, Agota spooned sour cream on her *kugelis*. "I got a statue of Saint Joseph for Jonas and he buried it in the front yard like you told me, but so far, no offer."

"Well, you wait and see." Odell seemed so sure of this remedy. She poured some beer, and the women toasted Ema Bartulis, proclaiming, "May she rest in peace." Odell wasn't so sure that Ema's ghost had gone for good, so she waited each night but no one appeared, and she never heard "Blue Tango" again as long as she lived.

The next day Jonas and Vida received an offer on their house and accepted it.

Agota marveled at the mystery of life and death and wondered if she would roam the earth after her death. Some evenings she would look around the room carefully, fully expecting to see her dead husband or her long-gone parents. Now that she knew that the very air she breathed was filled with spirits, she felt less lonely. Sometimes she even found herself in snatches of conversation with them.

Now and again Agota and Odell paid each other a visit. Sometimes, when the women sat companionably talking in Agota's front room and a loud boom box passed by on the street, they would both part the nylon curtains and cluck their tongues in disapproval. And sometimes, on balmy summer evenings, they just sat in Odell's backyard not saying much, just watching the lightning bugs blinking around them like tiny spirits.

Homecoming

Al Vitkus, 1991

A l Vitkus had reluctantly agreed to fly to Lithuania with his
mother and Magda. Though he'd spent his life hearing stories
about the old country, he had never really expected to see it. But
now, after almost fifty years of Russian occupation and separation
from the rest of the world, Lithuania was finally free again. The Ber-
lin Wall had fallen, and the Iron Curtain had lifted at last.

The Finn Air jet was filled with a tour group of Lithuanian-
Americans from Chicago. They were returning to visit their homeland like a disoriented flock following some genetic flyway to return
to their natal nests. Al, however, had mutated into some new thing,
no longer completely at home anywhere. The only reason he had
agreed to this trip was to accompany Magda and his recently widowed mother, who didn't want to make the trip alone. She was eager
to reunite with the sister she hadn't seen since the war.

Flying over the Baltic Sea, Al started to feel a mixture of apprehension and curiosity about Lithuania and the relatives he had
never met. As the plane began its descent into Vilnius, the group of
Chicago Lithuanians began cheering. Elena and Bronius Lankutis
both whooped for joy, which woke their young daughter. Agota
Janulis hugged her granddaughter, Amy, as she pointed to the spires

of the old city. Felius the Poet toasted the occasion with Valentinas Gediminas, lifting glasses to their homecoming. Then Felius began loudly reciting his latest poem, written en route. "My beloved motherland, your sons and daughters are returning to you at last..." When he finished, Silvia and Captain Eddie started to sing the long-forbidden Lithuanian anthem, and soon others joined in, tears flowing as they sang. Al twisted around to look at his fellow passengers, feeling like he was back at the Amber Tavern with all the regulars. Shifting uncomfortably, he whispered, "Motherland" hesitantly and found himself wondering how the White Sox were doing, suddenly longing to be back home with a cold beer, watching a game. Since Vietnam, he no longer liked to travel, and if he did travel, Lithuania would not be his chosen destination. Maybe Florida or Hawaii, or even California if he had to go someplace, but not the old country.

When the plane finally landed in this forgotten corner of the world, everyone descended the stairs and headed toward customs. Outside, a large group of friends and relatives waited behind a chain-link fence, holding armloads of flowers. A group of old men, wearing their college caps, held a sign for Felius the Poet reading: "Class of 1939 Welcomes Felius." Valentinas Gediminas knelt down to kiss the tarmac while Silvia broke from her husband Captain Eddie and ran to the fence, sobbing. "Mama, Mama." Her mother reached out to her daughter through the fence, "Oh, my child, my child," she said in a trembling voice.

Agota Janulis spotted her brother, Viktoras, and stopped for a moment, shocked to see how much he had aged in the years since she'd last seen him, before the world erupted into chaos. "Agota," he yelled through the fence to his sister, "you're home at last! I've waited so long for you." Al's mother, Regina Vitkus, watched these scenes, choked with emotion as she looked around for her sister, Violeta. She couldn't see her anywhere and began to fret to Al that she might not recognize Violeta after so many years.

After they got through customs, Regina heard her name called and turned in every direction, seeing families tearfully reunited. Magda was standing alone, flapping her hands the way she sometimes did. Al came over to take his sister's hand in an effort to calm her.

Suddenly Regina's arms were filled with red carnations as a plump old woman hugged her. It was Violeta, the sister she had last seen in her twenties. Regina held her tightly, shutting her eyes to keep in her tears, afraid that if she started crying, she wouldn't stop.

Violeta finally pulled back to get a good look at her sister. "Regina, how did you get so old?" she teased, shaking her head and shrugging. "My God, can I possibly be that old? I don't believe it."

Regina smiled, though her chin quivered with emotion. "But Violeta, you're older by three years!"

"Then life must be hard in Chicago," said Violeta, laughing as tears rolled down her cheeks like peas.

"And you lived the life of the manor, I suppose?" Regina played the familiar teasing game from their childhood.

"Must have," Violeta laughed, patting her gray hair coquettishly, "since I look so much younger."

Regina kissed her sister on both cheeks, so glad to be with her again, so filled with gratitude that her emotions finally gave way like a flood. Violeta held her, patting her gray hair and kissing her wrinkled cheeks until she calmed a bit. Then Violeta introduced her son, Linas, to Magda and Al. "Come, let's get your luggage," said the tall, lanky man in his forties. "You must be tired after such a long flight."

"I was tired until I saw you, Violeta. Now I feel reborn," Regina said, not letting go of her sister's hand.

Violeta lived in a tiny three-room apartment in one of the ubiquitous concrete apartment buildings that stood like giant tombstones in every former Soviet city. Her two grown sons and their families managed to squeeze into the crowded living room. A tablecloth was put on the cocktail table, and plates of veal roulade and open-faced ham sandwiches with cucumbers and tomatoes sprinkled with fresh dill were brought to the table. Al wondered how long his aunt had had to stand in food lines for this small feast. As Linas opened a bottle of champagne for the homecoming, filling everyone's glass, Al marveled that all of these strangers looked so much like family. Coming from a multicultural Chicago, he was amazed to see a city where everyone looked so Lithuanian, as if they could all be his relatives. In Chicago, so few Lithuanians had extended families. He had never given it much thought until he arrived here to find so many relatives who looked like his own small family.

Regina told them about Chicago, the stockyards, and her job at the Kool-Aid factory. No one had heard of Kool-Aid, so Regina went to her luggage and pulled out envelopes of the strawberry-flavored powder. She ripped one open, and everyone dipped a finger in and tasted the red powder. Violeta wrinkled her nose. "Smells good," she laughed, "but so sour it makes my uterus contract."

Linas raised his glass to toast the American branch of the family.

Regina frowned. "What do you mean, 'American'? We're Lithuanian also." This annoyed her.

Al wasn't so sure. "I was born in a DP camp after the war. What does that make me?"

"Don't worry," said Violeta raising her glass, "we'll take you DPs back. You won't have to wander the world anymore." Violeta had meant it as a joke but everyone looked so stricken that she regretted it. "A toast to the return of our family."

"You know," Al said, "in Chicago I grew up feeling so Lithuanian, even though I had never seen it, but my parents had talked about it so much that I used to yearn for my homeland. But strangely enough, now that I'm actually here in Vilnius I feel so American." That struck Al as funny until he saw everyone nodding and smiling sadly as if they felt sorry for him, as if life had played a dirty trick on him and now his family was cursed to be Chicagoans. One of the lost tribes. Al suddenly had that trapped feeling, like he'd like to call a friend back home, or maybe order a pizza. These were his blood relatives but they felt so Eastern Bloc, as if they had lived in a time warp, which, when he thought about it, they had—fifty years of isolation from the rest of the world.

He decided not to say any more. He sat back on the sofa and Magda leaned against his shoulder.

All his life, kids at school had given him a hard time about his accent, his clothes, and his strange school lunches. His parents wouldn't let him speak English at home, afraid he'd forget Lithuanian and not be able to fit in once they returned to the homeland. Al had never wanted to return, striving instead to become as American as he could. Now he realized how well he had succeeded. He was American through and through. Lithuania had regained its independence, but it was too late for his generation. Being here made him feel like a displaced person again.

Everyone drank and ate, and Regina told her sister how terrible the war had been for her family as they fled the oncoming Soviet Army. "We were so afraid of getting caught by the Soviets and killed or deported, or of my Jurgis getting taken by the Germans to the forced-labor camps, but the real tragedy for us was Magda. Allied bombs rained down on us until one hit near where we were hiding, burying Magda." Everyone turned to look at Magda, who hid behind Al's shoulder.

Violeta listened and nodded quietly, saying nothing for a few moments. "The war was terrible for us as well, but the post-war period was even worse, as the Soviets covered Eastern Europe like a shroud. The deportations to the Siberian gulags started up again—young men joined the partisan resistance rather than join the Soviet Army and fought a brave but futile war. The villages were emptied into collective farms. We were constantly watched by Soviet agents. One wrong move could get you deported. Russians moved into the homes left by those who had run away to the West. My husband, Simas, helped the anti-Soviet partisans and was arrested in 1952 and sent to a work camp in Arkhangelsk, Siberia. He suffered from the cold, hunger, and harshness of those conditions, may he rest in peace," she said, putting her face into her hands, trying to erase the thoughts.

⸻⸻◆◆◆⸻⸻

The next morning, a gray mist rose to cover the city, as Linas drove a borrowed Moskvitch to the outskirts of Vilnius, past Soviet-style apartment buildings. To Al, this was a grim landscape, as ugly and anonymous as any projects in the heart of Chicago. The rivers looked polluted; the stores looked empty. The Soviets had ruined the country. Regina was heartsick at the changes, seeing nothing she could recognize until in the distance she saw the familiar spires of the medieval old town of Vilnius. She rejoiced at finding the cathedral, the thirteenth-century castle of the Grand Duke Gediminas, and Vilnius University. When they strolled through the narrow winding streets of the medieval heart of Vilnius, Al saw the street that used to be called the Street of Jews. He realized that they were walking through what had once been the Vilnius Ghetto, where Jews had been brought during the war. He asked his cousin where the ghetto had been, but Linas didn't know. He stopped and asked at the shops, but they didn't know either. There were no memorial plaques, no commemorative sculpture—only small shops full of everyday items. His cousin told him that the history of what had happened to the Jews had been suppressed by the Soviets. Then down the street, he saw a group of teenagers in shorts, with Israeli flags on their backpacks. He went over to talk to the leader, who told him the students were there for a summer camp outside the city. They were spending their summer researching the archives to learn what had happened in the Jewish quarter during the war. Al shook the man's hand and wished him well. When he told his aunt, she said that there were plans to reopen the Vilnius synagogue and the Yiddish Theater. It pleased Al that their tragic stories would be researched and told.

Afterward, they drove to the Parliament Building, still barricaded on all sides with broken slabs of concrete to protect it from the Soviet tanks. Al and his parents had watched CNN as Soviet tanks had rolled into Vilnius in January 1991. People had stood outside in the freezing snow around the clock as human shields to protect the TV tower from the Special Forces flown in to take control of the media networks. The tanks had opened fire, killing peaceful demonstrators. Half a world away, in Chicago, Al's father had watched this on the news and taken it hard, angry tears gathering. Lithuania had declared its independence almost a year earlier in March 1990, the first of fourteen Soviet Republics to attempt this. His father had been waiting for this new declaration of independence ever since 1944. After that, even though independent Lithuania had been erased from the maps of the world, he still waited, but not long enough. Two months after the Soviet tanks rolled back out of Vilnius, his father died a quiet death in his sleep, having never seen his homeland again.

Near the Parliament, a group of school children had left notes of condolence for those who had died or were injured during those clashes, sticking their letters onto the barbed wire on the barricades in front of the Parliament Building. Three old women in babushkas lit votive candles and sang long-forbidden songs in thin, quivering voices. As Regina put roses at the makeshift memorial, she felt the weight of history that had rolled over their lives, blindly like tanks.

Later, as they were walking back to the car, Al thought he spotted someone familiar. She was standing near the barricades with an older man, reading the school children's letters. Al called his mother over. "Mama, could that be Mr. Matas standing over there?"

His mother took a few a steps closer. "Yes, I think it is. Let's say hello." Regina walked toward Mr. Matas, telling her sister about this neighbor from Chicago, while Al stood rooted to the spot, trying to work up the courage to go. Could that be Irene? Her dishwater-blond hair was sun-streaked and long, but he'd know that face anywhere, even though he hadn't seen her in years. He stood watching his mother greet Mr. Matas, when suddenly Irene turned to look for him. Surprised by the strength of his emotions, he wanted to run and hold her, yet he stood rooted to the spot. Until this moment, he hadn't realized how much he still cared for her. He thought he had gotten over her long ago. After all, Irene had moved away, had married someone else. Now here she was, older but still so like his old Irene that he found himself overwhelmed with longing. Taking a deep breath, he told himself what an idiot he was, that this was not a big deal. He smiled as she slowly walked over to him, her smile spreading.

"Al, I can't believe it," she said, hugging him warmly. "I never expected to find you in Lithuania."

"Irene, what are the chances of running into each other in Vilnius?" He swallowed hard, trying to tamp down his rising emotions.

"I came with my dad. He wanted to return to his grandfather's farm where he used to summer as a child. You know, it's strange. The minute I saw that farm I felt like such a Chicago city girl, but at the same time I felt so at home there with the cows lowing softly, the goats bleating." She laughed. "I felt as if I could move in and happily raise my son there." The wind blew her long hair over her face, and she pushed it away.

"I see your mom had the same idea." Irene smiled as she looked over at his mother.

"She wanted to see her sister again." He studied her face to see what had changed. Her eyes seemed more serious. She had always been so ready to laugh and have fun, but now she seemed quieter and more thoughtful. "It's been a long time, Irene."

"It's great to see you, Al." Irene touched his arm briefly. "It's been years."

Al couldn't stop smiling. "Yeah, really great," he repeated, drinking in her face.

Irene's smile had always warmed him. "Funny to finally see you here," she said. "I couldn't run into you on Michigan Avenue or something?" Irene stepped back to take a good look at him. He was wearing khakis and a blue oxford shirt, and his brown hair was shorter. "God, you look better than ever."

"Thanks, you always look great." Irene was wearing a summer dress with a sweater over her shoulders. "How are you?"

"How am I?" Irene laughed quietly. "Let's see, you got a couple of months to listen to my sad litany?" She looked away, toward her dad. "Listen, do you think we could get away from our families for a cup of coffee or a beer? I'd love to talk. There's a café over there." She pointed to a yellow building across the street. They walked over to Mr. Matas, and Al met Irene's five year old son, Nick, a bright-looking boy with blond hair. After clearing it with their families, they went off arm-in-arm to an old cellar that could have doubled as a bomb shelter. On the way, they passed another café and through the large windows

Irene was surprised to see Felius the Poet toasting a group of men. Al laughed. "We'll soon see the whole crowd from the Amber Tavern if we're not careful. I bet half of Sixty-Ninth Street is here."

As they sat in a dark nook, they noticed that all the waitresses were gathered in the back watching a telenovela from Mexico called *Los Ricos También Lloran,* Even the Rich Cry Tears, which everyone in Lithuania simply called Mariana, after the heroine. It seemed as if all of Vilnius was having its first glimpse of capitalism, and they were addicted. Irene said she had seen shop girls and waitresses, and even bartenders, watching Mariana's rags-to-riches story. It seemed campy to Al and Irene, who couldn't get a waitress to pull herself away from the televised melodrama long enough to bring them some coffee. Finally, one of the young waitresses turned around, annoyed that they were bothering them. "Wait, we just found out Mariana's pregnant." Only after the program finished did Al finally get someone to hand him two coffees and he brought them to the table himself.

Irene told him how she had been to Marquette Park before coming to Lithuania and how everyone had moved away but the poor old Lithuanians who couldn't afford it. "Our old neighborhood is gone," she said sadly. "Someday, we'll tell our grandchildren that there was once a place called Marquette Park, where all the Lithuanians fled after the war." She and Al talked about the neighborhood with the same nostalgia that their parents felt when talking about their lost homeland.

Al was amazed at how easy it was to talk to Irene as they caught up on each other's lives. She seemed to understand him effortlessly. He didn't have to explain himself the way he did to the other girls he had dated. As he sat across from his old love, he realized that he had been waiting for this moment for years.

"I've known you since I first came to America," said Irene. "Remember our old storefront and those Gypsies?"

Al nodded, laughing softly. "I used to think you were a scrawny nuisance."

Irene reminded him of the time he saved her from drowning in Miner's Lake at summer camp. She leaned over and kissed him on the cheek, thanking him. "I'm alive today because of you."

Al didn't say anything for a few moments, touched that she remembered that day.

Irene stirred her coffee. "Al, I wrote you two letters last year. Why didn't you answer them?"

He shrugged and folded his napkin into smaller and smaller squares, not looking into her eyes. "I didn't know what to say," he said honestly, but something inside ached.

When the waitress finally brought the bill over, Al took his wallet out and fumbled through it, looking for Lithuanian currency. As he pulled out a *litas,* a tattered photo fell out of his wallet. He tried to snatch it away quickly before Irene saw it, but it was too late. She stopped him and took it, examining it for a moment. It was so worn and stained that all that was left was her faded nineteen-year-old face, hair long and straight, eyes black with liner, staring straight into the camera with a sideways smile that hinted at amusement, but with warm eyes, obviously in love with the photographer. "I remember when you took this photo on my birthday." She smiled sadly and tried to straighten the creases. "Looks like it's been through hell."

Al shook his head, embarrassed that she had seen this relic. "I carried it all through the war."

"Why didn't you tell me?"

He raked his hand through his hair, wondering how much to say. "I was too raw then."

"Yes, I remember." Irene bit her lip. "You came back from Vietnam so angry, so quiet, and I thought that you no longer cared for me. It crushed me. I didn't want to be hurt."

Al shook his head and laughed softly. "You didn't want to be hurt." Al took a deep breath and ordered a brandy, asking her if she wanted one. She nodded. "Yeah, I was angry when I came back from Nam. You would have been too if you'd been there. You know, I still dream about it. I don't know how I got out alive but when I came back lame, I felt like an old man." He shook his head. "I'd seen too much." The waitress brought over the drinks. "Here's to love and war," he said and drank his down in one gulp.

"God," said Irene sipping her brandy, "why didn't we talk?"

"I couldn't." Al shook his head. "Maybe I was afraid."

"Afraid of what?" She touched his arm and he looked up.

Al swallowed hard. "Afraid to find out we had each changed too much to make a go of it." He looked deeply into her eyes. "Afraid to feel what I'm feeling right now," he heard himself say.

Irene took his hand. "Tell me."

"No, I don't want to be disappointed." He looked down at her hands.

"You won't be. I promise you." Her face looked so sweet as she spoke, more like the girl he remembered in grammar school, before the sixties catapulted them all into chaos.

As her words trailed off, Al realized how much he wanted her. When he looked up and saw the look in her eyes, he awkwardly leaned over the table and kissed her. "Well, I have to say this once and for all. The truth is that I still care for you, Irene, I always have." Al looked at her, letting the words settle in.

A solitary tear rolled slowly down her cheek. "I feel the same way about you, Al."

<hr />

Before they parted, Irene stopped at a kiosk that was selling amber souvenirs. She had spotted an amber heart, and she bought it for

Al. "See that dark streak running through it? Flawed like me." Irene smiled sadly. "Keep it and think of me until I see you in Chicago. I'm spending the whole summer there." Irene pressed the heart into his hand and kissed him softly. Al held her hand, afraid to let it go again, afraid that if he let it slip out of his, he would lose her once more.

She smiled and pulled away. "I'm not running away this time," she whispered as she walked away. Al watched her until she disappeared into the crowded street. "Thank you," he said quietly to the soft twilight. Holding the amber heart tightly in his hand, he walked away with the limp he'd brought back from the war.

The following day, Al's mother was eager to see her ancestral home and her village. Linas had borrowed a small former Soviet military minibus. It was old, and it rattled and sputtered, but it had room for all of them, even his seven-year-old daughter, Simona. Violeta warned her sister that so much had changed, and that she might not recognize her home, but Regina laughed at the idea.

"The villages are gone," warned her sister. "And the farms were bulldozed by the Soviets."

"Our land is still there, isn't it? Don't worry, I'll feel at home," said Regina. "Our birch woods are still there, aren't they?"

"Yes, of course," smiled Violeta, but she looked uncertain. "But first I want you to meet someone you once knew."

They drove to Kretinga, to the red brick church where Regina had been baptized and married. Regina wanted the priest to bless a cross she hoped to take to the Hill of Crosses. She walked into the dimly lit church that smelled of incense. Light filtered in through stained-glass windows and red votive candles flickered in ascending rows. Regina looked around and realized that the church was missing its statues. Only one broken statue of Mary stood in an alcove. Soon Violeta came in with a wizened old man with bright eyes and a stooped back. It was Father Jonaitis, who explained that this church, like so many, had been used as a warehouse during the Soviet era.

"You see the Communists finally gave me back my church, but they kept the statues. My only consolation is that those other statues are gone as well." The old priest looked around and saw that no one knew what he was talking about. "You know—the Lenins and Stalins are gone from the town squares, eh?" He wheezed a laugh.

Father Jonaitis had married Regina and Jurgis so many years ago. They talked warmly of times long gone, two remnants with more friends under the earth than walking on top of it. The old priest took a liking to Al and wanted to hear all about Chicago.

"Do you live near Al Capone?" the priest asked as they walked into the churchyard.

"No, he's long dead." Al laughed.

The priest nodded solemnly, on intimate terms with death.

Finally, they drove to the birch woods where Regina's village had been. When Linas stopped the minibus, Regina thought he must be mistaken, but her sister insisted that this was where they had been born and raised, even though when they looked around, there was nothing but an empty meadow. The gently rolling countryside stretched out before them and in the distance birch woods stood with white trunks gleaming in the sun, and beyond, a dark fir forest patiently waited. Regina told them how she had thought about her home so often while working in Chicago. It was what had sustained her in those long and hard years. She'd thought about it so often that it was more real than this empty meadow of wildflowers and weeds. Regina argued with her sister that this couldn't possibly be the place.

She walked the road back and forth as if trying to conjure up what was no longer there. From behind came a small voice. "Where's my house?" asked Magda suddenly, as if awakening from a long sleep. She was pointing to the empty field.

"Magda, you remember our house?" asked Regina.

"Where's the bathhouse?" Magda began pointing to familiar places, walking the outlines of what she remembered. "The well was here." Magda was agitated.

"Everything's gone," said Violeta, putting her arm around her niece.

"Bombs?" asked Magda, trying to understand why everything was gone.

"No, not bombs." Violeta patiently explained that their house had been burned by the Lithuanian Forest Brothers after Regina's family fled. It was in protest against the Russian family who moved in. The Soviets were mixing populations as part of a plan for Russification of the Baltics. The Lithuanian partisans burned such houses rather than let the Russians make themselves at home. "After a while, the Russians were afraid to move to Lithuania," she said proudly. "That's why so much of Lithuania is still Lithuanian, while poor Latvia and Estonia have so many Russians."

Al wondered if that was true or something they said to themselves to feel better.

"Mama, the stork nest," said Magda, pointing to the three oak trees that her grandfather had planted by the crossroads. Regina stared at this familiar landmark, and it finally allowed her to get her bearings. The oaks were almost a hundred years old, with massive trunks and a wide canopy. "Oaks can live for five hundred years," said Regina. "Long after our sorrows are forgotten, the land remains."

Regina walked the perimeter of her land, quietly crying and shaking her head, talking to her husband as if he were still alive, reminding him of his plans to return to Lithuania. Then life would begin again. Then they would take a free breath and be happy again. But he'd died too soon, and now she missed him so terribly. This land that held all of her memories now looked innocent, unused, with no history to tell, overgrown with weeds. Two small white butterflies chased one another through the Queen Anne's lace and purple clover. When she saw a few surviving rye stalks mixed with the weeds, she picked a stalk and saw the golden head was almost ripe for harvest. The land, the pond, and the oak trees were the same—only she had changed.

Now she could see where it had all been, where the cottage had stood. They had added a fine large room filled with windows, where the whole village used to gather in the winter for meetings, plays, and dances. Those had been good years, with everything paid for, even the new threshing machine. Money had been saved for the lean years. She looked around for the well, but it must have been covered over. The orchard was gone, with its apple and cherry trees. Regina walked to the edge of the property and down the slope. At the bottom, she could see two storks poking their long beaks into the marshy grasses, looking for frogs. The first sign of spring had always been the croaking of frogs. The second sign of spring had been the return of the storks. She watched as the pair of storks spread their wide wings, pushing back their long thin legs as they flew back to their nest. She remembered her father telling of storks pushing their babies out of the nest during a year of famine or war, and how they spent their winters on the Nile River, but came back to their same nests in Lithuania year after year. They were considered good luck. "They came back every year, but we couldn't," she whispered.

"Where's Magda?" asked Violeta, looking around.

"I thought she was over there," said Al, pointing to the wooded area. He called Magda's name several times, but she didn't answer. He ran over to the birch trees calling, but still no answer. His mother stopped for a moment, strangely reminded of the morning the Soviet Army was coming near. She had been preparing to leave when Magda had disappeared. She had looked for her daughter everywhere and then had found her in the bathhouse.

Regina turned to Violeta. "Is the bathhouse still there?"

"Has she gone to the pond?" asked Violeta.

Regina saw the remnant of the old path to the village bathhouse by the pond, and she pushed her way through the tangle of bushes. Al walked behind her, getting slapped by branches, trying to shield his aunt, who walked behind him.

"Why would she go there?" Violeta was winded from the effort.

"I don't know," Al said.

"Hurry up," urged Regina, panting and pushing her way down the familiar path. She finally saw the pond, overgrown with cattails on one end. There were still a few wooden posts where a small pier had once stood, but there was no sign of Magda. The small, weathered wooden bathhouse still stood, leaning over to one side. It would have fallen but for some birch trees holding it up. Al yelled for Magda and at last heard her answer. Relieved, he ran inside to find her digging a hole with a stick, scratching the packed earth.

"Magda, what are you doing?" asked Al.

"Digging," she answered resolutely.

"Why are you digging?" he asked.

"Papa gave it to me."

"Forget it, the ground is too hard. You'll never dig a hole in that packed dirt with your stick." Al tried to lift her.

"No," she grunted and jerked away.

"What are you looking for?"

"My box."

"You think you'll find something after so many years?" Regina came over and took her daughter by the elbow. "Magda, get up. You're getting dirty like some potato digger."

"No." Magda forcefully yanked her arm away.

"Magda, for God's sake, get up. Don't act like a child."

Magda whimpered but kept on digging.

"I'll help you," said Simona, pushing her blond braids with large red bows to her back.

"Let her be," said Violeta, taking her sister's arm. "What's the harm? Linas will help her too." Linas agreed and found a couple of sticks so that he and his young daughter could help Magda dig. They scratched and scratched but found nothing. After a while, Al found another stick and joined in. He had never seen Magda so determined. She was usually so quiet and docile.

The bathhouse was warm and dark, with some weathered benches piled in one corner. Violeta brought over one of the benches and spread a handkerchief on it so she and her sister could sit down. "When Regina and I were little, the whole village used this sauna. We would beat our skin with birch branches until it tingled."

"Those were golden days," said Regina.

"Maybe you and I could find a way to live here again?" asked Violeta, sighing. "Two old widows remembering our youth."

Regina smiled and shrugged, liking the idea.

The digging continued. "There's nothing here," Al said at last, throwing his stick away. He looked at the cobwebs and the dust, a broken lantern, and a child's canvas shoe abandoned in a corner.

Magda had given up on the first hole and had made several others. She was covered in dirt like some ancient crone, but she wouldn't stop digging. And then, to everyone's surprise, she hit something with a thud. Al and Linas laughed in amazement. Simona jumped up and down in glee. "I knew it," she said.

Violeta stood up and clasped her hands together. "I was praying she'd find something."

Regina stood to look over their shoulders as all four dug with renewed vigor until they removed a rusted tin box that advertised chocolates. Magda wiped it off as best she could with her hand but couldn't open it. Al tried but couldn't open it either, so Linas used his penknife to pry the rusty top off. Inside was a doll-sized china tea set in a delicate blue-and-white Dutch design, still carefully wrapped in a rotting linen towel.

Al picked up a toy cup in wonder. "I don't believe it."

"It's so tiny," said Simona, pleased and happy.

Regina broke down in tears when she saw Magda holding her precious tea set. When she stopped crying, she could only shake her head in wonder at life's strangeness. "Imagine, this is what survived from our past life. Magda's little tea set that Jurgis gave her when she was five years old. He had brought it back from a trip to Konigsberg. Jurgis would sit with her and drink tea from the tiny cups."

Al had never known Magda as a normal little girl. He had only known her as a slow and confused older sister, who used to embarrass him. He sighed for all the things that might have been.

They went outside to wash up in the murky pond. Afterward, Violeta went to the minibus and brought back a bag of food. She spread a blanket by the pond and passed out thick sausage sandwiches, while Linas sliced cucumbers with a penknife. The whole group sat at the edge of the pond for the rest of the day. The bees buzzed lazily over the dandelions. The sky was the color of cornflowers with clouds like delicate lace.

Magda sat at the edge of the pond with Simona happily washing every tiny dish, while Regina and Violeta sat under an oak tree feeling perfectly at home, as if world wars had never happened. Regina picked a cattail, brown as a cigar, spilling its seeds like down. She blew the seeds over the water and watched them float away. Violeta told her sister that she felt as if their ancestor spirits were happy at the return of their seed to the earth from which it had sprung—to the earth it would eventually return, like these cattail seeds, as if the natural order had finally been restored even if only for this brief moment of grace.

The light was golden as Al stood and slowly walked over to the murky pond. He, too, could feel a certain nostalgia for a way of life he had never known, the one his parents had summoned up for him. This simple life tugged at him and made him wonder how life might have been different had he grown up here and his parents' war had never happened. His life would also have been very different if his war in Vietnam hadn't happened. What was it in men's hearts that made them fight wars every generation?

In the late afternoon light, he leaned against a birch tree and thought about Irene. Taking the amber heart that she had given him from his pocket, he held it like a talisman, marveling at how strange it was to finally find her again in Lithuania, of all places. As he held the amber heart up to the sunlight, it shone like honey with a dark streak running through it. He smiled, wondering if all hearts were darkly flawed, yet, by some grace, still able to love.

Acknowledgements

The following stories have appeared in different form: "Blue Tango" in *Spectrum*, "Southside Miracles" in *West/Word*, "Secrets of Life" in *Story One*, "Sunday Dinner" and "Trains" in *Amoskeag*, "The Boarder" in *Lituanus*, "Carnival" in *Storyglossia*, "Those Chicago Blues" in *R-KV-RY*, "Frozen Waves" in *Banyan Review*, "Lachryma Christi" in *Citadel*, "Becoming American" in *The Smoking Poet*, and "Lucy in the Sky" in the anthology, *Bless me, Father*. Both "Carnival" and "Lucy in the Sky" were optioned for film by Columbia College Chicago. This collection was a finalist for the Sol Books Contest.

The road to publication is sometimes long and winding. I would like to thank those who helped me on that journey. I owe many people a debt of gratitude, but I would like to especially thank those in my writing groups who gave me such valuable feedback and who listened to countless versions of these stories. A warm thank you to Ausra Kubilius and Violeta Kelertas for their invaluable help and tireless support and to Vilija Karalius for her helpful contribution.

I am grateful to my wonderful family for letting me bounce the stories by them, and especially my children, Max and Anna, who patiently watched their mother write over the years, and to my late husband, Algirdas, for his unflagging love and encouragement.

CPSIA information can be obtained
at www.ICGtesting.com
Printed in the USA
LVOW12s1506070617
537270LV00002B/408/P